Praise for Steve Yarbrough's

THE END OF CALIFORNIA

"Surprising, even magical. . . . Yarbrough weaves the inner-workings of a small Southern town into a symphony of voices and scenes."
—*Pittsburgh Tribune-Review*

"A story rife with moral predicaments. . . . The tension is high. . . . [Yarbrough] writes with surprising subtlety about ordinary tragedies . . . and, without judgment, asks hard questions about righteousness."
—*Paste Magazine*

"Tense and vivid. . . . Yarbrough's piercing dialogue is as glittering and toxic as beads of mercury."
—*The Post and Courier* (Charleston, SC)

"[Yarbrough] has a sure touch with place and atmosphere and sensibilities. . . . [He] makes a small town the cauldron in which to mix the elements of guilt and redemption, race and religion, friendship and betrayal, alcohol, sex, and the possibility of grace."
—*The Advocate* (Baton Rouge)

"Yarbrough is a fine cartographer while guiding us through the maps of his characters' motivations."
—*San Antonio Express-News*

"The continuation of great prose from Yarbrough. . . . A tale of real people whose actions catch the reader in whirlwinds of passion, deceit, rage and death."
—*The Clarion-Ledger* (Jackson, MS)

Steve Yarbrough

THE END OF CALIFORNIA

Steve Yarbrough was born in the Delta town of Indianola, Mississippi, and now lives with his wife and their two daughters in Fresno, California, where he teaches at the university. The author of three previous novels and three collections of stories, he has won the Mississippi Authors Award, the California Book Award, and a third from the Mississippi Institute of Arts and Letters. His recent fiction has also been published in England, Holland, Japan, and Poland.

THE END OF CALIFORNIA

THE END OF CALIFORNIA

STEVE YARBROUGH

To Courtney —
with many thanks

VINTAGE CONTEMPORARIES
Vintage Books
A Division of Random House, Inc.
New York

FIRST VINTAGE CONTEMPORARIES EDITION, JULY 2007

The Library of Congress has cataloged the Knopf edition as follows:
Yarbrough, Steve, [date]
The end of California / Steve Yarbrough—1st ed.
p.   cm.
1. City and town life. 2. Mississippi—Fiction. 3. Domestic fiction. I. Title.
PS3575.A717E53 2006
813'.54—dc22
2005057750

Vintage ISBN: 978-1-4000-9570-4

Book design by Robert C. Olsson

www.vintagebooks.com

Printed in the United States of America
10 9 8 7 6 5 4 3 2 1

For Ewa

A SOURCE YOU CAN TRUST

UNDER THE CIRCUMSTANCES, he told himself, speeding made sense. He'd driven down through the San Joaquin Valley at eighty and eighty-five, crossed the Mojave with the Volvo's air conditioner blasting and the needle on the dash nudging ninety. Through Kingman, Flagstaff and Winslow, Gallup and Albuquerque, Amarillo, the vast nothingness of western Oklahoma, clean across Arkansas and over the Greenville bridge, and he'd seen more state police officers, deputy sheriffs and plain old small-town cops than he could have calculated, even if calculation came naturally to him, which recent events had proven it did not. None of them stopped him. It was as if they understood that while anybody who lived in California had good reason for wanting to distance himself from its borders, his reasons were better than most.

They hadn't been in Mississippi for more than three or four minutes before a gray patrol car pulled out of the lot at a bait shop and attached itself to their rear bumper. He glanced at Angela: stoic and silent, the picture of stillness, her eyes hidden behind sunglasses. Had she taken them off a single time since they left Fresno? If so, he didn't recall it. He'd noticed her wearing them in the motel room last night.

In the backseat, Toni said, "I think you'd better pull over."

"I think you're right, hon," he said, and stopped on the shoulder next to a cotton field where a young black guy was spraying herbicide from a Hi-Boy. Leaving the engine running and the air on, he climbed out and shut the door. Wet heat enveloped him in its familiar embrace.

The state trooper, a woman, was somewhere between thirty-five and forty. Trim and tan, with sandy brown hair and delicate hands that looked too small to wield the weapon riding her right hip. She tipped her own sunglasses up, and he saw a smooth lump below her left eye, the skin perceptibly discolored.

Her voice was husky but not abrupt or unpleasant. "You're a long way from home."

"Yes ma'am. I guess you could say that."

"Could I see your license?"

He pulled his wallet out, withdrew the license and handed it to her.

"Fresno. That's cotton country too, isn't it?"

"Yes ma'am."

She glanced inside the station wagon, nodded at Angela and Toni, then looked through the back glass into the cargo compartment, which in addition to luggage contained two computers, a couple printers, a bunch of medical books and the records from his former practice. "Moving?" she said.

"Actually, we are."

"Mind if I ask where?"

"Loring."

"Really?"

"Yes ma'am. The fact is, I grew up there."

She examined the license again. "Barrington," she said. "There are some folks by that name in Greenville."

"They're not kin to me, but I played football against one of them in high school."

"That'd probably be Carl, I'm guessing."

"Yes ma'am."

"He's tending bar now at the Holiday Inn. I used to stop in there from time to time with my husband. Carl likes to pour big ones."

"He was a pretty big guy, if I recall right. Not a bad ballplayer, either."

Something had disturbed her. Frowning, she looked through the window again—first at Angela, then at Toni, then at the stuff piled up in the back. She fingered the license once more. "Mr. Barrington," she said, "you were driving way too fast."

"Yes ma'am, I know that."

"Tell me this was an isolated incident."

"I'm sorry," he said. "I can't do that. The truth is, I probably slowed down some when I crossed the bridge. Just out of relief at finally getting where I was going. I've been driving like a bat out of hell for three days."

Her nose wrinkled as if she'd just inhaled an unwholesome odor. "Is something wrong?" she asked. "Why would anybody in this situation say anything like that?"

He'd ask himself the same question later. The best answer he could come up with was that a bunch of factors had converged to render him incapable of deceit. It also had something to do with her open, pleasant manner, the feel of that damp air on his skin, the sight of the black guy on the Hi-Boy, engaged with a fate that could have been his own. "I don't know," he said. "I've said and done a lot I can't explain."

Moving decisively, she led him some distance away—he was following her before he knew it. Halfway between the Volvo and the cruiser, she turned to face him, lifted the sunglasses off altogether and stuck them in her pocket. "You're driving a nice car," she said. "You've got what looks like your family in there. Is that who they are?"

He nodded.

"How old's the girl?"

"Fifteen."

"You mind if I ask what your profession is?"

"I'm a doctor."

"What kind?"

The words were easy to pronounce but hard to say. "Family practice."

She'd begun to sweat. Rivulets ran down the bridge of her nose and trickled over the unsightly lump beneath her eye. Her blouse was damp too. "Dr. Barrington," she said, "I'm going to ask you something. Do I need to run this license? Or should I just wish you all a pleasant journey?"

"Running that license won't tell you anything I haven't. My last ticket was about sixteen years ago, the car's registered in my name and there's no warrant out for my arrest."

She looked at the license one last time and then at him, as if to confirm that his face and the one on the card belonged to the same man. If only it were as simple as that.

"I'll just give you a warning," she said, holding out his license.

Before accepting it he touched her wrist. "That spot beneath your eye?" he said. "You need to have it looked at."

———

She gazes at the rearview mirror and sees the officer standing there. A nice-looking woman, just an inch short of pretty, probably friendly and smart too, and certain of her authority. Her heart misfires—not once but twice—robbing her of breath. She reaches for her purse, her hand closing around the plastic bottle of Toprol, in case she needs it.

As if the patrolwoman understands she's being observed, she reapplies her sunglasses, strides back to the cruiser and slides inside, slams the door, glances over her shoulder and wheels onto the highway, a plume of dust rising as she swings into a U-turn and heads back toward the bait shop.

After sticking his wallet into his pocket, Pete opens the door and climbs in beside her. The car shifts ever so slightly. On the trip he's added weight, the result of fast food and sodas, and she can see faint evidence of a belly. Soon enough that will be gone, once he finds a gym and starts working out.

"Well," he says, "times sure have changed. Used to be that anybody driving through here with out-of-state plates was already guilty. She didn't even write me a ticket."

"Did you really think she would?"

He takes every question seriously now, never sidestepping them or providing a facile answer. Tapping his finger against the steering wheel, he thinks for a moment and says, "I never assumed she wouldn't."

THE MOVERS HAD DAMAGED one leg of her piano, a Petrof Chippendale, not the best or most expensive instrument in the world but one you didn't see very often. Her tuner in Fresno had loved it. He always lingered beyond the terms of his engagement, unable to keep himself from teasing the keys with those long, slim fingers that coaxed magic from the cello at the Philharmonic. While he sat and admired it, they talked. She never hurried him away.

Now the piano stood in the corner of the living room in a house they'd rented sight unseen, and Pete and his friend Tim were kneeling there examining the crack, two tubes of glue and a piece of cardboard on the floor beside them.

"This industrial epoxy's strong as the Hulk," Tim said. "Mix the black goop with the white goop and you get some gray goop that will *not* let go."

"Yeah, that's what worries me a little. I'm scared the next time this thing's moved and somebody pulls the leg loose, a chunk of wood'll come with it."

She opened the sliding glass door and stepped onto the patio, the temperature in the mid-nineties and the humidity almost as high. A sluggish breeze stirred the leaves in an oak, casting jagged shadows on the surface of the pool. Tim had suggested this particular house because of the pool, knowing that where she'd grown up almost everybody had one.

She walked over to the deep end and mounted the diving board so she could see over the brick wall into the neighbors' yard. A charcoal grill stood next to a picnic table, and a German shepherd lying underneath the table pricked up his ears when he saw her. He looked as if, in cooler weather, he might be aggressive, but today he just studied her for a few seconds, then put his head down on his paws and closed his eyes.

Behind her the door opened again and Toni came out in her nightgown, shielding her eyes and looking up into the sky as though to make certain that at least one thing had remained unchanged. "God, this heat's awful," she said, "like there's something sticking to me all the time."

Angela stepped down off the diving board. "There is. It's your skin."

Toni rolled her eyes. "Yeah, right."

"What would you like for breakfast, honey? I could make you some scrambled eggs with tomatoes and green onions."

"I think I'll just have some cereal." She palmed a yawn. "I didn't sleep well last night."

"Again?"

"I feel like I'm still at a motel."

How to respond to a girl who'd said that? Empty reassurance might be offered, but why peddle goods the customer was too wise to covet? "I think I'll have some breakfast myself," she said. "I didn't eat anything yet either."

In the living room Pete had put a rolled-up towel on his shoulder, thrust it under the Petrof and managed to raise the damaged leg off the floor, enabling Tim to dab on epoxy. "Hurry up, man," he said, "before my rotator goes."

Tim's hair, speckled with gray, flopped into his eyes when he laughed. "Physician, heal thyself."

"Easier said than done, son." Pete gritted his teeth. "Ever tried operating on yourself?"

"No. Nor representing myself in court, either." He repositioned the leg and skimmed epoxy off the surface, then leaned back to admire his work. "Okay, I think that's got it. Go ahead and let her down easy."

Pete slid out from under the weight and wiped sweat from his face. "Who *did* handle your divorce trial?"

"Fred Alexander."

"Any kin to Donny and Mark?"

"Cousin."

"Do you any good?"

"Did what I told him to."

"Which was?"

"Roll over and play dead. He served my heart on a platter with all the proper trimmings."

"Bloody, was it?"

"Pure gore."

Tim was the first to see her standing there. Some kind of recognition dawned in his eyes, but he was having a hard time narrowing it down.

A different type of levity seemed to be called for, so she supplied it: "Know what you call a doctor whose best friend's a lawyer?"

He pulled a rag from his pocket and wiped his hands on it. "Aw, who the hell doesn't?" he said, grinning. "The accused."

———

At the kitchen table, she and Toni ate while the men drank coffee. Tim gasped when he took the first swallow, then said it was good but way too strong, that if like him you sat around the courthouse drinking it all day long, it'd make your heart do side-straddle hops. He knew one lawyer who drank fifteen or twenty cups before noon.

"He'll die of stomach cancer," Toni predicted.

"Maybe," her father said. "Then again, maybe not. The coffee probably *is* having a bad effect, but there's at least a slight chance it might also be preventing something worse. Sometimes you rid folks of *H. pylori,* which really does lead to stomach cancer, and in no time they've got cancer of the esophagus. Bacteria eat acid. When they're no longer there to consume it—bam." He leaned over and gently pinched her arm. Without even looking at him, she slapped his hand, hard.

Pete didn't wince, but Tim did. "Oooh," he said, "she's a tough one. We could use a strong safety on the football team this year. Reckon she'd be interested?"

The back of Pete's hand was red. "You'll have to ask her," he said.

"Speaking of which, have you had time to reconsider my little proposal?"

"Can't do it."

"Can't, or won't?"

"Can't."

"John Berryman," Angela said, "once claimed *it* was the filthiest word in the English language. I prefer my mysteries in hardcover."

"I don't know any mystery writer called John Berryman," Tim said, "but it sounds like there's something your husband hasn't let you in on."

There was plenty he hadn't let her in on, and plenty he had. The only question was whether he'd let Tim in on any of it. Her best guess, based on twenty years' evidence, would have been no. His friend was incorrectly configured.

"I'm helping out this year," Tim said, "with the high school football team. Coaching the DBs."

"DBs." She turned the phrase over. "That means . . . *diamond-backs*?"

Tim shook his head. "Man, I love her," he told Pete. "You married one great lady."

Toni crunched the last of her cereal, tossed the spoon into the bowl, deposited the dish loudly in the sink and left the room.

No one but her father watched her go. "DBs means defensive backs," he finally said. "But I don't have time, Tim, much as I'd like to. Got to get my office up and running, on the off chance I might acquire some patients."

Tim turned to her, suddenly imploring. "See, problem is the school district's broke. They fired two full-time coaches in May, so now there's only the head coach and an assistant who never even played football—they hired him just because he was cheap and can teach history. Practice starts at three-thirty, but I can't get there till four-fifteen, and I'm thinking Pete could come in at four-thirty or so to work with the tight ends and defensive line for half an hour or so. You know, get back in touch with the community, helping out your daughter's new school. Plus, attract some new patients."

"Sounds like a good idea to me," she said. "The perfect combination of business and pleasure."

"See? I told you she was a great lady." He slapped the tabletop. "So what do you say?"

"I need another day."

She knew then that he'd already made his decision, the choice of where to spend his afternoons being all that easy. Later, after Tim left, in the obligatory scene, he would ask if she'd really meant what she said, whether she truly did consider his helping coach a good idea and wouldn't be angry about the hour or so it would take each day. Because if she didn't really mean it, he'd say, then he would simply not do it.

Tim forced down the rest of the coffee and glanced at his watch. "Time to go hose myself off and get down to the courthouse."

Pete shrugged. "Big case under way?"

"Just the usual. Fellow with an IQ below the freezing point starts a fight with his druggie girlfriend, and ducks when she throws the butcher knife at him."

"Sounds like rational behavior."

"Except he didn't duck far enough. First time I see him he's sitting on a gurney at the hospital, handcuffed to the railing, with his head bandaged up like a mummy and the handle of that butcher knife sticking straight up in the air. Had to wait on a neurosurgeon to drive up from Jackson and put him under a sonogram and pull the blade out."

"Otherwise," Pete said, "some of his gray matter might've come along with it."

"Yeah, and this guy didn't have any brain cells to spare. He and this chick were fighting because he'd been playing with her baby, bouncing it up and down on a pillow, until it rolled off and broke an arm. Now, since he has two priors already, he'll be doing three to five at Parchman. Today's the sentencing, and that shouldn't take long."

Once he'd gone, Pete rose and rinsed his coffee cup, then came back and, standing behind her, softly placed his hands on her shoulders. "I want to thank you for saying I could help coach," he said. "I didn't bring it up because I didn't believe you'd want me to do it. But

I'd really love to, and since you agree it's a good idea, I'll say yes. Maybe you'll even come to a few games."

His hands were as warm as the room, and her stomach was full of hot coffee. So where did this cold rush originate, if not in the fear he might never lie again? He was wielding a new weapon—truthfulness—that was pointed right at her.

———

That evening the T-shirt rose over a still-hard stomach covered by a layer of down that grew wiry and dark as he pulled the fabric higher, revealing his massive chest. He drew it over his head. "I keep looking for the wicker chair over here," he said, "but now it's over there." He tossed the shirt on the chair and bent to step out of his briefs.

A collection of poems by Adam Zagajewski lay facedown on her stomach: *Try to praise the mutilated world. Remember June's long days, and wild strawberries, drops of rosé wine.*

He sat down on his side of the bed. The mattress sank beneath his weight, the world tilting again in his favor, and he yawned. "I haven't done much of anything all day, but it's like I just ran a marathon. Not adapted yet, I guess, to the new time zone." He lay back and shut his eyes. "Go ahead and read as long as you want. It won't bother me."

"That's all right," she said, "I'm finished." She closed the book and laid it on the floor, then reached up and switched off the lamp.

Every day for fifteen years, except for weekends and major holidays, Alan DePoyster had unlocked the back door at the Piggly Wiggly at seven a.m. and stepped into the storeroom. On Tuesdays and Fridays, two kids off the night crew would be back there burning paper and cardboard in the big incinerator while a couple guys out front swept up and mopped the aisles and the crew chief finished keying in their stock order on the computer.

These days almost the entire night crew was black, as were most of the checkout clerks and sackers, even the assistant manager. Few of them worked at the store for more than a year or two, and many moved away, but some would come back later for another stint. The word around town was that DePoyster treated people right regardless of color, even paying Christmas bonuses out of his own pocket.

If anybody had thought about it—which no one ever did—it might've been easy to think Alan's own background made him sympathetic to his employees. When he was in eleventh grade, his father had dropped him off in front of the high school, taking time to wish him good luck in the basketball game they both knew he wouldn't be playing in that evening unless Loring went ahead by twenty or thirty points. Then he drove back home, packed his suitcase and disappeared from Alan's life forever. It was easily the biggest scandal of the year, his dad having been a successful insurance agent as well as a member of the Chamber of Commerce and the Rotary Club.

He'd left some funds in a savings account, but a lot less than people suspected, so it wasn't long before money became a problem. Edie DePoyster hadn't finished college, and for a while Alan assumed that was why nobody wanted to hire her. Then, when people started talking, he learned it was not lack of education that had disqualified her.

At the beginning of his senior year, he moved to Greenville to live with his aunt and went to work as a stockboy at the Piggly Wiggly there. The following year he moved up to crew chief, and a year later to assistant manager. By then he'd given up the notion of going to college himself, understanding that he'd eventually be named manager at either the Greenville store or one nearby. Besides, he'd already met Nancy at a church camp, where they both served as counselors. He wanted to marry her, to start a family, and having a steady job was essential.

He was thinking about steadiness when he parked at the loading dock that mid-August morning, got out and climbed the steps to unlock the back door. Fifteen years ago, when offered the store in Loring, he'd wondered not only if he could stomach living in his hometown again but also if he could handle all those responsibilities, whether the store and his family would flourish or he'd make a mess of both. Mason had been six months old back then, dogged by asthma, unable to sleep at night, and Nancy had fallen into some kind of depression he couldn't understand. She frequently cried for no reason at all, and sometimes, when both she and the baby got going full blast, he wanted to run off just like his father had. He wasn't the running kind, though, and in the end everything worked out. The store kept expanding, as did his bonuses. Nancy got a job she liked as a receptionist at Southern Prime Catfish, and Mason, a sophomore now, was on the honor roll every semester. Things had gone according to plan. They usually did, he believed, if you kept a steady hand.

When he walked in that morning, Reggie McDonald, the high school's star tailback, was standing in front of the incinerator examining his forearms, which had something white all over them.

Seeing his boss, he grinned. "Mr. Alan, you went and caught me."

"Caught you doing what?"

Reggie's sidekick, Wayne Collier, stepped out of the incinerator room. "He just beat me out of five dollars, Mr. Alan. You know what that is on his arms?"

He stepped over and took a closer look. Whatever the substance was, it had formed a hard crust. "Don't have the faintest idea."

"Being a regular whirlwind, I get to sweating like a hog every night over in that flour aisle," Reggie told him. "And every time I bust one of them bales of Pillsbury or Martha White open, a little bit of flour dust fly up, and because my arms is so wet it stick to me. Come back here and start burning trash, and when that fire get to roaring, the stuff on my arms bake. I told Wayne, but he keep saying no way, so we done a little experiment. I busted open a whole bag and rubbed it on my forearms real good and stayed in there ten minutes, and what you looking at on me right now ain't a thing in the world but bread." He stuck an arm out. "Want to take you a little bite?"

"I think I'll decline."

"I hope you ain't mad about us busting that bag. I mean to pay for that out of Wayne's five dollars."

"You just hang on to your money," Alan said, "since it was done in the name of science."

He pushed open the door to the meat market and walked through, verifying that all the surfaces were clean and the butcher trays stacked and ready. Then he strolled each aisle and made sure they were neatly fronted, so when you rolled your cart along you'd see a solid wall of labels. There were a couple snafus, though: on aisle three, a box of Grape-Nuts was standing in the Cornflakes section, and on aisle four, Wayne had left a gap where a sack of Purina Puppy Chow should've been. He jotted this down in the pocket notebook he always carried, and before leaving this evening he'd walk the floor again, then pin the day's notes to the bulletin board back by the bathroom.

His assistant manager appeared at seven-thirty, the checkers and sackers were in place at five till eight, so at seven fifty-nine he opened the front doors. He always made a habit of speaking to the early customers, who tended to be the same from one day to the next. This morning he talked to Norma Salter, whose daughter he'd gone to school with. Mr. Salter had died four or five years ago, and she usually bought nothing more than some cereal or granola bars and a small carton of two percent, but today she'd filled her basket with a few pounds of bacon, two dozen eggs, pancake mix, two gallons of vitamin D milk, two loaves of bread, a gallon of orange juice, a family pack of ground beef and two bags of hamburger buns.

"Company?" he asked, eyeing the provisions.

"My grandkids are coming tonight."

"How many you got? Three, is it?"

"That's right. But each one has a little friend, and they're bringing them along."

"Mighty nice of you to invite the whole posse."

"I wouldn't say I invited them. I just didn't say no once they'd announced their plans. You wait, Alan. When Mason marries and sows his garden, a good part of the time you'll be the one tending the vegetables. You get two shots at parenthood. The first one you bring on yourself. The second one brings itself on you."

He laughed. "Twice blessed is how I'd put it."

"I'm glad you would, Alan." To his dismay the corners of her mouth began to tremble. "When I was twenty-one and pulling off my clothes in the Pontchartrain down in New Orleans, I could see ahead to forty. But I couldn't see ahead to the day when I'd be sixty and by myself and just the easiest solution to somebody else's problem." She stood back from her remarks as if waiting to see what response they would draw, this slim woman in freshly pressed jeans and a white blouse, her makeup so carefully applied.

When she realized he wasn't going to say anything, she smiled and reached out and patted his hand. "Alan, this is the best-run grocery store in Mississippi. You tell your wife I said hi." Then she rolled her cart down the aisle to the checkout stand.

He took the notebook from his pocket and, on the page after the one where he'd recorded the cereal and pet-food problems, he wrote down her name. Tonight, when he was alone in the far corner of his backyard, sitting on the overturned washtub, she would be included among the people he prayed for.

———

After his encounter with Norma Salter the morning passed uneventfully, just how he liked it. He wrote one check to Mississippi Power and Light, another to the city of Loring, a third to the *Weekly Times* and a fourth to the Loring County Sheriff's Department, whose efforts to start a drug-awareness program in the county schools he'd agreed to support. At eleven o'clock he stuck those envelopes in his pocket and went back to tell his assistant manager he was running a few errands, then walked out the same door he'd entered at seven that morning.

Most of the employees probably thought he was going home to grab a cup of coffee, though once he left the building they most likely didn't think of him at all. They were generally pretty busy along about then and didn't have time to ponder his absence or anything else, either.

He climbed into the truck and pulled out of the parking lot, then drove down Front Street to Loring Avenue and took a left. On his way out of town he always passed the house he'd grown up in, a neat English Tudor at the corner of Loring and Sunflower, and while the sight of it used to cause a twinge in the pit of his stomach, now he barely noticed the place.

He crossed the highway and drove out into the Industrial Park, inappropriately named thirty years ago, back when the town thought manufacturers would relocate anywhere if the taxes were low enough. The Southern Prime plant stood at the end of the road, and its corrugated roof always reminded him of a cotton gin. A few workers off the kill line milled around inside the fence wearing blood-stained aprons and white hairnets, some of them smoking or drinking coffee. He was a couple minutes early so he sat there with the engine idling. None of the workers paid him any mind. They were used to seeing him.

At exactly eleven-fifteen the main door opened and Nancy emerged. Tall, auburn-haired and a little heavy these days, she strode along purposefully, her skirt parting once or twice to give a glimpse of calf and thigh. She stopped near the flagpole, raised her hand and waved at him, her broad face breaking into a smile as it did every weekday morning at eleven-fifteen, come sunshine or shower. He smiled and waved too, and she glanced to see if anyone was looking before she puckered her lips and blew him a kiss, which he promptly returned on the air.

She went back inside. He made a U-turn and headed for the highway.

———

Out of stamps, he parked in front of the post office. Later, he'd recall that he'd just shut the engine off when he saw him. But no sooner had that detail come to mind than he began to wonder why it seemed significant enough to dredge up. What did it matter that he'd just shut off the engine? That's what anybody would do if he intended to leave his truck parked on the street and go into the post office to buy stamps. He finally decided that the significance, if there was any, lay not in shutting off the engine but in what he did next—or didn't do. Because instead of going inside and buying a book of stamps from Mary Pelossi or Bubba Jenkins or the young clerk whose name he couldn't remember, then shooting the breeze for a few minutes about the upcoming mayoral election, the sad state of affairs in Iraq or the cold front that had somehow gotten diverted and missed the Delta entirely, he sat there in the truck with the engine turned off, watching in stifling heat while Pete Barrington stood on the front steps, read a couple pieces of mail, frowned once or twice, then tossed them in a trash can and finally, mercifully, walked over and climbed into a Volvo wagon displaying a new Mississippi license plate, started the engine and disappeared down the street.

SHE OPENED THE REFRIGERATOR door, and light spilled out, pooling on the floor. Inside, where she'd put them the night before, were a bag of grapes and a ham and cheese on rye. These she stuck in a brown paper sack, along with a bottle of Evian.

The wall clock said five-thirty, so she had time to drink some coffee on her own before waking Toni. She dumped the coffee—ground last night—into the basket, filled the reservoir with water and turned it on. While it brewed she cracked eggs for an omelet and diced an onion, a bell pepper, some ham and a handful of mushrooms and left them on the cutting board. Then she opened the cabinet above the refrigerator, pushed a stack of paper plates aside, removed the Toprol bottle and shook a pill into her palm. About twenty-five remained. How she'd get a refill was open to question.

She poured herself a cup of coffee and took a sip to wash down the beta-blocker, then opened the sliding glass door and went outside.

Around here you interacted with the atmosphere. The warm wet air wrapped itself around you. The first time she'd felt heavy air, she'd reacted like Toni had, as if something thick and alien had attached itself to her and needed to be washed off. That was a long time ago, when Pete first brought her down to visit his mother and grandmother—his folks, so he called them.

The word *folks* had seemed so quaint, suggestive of Appalachian hollows filled with moonshine stills, revenue stalkers and barefooted cretins plucking banjos on the porches. There were no hollows here, however, the land was so flat you could see for miles and this made it a dubious place to hide. Especially if what you wanted to hide from had come along with you.

She sat on the diving board sipping the coffee, letting her feet dangle above the surface of the pool. She liked being awake when no one else was, and derived from this a sense of advantage. Sleeping people weren't aware of what trouble might be bearing down on them, or worried that they might disappear entirely. She preferred to know what was coming.

Hearing a noise beyond the brick wall, she set the cup down on the concrete and tiptoed across the grass. Three or four days ago she'd spotted a hole, perfectly round and perhaps two inches in diameter, about two feet above the base of the wall, partly hidden on her side by a bush. The hole must have been made with a drill, by someone who wanted a certain kind of access to his neighbors' yard.

Squatting, she pressed her eye to the opening. On the far side an eye looked back. Then it was replaced by something wet and warm. She was gazing right into a pair of nostrils.

The dog whined, softly, as if aware that this was a secret transaction.

"All right," she said. "Will you just wait?" She hurried across the yard, slipping once in the dew. On the mat outside she wiped her feet off, then went to the kitchen, got a slice of ham out of the refrigerator and carried it back over to the wall. "Are you still there?"

Another whine.

She pushed the ham through and heard an immediate sound of gratitude. Pressing her eye to the hole, she saw the dog's muscular shoulders bobbing up and down. When he finished eating, he whined once more.

"Did somebody over here make the hole so they could feed you?" she asked. "Or for some other reason?"

The dog backed away, cocking his head, apparently puzzled.

"Maybe somebody was watching your owners," she said. "Is something scandalous going on over there? Are the people in your house thankful you can't talk?"

She woke her daughter late—the time having slipped away. It was five till seven and Pete was already in the shower.

"Jesus, Mom. I mean, my God. Jesus Christ and all the angels."

Her daughter's first day at a new school. Pete's first day at his new practice. Her first day alone in a rented house two thousand miles from home.

Toni pushed past her and ran down the hall, one slipper coming off as she scurried into the bathroom and slammed the door behind her. She emerged ten minutes later, her hair wet and tangled, her mood even worse. "If you're fixing me some kind of big Denny's breakfast," she yelled, "one of those Super Grand Slam All-American five-egg Baja whoppers, you can just forget it. I don't have time." With that, the door to her room banged shut.

Angela stood at the stove over the perfect omelet she'd just made. Using the spatula, she sliced it in two. She lifted Pete's half out and laid it on a plate. Then she tore off a paper towel, folded it double and laid the rest of the omelet on it. She carried it across the yard and fed the dog.

FOR MOVING AROUND TOWN he'd bought an old pickup at Sonny's Discount Auto. The truck had 153,000 miles on it if you trusted the odometer, but he didn't. The vehicle was so old that the factory-installed stereo played only eight-track tapes.

The day he bought it, he'd taken his only drive out into the countryside past the house where he'd lived when his father died. They'd been farmers, his family, the kind that rented land from the county and had to worry every five years if their leases would be renewed. Both his grandfather and his father had suffered heart attacks—his dad making it only to forty—and it was the constant fretting, as much as any physical ailment, that killed them. Consequently, he hated the sight of a cotton field and was actually relieved to find that every inch of the ground his folks used to slave over was currently underwater. Somebody had turned the fields into fishponds.

———

"Watermelons 'n More?" Toni said. "Christ Jesus."

The sign was anchored to a boat trailer parked in front of a low flat-roofed building. Despite the funny name, the art deco trim, the fruits and vegetables stacked high in bins out front, the structure hadn't quite transcended its filling-station past. There was still a concrete slab where the pumps once stood.

"That used to be a gas station and repair shop," he said while they waited in his truck for the light to change. "Owned by a man named

Casey Roe. When my grandfather brought me to school in the morning, he'd take me in there sometimes and buy me a Holloway sucker."

If that information interested her, she didn't show it. She pulled out a brush and went to work on her hair for the third or fourth time that morning—not so much brushing it as tearing at it, each stroke sizzling with static.

"Mr. Roe repaired our tractors," he said, deciding to plunge ahead. Since she disliked most of what she thought she knew about him, things could only improve if he told her more, assembling a second set of facts to compete with the ones already at her disposal. "Only our tractors, no one else's. Mr. Roe wasn't in the farm-implement business. But he and my grandfather had both moved to the Delta from over in east Mississippi and were part Choctaw, and they did each other favors. Every year at hog-killing time Grandpa carried the Roes fresh sausage."

The light changed, and he looked in each direction before pulling onto the highway.

"There used to be a lot of wrecks back there. Including a famous one in the mid-'60s. An eighteen-wheeler was coming from Greenville loaded down with new cars, and it ran right through that light one night and smashed into a car with a bunch of kids out joy-riding. Killed all of them, including that year's homecoming queen. Over the next week we went to six different funerals."

She opened her red vinyl purse, stuck the brush inside and jerked the zipper shut. "Did anything *happy* ever happen here? I mean, other than your grandfather buying you those suckers?"

She was looking at his hands, which were locked around the steering wheel so tightly his knuckles had turned white. A smile played at the corners of her mouth. He almost told her that there used to be a picture in a scrapbook of her grinning like that while he stood nearby with a soiled Huggie in his hands, looking like a man who believed the substance contained by the diaper and the remains of his life were the same. Events led to the removal of that photo. Angela purged all images of an ambiguous nature, leaving only those that depicted family life as she'd always hoped it could be, even as the dream slipped away. "Yeah," he said, "a few happy things happened here too. Quite a few."

"Like what?"

"You really want to know?"

"Jeez." She tossed her head as if she were the one confronting an obtuse child. "No, I don't want to know. That's why I asked."

Fortunately it was a quarter till eight, the highway as busy as it ever got, folks going to work or carrying their kids to school, both lanes full, trucks and cars vying with tractors and module transports headed for the gin, and the shoulder was too narrow for him to pull over and shake her like he wanted to. That's what she wanted too, for him to shake her or yell at her or tell her to get her ass out and walk. This would keep her from dealing with alternative facts, allowing her to see him as she had for a long time now: a man concerned with something other than herself.

"Well," he said, "one fall, maybe three or four weeks later than this, a circus came to town."

"A circus?"

"Yeah. A very small one."

"A very small circus."

"One tent, a few rides, a few animals, a handful of performers."

"But it was a big deal."

"That's right. The rarity of the circus combined with the smallness of the town to make its presence here a thing of wonder. We discussed it for weeks before it came and weeks after it left."

"I suppose they had a tractor pull?"

"A slight variation, a tractor slash elephant pull."

"And you expect me to believe the elephant won."

He sometimes thought that if their ages were about the same and they met as strangers on a plane or at a medical convention or even at a party, they'd enjoy every moment they spent together. Unfortunately, that level of involvement wasn't possible. They were strangers, all right, but of the wrong type. "No," he said, "I don't expect you to believe the elephant won. Not even for a minute."

"Nevertheless, that's what happened?"

He drove into the parking lot, pulled into the queue and began to creep forward. In a minute it would all be over, at least for today. If she just wouldn't say another word.

"Well," she said, "is that or *is that not* what happened?"

He held his tongue until they'd reached the front of the line and he'd planted his foot on the brake. "At orientation the other day," he asked, "did they show you where the library is?"

"Yeah."

"Does it have old newspapers in it?"

"I guess so."

"Then look up the third or fourth week of September, in '68 or '69, and find out if the elephant won or not—from a source you can trust."

The truck door slammed so hard the duty teacher jumped as though a gun had just gone off. Toni left him as he'd once left her, sitting alone in a motionless vehicle, and there was nothing he could do but watch her disappear inside. He knew without being told that none of her classmates would call her by name anytime soon, that when they referred to her at all she'd be *the girl from California*. Then, next week or the week after that, as they grew used to seeing her in the hallway, the tag would be shortened to *California* and she'd be reduced to the place she came from, a fifteen-year-old girl who'd stand for bright lights, wide highways, blue water, white sand and a permissive attitude toward chaos.

IT HAPPENED TO me last fall too," the elderly woman said, heaving her legs onto the examination table. "I went to see Donny Alexander but he acted like he thought I was hysterical. The thing I can never quite forget about Donny is that I had to give him a D in American history. He got his medical degree in Manila because once they saw his Ole Miss transcript, no school in the Western Hemisphere would take his daddy's money. I don't know what possessed you to come home, but a bunch of us are mighty glad you did. Chester Kilgo hasn't been in yet, has he?"

"No ma'am. The truth is you're my first patient."

"Well, Chester'll be here soon enough, and I'll warn you ahead of time, he's Medicare's worst nightmare."

"Gets sick a lot, does he?"

"That old man's got the constitution of a horse and the psyche of a tulip. For thirty-five years, every time a student looked at him the wrong way, he was knocking on my door asking for 'coping strategies.' Once they made him retire he quit worrying about students and started worrying about his health. Donny never could find anything wrong with him, but Chester's convinced you will because, as he put it, there's a brain lodged in *your* head."

When she rolled onto her side as he'd instructed, the back of the gown fell open, revealing a diamond-shaped scar an inch to the left of her spine. "Looks like you had some kind of surgical procedure back here," he said, gently touching the red spot.

"I had a cyst removed six or seven years ago. It had been there for ages and never bothered me. Then I went on a canoe trip in North

Carolina with a seniors group, and it kept rubbing against the seat back and got infected. Can you imagine me in a canoe?"

She'd been big when she taught him. She was even bigger now. Dimpled fatty tissue clung to her buttocks and thighs. "I can imagine you in a canoe just fine," he said. "Though I can't imagine myself in one." He slipped on a latex glove and reached for the K-Y jelly.

When he inserted his finger, she tensed. "Bear down for me," he said, "as if you were trying to have a bowel movement." He felt around, checking for lumps or swelling. "Is that tender?"

"Why, hell yes, Pete. Where you think you are? On the San Diego Freeway?"

They both laughed. When he'd finished he pulled the glove off, tossed it away, washed his hands and told her she could sit up.

She sat on the edge of the examination table, the loose gown riding up over legs crisscrossed with varicose veins.

"To be on the safe side, I'm going to send you over to Greenville for a sigmoidoscopy."

"Sounds Freudian."

"Depends on how you define it. They put a scope with an eyepiece on it into your rectum and go up into the last third of the large intestine."

"An epic voyage."

"If you've got any growths of any kind in there, they can see them and then extract tissue and get it biopsied."

"I hope the eyepiece stays outside."

Unlovely and sardonic, never married and, he suspected, seldom kissed, she'd been among the least popular teachers at his school, but he'd always liked her and now he knew why. Because she was unlovely. Because she was sardonic. Because, having recognized a certain deformity in herself, she'd somehow learned to make light of it. "The eyepiece stays outside," he said.

"You're thinking we may be talking cancer?"

"No, I'm thinking we're almost certainly talking internal hemorrhoids. You said the blood you saw this morning was red?"

"As a fire engine."

"That's a good sign. If it had been coming from higher up in the

GI tract, it would have gotten digested and then you'd be seeing black stool. You haven't noticed anything like that, have you?"

"No. If I had, you'd be treating me for a fractured skull because I'd faint and fall over."

He laid a hand on her knee, broad as a watermelon. "Take it from me, Ms. Marsh. You don't want me treating you for a fractured skull."

"Pete Barrington," she said, in the same voice she'd once used to call on him in class after everybody else gave the wrong answer, "I'd trust you to treat me for a fractured skull or a blocked artery or an ingrown toenail and just about anything else—up to and including the blues."

————

When he walked onto the practice field that afternoon, the team was running nine on seven—the offensive line, backs and tight end against defensive line and linebackers. He stood and watched for a few moments, listening to the grunts of the linemen and trying to recall what it felt like to practice football in late summer, fall coming on and the first game around the corner. If he'd had to find a word for how he felt then, he probably would have settled on *expectant*. There was always the next game and then the game after that. Down the road a few miles, after the final whistle blew, manhood lay waiting. Whatever it demanded of him, he must have thought back then, wouldn't be any tougher than trying to hang on to a badly thrown ball when you knew the strong safety was about to spear you with his headgear, slam that Riddell in the pit of your stomach. In a sense he'd been right. Learning not to drop the ball had been the hardest thing for him as a man too.

Over the weekend he'd attended a meeting with Tim and the head coach, Rashard Killingsworth, and the other assistant, Brandon Robbins, who cheerfully announced that his main duty was to mix and dispense Gatorade. Killingsworth said they'd gone four and six last year but now had a couple of legitimate college prospects at tailback and defensive end, and though the schedule was by no means soft, he expected to win more than they lost. It would help a lot, he said, if

Pete could work with the tight ends and then spend a little bit of time with the defensive line.

Spotting him now, the head coach clapped his hands and called the team together, then motioned for Pete to join the huddle.

"We've got a new member of our staff here today," Killingsworth announced. "His name's Pete Barrington. Now I want to tell y'all a thing or two about him. First thing is, when you go see him at his office seeking medical treatment, he's *Doctor* Barrington. Sometime you might want to ask him what it took to earn that title because they don't give it away. When you see him on the football field, he's *Coach* Barrington. And he's earned that title too. Y'all understand me?"

Thirty-five headgears nodded.

"All right. Now if you grew up in this town, chances are you heard your daddy tell about Coach Barrington. How many did?"

Several hands went up.

Killingsworth called on one of the players. "What'd your daddy tell you about Coach?"

"Said he got a football scholarship someplace out west. Went out there and played on TV."

"That's right. Fresno State. Trent Dilfer, David Carr, Michael Pittman. Any of y'all ever watched them?"

A few more hands went up.

"All right. Now I hope Coach won't mind me saying this, but when he was young his daddy died. His momma got a job as a store clerk, but they had a tough time making ends meet. My point is, Coach needed that scholarship. Isn't that right, Coach?"

Pete nodded. He'd needed it for lots of reasons, and the most important ones had nothing to do with his desire to play football.

"And now he's a doctor. Made a bunch of money out in California, got a car came from Sweden, got himself some stocks probably and some bonds and some TSAs and some IRAs, been overseas a bunch of times, to Paris and London and Tokyo, and football started it all. Right, Coach?"

"That's right. What I learned playing this game's helped me throughout my life."

"Yes sir," Killingsworth said. "And now he's here to pass it on." He clapped his hands again. "All right, men. Let's do a little full-scale scrimmage. We'll show Coach Barrington who's made from sugar and who's made from salt."

While the team scrimmaged, Pete stood next to Tim. "Who told him that about my father dying and me growing up poor?"

His friend spat tobacco juice. "I got a feeling it may have been me."

"What else did you tell him?"

"Told him you could really clean a linebacker's plow when you blocked down." The tailback broke a long run, stiff-arming the safety as he turned the corner, then cruising into the end zone. "That's Reggie McDonald," Tim said. "Got loads of ability but he's in grade trouble all the time, mostly because he works at night and doesn't get enough sleep."

After the first-team offense had run ten plays against the second-team defense, they switched up. The kid playing tight end for the scrubs probably didn't weigh more than 170, yet on several plays he was being asked to block a first-team lineman who'd tip the scales at 280. Nobody knew better than the end that the task lay beyond his modest talent. Rather than fire off the ball, he stepped sideways, trying to set up and position block, but every time the result was the same—the big defensive lineman blowing into the backfield and leveling the number-two tailback.

"Awful!" Killingsworth screamed after one inept effort. "Depot, you're behaving in a feminine manner."

Brandon Robbins finally rolled out the Gatorade and a short break was called. The kid pretending to play tight end wrenched off his helmet. Sandy hair, intelligent eyes, a big ugly scab on the bridge of his nose.

Pete walked over. "What happened to your nose there?"

The boy shrugged. "Tried to block Shontell a few days ago. He hit me with a forearm, and my helmet came down over my eyes and cut me."

"And Shontell is?"

"Our best defensive lineman." He pointed at the big player he'd just been avoiding.

"That why you're refusing to stick your headgear into him?"

The kid looked over his shoulder. The other players were drinking their Gatorade, wrapping ice towels around their necks or just sprawling on the ground, exhausted. "Well, to be honest, Coach," he said, "I'm not real enthusiastic about getting hit like that again."

"Makes perfect sense to me."

"It does?"

"Sure does. But football's an insensible sport." He let the boy ponder that for a moment. "Why don't you and me make a little deal? If you ever decide you want to spare yourself some embarrassment and lay a hat on Shontell, you tell me and I'll show you how to do it. You won't stop him, but you might at least retard his progress."

"You're not going to yell at me or anything?"

"No, because yelling won't do any good. Your sense of self-preservation's telling you to stay away from him, and until you overrule it Shontell's going to maintain a presence in our backfield."

"I don't think I'm going to overrule it."

"You never can tell. You may surprise yourself."

When Killingsworth blew his whistle, the kid picked his helmet up and pulled it down over his ears. Before trotting after the others, he said, "Thanks, Coach."

"Hey, son, what's your name?"

Over the shoulder: "Mason DePoyster."

Pete was still standing there a minute later when Brandon Robbins rolled the Gatorade by, took one look at him and said, "Coach? Everything okay?"

Practice ended with the team running twenty forty-yard sprints, one after another, the bigger linemen swooning, one or two of the more devout ones beseeching Jesus to deliver them from such agony. Afterwards, in the parking lot, Tim asked Pete what he thought.

"Our tailback can motor, but the offensive line's a little slow off the ball, and it doesn't look like we've got much depth." He opened his truck door but didn't climb in. "That kid playing second-team tight end? The one they call Depot?"

"Yeah?"

"He wouldn't be Alan DePoyster's son, would he?"

"As a matter of fact, he is."

"How come you didn't mention it?"

Tim reached to put his hands in his pockets, then realized he had on gym shorts and settled for sticking his thumbs under the waistband instead. "Well," he said, "why would I?"

"I thought Alan moved away."

"He did. And then, about fifteen or sixteen years ago, he moved back. Just like you have. He runs the grocery store."

"Which one?"

"Piggly Wiggly. Same place Reggie McDonald works at. Why?"

"I just hadn't thought of him in a while." He glanced at his watch. "Hell, it's time to get home. Angela probably has dinner ready."

But instead of going straight home as he'd fully intended, he found himself turning off the highway onto Sunflower Street, driving past the old Ellsbury mansion with its twin cupolas, past the Methodist church and the library and then across Choctaw Creek. At the intersection of Sunflower and Loring Avenue, he pulled to the curb and looked across the street at the small English Tudor. A green Honda Accord was parked in the driveway, and a red tricycle with pink streamers on the handlebars stood near the steps. Somebody had painted the house beige now, with bright yellow trim around the windows. He was ninety-nine percent sure that it used to be white with beige trim, but there was at least a slight chance he'd gotten that backwards. If you'd told him twenty-five years ago that he'd ever forget a single detail about the place, he would've bet everything against it.

He'd made love for the first time sitting on a ladder-back chair in the basement. It was summer, her son at church camp, her husband in Memphis for a regional meeting of insurance agents. Still, she took no unnecessary chances. "If you know what you're doing's wrong," she said, reaching around to unhook her bra, "at least you should try to hide it."

The air-conditioning unit stood in the basement, a cold pipe running above their heads to the fan on a slab outside. The pipe was sweating. Drops fell onto his neck and shoulders.

"If you really thought it was wrong," he told her, "you wouldn't do it. We learned about Aristotle last semester in Western civ. You think what you're fixing to do'll bring happiness, else you wouldn't be here. You've defined it as *the good*."

Her breasts spilled out, the first ones he'd ever seen except in pictures or on a movie screen. It seemed like putting his hands on them would be okay, but he couldn't bring himself to do it. So she put them there herself. Then she closed her eyes, and her lips formed a word she never spoke.

She opened her eyes again. "I haven't studied Aristotle. Does he ever say anything about the difference between people and animals?"

His hands roamed, his thumbs exploring her nipples. The left one was bigger than the one on the right and darker in color. For the first but by no means the last time, he marveled at the level of detail that comprised a woman's body. "Yeah," he said. "Somewhere, I think."

"Well, we're animals right now. We're not thinking about the good. We're not thinking, period. Later on, when we go back to being people—well, that's when all the thinking'll set in. And then this won't be *the good* anymore."

"Then I don't want to go back to being a person," he said.

She lowered herself onto him and he buried his face between her breasts, which had begun to sweat too, like the overhead pipe.

"You won't have any choice," she said, beginning to move, the soles of her feet slapping concrete. "That's always the problem for folks like us. You have to live like a dog to have any fun at all, and then you go back to being a person when all you really want is to find another bone."

He was her bone all through the fall and winter and into the following spring, this woman whose first name he hadn't known when he started seeing her at the jogging track. She'd walked while he ran, and after a few days she began to speak to him each time he passed her, silly stuff at first—*nice stride . . . come on, you can go faster,*

I know you can—and then one day she'd strolled over and sat down beside him while he slumped on the bottom bleacher gasping for breath. "You've got the finest physique I've seen on a young man in a long time," she said, and he said, "You're Alan's mother, aren't you?"

"That's one way to look at it."

"Is there any other?"

"Now that's a conversation for another day." She glanced around the stadium, making sure it was empty. Then she ran her fingers through his wet hair and left.

One afternoon the following week she came into the United Dollar Store, where as far as he knew, she'd never been before. He was working there that summer, his mother the assistant manager doubling as checkout clerk, his grandmother walking the floor trying to pretend for the benefit of the poorest of the poor who shopped there that there was a qualitative difference between one piece of junk and another.

"Running today?" She lifted a can of Comet off the shelf.

"Yes ma'am."

"Yes *ma'am*? That's no way to talk to a woman who's crawled so far out on a limb."

"I don't know your first name."

"You don't need to. You just need to know it's not *ma'am*."

Her first name was Edie. The following year she did the same thing with another high school senior, and it must have been a lot easier since by then both her husband and her son had left town. He'd left town, as well. When he heard about what had happened, he couldn't help but wonder if she'd taken the other kid into the basement.

————

He was dimly aware as he put the truck in gear and headed toward home that another pickup stood at the opposite curb, not directly in front of the Tudor but a few feet away. He even registered the presence of a driver, though he didn't take the time to look at the man's face. He knew perfectly well what was going on. It was just some guy waiting for his wife to emerge so the two of them could go out and have dinner, maybe take in a movie and then stop off for a drink, spend an entire summer evening pretending their lives were still exciting.

ALAN REACHED UP AND pressed the button on the sun visor, opening the garage door, then drove in and parked beside Nancy's Pontiac. Normally he would've climbed out of the truck and, before stepping into the laundry room, closed the door by punching the wall button, but tonight he pressed the one on the visor a second time, sitting there until the door descended and the garage grew dark.

His shirt was soaked. He unsnapped the red-white-and-blue bow tie he'd worn to work every day for the last two years, ever since September 11, and tossed it onto the truck seat. He opened his collar too, but that didn't help much. Still he didn't get out.

He was clueless as to why he'd driven by the old place tonight and parked on the street. He hadn't done it the other day when he saw Pete Barrington on the steps of the post office, and he hadn't done it on any of the intervening days. He knew the family that lived in the house now, Ben and Lisa Paxton and their children, Ben Junior and Gracie. They shopped at his store and attended First Baptist church, where he served as a deacon. He'd never told them he'd once lived there, so he didn't know whether or not they were aware of it. He knew who'd lived in his current house right before he bought it, but the house had been standing for close to sixty years and he had no idea who'd lived in it in 1945 or '55 or '65, and he didn't care.

Neither did he care that the Paxtons occupied the house he'd once called home. They were a nice young couple—Ben a tractor salesman at Delta Implement, Lisa a dispatcher at Loring Heating and Cooling—and if he'd wanted to, he suspected, he could have knocked on their door any day of the week and told them he'd grown up there and that he'd gotten sentimental or something and been overcome by an urge to walk through those rooms again, and the Paxtons would have invited him right in. But the last thing in the world he felt any urge to do was walk through those rooms. And so it made no sense to him that he'd parked there on the street, where anybody who drove by or looked out their window could see him and wonder what in the world Alan DePoyster was doing sitting in his pickup at six o'clock on a weekday evening and staring at somebody else's house. It was the kind of thing only a criminal would do.

Yet somebody else was doing it too. When the other truck—an old GMC that had probably once been blue but was now so rusted out and dinged up that you couldn't really call it any one color—stopped at the opposite curb, he assumed it was somebody's yardman, that a black guy in dusty clothes would climb out and unload his lawn mower and get to work. But nobody climbed out. And in a moment his attention had been drawn away from his old house.

Light suddenly hit him in the face as the door to the laundry room swung open. "Dad?" Mason said. "Are you coming in?" He sounded alarmed, as Alan would have been if his son had sat alone in the garage for however long he'd been sitting there.

"Sure am." He climbed out and closed the truck door.

"What were you doing out here?"

He walked over and threw his arm around Mason's shoulders. "I was listening to the news on the radio," he said, which wasn't a total lie because he *had* been listening to it before deciding to drive by his boyhood home.

————

The dining room table was loaded down with fried chicken, coleslaw, baked beans, fresh tomatoes and corn bread. Somehow, in between now and five o'clock, when she got off work, Nancy had managed to ride the exercise bike for half an hour, shower and change into jeans and the white lace blouse she knew he loved, cook a meal and set the table. When he and Mason walked in, she said, "I was starting to get worried."

"It was a slow day. Started slow and ended slow. And then I heard a report about some more kids getting ambushed near Baghdad and got caught up in that."

He took his place at the end of the table, and she and Mason sat down on either side.

He knew a lot of people said the same mealtime prayer day after day, but he didn't believe in doing that. Every day was different—a different set of blessings, different set of worries—and he'd always tried to account for both in the prayer he said at supper. Today, however, he couldn't address what worried him, because he'd never said one word to either Nancy or Mason about Pete Barrington and the role he'd played in his life. He'd never expected to lay eyes on him again and couldn't even understand why he should be troubled that he had. No matter what pain Pete had caused in the past, there was no chance he could hurt him now. "Dear God," Alan began, "we thank you for this food and we ask that the energy it'll provide our bodies be put to good use. We pray for the two soldiers who were killed today, as well as for their families and loved ones, and we pray that peace will soon be restored to the Middle East. We pray for those who are suffering in all parts of the world."

He broke off with a vague sense of uneasiness at having held something back, and Nancy took her turn. "Our father," she said, "thank you that Mason wasn't hurt again at football practice. Also, thank you for helping me find the strength to keep my weight under control. Please take care of the woman who got cut today on the filet line and help all the workers who've been laid off."

When Mason understood that his mother had finished, he said, "Well, I'm every bit as thankful as Mom is that I didn't get hurt. Thanks for keeping me out of Baker's lab this year too, and please help that girl who looked so miserable in McCann's class this morning."

Traditionally Alan pronounced the closing words. He knew that if he didn't say more now than he'd said earlier, it would bother him all evening and he'd end up having to deal with it later when he sat alone in the backyard. "Dear God," he prayed, "we ask that any darkness which might be hiding in our hearts not be allowed to erupt, that you keep us from being mean-spirited or giving in to anger, that above all we continue to wish others well and never bear them grudges. Amen."

Mason lifted his fork and speared a drumstick. "We've got a new volunteer on the coaching staff," he said. "A really cool guy named Pete Barrington, who's also a doctor." He looked at his father. "You ever heard of him, Dad?"

Lying in bed that night with a Stephen Ambrose book, he considered the curious nature of war. Young men—eighteen, nineteen years old—went about the business of killing one another, yet many years later, when they gave their oral histories to Ambrose, the one emotion they rarely mentioned was anger. They'd experienced plenty of fear, sometimes pure terror, but again and again they spoke of the enemy with respect and compassion. Some of them had actually become friends with the Germans they'd once fought, meeting them on the anniversaries of famous battles, strolling arm in arm over the very ground where they'd slaughtered one another's comrades.

He laid the book on his bedside table, opened the drawer and pulled out his Scofield Bible and flipped to the concordance. Somewhere—the source escaped him right now—there was a verse that said something about how anger rested only in the bosom of fools.

He'd just thumbed the parchment when one eye registered motion. He looked up to see that Nancy had stepped out of the bathroom stark naked. The sight of his wife without her clothes on never failed to bring a rush of heat into his cheeks. Immobile, she stared at him, her hands hanging at her sides, hiding nothing. In the last couple of years she'd put on fifteen or twenty pounds, couldn't lose it no matter how hard she tried, and even though her weight gain had been arrested, she was ashamed of the extra girth of hips and stomach. The fact that she made no move to conceal what embarrassed her enflamed him now to the point of madness. "Nancy," he said, his voice weak, raspy. "Just look at you. Oh, just look at you."

She did move then, stepping around the foot of the bed, never losing eye contact, finally reaching down and lifting the cover.

Toni's locker was the last one on the bottom at the end of the hall, right next to the breezeway between the main building and the gym. Number 640. Most of the paint had been chipped off the door, which looked as if somebody had tried to kick it in. The first few days she'd had trouble opening it, but this morning she gave it a good jerk and it swung right out. She pulled her lit book from her backpack, shoved the backpack in and slammed the door shut.

Rather than succumb to the urge to move fast and keep her head down, she lingered in the hallway, looking at the pictures that hung on the walls, as if perusing them with a critical eye. Portraits of all the valedictorians going back to 1921, pictures of the old high school that had stood downtown, action shots from sports events, parades, graduation ceremonies and senior proms. Where the east and west wings of the main building met, not far from her English classroom, stood a big glass case filled with medals and trophies, and in one corner of that case there was a large framed photo of interest to her, though she glanced around and made sure no one was watching before she examined it more closely. In the photo a football player with the number 88 on his chest had just caught a pass and was in the act of tucking the ball under his arm and turning upfield. Because of the face mask, you couldn't see much besides his eyes, which had an expectant look in them as if he knew he'd just become the object of everyone's attention and relished the scrutiny. Underneath the photo, an inscription: *Pete Barrington, All-State Tight End, 1979.*

A voice said, "That's your dad."

It was the kid from her English class who always knew the answers but never raised his hand. Sandy hair, gashed nose. Generic-looking sneakers, washed-out 501s, a blue short-sleeved pullover with the silhouette of a church steeple on the pocket and beneath it, in script, *2003 Mississippi Baptist Convention Youth Delegate.* Depot. Even the teachers called him that.

"That's not who my dad *is*," she said. "That may be who he *was.*"

Depot whistled. "Wow."

"Wow what?"

"That's a weighty kind of talk. In California they must teach philosophy in high school. I mean that sounds, like, existential or something."

"Just the truth," she said, looking at the picture again. "He was seventeen then. He's forty-two now. Imagine I took your picture right this minute. You think that when you're forty-two you'll have much in common with the current version of yourself?"

He hung his head. "I'll never be forty-two."

"Why not?"

"I've got a genetic disease."

"Jesus."

"Yeah. They say I'll only make it into my late twenties. Maybe early thirties, if I'm lucky."

"Are you serious?"

"Afraid so. Some folks die from it when they're even younger. And the sad thing is, they've been researching it for decades but there's still no cure in sight."

"What's the disease?"

He grinned. "My heart melts."

Her facial muscles froze. She must have presented the perfect image of stupidity and gullibility. Caught for all time, at least in his mind, just as the photographer had caught her father. She lifted her right foot and brought the heel down hard on his toe.

"Aw!" he yelped, dropping his lit book, drawing stares from both ends of the hall. "Why'd you do *that*?"

She refused to move her foot, every ounce of energy she could muster went into keeping him pinned. "This is a photo op," she said. "In my mind I'm taking your picture like you look right now, with your eyes bugged out, your nose busted and your mouth screwed sideways from pain. I'm even composing a caption like the one underneath that silly church steeple you're wearing right above your melted heart. Want to know what my caption says?"

He swallowed once, then gnawed his lip.

" 'September seventh, 2003. A Young Creep Weeps in a High School Hallway.' "

———

In English they'd been sitting in adjacent rows right in the middle of the room, a couple of seats from the teacher's desk, but today he sat by the window and she grabbed a desk by the door. Just as far from each other as they could get. His cheeks, she could see when she glanced over, were bright red. He never looked up from his book but must not have been following along, because when Mrs. McCann, who regarded him as her pet, called on him to read the first three stanzas of "When Lilacs Last in the Dooryard Bloomed," he didn't react. "Depot," she said. "Did you *hear* me?"

"Yes ma'am. I mean, no ma'am."

"I guess maybe your star's been drooping in the west too. Are you thinking of her you love?"

The classroom dissolved into squawks and giggles.

He recovered quickly—Toni admired him for that. "You're quoting from the poem," he said, "but distorting it. This particular poet never thought of a *her,* he only thought of a *him.* It doesn't say it in this anthology, and you haven't told us, but he was gay as blue blazes."

"Aw, naw!" another kid hollered, banging both hands on his desk. "This the first shit I liked and now you telling me *that*? Depot, why you want to ruin things?"

"James," Mrs. McCann said, "I've warned you about these outbursts."

"My folks don't want me reading stuff by no *gay* guy. They sing in the Mount Zion choir."

At lunch, sitting alone as she had for each of the last three days, she noticed him watching her from his regular place. He was one of the few white kids in the school who ate lunch with blacks, the same ones each day, three girls and one guy. All of them brought stacks of books to the table and seemed to be quizzing one another between bites. When his gaze met hers, he looked away fast.

She got out of the lunchroom as soon as she could and, with nothing else to do, walked down the hall to see if the piano in the music teacher's classroom was free. When the teacher got over the shock of hearing her play the other day, she'd said Toni could use the instrument anytime she wanted, as long as class wasn't in session.

The door was open, the room empty, so she walked over to the piano and sat down.

Initially her mother had tried to interest her in her own favorite composers—Scriabin and Rachmaninoff—so Toni focused on Bach. Then she encountered the head of the music department at University High, whose dislike of Rachmaninoff was legendary, so she trimmed sail and began to play the work of the Russian composer at every opportunity. Hearing her storming through the last variations of the *Rhapsody on a Theme of Paganini,* the department head would holler, "That's diabolical."

She never lost the rhythm. "It's supposed to be. Paganini sold his soul to Satan."

"That doesn't mean you've got to sell yours to Rachmaninoff."

Now, with no one to annoy, she could just play what she wanted, so she chose Shostakovich. She was making a mess of the A Minor Prelude with its confounding semiquavers when she became aware someone was watching her. She looked over at the door and saw him standing there, one hand against his forehead.

She lifted her fingers off the keys. "Is my playing giving you a headache?"

"No. It's really beautiful." He crammed the offending hand into his pocket. "I mean, my gosh. I never knew anybody who could play like that."

"You should hear my mother."

"She's better?"

"No, she's worse. But she can *play like that,* as you put it."

"What kind of music was that?"

"An abstract composer's approach to the baroque."

He sat down on a stool behind a pair of congas. "That doesn't tell me a heck of a lot. My idea of music's Metallica. I'm afraid I'm fairly ignorant."

"If you're listening to Metallica, you must be."

"I didn't say I was *listening* to them. My folks don't like that kind of music, and it'd bother my dad if I played it at home, so I don't."

"If you like it, why not?"

"If your dad didn't want you to do something, would you make it a point to?"

On the defensive for the first time, she said, "I might. Or I might not. It would depend."

"On what?"

"On how bad I wanted to do it."

"Well, there aren't many things I want to do bad enough to annoy my dad."

"Why? Are you that scared of him?"

He thumped a conga once or twice. "I'm not scared of him at all. No reason to be. He's a nice guy. So's your dad. I probably would've quit playing football this week if it hadn't been for him. Now I think I'll stick it out."

The bell rang. It was followed by the sound of voices in the hall-way, lockers creaking open and clanging shut.

"Listen," he said, "I was being stupid this morning. I'm really sorry. I just figured out yesterday that Coach Barrington was your dad. I like him, and when I saw you looking at his picture, I thought I'd introduce myself. But I don't know, I got nervous or something, and that's why I made that dumb joke. It's not like me. Really. I don't do stuff like that."

With her right hand she played the first few notes of a melody without knowing what it was. She meant to buy a little time in which to decide if she should follow his confession with a put-down or tell him not to worry. There were arguments for each response. On the one hand, nobody else around here had tried to talk to her, and she knew he wasn't stupid and even liked his looks except for the gash on his nose, and that would eventually heal. On the other hand, he was wearing that shirt with the church steeple on it, he'd outed Walt Whitman and his idea of a good time might be some prayer meeting. Before she could come down on either side of the issue, the music teacher walked in, so they both got up and left the room together.

Outside, moving along through the crush of rushing bodies, he said, "My name's Mason—Mason DePoyster. But everybody calls me Depot."

"Do you like that nickname?"

"Hate it."

"Then I won't call you that."

"You plan to use my name much? You think you'll have occasion to say it fairly often?"

They'd reached her locker. She bent down, spun the dial on her lock, opened the door, pulled out her algebra book and handed it to him, then squatted and began to rifle through her stuff, pretending to look for something. The bell rang again, indicating both of them were late. Beside her, the weight in his sneakers shifted, but he never moved his feet, never said he'd better get going, just patiently continued to stand there.

ON SATURDAY MORNING around nine o'clock, while Mason and Nancy slept in, Alan drove his pickup across the railroad tracks just as he'd promised and parked in front of the little white house where Reggie McDonald lived with his mom and sister.

Reggie was waiting on the front porch, yawning and stretching, his wiry muscles rippling. "Sure do appreciate you doing this for me, Mr. Alan," he said. "First thing I mean to do if I ever sign a pro contract's buy two pickups just like yours. One for me, one for you. You gone could use a new one by then."

Reggie stood five-eight and weighed about 170. Alan had watched him play a few times last season, and while he didn't know much about football, he knew enough to see the kid had real talent. He also knew he'd probably never be big enough for the NFL. As for college, well, there was always the issue of his grades. Twice last year Alan had put him on paid vacation, over Reggie's protests, telling him to take off for a week and study. In both instances, Alan stayed late and stocked Reggie's aisle himself. "Before you worry about buying us trucks," he told him now, "you need to take care of your momma."

"Why? She ain't sick."

"She's not sick now. But later on it may be a different story. Working on that filet line day in and day out's rough on a person. The time may come when she'll need to move into whatever mansion the Dallas Cowboys bought you."

Despite the fact that Alan was older and white, Reggie felt comfortable enough to take issue with him. "I ain't notice your momma living with you."

Alan paused near the foot of the steps, pulled his cap off and began to fan himself. "She doesn't want to live with me. Got a big house of her own up in Memphis." He ran his fingers through his hair before putting the cap back on. "Now, where's that pile of junk that needs moving?"

Reggie looked like he was going to say something else, then evidently changed his mind. "Back yonder in the shed." He hopped down off the porch, and Alan followed him around the corner of the house.

The shed door had a rusted padlock on it, but rather than unlock it Reggie pulled a nail from each hinge with his bare fingers and swung the door open backwards. "The padlock's just discouragement," he said. "We ain't got the key."

Inside, a long workbench was covered with tools, electrical meters and circuit panels. Near the back, stacked almost up to the ceiling, were some old television sets, radios and stereos. A pile of picture tubes took up one corner.

Alan whistled. Reggie hadn't specified the nature of "the junk" that needed moving. "How'd you come by all this stuff?"

"It ain't what you think."

"How do you know what I think?"

"Well, maybe *think* ain't the right word. Maybe more like *suspect*. But I ain't stole it. My daddy left that stuff in here."

The only thing Alan knew about Reggie's father was that he'd been killed eight or nine years ago when a tractor flipped over on him as he tried to pull a stump from some bottomland the man he worked for was clearing. "I didn't realize he repaired audio-visual equipment."

"He was learning to. Had him a bunch of manuals he ordered from someplace up in Ohio and was studying to get certified. That was his main word. *Certified*. He knew every different form of it—*certificate, certification*. Only thing he talked about. Said when he got it he was gone open up a shop and we'd move over town. Just think, Mr. Alan. You and me might of been neighbors."

Even with the door open, the light in the shed was poor, but that now struck Alan as a fortunate circumstance: his throat suddenly felt constricted, as if a blockage had developed somewhere in his larynx.

"I don't know what use anybody'd have for this stuff," Reggie was saying. "But Kawika Fordyce told Momma he'd give a hundred dollars for the load."

As far as Alan knew, he'd never met Reggie's dad. But he could feel his presence in this hot little shed, could almost see him standing over the workbench with a manual spread open beside him, a dim light dangling from the ceiling where now there was only an empty socket. A dark-skinned man in his late twenties, clad in dust-encrusted khakis, no education to speak of, no future that anybody else could envision, a young man determined to do right by his wife and kids, to set himself up in business and move to a better part of town. Only a terrible accident could beat a man like that. Something big and heavy coming down.

"I ain't crazy 'bout being out here. I seen a snake crawl under the door one time. Probably a chicken snake, but I got adverse feelings for the whole reptile kingdom."

They took the larger items first, both of them gripping the consoles by the edges, straining and sweating as they carried them across the yard. Reggie said his mother would've helped but had to pull a shift today, and his sister was over at a friend's place. Then he asked if Alan was going to the father-son banquet that evening, which the coaches always threw for the team on the Saturday before football season started.

Alan had been looking forward to this for months but now wished he could avoid it. Distracted, he lost his grip on the big Zenith they were carrying, and one of the legs smashed his toe. "Damn," he sputtered.

Reggie dropped his side too, more from amazement than anything else. "Mr. Alan! I didn't know you cussed."

Alan gritted his teeth. His toe felt like it had been hit by a hammer. "Most folks'd cuss if that happened to them."

"I'd sure cuss. Just didn't know you would."

"There's lots about me you don't know."

He thought about that statement later, after they'd made two trips to Fordyce's liquor store and Reggie collected his mother's hundred dollars and got dropped off back at his place. The kid had just laughed when Alan said that, and a moment later he was chattering away about some cheerleader he knew was going to break up with Shontell Clemons any day now and start going with him. The curiosity he'd expressed when he heard Alan curse didn't extend very far—certainly not far enough for him to wonder what there could possibly be to Mr. Alan that didn't meet the eye, or what things you might learn if you followed him around after he stepped out of the grocery store and pulled off his bow tie.

———

That afternoon he took a shower, then lay down on the couch in the den and tried to sleep. But Mason was in the next room doing homework, and Alan could hear him typing on his keyboard, and whenever he quit for a while and the screen saver came on, the computer started making weird noises like the ones you used to hear when the submarine dived in *Voyage to the Bottom of the Sea.*

Through the window he watched Nancy pedaling the exercise bike, her hair done up in a bun, some kind of women's magazine clutched in her hands. After a little while she began to get tired, closed the magazine, dropped it on the patio, then bent over the bars and pumped even harder.

She was the only woman Alan had ever made love to. The popular perception seemed to be that everything got worse between two people after all the newness wore off, but what happened between the two of them in bed had only gotten better and better. And it had been good to begin with.

It had been good despite the fact that, as she'd told him one evening about a week before their wedding, her brother had abused her when she was fifteen. Before Alan could say a word, mouth gaping open and lungs empty, she corrected herself. "I shouldn't put it that way," she said. "Because I never said don't. He should've known better. He didn't, but abuse is not what it was." When he remained mute, she said, "Would you please say something, Alan? The look on your face frightens me." Her brother was in Germany, serving in the military, and Alan had never met him. And it was a good thing right then that the Atlantic lay between them and he couldn't afford to buy a plane ticket and didn't have a passport.

It was another two years before the dreaded encounter finally took place, at a family reunion down in Raymond, and he couldn't believe how normal the guy seemed. He was just an ordinary young man in his mid-twenties, with a military haircut and an unassuming manner, and if he bore any ill will toward the man who'd married his sister, Alan couldn't detect it. Jimmy walked right over to the table where Alan was hovering over a big bowl of coleslaw, begging God to help him get through the day, and introduced himself. Then he did exactly what Alan had feared he would do: he gazed at his sister. She was surrounded at that moment by younger female cousins, their eyes glittering with envy, all of them probably hoping they'd grow up to be just that tall and trim and beautiful. "She sure does look happy," Jimmy said. After making that observation, he glanced down at the small, thin blonde who'd materialized at his side. "I hope I make you look that happy," he said, then introduced Alan to this German girl who'd just agreed to become his wife. Before the day was over, the brothers-in-law had teamed up to surrender sixteen runs in a losing softball match.

They borrowed money from each other once or twice down through the years, and in 1998 their families spent Christmas together at Gulf Shores. While the two of them had never become close, neither had they ever come close to blows. And Alan knew as surely as he'd known anything that if he called him up right now and said, "I'm in trouble, I need your help," Jimmy would bid good-bye to his wife and their two little blond girls who spoke perfect German, and then climb in the car and make the long drive from Atlanta, no questions asked.

Alan had never learned anything about him that would excuse what he'd done. His father hadn't beaten him, his mother hadn't clung to him, and he'd never had any particular trouble finding a date. But one night, when he was seventeen and alone with Nancy, he'd done something abominable. Still, as horrible as that action was, it hadn't foretold the kind of man he'd become.

Alan got up off the couch and waved at Nancy, who smiled and pinched her hip, as if to suggest that until there was less of her, the self-torture would continue. He walked into the hallway and said, "Son, are you still on the computer?"

"No sir. I'm through for now."

"Mind if I boot you out of your digs a few minutes?"

Mason came out yawning. "No sir. I'd like to catch a little of the Ole Miss game anyhow."

"What channel are they on?"

"ESPN."

"Well, soon as I get done doing a little research, maybe I'll join you."

Once in his son's bedroom, he closed the door. He sat down at the desk, moved one of Mason's textbooks aside, clicked the Explorer icon and, in the search bar on Google, typed: doctor pete barrington fresno california.

He would never know if the line from Ecclesiastes had really come to him then, like some celestial pop-up, or if through hindsight he'd only convinced himself it had. He wasn't that big on the Old Testament. It emphasized retribution over forgiveness, which seemed to him something most folks needed more of. He knew he did. So while he could quote plenty of Scripture from the Gospels and the Pauline epistles, he would've been hard-pressed to recite much of anything else. Yet he felt, before the machine flashed its first list of results, an unmistakable warning:

He that increaseth knowledge increaseth sorrow.

———

In the gym, tables had been arranged in four long rows with name cards in front of each place setting. His was flanked by Mason's on one side and Shontell Clemons's on the other. Cody Blackstone, the starting quarterback, and his dad would be seated across from them. Reggie, who at that moment was busily ragging Shontell, unfortunately had been assigned a different table. It looked as if the plan was to make sure the boys whose fathers weren't present got spread out so everybody would have a dad nearby, even if it wasn't his own.

To his relief, Alan noticed that the coaches would eat at their own table, along with the team captains and their fathers and the high school principal. Though Pete wasn't there when they walked in, he appeared soon enough, wearing a pair of cleanly pressed khakis and a white dress shirt with the sleeves rolled up. When you saw him up close, his size was hard to ignore. He'd put on weight since high school but not much. Alan would have pegged him at 230, maybe 235, and it was obvious he still worked out, his whole body rock solid.

He'd never been anybody to mess with. Alan had played football only one year but still remembered an incident during two-a-days. The weakside linebacker on the second-team defense, he'd been giving halfhearted chase behind a sweep when the ball carrier ran out of room near the sideline and reversed field. Alan planted his foot, spun, reversed field himself—and caught a helmet right in the sternum. The next thing he knew, he was flat on his back, his head aching as if somebody had hit him with a baseball bat, salty blood trickling into his mouth and a coach's voice hollering, "Way to go, Barrington! Goddamn!"

Pete moved among the players and their fathers, shaking hands, clapping one or two kids on the back and, in one case, dropping into a three-point stance to illustrate some technique while a kid looked on with stars in his eyes. Alan started talking to Marvis Blackstone, doing his best not to look in Pete's direction. He overheard him asking one of the fathers if the new blood pressure medication was causing him to sweat excessively. Rumor had it that the moment he opened his practice, he'd begun drawing patients away from the Alexander brothers. You couldn't really blame him. The Alexanders were incompetent.

Alan had hoped everybody would sit down before Pete got around to him and Cody's dad, but the inevitable finally occurred.

"Hi, Alan," Pete said, holding his hand out.

Alan offered his own, knowing Pete couldn't help but detect the moist palm. "Hello, Pete. You know Marvis Blackstone?"

Marvis laughed. "Knows me inside out. How you doing, Doc?"

"Doing just fine." Pete gestured at Killingsworth, who was chatting with Tim Kessler on the far side of the room. "Better not call me Doc around here, though. That drives Rashard crazy."

"The first syllable of that man's name's very well chosen," Marvis said. "Because he ain't nothing if not rash. He pull my boy out this year after every interception, me and him gone set down and talk."

"Between the two of us, I'd have that conversation with him on the phone, Marvis."

Grunting, Marvis glanced at his watch, said he guessed he'd better take a leak before dinner and wandered off toward the restroom.

Pete watched him go. "The thing is," he said, "Cody rushes his passes when the protection breaks down. And it's going to. The game's changed since we played it. Even high school teams do a lot of zone blitzing now, dropping ends and tackles into coverage and bringing the safeties and corners, and some of our linemen aren't picking it up." He crossed his arms over that huge chest. "How've you been, Alan?"

Maybe because his pores had opened up and his armpits, legs, back and neck were streaming sweat, Alan felt he'd become less substantial, as if even the facts of his physical existence were entering a state of flux. It came to him that he was not by nature a generous person. Generosity was a gift that had been bestowed on him, and now he felt it slipping away. Until this afternoon he'd been trying to believe Pete's presence across the street from his old house a couple weeks ago indicated that what had happened back then left its mark on him too, that it was still something he thought about, that it had the power to wound him just as it had wounded Alan. If you made that kind of mistake once, Alan had been telling himself, you wouldn't make it again. You'd do like Jimmy, his brother-in-law, and lead the straightest life you could, trying every day to give back more than you took because you'd once taken far too much.

This gift of generosity had allowed him to make up with his mother not long after Mason was born. He and Nancy had bundled him up and driven to Memphis, where Edie DePoyster was living openly with a rich man who, like her, was still legally married to somebody else. The gift had also enabled him to continue loving the memory of his own dad, even though as a parent himself he couldn't imagine a more monstrous action than abandoning a human being you'd brought into the world, no matter how badly you'd been hurt.

For years, the same gift had made it possible for him to imagine a future in which Pete Barrington, who'd gone on to become a rich California doctor, fielded a character as solid as his body. But Pete's character, he'd learned this afternoon, was still porous. Whatever good he'd done, he still continued to wreak havoc in other people's lives.

Now here he was, the two of them standing face-to-face. And something had to be said.

"I've been just fine," Alan told him, "for almost twenty-five years."

THE LOSS OF SENSATION

More often than not a bell woke Tim Kessler. Sometimes it was the bell on his alarm clock, the Sears Roebuck special he'd owned as a boy, one of the few things he'd insisted on keeping when he and Jena split up. Other times it was a bell at the fire station, which stood just a block or so away. More frequently, it was the telephone. Repeat offenders called so often that he could usually identify them the moment they said, "Mr. Kessler?" They spoke his name tentatively, just as he would have if he'd been them.

When the phone rang that Tuesday morning, it took a while to penetrate the dense fog he'd slept in. The first thing he saw after opening his eyes was the Bushmills bottle. He could see right through it. Groaning, he swung his legs off the couch, bashed his knee against the coffee table, but still managed to grab the receiver before the caller hung up.

Which was a good thing, because the voice on the other end said, "Daddy?"

"Susan. Where are you, honey?" He glanced at his watch. Eight twenty-five. "Shouldn't you be at school?"

"I am at school."

"Where?"

"In *Jackson,* Daddy. That's where my school is."

"I know that, sweetie. I mean *where* at the school? Don't you have a class now?"

"Oh. I'm in the bathroom. In a stall."

He carried the phone over to his lone armchair. When he settled into it, a dust cloud arose. He'd been meaning to have the place cleaned. He'd intended to do that and also to buy some groceries, an actual chicken, maybe, or a package of rice and some potatoes and lettuce and green beans, start cooking real food rather than continuing to live off McNuggets and fries. Yesterday, for lunch, he'd made a mayonnaise and potato chip sandwich. "What're you doing in the bathroom stall?" he said.

"I told my teacher I was feeling sick."

"Are you?"

"Sort of."

"Sort of how?"

She lapsed into silence. He heard a clattering noise in the background and then a sound like rushing water.

"Susan? Are you still there?"

"Jesus," she whispered. "I didn't know anybody else was in here."

"Are you in some kind of trouble?"

Another whisper: "Hold on."

He sat there clutching the receiver until she sighed and said, "They're gone."

"So answer my question, honey. Is something wrong?"

"I want to come home."

Hearing her call this place *home,* on a morning like this, was about as bad as driving down the road and seeing a billboard with his face on it above a list of all his shortcomings, either a huge billboard or very small print. "Well, you can't do that, sweetie," he said. "Much as I'd like it."

"Why not?"

"Because the sovereign state of Mississippi casts a hard eye on the wayward, and that's what they've decided your daddy is."

"Can't you just stop drinking?"

"Sure I can. Sometimes I stop for two or three weeks straight. Only time I've ever been drunk in court's when I was on trial. So to speak."

"You're on trial now. With me."

He closed his eyes for a few seconds, then opened them again. While they were shut nothing had changed. Their conversation was real, not part of some drunken dream. "Football season starts Friday night," he said. "Why don't you ask your momma if you could visit one of these weekends? Think you could do that? I'd drive down and pick you up. An old friend of mine's just moved back here from out in California—Pete Barrington, you've heard me talk about him—and he's got a daughter about your age. You could come to the game and watch me coach, and then on Saturday we'd all have a cookout."

"She won't let me. You wouldn't believe how mean she's been."

"Want to tell me what the source of your problem with her might be? It wouldn't be Kent, would it?"

"No, it's not Kent. He's okay. He even took me to a movie the other day while she went shopping. He's not a bad guy at all."

He was a dull guy, Tim had heard, just as bland as Nebraska, an accountant in north Jackson, the kind of fellow who'd give the Republican Party a thousand dollars for the chance to watch Haley Barbour stuff himself with pancakes. "I never said he was bad."

"But neither is he my daddy."

He bowed his head after that one.

She sniffled. "What happened is that my friend Mandy's been using an alias and having Web chats with this guy at our school named Van, who she thinks is cute. He doesn't have the faintest idea it's her he's chatting with, he believes it's somebody in Florida, so he's saying all kinds of crazy things and then she says crazy things back. Well, the other day she e-mailed me one of those chats, and it had some dirty stuff in it."

"What kind of dirty stuff?"

"You know."

"If I knew, I wouldn't be asking."

"They were, like, talking about the kind of stuff Monica Lewinsky was doing with Bill Clinton."

"Your friend was saying she'd do that with Van?"

"Yeah, and I was dumb enough to print it out, and Momma found it in one of my drawers. She shouldn't be going through my things like that."

"She went through my drawers too," he said, before he could stop himself.

"Yeah, I remember." Dead silence. "So anyhow, after she found it, she sat me down—in front of Kent, Daddy, that's what was so awful—and asked if I'd been doing stuff like Mandy was talking about. I told her I don't even know what those words *mean,* and I bet Mandy didn't, either. So she says, 'How can you use them if you don't know what they mean?' and I told her, 'Well, you don't have to know how to dance just to say *ballet.*'"

He burst out laughing.

"See? You think it's funny. But she just started sobbing and pulling her hair, and Kent made her go lie down. And now I can't use the computer, and she even took away my cell phone and says I can't see Mandy or any of my other friends except at school. For all practical purposes, Daddy, my life is just *ruined.*"

The full import of her statement took a moment to sink in. "Honey," he said, "if she confiscated your cell phone, what are you calling me on?"

Silence again. "It's someone else's phone."

"Whose?" His head began to pound even before she supplied the answer.

"Well, to be perfectly honest, Daddy," she said, "the sovereign state of Mississippi would probably consider it stolen."

SEEKING A SYMPATHETIC HEARING, and aware that Pete would be at work, Tim went to their door. As Angela stood back to let him in, he apologized. "I could've at least taken a shower. I mean, there's a certain amount of botanical activity going on in the stall, I don't deny that, a regular garden growing on the tile, but that's no excuse."

"Really, Tim," she said, "it's all right. You look fine."

He looked anything but. His eyes were streaked with red, and his shirt was misbuttoned. She could smell whiskey on him, as well as something she identified as emotional residue.

In the living room she watched him take in the music spread out on the floor around the Petrof, the cup of tea standing on an end table beside the couch, the book of poems open on the glass-topped coffee table.

"I feel like I'm at Lincoln Center," he said. "Understand, I've never been there, but I associate the name with pianos and the kind of tea you drink out of a cup and itsy little books like that one over there."

"Would you like some tea? I can bring you a glass with some ice cubes in it."

Alone in an honest-to-God house with a grown woman: a kind of reverence came over him, as if he were in church. But this type of reverence, he found, demanded something besides tea. "I'd be more inclined to say yes to a beer."

"A beer it is."

"But don't put it in a glass. That spoils the flavor."

In the kitchen she rummaged through the refrigerator until she found a long-necked Bud and went back to the living room.

"Thank you, ma'am." He nodded at the piano. "You play?"

"Since I was four."

"I knew Toni did. But Pete didn't tell me about you."

Every omission assumed significance. In defiance of mathematical logic, minuses did add up. "Actually, I taught her."

"How was that?"

"Hard sometimes. When she was younger she'd cry if I criticized her. Then, as she got older, she'd make me cry. She's really good, though. Last year she placed second at the Southern California Bach festival. The winner's at Juilliard this fall."

"Damn." He began to drag his thumb back and forth over the Budweiser label.

"Are you going to start peeling that off?" she asked.

Absurdly, he thought of the night he'd gone to visit his college roommate, whose mother was a dentist down in Gulfport. In the guest room of a big Victorian, his friend gestured vaguely at the hallway and said the bathroom was out there. After waking the next morning with his bladder about to burst, Tim slipped into the hallway stark-naked and opened the first door to discover a roomful of patients staring right at him. Nobody had told him the dentist worked at home.

He felt just as naked now. "Hadn't really thought about it. Why?"

"I've never actually seen anybody peel off a beer label. But they sing about it all the time in some of the music Pete likes."

"That'd be music by folks called Merle or Buck. And if you don't mind, I believe I will peel this label. Give my hands something to do."

While he scratched off bits of coated paper and rolled them into tiny cylinders he dropped onto the glass table, he talked about his daughter's phone call and how worried he was. Since she and her mother had moved to Jackson, her grades had gone to hell and she'd made a bunch of bad friends and even been threatened with suspension. "I mean, don't get me wrong. She's a great kid. Got the kind of wit I just love—*acerbic,* I guess is the word—and there's times I wish

I could've known her when I was the same age. Now I know that sounds a little like reverse Oedipalism or something, but that's not how I mean it. I just would've liked to hang out with her, be her buddy." He shook his head. "Hell, we used to have a fantastic time. That girl knows football inside out and makes the meanest barbecue sauce I ever tasted. Won't tell a soul what's in it."

"Why'd your marriage fail?"

"I don't think it was anything I did. More like everything I didn't do. What I did was just the pretext Jena used. I even think maybe I sabotaged myself on purpose, just so she'd have a reason to get rid of me." Closing one eye, he gazed into the bottle as if gauging its contents. "You know what she said was her happiest memory of me? It's one night when Susan's about three years old, and they're both waiting in the car, and I come out of Piggly Wiggly in a driving rain, carrying a grocery sack in one hand and a gallon of milk in the other. She said for just that one moment there, she thought I might actually grow up."

She was noticing details now such as his front tooth. "Did you get into a fight last night?"

"I don't think so. Why?"

"Your tooth's chipped."

"That happened years ago. At Ole Miss. Me and a bunch of my buddies were at Kroger getting some beer, and I was pulling out to the street when I noticed a carload of Tri-Delts turning into the parking lot, so I stuck my head out the window to give a Rebel yell and ran smack into a light pole. Would you have spent five minutes on a guy who did that?"

He looked as if he were going to laugh, so she mustered a smile.

It was his task to watch that same smile fade when instead of laughter he produced something closer to a sob. He presumed, incorrectly, that she lacked experience dealing with nerves frayed by alcohol.

"Tim?" she asked. "Are you all right?"

"Absolutely not. Are you?"

The pile of paper strips accumulating on the coffee table caught her eye, which was searching, right then, for something to be caught by. There had been so little real conversation for so long that she felt incapable of it. She wondered once again what she was turning into, where the steady erosion of character would stop. When she was in shreds like that label? "There's a critical essay," she said, "to be written about those strips of colored paper you've peeled off that bottle. Lots of people do it, I gather, so there must be some common need they give in to."

He knew then that the decent thing to do was let the moment slip away. His decision, though arrived at instantly, occasioned no small measure of regret. She had her own wounds, and they might well be as deep as his. "The common need," he said, "to be immortalized in music. By the world's Merles and Bucks. Yes ma'am, I see what you're driving at. Sociology of label-peeling." He broke into song.

> I sit right here
> in real bad cheer
> pulling paper off my beer
> without no fear
> of folks thinking I'm queer
> oh I'm just a seer
> without no crystal ball.

He believed he could calculate the effect of his buffoonery, that as far as she was concerned, he might as well have painted his face white, rouged his cheeks and put on a pair of oversized slippers, since he'd already been filed under Clowns I Have Known.

But he was wrong. Instead he'd made her remember the night she'd met Pete. A Halloween party in north Fresno, hosted by the parents of her best friend's boyfriend. Everybody dressed up, she as an angel—the only suitable disguise, her friend claimed, for anybody with her name. The boyfriend brought along some guy in full Fresno State football regalia: red pants and red jersey, helmet, shoulder pads, the whole works, right down to the cleats, which left scuff marks on the marble floor. "Meet my friend Pete," the boyfriend said while she searched for human features behind the barred face mask. "He doesn't play football anymore. He's in medical school at USC. Pete, meet an angel."

Behind Tim's stupid lyrics, the twisted rolls of paper, all the talk about Lincoln Center and itsy little books, she sensed the presence of a person. The question was, would it be the same person from one day to the next, or did he also traffic in disguises? "If I go get a couple more beers," she said, "do you think you could teach me to strip off the label?"

Something in his chest twisted and turned over. "Damn straight. And I'll tell you one thing ahead of time."

"What's that?"

The broken tooth flashed. "Be a hell of a lot easier than learning how to play the piano."

A FRIDAY MORNING, the air not yet crisp though cooler than it had been and laced with the odor of defoliant. Pete was allergic to the stuff, would have a headache by afternoon, but he didn't care. They'd play their first game of the season that evening against a team from Yazoo City that would probably pound them. Still, there was always a chance they might win, and even if they didn't somebody at some point would make a play he had no business making, transcending his own limitations, and the sheer joy of knowing he'd get to watch it, to exult in the surprise, left him giddy. Even Toni's stiff presence beside him in the pickup couldn't ruin this day.

He pulled up in front of the school, reminding himself to warn Shontell Clemons once again that Yazoo City would most likely try to trap him, since he barreled into the backfield as if bound for a steak dinner.

He was surprised, nearly shocked, when Toni said, "Do you think we'll win tonight?" She was working on her nails, which she'd never done before in his presence. Her normally pale lips displayed real color.

"I don't know."

"I know you don't. You're not God."

The implication, he supposed, might be that he was Satan. But implications could always be ignored. "Well, they were eight and three last season and made it to the first round of the state playoffs, plus they're returning twelve seniors. So the odds are on their side. You never can tell, though. Stranger things have happened."

"If either team gets a big lead, will our reserves play?"

"That's up to Coach Killingsworth. Why?"

She stuck the nail file into her purse and slung the strap over her shoulder. "I feel sorry for the ones who can't do anything but sit there. Everybody in the stadium knows they aren't any good."

He pulled up at the drop-off point, and she grabbed her backpack and opened the truck door.

"Hey," he said, "hold on."

She got out but didn't shut the door, just stood there looking at him as if anticipating his next inanity.

"You want to come to the game? I can make sure you get a seat right on the fifty-yard line."

She glanced over her shoulder at the duty teacher, who was starting to act impatient because they were holding up traffic. By the time she looked back at him, the intensity of her gaze suggested that some new decision about his abject status might have been reached. If so, its announcement was being deferred. "Maybe," she said. "And then again, maybe not."

When she closed the door, at least she didn't slam it.

The day brought a stream of new patients, most of them black, many of them aged. The quarterback's father, Marvis Blackstone, whom he was already treating for chronic prostatitis, showed up with his mother, a short, thin woman who was seventy-eight years old, she said, and still capable of picking cotton all day if she had to. Her skin was a good bit lighter than Marvis's, and the arch of her cheekbones suggested Native American blood, which made sense to Pete once he had a look at her newly created file and discovered that she, like his grandfather, had been born in Webster County. She wore a bright blue dress with a quarter-moon pattern on it and sported black stockings rolled down to just above her sneakers. When he asked what was wrong, she said, "Sometime my head swim."

"Swim, my booty," Marvis said. "She been blacking plumb out. Cody came home yesterday from practice and found her sprawled out on the porch."

"Never sprawled once in my life. Sprawling ain't the kind of thing a lady do."

"This been going on now for close to a year. Took her in to Dr. Alexander, and he stick a flashlight in her eyes, thump her on the knee and say she must of fainted." Rocking on the balls of his feet, Marvis shook his head. "Now what kind of doctor is that? I watch a movie about cops, I want it to tell me something I don't already know from going into the Western Auto and looking at a pistol."

Pete asked if she'd felt any numbness in her legs or feet, and after first quibbling over his syntax—"How a person spose to *feel* numbness?"—she admitted that she sometimes experienced a tingling in her left foot and calf and had trouble controlling that leg. "But the way Marvis carry on"—she glared at her son—"I hate to tell him anything."

"I'd say his carrying on's a sign he loves you. Wouldn't you?"

"I might, if I wanted to waste words. But a person only draw so many breaths in their life. And every time you say a word, it cost you oxygen."

He couldn't argue with that assessment. He checked her pulse and blood pressure, listened to her heartbeat and then scheduled her for a CAT scan the following week. Before leaving, she reluctantly offered Pete her hand.

He treated a pond worker who'd been finned by a catfish, prescribed penicillin for the police chief, who'd developed septic bursitis in his elbow, saw a truly horrible case of shingles that had spread into a woman's vagina, and immediately got on the phone with a neurologist after a retired farmer was brought in by his wife, who said, "All he can tell me is his face won't move." Bell's palsy, quite possibly.

At a quarter past twelve—already late—he told his nurse-receptionist he'd be back before two and went to meet Angela at L'Arc de Triomphe, "Loring's First French Restaurant," opened the previous week by a former classmate, Sandra Jean Sturdivant, where her dad's barbershop used to be. He wasn't exactly expecting Chez Panisse.

Angela was sitting at a lonely table in the rear. Forty years ago, while his grandfather told some genial hunting lies, Pete had gotten his first professional shoe shine right there from a black man everybody called Buff. Now, as he stood surrounded by empty tables and looking at his wife, who kept her eyes focused on her wineglass as though she feared that whoever had just opened the front door wasn't him, that she'd have to sit waiting for another twenty or thirty minutes, in a place she'd never belong, the urge to flee almost overpowered him. It wasn't Angela he wanted to run from but that small boy perched on the shoe-shine throne, a memory that seemed to threaten his existence.

Rescue of a sort emerged from the kitchen, and Sandra Jean floated toward him. "Aw shit, Pete. Goddamn. I'm so happy to *see* you!" She threw her arms around him. She was saying something about her daddy, how he'd gone peacefully in the night, though she knew in her bones Pete could have saved him. After all, Donny Alexander had made that D in math.

"American history," he said.

"Say what?"

"American history. Ms. Marsh gave Donny the D."

"Who gives a shit who pinned the D on Donny? I want my doctor making *A*'s. Is that your wife back yonder?"

Angela was already rising, waiting for the introduction to be inflicted. Recalling Mrs. Blackstone's observation about wasted words, he held his remarks to the minimum. "Angela, this is Sandra Jean. Her daddy used to cut my hair."

"Honey, I bet you've eaten in a lot of real French restaurants—just one look at you and I can tell." Sandra Jean poked Pete in the ribs. "You did a lot better in married life than me. You remember Dale DuClos, don't you?"

"Yeah. He was what—two years ahead of us?"

"Three. And anybody with half a brain should've seen that he was born to drive a tractor. Thing was, he had too much status for that, so as soon as his daddy retired and put the farm in his hands, Dale contrived to lose it. Can you believe he wrote the IRS a bad check for a million point two? That kind of revived my interest, and we stayed together another year or so."

To be polite, he asked, "What's he doing now?"

"Works at the Lady Luck over in Greenville. The casino pays him to hang around and talk to folks just like him while *they* lose all their money." The front door opened again and she began to levitate. "Goddamn. Four whole people coming to eat at the same time? Y'all ex*cuse* me."

When the hubbub died down and Sandra Jean had retreated to the kitchen—to wake the help, she claimed—Angela asked, "Was she always so . . . effusive?"

"No."

"I didn't think so."

"Believe it or not, she was the brightest girl in my class. Got a full scholarship to study French at Vanderbilt, but Dale talked her into quitting after a year and getting married."

"Did you date her?"

"Took her to a movie once or twice."

"Which was it? Once or twice?"

"Maybe three times. Four, tops."

At a table up front, the recent arrivals, two women who looked vaguely familiar, were talking about an awful dress someone had worn to church the previous Sunday. The sparkles on the back of it kept coming off, one of them said, until they lay all *over* the damn pew.

"There was a phone call this morning," Angela told him. "From Fresno."

The prepositional phrase achieved physiological effect. Breakfast was hours ago, but he could taste it. "What kind of call?"

"Heinz Properties."

Trying to hide the drop in tension was pointless, so he went ahead and let his shoulders relax. "We got an offer?"

She nodded.

"How much?"

"Oddly enough, one point two."

"And what did Brad say?"

"Not a lot. My impression was he thinks we should accept the offer without trying to bargain."

"Well, I think so, too. And you?"

She took a sip of Merlot and held the glass aloft, and the thought occured to him that she was deciding whether to throw it. He wouldn't have blamed her one bit. She loved the house, which stood on the bluffs overlooking the river. Now it was all but gone, and it wasn't even the most important thing she'd lost.

Instead of throwing the glass, she took another sip of wine and set it down. "I don't think I want to own another house," she said. "Let's just buy a Dumpster, since our lives have turned to garbage."

For a long time he'd assumed the cotton sacks he'd dragged as a boy were the heaviest loads he would ever pull. But some burdens weighed even more, and these you couldn't shed at the end of the row.

He noticed the red ring on the tablecloth, next to her glass. "How long have you been here?"

"I'm not drunk, if that's what you're implying." Her mouth twisted into the wry smile he used to love. "But I'm not entirely sober, either."

"Are you still taking Toprol?"

"Sometimes."

"Did you take it today?"

"Maybe."

"Then you shouldn't be drinking. Nor should you take Tums, and I saw you pop a couple of those after breakfast. Jesus, Angela. Toprol slows your pulse rate down to a crawl, and your heart barely beats to begin with."

His last statement must have sounded just as bad to her as it did to him. "What do you know about my heart?"

"I know nobody should've written you a prescription for a beta-blocker. To my mind, that's damn close to malpractice."

"Now there," she said, "is something you *do* know a lot about."

As his face caught fire, a young black woman with a pad and pen in hand approached their table. "Y'all decided what you want yet?"

Angela said, "I'll take the Swiss chard omelette."

He hadn't even looked at the menu, and now didn't intend to. "I'll have the omelette, too."

"Anything to drink for you?"

"Just water."

His wife waited until the waitress had disappeared into the back. "Look," she said, "I'm sorry." To his amazement, she reached across the table and laid her hand on his. He sat there staring at it, struck by the loss of sensation.

How a person spose to feel *numbness?*

As if she knew exactly what he was thinking, she removed her hand and closed it once more on the stem of the wineglass. "I think we should take the offer," she said. "It might not be what we hoped for, but it's still a lot more than we paid."

She didn't say anything more, and for the longest time he couldn't. Then both of them spoke to make the same point, but he got it out first: "Remember when we bought it?"

After that there was really nothing left to say, nothing they could do, either, except sit there as though in mourning, while the women at the table up front argued about what breed of dog the husband of a mutual friend would have been if the good Lord hadn't made a mistake and let him try to be a person.

AT A QUARTER TILL FOUR, half an hour later than she should have been picked up, Toni walked across the parking lot and sat down on the concrete block where the flagpole was embedded. The question of what to do now absorbed her. Glaring down the road that led to the highway was out: though furious with her mother for failing to show up on time, she refused to appear anxious. She couldn't look back across the parking lot either, because a few other kids were still waiting for their irresponsible parents and she didn't want them considering her one of their number. She certainly couldn't stare at the ground—anybody who saw her would think she was on the verge of tears. She was, but they didn't need to know it. So she pulled out the David Guterson novel she'd finished during fifth period and reread the last few pages.

This had been the worst day yet, the entire school addled by football fever, from the teachers and students on down to the custodians. Almost everyone wore black and gold. Streamers of the same colors hung from overhead lights and dangled off doorknobs, and the cheerleaders had cut out little gold football-shaped name tags and taped them to the players' lockers. *Good Luck, Cody. Beat Yazoo City!* Two of her teachers didn't hold class at all, just graded papers or read while letting the students do whatever they wanted. The afternoon culminated in a mandatory pep rally, the entire student body in attendance, the band playing in about three keys at once, the team sitting together at one end of the gym while the head coach and captains rose to make speeches promising victory. The last moron to approach the microphone broke down and cried and swore to win for the sake of his grandfather, who'd died six years ago last week. She'd never seen anything like it.

Afterwards, falling into step beside her as she went to get her stuff from her locker, Mason told her he didn't expect to play, but he actually thought they had a chance to win, even though the other team was stronger. When she asked him why, he said, "Your dad."

"Oh? Are they going to suit him up?"

He grinned. The gash on his nose was starting to heal, so you could appreciate his features: warm, walnut-colored eyes, perfectly symmetrical cheekbones, a delicate chin, not one of those big square blocks. "No, he won't suit up, but I think Coach Killingsworth's going to have him calling most of the plays. He'll be in the press box wearing the headset. Speaking of headsets, there's a dance next week. Are you going?"

"What does a dance have to do with headsets?"

"Well, you know—sound. There's music at a dance, and sometimes you listen to music on a headset."

"But not the kind my dad'll be wearing."

He stopped before they reached her locker. "You know what?"

"What?"

"You're awfully literal."

She liked the response. Standing there in the hallway, she got ready to come up with a nonanswer to the question of whether she'd go to the dance with him. Instead of posing that question, he glanced at his watch and said he guessed he'd better head on home, that he needed to take a nap before the game.

At four she gave up waiting for her mother, stuck the novel into her backpack and set off toward the highway, walking behind the tall pines lining the road, treating them as a shield against the curious. She was loath to use her cell phone. If her mom couldn't remember she had a daughter, the hell with her. And with her dad, too.

Hoping to find a shortcut, she veered off to the right before reaching the highway and walked through tall grass behind the Wal-Mart, then stepped down into a deep drainage ditch and climbed up the other side, slipping once on the crumbling bank and getting black dirt all over her capris. After she'd pulled herself over the edge, she hurled her backpack onto the ground and said, "Shit."

Somebody laughed. "You got a saucy mouth, ain't you?"

A few feet away, off to the left against a green board fence, sat a guy with a rucksack. He was smoking a cigarette, knees drawn up close to his chin, a quart bottle of beer beside his right foot. Stubble covered his face but you couldn't really call it a beard. He wore a dirty cap with a picture of Winnie the Pooh on the front.

She lifted her backpack and slipped into the straps.

"Sweet little sixteen," he said.

Her heart pounded like the bass drum at the pep rally. "I'm not sixteen."

"Are you sweet?"

The fence made an L a few feet to his left, then extended about fifty or sixty yards in the direction of the high school. The only way out was around that distant corner, unless she wanted to go back through the ditch, and she didn't. "This fence needs work," she said, doing her best to remain calm. "It looks half-rotten."

"You know what's inside there, don't you?"

Through a gap between boards she saw a stack of old tires. "Sure," she lied.

"Biggest junkyard in Loring County. I live in there."

"Really?"

"Me and two other guys. Jump the fence before daylight, stay out of sight till it gets dark, then jump it again. I got the best digs—a 1990 El Dorado. There's blood all over the front seat but I sleep in the back." Continuing to stare at her, he puffed out smoke. "You got nice ankles."

She knew she ought to run and that she'd be a lot faster without the backpack. What in the world had made her put it back on?

"You weren't born here, was you?" he asked.

"Why?"

"You just don't sound local."

She slid one of the straps off her shoulder.

He chuckled. "Getting ready to run, ain't you?"

"No."

"You're lying." He dragged on the cigarette once more, then tossed it aside. "Ain't no reason to run from me, though. I'm the only person I pose any threat to. You looking at a dude's been batting zero forever."

She wanted to believe she knew the truth when she heard it, and she needed to believe she was hearing it now, that he wouldn't rape and kill her, then cut her up and bury the pieces, if only because he lacked the energy. After all, he'd scared her half to death just by sitting on the ground and smoking a cigarette. Substantial returns on a minimal investment—that's what his kind wanted.

"You could get a job," she said. "I bet someone would hire you. Sitting around all day isn't doing you any good."

He laughed and lifted his quart bottle. "I got too good at it." He took a swallow. "Practice makes perfect."

She slipped the strap back onto her shoulder. "I've got to go home. My dad'll be out looking for me."

"You're lying again, hon. Ain't nobody out looking for you. Ain't nobody interested in you right now but me."

She did know the truth when she heard it. Turning, she began to walk along the fence, and once she got around the corner, she'd head straight for the highway. She didn't give a damn who saw her.

"Hey," he called. "Hey, there—wait."

She looked over her shoulder, hoping he wasn't on his feet and running after her. He hadn't moved an inch. "You going to the ball game tonight?"

"What?"

"The football game. I ain't got the money for a ticket, but there's a wrecked Hyundai in there"—he gestured with his thumb at the junkyard—"with a good radio in it. Me and my buddies'll be listening till the battery gives out. Being a dreg of the earth don't mean you can't root for the home team."

The front door was locked. She didn't have a key and wouldn't have used it anyway, because that wouldn't make much of a statement. She whipped out her cell phone, dialed their home number and heard ringing in different parts of the house.

"Hello?"

Her mother sounded sleepy, confused. Possibly—though she'd seen this only once or twice—drunk. "Will you let me in?"

"Toni?"

"No." She fought back tears. *Ain't nobody interested in you right now but me.* Even a bum could see through her. "This is Little Red Riding Hood. The wolf ate Toni."

"God, honey, I'm sorry I didn't pick you up. I met your father for lunch, then came home and fell asleep."

"Just open the door—I'm outside."

Angela did as she'd been told, gasping when she saw her daughter standing there with mud all over her knees.

Toni walked into the kitchen, pulled her backpack off and slammed it down on a chair. Then she went over to the sink, pulled a glass from the drying rack and turned on the faucet. She never stuck the glass under the stream, though. She was shaking.

"Honey?" Angela laid her hand on her daughter's shoulder, and Toni spun around sobbing. Her mother pulled her close, smoothing her hair, whispering that everything would be all right, not to worry, everything would be just fine, and all the while wondering what had happened. "What's the matter, honey? Can you tell me?"

Toni stepped away. She brushed her bangs from her face, then tore off a paper towel and dried her eyes. "I want you to take me to the ball game," she said. "Let's just *go* to the damn thing like everybody else."

———

In the ticket line that night Angela noticed that while quite a few kids glanced at Toni, none of them spoke to her. She'd had no shortage of friends back home, bright girls whose parents took them to openings at MoMA in San Francisco or held season tickets to the Philharmonic, and she'd spent a lot of time with one in particular, a cute brunette named Lindsey. The two of them would study French or physics together for a couple of hours, then waste a couple more mooning at pictures in a Prince William biography. That had all stopped back in the spring, though, when the girl quit coming over.

"Your dad would've given us tickets," Angela said while they waited, "if he'd known ahead of time that you wanted to go."

"Well, I didn't know I wanted to. I mean, I don't want to, not really. But what else is there to do?"

They bought seats in the reserved section and paid for a program, then walked to the gate, where it turned out the music teacher was on duty. "Your daughter," the woman said, "well, she's a once-in-a-lifetime find." She tore their tickets in two. "I was walking down the hall the other day after lunch and heard someone playing 'March of the Trolls.' And my first thought was it had to be Public Radio, because I don't have that on CD. But it wasn't the radio or a CD either. It was *her*." She shook her head in wonder. "Probably the first time that piece was ever played in Loring, Mississippi."

"But hopefully not the last."

"I'd say that depends on Toni," the teacher said. "I sure can't play it and nobody else around here ever heard of it."

Inside the fence, small boys roamed in packs beneath the bleachers or tossed miniature footballs at one another, and the smell of hot dogs and popcorn hung in the air. "Want some junk food, honey?" Angela asked.

"Jeez, Mom. *No.*"

Their seats were about fifteen rows up and close to the aisle. Down below, the teams had finished their pregame warmups and were milling around on opposite sidelines, the visitors across the field a lot bigger than the locals. Angela saw Tim squatting in front of Loring's bench talking to three or four players, all of his problems temporarily forgotten. The head coach was down there too, yelling and clapping his hands while the other assistant peered anxiously into a barrel of Gatorade, but Pete was nowhere in sight. Rather than come home for dinner tonight, he'd eaten with the team. At least he said he was going to. "Do you see your dad?" she asked.

Toni was studying the program as if searching for something in particular. "No," she said, "but I know where he is."

"Where?"

With her thumb Toni gestured at the press box. "Up there."

Turning, Angela saw him fussing with a set of headphones, putting them on and pulling them off again and making some kind of adjustment. If he'd noticed her and Toni, he didn't show it.

Everybody rose, the band played the national anthem, then Loring lost the toss and kicked off. A Yazoo City player took the ball close to his own goal, eluded a would-be tackler and raced toward the far sideline. A groan arose as the home crowd realized nobody would lay a hand on him.

"Ninety-eight yards," the announcer intoned, and somebody behind them growled, "I wish Rashard Killingsworth'd come down with terminal cancer."

———

From Pete's vantage point the game looked far from hopeless. Yazoo City, though the more talented team, quickly began to display some of the telltale signs of poor coaching, jumping offside twice on Loring's first drive, which ended with a punt but established that as long as Reggie McDonald remained in the lineup, the home team could at least move the ball.

Early in the second quarter the visitors scored again when Tim's cornerback froze on a pump fake and let the receiver haul in a long pass. But the pall that settled over the crowd lifted on the next series, as Reggie broke runs of twenty, sixteen and forty-one yards, then carried the ball in from the two. At the half they trailed by only seven in a contest that should've already been decided.

Leaving the press box, he saw Angela and Toni sitting together beside an aisle. "Didn't know you two were coming," he told them.

"We didn't either," Angela said. "Toni wanted to."

"Are you enjoying it?"

Toni shrugged. "It's okay. The other team looks better."

"They are. But they may not be so much better that they can beat us."

When he walked into the field house, Donnie Alexander was over in one corner, wrapping tape around Cody Blackstone's knee, and Killingsworth was glaring at the team, two halves of a clipboard on the floor near his feet. Even the black kids looked pale. Seeing Pete, the head coach asked, "How are they blocking that goddamn counter play?"

Pete grabbed a piece of chalk and sketched the X's and O's. "Onside tackle doubles down on our DT, then slides off on the Mike linebacker, and they pull the offside guard to trap Shontell. The thing is, the guard hasn't had to block him yet, because by the time he reaches the hole Shontell's six yards in the backfield."

"Shontell," Killingsworth said, "next time that tackle blocks down, don't you move. I want your ass parked in the hole like a goddamn Winnebago."

They diagrammed three or four variations on pass plays, hoping to get one-on-one coverage on Reggie flaring out of the backfield. Then Killingsworth worked himself up again and disputed everybody's gender for three or four minutes before telling them they still had a chance to win if somebody besides McDonald woke up and played ball.

For a while no one did. The first time they tried to hit Reggie downfield, Cody Blackstone got sacked, aggravating the knee that he'd twisted in the first half. The second time, he threw an interception. As for Shontell, he took Killingsworth's admonishment to heart and basically stood around doing nothing.

Near the end of the quarter, a Yazoo City running back fumbled and Loring recovered on the visitors' twenty. From there they gained only eight yards but were close enough to kick a field goal. They entered the final period down by four.

With three minutes left in the game, Reggie fielded a punt on his own fifteen, juked the first man downfield, then wove through the Yazoo City coverage, back to his own forty-eight, where the punter caught him by an ankle. Over the headphones Killingsworth said, "Pass it? Or just hand it to Reggie and hope he shakes loose?"

Pete's heart pounded pleasantly in his ears. Whatever happened, they'd stayed close against a more talented team, and he hadn't worried about much of anything for almost three hours. The only thing that would make the evening even better was a win. "Think Cody can hang in there long enough for us to run that screen off the fake draw?"

"Might as well try it," Killingsworth said, then put his hand on Cody's shoulder, told him what to call and slapped him on the butt.

The play worked perfectly: Reggie's halfhearted fake fooled no one, so he managed to slip out into the right flat and pull down Cody's wobbly pass right before a wave of rushers buried the quarterback. Reggie followed his blockers well, a black-and-gold wall, to the thirty, before breaking into the middle of the field, the safety bringing him down on the eighteen. Two and a half minutes left.

They ran Reggie off tackle for six to the twelve. Reggie on a sweep to the other side for three. Then Reggie on a dive that went nowhere. Fourth and one. Cody signaled time-out and limped over.

"Got less than a minute left," Killingsworth said over the headphones. "One time-out. Try to run Reggie for the first down, then fling it into the end zone four times?"

"How about play-action right now to the tight end?"

"It goes against my nature."

"They're not worried about a thing in the world but Reggie. A good fake'll suck everybody up."

He heard Killingsworth sigh, then give Cody the play: "Jet left, thirty-three bootleg, Z drag."

Reggie hit the line hard and, just as Pete had predicted, the entire defense rose to meet him. Cody hid the ball behind his hip, and Pete's tight end slipped past the linebackers. Everything worked perfectly until the quarterback planted his left foot to pivot, then staggered and almost went down, recovering by putting his hand on the ground and pushing off. By that time everybody knew where the ball was. A big defensive lineman broke free and charged into the backfield.

Cody threw leaning backwards. The tight end, who'd broken

across the goal line, had to come back for the pass, but he hauled it in a foot off the ground and was preparing to celebrate the pending touchdown when the left corner peeled off his man and put his head-gear into the kid's sternum.

Somehow he held on to the ball. What he couldn't hold on to was consciousness, sprawled on his back about a yard from the goal line while Donny Alexander and the trainer ran onto the field.

"Got his bell rung," Pete said.

"At the very least. You know where this leaves us, don't you? We don't have anybody to stick in there now but Depot."

"Depot'll do just fine."

The kid on the ground didn't move for several minutes. After Donnie finally woke him up, a couple of his teammates helped him off the field.

Headgear under one arm, Mason DePoyster waited near Killings-worth. "Let me talk to Depot," Pete said, so Killingsworth handed the boy his headset.

"Yes sir?" You could almost hear his teeth chattering.

"Listen," Pete told him, "we're going to run thirty-two blast—three times in a row, if that's what it takes. They'll probably be in an eight-man front. You'll have that end on your inside shoulder. He's not Shontell Clemons. He couldn't take your head off if he spent all night trying. But he's probably going to close pretty fast, so you've got to tie him up. You come off at a forty-five-degree angle, stay low, get in his legs and don't let him beat you inside. We're going behind the guard, so all you've got to do is slow your guy down. Reggie'll take care of the rest."

"Yes sir."

"And Depot?"

"Yes sir?"

"Have fun." Though he knew it was inappropriate, and maybe even a little unseemly, he added, "I wish I could be you right now."

"Well," Mason said before pulling off the headset, "I do too."

When Toni saw him run onto the field, she closed her eyes for a moment and prayed he wouldn't make a fool of himself. Then she immediately had to account for her willingness to address God on his behalf, and she did so by telling herself that it wasn't really him she'd prayed for but the Displaced, all those who didn't belong where they were on this sad Friday night in September. She prayed for the world's immigrants, the cabdrivers in Manhattan articulate only in Farsi, the Gypsy bands playing "Melodie au Crepuscule" all day in Krakow, the children of migrant laborers in the San Joaquin Valley who switched schools at least twice a year—starting the fall in Bakersfield, ending the spring in Stockton. The rootless and the disaffected, those lost or rejected, the budget travelers who'd been bumped up to first class and were uncertain how many free drinks they could order. She prayed for the guys listening at the junkyard.

He broke the huddle with his betters, pretending he belonged in their midst. The noise from the crowd was worse than Papa Roach. She covered her ears as Mason dug in, the player on his nose twice his size, three times even, number 54, his enormous forearm swinging back and forth in Mason's face.

In the press box, Pete watched it unfold, the eye he'd been blessed or cursed with breaking the play down into a set of actions not quite simultaneous but not quite separate either. Cody took the snap and spun, the H-back plunged past him into the line, Reggie cradled the ball against his navel and his Pumas left the ground. The guard and tackle's surge was tremendous, driving the submarining linemen over the stripe.

And as for Mason DePoyster, he did all he'd been asked. He came off hard and fast and low, concerns for own safety discarded, and number 54 blew right by him like a heat-seeking missile, nose cone honed on the ball. It popped loose an instant before Reggie's body soared over the goal line.

Someone in the wrong color jersey reached out from the pile of trunks and appendages and pulled in the fumble.

Pete left the press box before the gun sounded and still got caught in the crush of bodies. He wanted to put his arm around Mason, tell him he had nothing to be ashamed of because he'd conquered his fears and stuck his head in there just like he'd been taught and that was all anybody could ask and all he should ever demand of himself. But he never got to say any of that, because somebody else reached the boy first. So he stood beside Angela at the foot of the bleachers and watched while Toni leaned over the fence and whispered something to the evening's goat, whose cheeks were glistening beneath the stadium lights.

Whatever she said must have made Mason feel better: his face broke into a smile and his mouth formed the word *Really?* She nodded and he said *Wow* and reached out and laid his hand on her forearm.

"Is that boy Toni's talking to a nice kid?" Angela asked.

"About as nice as they come."

"Smart?"

"That, too."

"He'll need to be if he's going to deal with her."

They stayed right where they were, not wanting to crowd Toni or Mason, who now was grinning as if he'd scored the winning touchdown. So neither of them saw Alan DePoyster over by the fence—looking first at his son, and then at their daughter, and then directly at Pete.

FOR THE PAST COUPLE OF MONTHS, ever since a group of kids got arrested for spray-painting obscene drawings on the exterior of the courthouse, Reverend Phelps at First Baptist had built his Sunday morning sermons around front-page items in the *Weekly Times.* The topic today was stealing. The previous Tuesday evening, in the space of three or four hours, a number of cars parked in residential areas had been ransacked, stereos ripped from dashboards, glove compartments emptied. A few tires had even been slashed, apparently because nothing worth taking had been found inside.

Alan had heard a little grumbling about the sermons. People *knew* the news, some folks said, and it was almost always bad. You didn't need a preacher to tell you what to think about it. The preacher's job was to uplift sagging spirits.

He didn't add his voice to the chorus of complaints because, for one thing, he loved and admired Wade Phelps. And for another, he happened to know that the minister, who was all of thirty years old, had been working in a convenience store down in Hattiesburg about ten years ago when a guy wearing a ski mask walked in pointing a gun at Wade's chest and ordered him to empty the register.

Recounting the awful event, Wade had told Alan he wasn't trying to be brave and didn't have the slightest intention of resisting. Too scared to move, he tried to speak but couldn't. He knew that even if he handed over every last bill in the register, he was about to die.

"Are you stupid?" the man finally asked him.

"I'm scared," Wade managed to reply. "You're going to shoot me no matter what."

"I bet you're a college student, aren't you?"

Wade nodded.

"So you think I'm predictable. Well, in your intro-to-psych course they didn't teach you anything worth knowing about what I will or won't do. Now step away from there." Wade backed up and the burglar stepped around behind the counter. Pointing the gun with one hand, he punched the Cash key with the other and the register popped open. He reached in and grabbed the tens and twenties and stuffed them in his pocket, then added the singles and glanced at the street, which at three on a weekday morning was predictably empty. He stepped out from behind the counter and gestured with the handgun. "Walk over there to the potato chip rack."

Wade told Alan he'd walked past the gunman, stood next to a Frito-Lay display and seen his face reflected in the door to the ice cream freezer. His skin looked dull and gray.

"Now pull your pants off," the burglar said.

Wade remembered reading somewhere that murderers often liked their victims to be naked when they killed them. Shaking, he unzipped his Levi's and pulled them down.

"Now the shoes—unless you think those pants'll slide over a pair of size twelves."

Bending, he untied the laces, expecting a bullet any minute. He kicked the shoes off, still shaking, then pulled his pants off too.

"And the shirt."

He unbuttoned it and let it fall to the floor.

"Underwear?"

They fell to the floor too.

"Now take three steps backwards." When Wade did as he'd been told, the guy stooped and balled up the clothes and tucked them under his arm. "Now I want you to stand on your right foot, like this." He demonstrated, then gestured with the handgun, and Wade raised his left leg into the air. "Reach around and stick your left thumb in your right ear." He did that too. "So tell me one thing," the guy said. "Could you ever have predicted I'd make you do this? Does this enter into your college-bound conception of what a convenience-store robbery is? Answer me."

"No."

"That's the right response, the first smart thing you've said tonight. Now here's one more question. If by some miracle you *had* been able to predict I'd make you stand there like that, with your pecker shriveled past the point of no return, how would you have expected to feel?"

"Foolish."

"And do you?"

Wade nodded.

"So which one of us is predictable?"

"I am."

"That's right. *You* are." He walked over to the door and pushed it open. "Now you stand right there just like that for as long as you can because the Hattiesburg Police Department's hired a bunch of women cops and you're one hell of a sight."

The funny thing, Wade told Alan, was that when he finally decided it was safe to call 911, the notion of being discovered by a female cop made him ask the dispatcher, a woman herself, if she could please send a male officer. A person might think that wouldn't matter, given what he'd been through, but to him right then it did. He still didn't know why. It seemed silly now.

Even though many years had passed since that night, it must have been on Wade's mind a lot lately. Because he'd said a good bit these last few weeks about the different forms of crime and how believers ought to respond to them. Some of what he said came from the Bible, but many of the most thoughtful remarks were his own.

Today, as always, he led off with Scripture, citing the fourth chapter of Ephesians. " 'Let him who steals steal no longer. But rather let him labor, performing with his own hands what is good, in order that he may have something to share with him who has need.' " He paused and closed the Bible, a sure sign that, having stated his theme, he was ready to begin the improvisation. "My father used to say that if we turned loose everybody at Parchman who'd stolen something for the sake of love, three-fourths of the cells would be empty. Well, Dad was a smart man, but I've always thought he got this wrong. It's not love that makes people steal. If anything, it's the lack of it. Some folks are just bottomless. Love might fill them up—love of many different kinds, the love of God, if they'd accept it . . . the love of a husband or wife, or a friend, or even a pet. But they either can't find it or they won't accept it, and because of those big empty spaces inside themselves, they take what belongs to somebody else, in an effort to fill the void. It's as simple as that.

"But you say, 'Brother Phelps, of course it's simple. Identifying the problem's rarely hard. Coming up with a solution—well, that's another matter.' And you're right. That *is* another matter. Because a man who's lost, one who sees nothing wrong with smashing in a window and stealing some kid's stereo and his CDs and his cell phone, a man who'll walk into a bank and point a gun at an underpaid teller with two children at home and either shoot her or scare her to death—that man's not going to wake up one day and say, 'Yes, Jesus loves me, the Bible tells me so.' Oh, no. That man, if he's going to find the love of God, is going to have to find it first in another human being. Somebody's going to have to love the crime right out of his heart before *he* can do what the Scripture says and perform with *his* own hands what is good and share it with another. And who is that somebody who's going to love the thief? Brothers and sisters, look around." He waved his hand in the air. "That somebody better be you. And it better be me. If Jesus can love the thief—and we know He did—then why can't we? What excuse can we possibly produce for just hating the criminal? The criminal's the last person on earth we should hate. Because, brothers and sisters"—his voice fell to a whisper—"he's the one most desperately in need of love."

Judging from the expressions on people's faces, Wade might as well have announced a fund-raiser for Al-Qaeda. Alan saw a couple other deacons look at each other and shake their heads.

By the time the hymn of invitation rolled around, Alan himself had formed some serious questions about what Wade had said. At some point, he thought, you had to draw the line. Maybe you should forgive a hoodlum for walking in on you one night, pointing a gun in your face, making you strip naked and stand on one foot and stick your thumb in your ear. But should you forgive that same hoodlum if he did it again the following night? Or what if he didn't do it to you but to somebody else? In the absence of any serious consequences, he might have somebody standing naked on one foot every night for the rest of his life.

When the service ended, Wade walked down the aisle and stood in the vestibule to shake hands with folks as they left the church. Alan reached in his pocket and handed Mason the car keys. "Why don't you and your mom go on home," he said, "and I'll just walk back. I need to discuss something with Wade."

"Anything wrong?" Nancy asked.

"No, there's just a couple things I need to go over."

She looked at him strangely, then she and Mason filed out with all the others.

He waited in his pew, paging through the church bulletin to avoid people's glances. He had never ceased to be bothered that folks behaved differently in church than they did anywhere else. Nobody here, if they saw him at Wal-Mart Tuesday evening, would call him Brother Alan or Brother DePoyster, as all of them would now if their gazes happened to meet. He knew for a fact that when in the company of males beyond the confines of this sanctuary, one deacon could scarcely say a sentence that didn't include the word *shit*. Everybody knew how he talked, and while many people probably disapproved, that hadn't kept them from electing him deacon. The assumption, though most members of the congregation would've denied it, seemed to be that you were one person here and another person out there. Little things gave the lie away.

Eventually the voices in the vestibule faded and he heard Wade close the double doors and start back up the aisle.

The minister stopped near Alan's pew. He was tall and fit, a former distance runner who could still be seen jogging around town every day of the week save this one. "Something's troubling you, isn't it, Alan?" he asked.

Alan folded the bulletin and stuck it into the hymnal rack. "How come you didn't call me Brother just now?"

Wade slipped into the pew and sat down beside him. "Because it goes without saying," he said, crossing his long legs. "You know we're brothers and I know we're brothers, and I have a feeling we're about to engage in a conversation in which the reserve invoked by formality would be hard to maintain and counterproductive as all get-out." He grinned. "What's on your mind, bro? Got a problem with my sermon?"

"Maybe. I mean, gosh, Wade—isn't there a point when you have to say enough and no more? Otherwise the criminal just keeps right on sowing misery left and right."

"No," Wade said, "there's no point at which you have to say enough and no more."

Alan sat there looking at the younger man, feeling, for the first time in the two and a half years he'd known him, a measure of resentment. The previous minister had been sixty-six years old when he retired, a stolid man who wore granny glasses and began almost every prayer by asking God to look after the fortunes of all the local farmers, bringing sunshine, rain, higher prices or lower labor costs, whatever they claimed they needed. That was the kind of minister a lot of people wanted, and when Wade came for his interview a great many of them worried that he might be too young and inexperienced to serve the needs of this particular church. But Alan had liked him the instant they met. He sensed that Wade was looking hard for answers, that he wouldn't just stand in the pulpit week after week pretending nothing could ever go wrong as long as you knew your Scripture. Things could go wrong and they did go wrong, and while knowing Scripture and hanging on to your faith could help you deal with that, to pretend the world wasn't full of pain and suffering struck Alan as downright sinful. So in board meetings he argued long and hard that Wade was the man for the job, and eventually he convinced a bare majority of the voting members, including a couple very wealthy and influential folks. Now, though, he wondered if maybe Wade was exuding a different kind of false optimism: love the murderer into volunteering for the Salvation Army.

"There's not a point," Wade said again, speaking more softly this time, "at which you or I, or your wife or mine, or any other member of this or any other congregation, needs to say enough and no more. You know why?"

"You're going to tell me that's God's job and His alone. And I bet you can quote some Scripture that'll back you up."

"That's right. And you know what? I bet you can quote some Scripture to contradict me. If you can't, I can."

Heresy hovered close by. "So then what's the Scripture worth, Wade? You trying to shake the whole foundation?"

"Let's say you're sitting in front of a computer," Wade said, "and you want to know something about catfish. So you type that word into one of the search engines, and what happens? About four hundred thousand results come up. So what do you do next? You either start going through them item by item, which'll take forever, or you narrow the search by including more info than just catfish. Maybe you decide that you really want to find out something about the processing plants, so you type that whole phrase in and this time you get only about a thousand results, which is still a heck of a lot. So you define the search more and more narrowly until you reduce the number of results to something manageable. Say fifty. But even when you get it down to fifty, you still have to decide what to do with the information, right?"

The reference to computers and search results made Alan uncomfortable. In his safe at work there was a manila file folder containing several articles he'd printed off the *Fresno Bee*'s Web site. The first detailed how some months ago, an attorney had walked into the office of a local doctor, pulled out a gun and fired two shots that somehow missed their mark, even though the target was standing just a few feet away, handing a file to his receptionist. Follow-up articles made it clear that the attorney, who'd been wrestled to the floor by the doctor, was married to one of his patients. A bit of research on the California Medical Board's Web site revealed subsequent disciplinary proceedings against the physician, though no cause was ever specified. Alan hadn't yet decided what, if anything, to do with this information. He hadn't prayed for guidance in the matter and was puzzled, even troubled, by his own unwillingness to do so. "What are you getting at, Wade?" he asked. "I'm afraid I just don't see the point."

"Well, to me, the point is that even when you know plenty of Scripture, you still have to decide how to make use of it."

"Yeah, but since our nature is corrupt, left to ourselves we make corrupt choices. Isn't that right?"

"That's what it means to be saved, Alan. It means you walk in the light, not in the dark, and because you walk in the light you can see better than some other folks. And you have to trust yourself to make wise use of Scripture. If somebody came up to me tomorrow and said, 'I'm the guy that held up that convenience store down in Hattiesburg ten years ago,' I'm not going to slug him in the nose, though I can find some Scripture back in the Old Testament that'll substantiate my right to do it. Instead, I'm going to invite him to lunch. Now it's true that you might drive by my house an hour later and find me out in the yard naked and barking, with a leash around my neck, but I'd get over the embarrassment."

"What if I drive by your house," Alan said, "and find you naked and hanging from a tree with a *rope* around your neck?"

Wade rose and clapped Alan on the shoulder. "Well, then you'll say, 'I told you so,' Alan. And there won't be much I can do except look down from heaven and nod."

———

That afternoon he turned on the TV and tried to focus on a ball game—the Saints and the 49ers—but before long he dozed off. He woke when a truck door slammed. Opening his eyes, he looked out the window and saw Mason sitting behind the wheel of his pickup, staring down at the dashboard and fooling with the radio dial. Nancy picked precisely that moment to walk through the living room, running her fingers through his hair as she passed his recliner. And without really being concerned, he asked, "Where's Mason headed?"

"Going over to a girl's house to study for a quiz."

"What girl?"

"That new doctor's daughter. You know, the one who helps coach the team."

He was already on his bare feet then, rushing by her so fast he knocked the Sunday magazine supplement from her hand.

"Alan? What's the matter?"

He threw the screen door open, and the metal frame crashed into the wall. Mason was backing out, looking over his shoulder, so he didn't see his father bounding down the steps. "Hey!" Alan yelled, but his son couldn't hear because of the awful music pounding in the cab. "Mason!"

At the foot of the driveway, Mason spun the wheel and the pickup rolled into the street. He tapped the brakes and put the truck in drive. He must have entered a world of his own creation, one filled with noise and flashing lights and smoke, because he remained unaware that his father was running barefoot through the yard.

"Mason!"

The truck lurched forward just as Alan slammed his fist into the passenger door. Mason's mouth popped open and he stepped on the brakes, but by then it was too late. His father had pulled the door open. While Metallica played full throttle, prompting the neighbor across the street to stick her head out the window, the man he loved most in all the world, the one he'd looked up to since the day he understood that adult behavior was not necessarily superior to that of children, that some fathers were lousy but his was and always would be the best—that very man was standing beside the truck in bright sunlight, his face resembling nothing so much as a fat purple plum, and he was punching the seat cushion and yelling, "I need the truck, goddamn it! Now turn that shit off!"

THE FOLLOWING MORNING he was waiting beside her locker, his backpack on the floor. A khaki-colored Jansport, it must have contained a cheap thermos filled with coffee or tea because when she kicked it, something shattered and a brownish stain seeped into the fabric.

"Why'd you do *that*?" he asked.

Some kids walked by, shaking their heads. She heard one of them say, "California for you."

"Because your backpack was in the wrong place." She leaned over, spun the dial on her lock and wrenched the door open. Inside, on top of her books, lay a small square package wrapped in silver paper, with a bright red ribbon tied around it. She reached in and picked it up. "How'd you open my locker?"

"Memorized your combination." To her surprise, he snatched the package out of her hand.

"Give me that—it's mine." She grabbed it back.

"I need to return it," he said, "and start saving money to buy myself a new thermos and backpack."

She tugged the ribbon loose, then tore off the paper. A CD. One of those unclassy classical samplers. A string serenade from Mozart, a Beethoven bagatelle, Vivaldi's "La Primavera," a piece of Tchaikovsky's ear candy and something simply labeled "An Irish Tune." No performers named.

"They don't have much to choose from at Wal-Mart," he said. "That *is* the kind of junk you listen to, isn't it?"

On the shelves in her room stood boxed sets containing Simon

Rattle's Beethoven cycle, Idil Biret's Rachmaninoff and Brahms, the complete Deutsche Grammophon Chopin collection, as well as almost all the work of Pollini, Argerich, Gould, Uchida, Ax and Ashkenazy. She'd chosen everything in the collection herself, had begun building it when she was seven. She knew where every single item in it had been bought, what it had cost, how it related to each of the others. None of it, right then, was worth anything at all. "I guess this means you had a good reason for not showing up yesterday."

"Yeah. I did. And I'm willing to listen and see if you had a good reason for kicking my backpack."

Just say it, she coaxed herself. *Don't lie. Try it.* "You hurt my feelings."

"That's not a good reason." He grinned then. "However, it probably seems like one to you, so your apology's accepted. You can keep the CD."

Rather than point out that she hadn't apologized, she asked, "Where were you?"

He stuck his hands in his pockets. "My dad wouldn't let me come. He said he had to go somewhere in the pickup, then he left and took Mom's car keys with him. I should've called you but I was embarrassed. I had to walk across town to buy that CD."

"If you could walk to Wal-Mart, why couldn't you walk to my house?"

The bell rang. Lockers clanged shut, and late arrivals ran past them hurrying to class. Down at the far end of the hall the vice principal hollered, "Y'all quit running. This is *not* a track meet!"

"My mom," Mason said, sounding more than a little disturbed, "thinks my dad's got some kind of grudge against yours."

THE SECOND GAME of the season was played on a sloppy field after three straight days of rain, but the conditions didn't stop Reggie McDonald from scoring four times before the half. At the beginning of the fourth quarter, Loring led 41–14, and the reserves went in. A few minutes later, with the ball on the opponents' ten-yard line, Pete talked Killingsworth into a slant to the tight end.

The backup quarterback hit Depot right in the numbers, and he lunged across the goal line. Down below, where she sat beside her mother, Toni raised both fists into the air and Pete heard her holler "Yes!" She rose and cheered while Mason ran off the field trying to act as if he was used to scoring touchdowns. As soon as he reached the sideline, she turned and looked up at the press box where Pete tried to act as if it were no big deal for him to call that particular play. And no big deal for her to look up there.

Afterwards, the kids met at the fence again. This time Angela spotted the man in the yellow rain slicker frowning at them. "Who's that guy looking at Toni and her boyfriend?" she asked when Pete joined her.

"I don't know that she's got a boyfriend. But if she has, then that guy's her boyfriend's father."

"I don't like the way he's looking at them. What's his problem?"

He didn't want to get into it just then. In fact, he didn't want to get into it at all, because that might entail getting back into something else too. "Alan's all right," he said. "He's always looked like he's got heartburn."

THE LORING COUNTY COURTHOUSE stood across the street from the Methodist church. Back in 1968, Tim had told her, not long before the assassination, Martin Luther King spoke on the front steps. The only white folks in evidence that day, he said, besides the cops, were Pete and him. They'd slipped off from school to see the man everybody was talking about, and when they went back they got paddled by a coach.

She'd heard the story before. But as she paused at the top of the steps that morning and looked down onto the courthouse lawn, trying to envision two young white faces in a crowd of black people, she discovered she could summon only one. What she'd attempted to call up was a portrait of innocence, and it was difficult, if not impossible, to think of her husband in that context.

The lobby was empty except for the row of plastic chairs outside the office of the circuit clerk. Feeling furtive, as if she were guilty of criminal activity herself, she walked on through, looking for the staircase, and finally found it near the rear entrance, where a young black man stood mumbling into the pay phone.

When she walked into the second-floor courtroom, Tim and another lawyer were standing before the bench whispering to the judge, a petite blonde. Next to her gavel stood a styrofoam cup and a quart bottle of club soda. Once or twice, while the attorneys advanced their arguments, she lifted the cup and sipped. She seemed to be enjoying herself, and the lawyers acted like suitors competing for her favor. Something Tim said made her laugh.

Angela took a seat at the rear. There were twenty-five or thirty people in the courtroom, all but six or seven of them black. One of the few whites in attendance was Tim's client. Every couple of minutes he turned and glared over the railing at a woman who sat three or four rows behind him with a baby in her arms. The baby never made a sound.

Finally both counselors returned to their respective tables. Before he took a seat, Tim saw her there and smiled.

The judge addressed Tim's client. "Mr. Autrie," she said, "you're several months behind on your child-care payments, and this six-year-old's going to school without adequate clothes. Before long it'll start to get cold in the mornings. The child has no coat, her shoes are too small, she doesn't even have an umbrella. And in spite of this you're worried about a missing basketball. Is there anything you'd like to say for yourself before I tell you what's going to happen next?"

Tim whispered to his client. Autrie shook his head with such energy that his hair flopped into his eyes, forcing him to sweep it aside. Tim said something else and he shook his head even harder, at which time his lawyer made a hands-up gesture and leaned back in his chair.

Autrie stood. "Your honoress," he began.

The judge said, "*Your honor* will suffice."

"Your honor. The thing is, I've known that basketball longer than I've known my wife."

Two or three people giggled. The woman with the baby said, "I'm not your wife anymore."

The judge lifted the gavel but didn't bang it.

"I got that basketball from my daddy on January sixth, 1983. He gave it to me on my eighth birthday. Four days later he got crushed when his tractor-trailer rig got caught in heavy fog. It was one of them big pileups on the interstate and lots of folks died, I forget exactly how many.

"That basketball was the last thing I got from him. Other than that there ain't nothing special about it. Michael Jordan never signed it, I never scored forty points with it, in fact I never hardly played with it at all because I don't give a hoot for basketball. But the goddamn ball, Judge, is mine, and ain't nothing you nor that woman sitting behind me back there nor my worthless lawyer can ever do to change that. I ain't paying nobody nothing till I get it back. And if I ever find out where it's at, I guarantee you whoever's got it's fixing to get fouled."

The judge laid her gavel down and poured some more club soda into her cup. She didn't drink it right away, just sat there holding it as a smile formed on her face. Finally, as if sampling some great Bordeaux at a tasting, she took a dainty sip, then set the cup back down. "Your ball," she said, "has been impounded."

Autrie remained standing. Angela could see Tim's shoulders starting to shake, and most of the people in the courtroom were laughing along with him. A woman sitting off to one side said, "Put his other balls in that pound, too. Them's the ones what caused the problem."

Once the laughter died down, the judge said, "Mr. Autrie, I'm going to have you jailed—unless you pay Mrs. Autrie what you owe by five o'clock today. In which case I'll give you back your ball."

Meekly, Autrie said, "Well, I might go ahead and do that. I'll have to see."

"You've got exactly ten seconds to make up your mind."

"Well, I guess I'll pay then. Though it still don't seem quite right."

"You're certainly free to disagree. You'll find the clerk's office downstairs in room one-fourteen. I'd hurry, if I were you. They're about to close for lunch."

When Autrie trudged past, Angela got a good look at his face: gaunt cheekbones, a jaw that looked far too loose without a chaw of tobacco to keep it company, too many veins visible in his nose. A man who sought to wash himself in the waters of sentimentality.

Tim shook hands with the other attorney and, down the aisle, stooped over and said something to Autrie's ex-wife. The young woman nodded at him. Before he straightened up, she reached out and touched his hand.

On the landing, Angela said, "Whose side were you on?"

Tim crammed some papers into an overflowing briefcase. "Well, I'm on the side of justice."

"I think your client realized that. It's why he called you worthless."

"We had to stage the dog-and-pony show to help him see the light."

"The judge was great."

"Lana? She's all right in there."

"But elsewhere?"

"Elsewhere, I don't think she knows how to be herself. She comes into her own when she sits up higher than everybody else and holds a hammer and has to be approached with care. And out in the big old R and W, things just don't line up like that."

They went downstairs and through the lobby, which was suddenly full of people. All of them seemed to know Tim. A deputy sheriff slapped him on the back and told him his DBs looked like they weren't scared to death this year. A secretary leaving one of the offices asked when his daughter was coming for a visit, and he told her it wouldn't be long. An elderly man he called Reverend Fulcher shook hands with him and announced that their mutual reclamation project had attended church six weeks in a row. Everybody gave Angela the once-over.

On the front steps Tim paused and gazed off across the parking lot, as if posing for a campaign poster. "Up for lunch?"

For some odd reason she loved it that he couldn't look directly at her while asking the question. "That's why I'm here," she said.

"Thought you'd come to witness a display of fiery oratory worthy of William Jennings Bryan."

"I came because I'm hungry."

"You like barbecue?"

"If it's good."

"Mind if we go down across the tracks?"

"Not," she said, "unless we're going to be hit by a train."

———

Montrose's stood on a street that had been paved at some point in the distant past, though by now the only evidence of that was the occasional patch of asphalt. The restaurant smelled of hickory smoke, and a layer of grime covered the floor and tabletops. They were the only customers.

Montrose himself walked over to their table, a pad clenched in one hand. He was an enormous black man wearing a dirty apron whose pouches, each holding a plastic bottle of barbecue sauce, were labeled Hot, Extra Hot and Flaming. Tim had already warned her that if you asked for Mild, you'd get it but he'd never bring you a drink, no matter how many times you reminded him, and would make you wait all day for the check.

His voice was deep, sonorous. "This gentleman you're with," he informed her, "is good for one thing and one thing only—keeping somebody out of jail who belongs in it."

"I kept your nephew out of jail," Tim said, "and you paid me to do it."

"Because my wife threatened to deny me my conjugal pleasures. The young man's a hoodlum, pure and simple. He belongs under lock and key. Thanks to you, he lives with me." Montrose looked at her. "What would the lady like?"

She glanced at the menu.

"The pulled-pork plate's hard to beat," Tim said.

"Well, then I'll try that. What comes with it?"

"I recommend cole, coleslaw for those with hard, hard hearts," Montrose said. "If your heart's not hard, I suggest my tangy baked beans, which will rectify that problem. Either one goes just fine with my french fries. If you want anything else, I'm afraid I can't provide it."

Tim grinned at her, and she saw the chipped tooth again. "Your heart hard or not?"

"Not hard enough. I'll take the beans."

"Me too." He handed the menus back to Montrose. "Can you bring us a couple Bud Lights?"

"Most certainly." Montrose crammed the pad into his pocket without writing anything on it. He looked at Tim, then at her, then shook his head and muttered, "What a waste, what a waste," as he walked off.

When the door to the kitchen closed, she said, "What was that about?"

"It's how he shows affection."

Men amazed her. The best among them maintained barriers between themselves and other men, revealing their true feelings only to women. The worst, on the other hand, never gave in to anything she would label a feeling. They functioned at the level of impulse, like jackrabbits.

Montrose brought their beers. Tim lifted his bottle and clinked it against hers, then turned his up and drank about half of it. Three-point-two beer hadn't provided him much of a rush for years, but it did sometimes calm him. And today that's what he needed. Sitting in the truck beside her, he'd experienced something he figured was a panic attack. His palms began to sweat, his chest tightened and he came within an inch of telling her they ought to turn around and head back to the courthouse, where he'd drop her off, let her climb into her Volvo and drive herself home. Because home was where she belonged. Not here with him on the south side of the tracks, where the only folks who might see them would keep their mouths shut.

Montrose brought two big plates heaped high with barbecue and beans and fries and slapped them on the table. "Sauce?" They both asked for Hot, so he grunted and squirted it onto the meat, then disappeared into the kitchen.

The food was good and they both enjoyed it, but it was not the only thing on the table. Each of them had decided there was one topic they wouldn't discuss, so for a while they talked about everything else. His daughter's school. Her daughter's taste in pianists. The merits of California cotton as opposed to the Delta variety. The birth of the blues. The death of Emmett Till.

Then their plates were empty. And simultaneously they broached the forbidden. "I've known old Pete—" he said just as she said, "The year I met Pete—"

She lowered her head and felt her face turn the color of an August sunset.

He grinned like an idiot and said, "You know that's what Robert E. Lee called James Longstreet?"

She just stared at him. She couldn't decide if she wanted to slap him, or shake him, or kick his shin, or just tell him to quit acting like too many other men.

"*General* James Longstreet. The fellow that cost us—I mean, the Confederacy—the victory at Gettysburg. You know, by dragging his feet before giving Pickett the order to charge? Bobby Lee called him 'Old Pete.' "

"Why bring up the Civil War now, Tim?"

"Because I'm emotionally challenged?"

"I don't think you are."

He wondered if what was happening to him might possibly be happening to her too. He used to be able to tell, but these days the only minds he could read belonged to criminals. "Well, then, could it be that I'm scared to be sitting here with Pete's wife?"

"Scared of *him*?"

"No, scared of me. And you."

"Well, I'm scared too."

He hadn't tossed caution aside very often since the day he took his shoulder pads off for the last time, some twenty-five years ago. But he tossed it aside now. He hurled it away.

"Since sitting here's so scary," he said, "want to go someplace else?"

———

The pickup stank of sweat and hot vinyl. He switched on the air conditioner, then leaned over and rummaged under the seat until he pulled out a CD. "My favorite," he said, showing her the cover. *Sad Songs and Waltzes* by somebody named Keith Whitley, a haunted-looking guy with an acoustic guitar. "Greatest country singer ever. Only problem is he drank himself to death. I think he was thirty-three. A good bit younger than me." He popped the disc in and, after a pianist pounded out the intro, the singer wept his first words.

> *I can't stand to see*
> *A good man go to waste*

One who never combs his hair
Or shaves his face

A man who leans on wine
Over love that's told a lie
Oh, it tears me up to see
A grown man cry

"My God, Tim," she said. "Do you listen to this kind of thing often?"

"Day in and day out. For my purposes, just about every song on this CD's thematically on target."

By the time they pulled into his apartment complex, she'd been treated to such gems as "(I've Always Been) Honky Tonk Crazy" and "Where Are All the Girls I Used to Cheat With?" Despite the air-conditioning, the back of her blouse was soaking wet. Her shoulders itched and so did her knees. But for all the physical discomfort, she'd found a small zone of emotional security. She could say whatever she wanted to. Whatever was going to happen would, and for once she'd be the one to hand down the decision. "Have you cheated with a lot of girls?" she asked as he turned off the motor.

"The whole time I was married, I never slept with anybody but my wife."

"Since then?"

"Since then, I've left a real trail of disaster. And mostly, I'm afraid, it involves only sleep."

On the landing outside his apartment was a charcoal grill. Ashes were sifted all over the concrete, and the grill's hood was so rusted you could actually see inside.

He stuck the key into the door lock but didn't turn it. "I warn you, it's a real cave in there."

"Why didn't you clean it up, if you knew I might be coming over?"

"Never in my wildest dreams did I think you might come over."

She took his free hand in hers and exulted when he flinched at her touch. "Tim," she said, "if there's one thing life has taught me, it's how to tell when a man's lying. And you're lying now."

"Well, there're better lies and worse ones. I hope you don't think mine's too bad."

"It's the nicest one I've been told in a long time."

The door swung open to reveal a pair of dirty jeans spanning the void between coffee table and armchair and another pair balled up on the floor. Copies of *USA Today, Sports Illustrated* and the *Loring Weekly Times* lay everywhere. Bottles, however, were the true lords of this realm—the clans of beer, whiskey and wine. In every other respect a nightmare, his apartment represented a treasure trove for the enterprising recycler.

"This is how I live," he said. "What do you think?"

"I've formed a preliminary impression, but I imagine it's going to get a lot worse." She walked past him into the kitchen, which to her surprise proved fairly clean. You could tell something had boiled over on the stove—a large stain spread out around one of the eyes—but no dirty dishes were piled in the sink, and the countertops looked like you could probably touch them without getting stuck. "It's actually not *that* bad," she said.

"You don't need to go to the bathroom, do you? Because that's pretty much the nadir."

"I guess if I need to go to the bathroom, you could drive me over to the Shell station."

It was not like she'd imagined. She stepped forward, he stood still. She actually had to push his arms away from his sides, but once she'd done so they began to work of their own accord, and he was holding her, and then his hands began to roam over her spine, up her shoulders, into her hair, and she was back in the world of male odor—perspiration, aftershave, a whiff of desperation.

His cheek grazed hers. Her left hand slid inside his shirt, her fingers feeling for the wiry hair she expected on his chest, but instead she found smooth skin.

"Why?" he said.

"Why what?"

"Why me?"

"I don't know why. I don't care why."

In the bedroom, a picture of a girl with strawberry blond hair stood in a frame next to an ancient alarm clock. A large sack of Purina Puppy Chow was propped in one corner, though as far as she knew Tim didn't own a dog. When he kicked off his shoes, a bottle rolled across the floor.

He sat on the side of the bed, ducking his head as she began unbuttoning her blouse.

"No," she said, "watch me."

"You're brassy."

There was no brass inside her, no hard metal that might have stiffened her will when circumstance required. But she remembered how the man who sat staring at her now and the one who hadn't stared at her in ages had mixed the epoxy and repaired her piano. Two soft substances forming something hard and strong.

She tossed her blouse onto the bed, then picked it up and laid it on the bedside table. She undid her bra, pulled it off and laid it aside, then stepped out of her skirt and panties and stood there as if she were being auctioned. "If I'm too thin and insubstantial for your taste," she said, "tell me now."

He sat there thinking, as he so often had before, that marriage was the most brutal institution of all. It demanded too much, gave too little back, both demystified and commodified longing. For him the only mystery left in marriage was how anybody survived it. He and Jena sure hadn't. It didn't look like Angela and Pete would either. Not without a lot of help. "Come here," he said.

"No," she replied. "You can come to me."

He stood and slipped off the rest of his clothes, revealing a body that she could tell had once been athletic but was now soft in the same spots where Pete's remained hard. Stepping forward, he put his arms around her and began to stroke her hair, but he never pressed himself against her the way Pete used to. So she pressed herself against him.

"I've been having a lot of trouble with women, Angela," he said.

"I know that."

"It's not just the drinking. It feels like something in me's withered."

"Something in me, too. I assumed you knew."

She couldn't remember later if he'd turned back the sheets or she had. She did remember being surprised that the fitted sheet was pink. The top sheet was white and made of coarse fabric, and the speckled pillowcases matched neither one. He climbed into bed first and she followed. Settling into his arms, she immediately felt him grow hard.

"Jesus Christ," he said. "This can't be happening."

Her thought exactly as she swept aside the covers, pressed his shoulders flat against the mattress and climbed on top of him. Right before she closed her eyes, as she began to move and felt the tremor pass through his body and into her own, she had another thought.

This is it. This is what Pete knows that I never knew until now.

LAURA SUMMERALL," Fran said. "Mid-to-late thirties? Forty, tops?"

He paused in the hallway, holding a chart. The name meant nothing. Could be somebody he'd known growing up, and it wouldn't be the first time since he moved back that a patient he didn't remember came to see him. Sometimes, when he saw their faces, he recalled who they were, sometimes not. It seemed as if nobody had ever forgotten him. They just showed up, history in hand. "She wants to make an appointment?"

"She says she needs to see you, that she doesn't live here and this is her only day off this week." Fran did a few things that annoyed him, like praying audibly over her sandwich at lunchtime, but he'd hired her because she exhibited one of the most important qualities a person in her position could possess: an overall skepticism that any truly urgent situation was likely to arise at any given time, ever. Yet something about Laura Summerall, whoever she was, had convinced her to interrupt him. "She said she could wait as long as need be."

He glanced at his watch. Almost four. He still had to see two more patients, and he hated to be late for practice. Football was the main thing he looked forward to. The team had won two in a row now and the kids were starting to think of themselves as something more than losers. "Okay," he said, "tell her I'll see her just as soon as I can, but I'm running short of time. If she needs more than three or four minutes, tell her to schedule an appointment and come back another day."

She was waiting in the last room at the end of the hall, standing with her back to him and looking at a wall chart detailing the workings of the circulatory system. She wore a maroon skirt, a white blouse and a pair of very sensible shoes. Her purse rested on the plastic chair.

When she turned around, at first he failed to recognize her. Then he noticed the purple indentation beneath her left eye. "You're out of uniform," he said.

"Well, that's because I'm off duty. I've got my piece, though. It's in my purse."

"You won't need to use that on me."

She laughed. "The last time I saw you, you were going eighty-one miles an hour."

"You made notes?"

"Not on paper." She'd locked her hands together near her waist. She was sweating, he realized, as she was that afternoon south of Greenville. The fabric beneath her armpits had turned a darker shade. "You *knew* you were in trouble," she said, "but I didn't know I was."

Her mouth twisted wryly when she spoke, and he knew then why he'd felt the urge to unburden himself to her after she caught him speeding. She'd reminded him of the night he met Angela, at that ridiculous Halloween party when he'd worn the football uniform. His future wife's mouth had twisted in the same manner when she looked at him and shook her head, as if to say that on an evening when everyone was pretending to be someone else, he was, by virtue of having come disguised as himself, the biggest phony of all. When a woman looked at you like that, you had to make sure she left knowing who you were. Or at least who you thought you were. At that moment.

"Why don't you sit down?" he said to Laura Summerall.

He'd intended for her to take the chair. Instead she placed both palms flat on the examination table and boosted herself onto it. He waited until she'd gotten settled, then stepped over and took a look at the spot under her eye. She was wearing perfume, but just a touch.

"Basal cell carcinoma?" he asked.

She nodded.

"Well, whoever removed it did a good job. Who was it?"

"Dr. Finley. Frank's his first name, I think. Looks too young to be a doctor? Real skinny with the kind of black-rimmed glasses nobody wears anymore?"

"At DMC?"

"No, he's down in Jackson. That's where my regular doctor sent me."

He picked up her purse and placed it on the counter, then took the chair himself. "I'm sure they told you it's not life-threatening?"

"Yeah, they did," she said, resting her hands on her knees. He noticed that she wore no wedding ring. Yet back in August, she'd said something about drinking at the Holiday Inn with her husband. "They also told me," she said, "that because it was so close to my eye, it could have eventually destroyed my vision on that side. If I hadn't had it checked. And I wouldn't have if I hadn't run across you."

"I think I was the one doing the running that day."

"Something *was* wrong," she said. "Between you and your family. I could tell. I hope you won't think I'm prying."

He wanted to tell her what had been wrong then, that it was still wrong now and probably always would be because some wrongs just couldn't be made right. But telling her any of that would constitute another wrong, and they were starting to add up. "You know how it goes," he said. "Moves are stressful for all concerned. We'd been driving three straight days, it was hot, I was tired, my foot got too heavy on the pedal. *Voilà.* A speeding ticket, which you were kind enough not to give me."

"I couldn't. Till this day I didn't know why. I've seen a lot of wrecks, a bunch of mangled bodies, and I generally don't hold much sympathy for folks that drive that fast. I may have written more tickets in the last couple of years than anybody in the state. But I couldn't bring myself to write you one."

"Well, I'm glad you stopped me, since it helped us catch that medical problem. And I'm glad you let me go." He glanced at his watch. "Now, you may not believe this," he said, rising, "but I'm not just a doctor, I help out with the football team too, and I'm afraid I'm about to miss practice."

She reacted instantly, sliding smoothly off the table. "I don't know what would have happened if you hadn't said what you did that day," she said. "Nobody else had said a word. Not my momma or my sister. Not my neighbors. Nobody I work with. Folks appear when you need them. That's something I try to believe. If you don't mind, I'd like to give you a hug."

When she stepped into his embrace, he smelled the smoke in her hair. She pressed her cheek against his chest and, as he held her, he suddenly saw himself standing two thousand miles away in another small room, under a different set of fluorescent lights, with a different woman in his arms.

A grown man reduced to late adolescence by urges he'd never quite mastered.

———

Ten minutes later she was sitting in her car, smoking a cigarette and trying to calm down, when she saw him leave his office. He had on black sweatpants now and a long-sleeved white T-shirt, a black-and-gold baseball cap and a pair of white running shoes. He walked over to an old pickup in the far corner of the lot and climbed in.

She assumed he'd start the motor and drive off, but instead he sat there, just as she was sitting here, and then he wrapped his arms around the steering wheel and rested his head against it. She'd seen men do all kinds of strange things, to themselves and to others, but until now she'd never seen one hug a steering wheel like that, and it would be a long time before she forgot it.

Once a month, for more than two years, ever since his mother suffered her stroke, Alan had driven up to Memphis on a weekday and met her for coffee at the Davis-Kidd bookstore. He wasn't opposed to visiting her at home, in her big house on Park Avenue, but she said it did her good to get out, and Davis-Kidd was the place she liked best.

He usually got there before she did. But when he pulled into the parking lot today, Veasey's big Cadillac was already parked in front of the store.

Veasey himself was in the café, standing behind the woman he'd lived with all these years, his hands gripping the handles of her wheelchair. Edie had her back to Alan—she was facing the counter, ordering her double decaf extra-hot latte—and while he stood there watching, Veasey lifted one hand off the wheelchair to smooth her hair, iron gray now, thin and wispy.

At one point in his life, Marlon Veasey had made a lot of money doing something, but he either couldn't or wouldn't tell you what it was. Alan had been given to understand that he owned a lot of land in north Mississippi, some of it over near Tunica, and had profited mightily in recent years from the incursion of the casinos. He supposedly owned several buildings on the square down in Oxford, as well as a good bit of commercial real estate in Batesville, Senatobia and Corinth. In his seventies now, he still wore too much cologne and talked too much, but he'd doted on Edie for years, never more so than since the stroke. Sometimes, she'd told Alan, she had to make him leave her alone, just so she could read or entertain a stray thought.

This morning, when he saw Alan, Veasey shook his hand, then slapped him on the back and said, "Hey, boy, how's things in the grocery business?"

Alan had never liked being touched by other men. "About the same," he said.

"Well, like I've always told you, people have to eat."

He'd never told Alan any such thing. He was always making references to one thing or the other he'd told you, and it was never anything he'd actually said.

Edie got her latte and, while Alan ordered a cup of coffee, Veasey rolled her over to a table near the door, where she could look out onto the patio. He told Alan he was going to get his hair styled and have his shoes shined and pick up a bottle of something really special. "I'll loan her to you for an hour," he said, throwing his arm around Alan's shoulders, "and then she's mine again."

When he'd left, Edie pulled a cigarette out of her purse and lit it. You weren't supposed to smoke in the café, but she always did anyway and nobody ever said anything about it. "He's got health problems," she said.

"Marlon? He looks fine to me."

"His hip hurts so bad at night he can't sleep. They give him medicine that eases the pain, but it knocks him out, so he won't take it because he's scared I'll need to go pee or something and he won't wake up and I'll wet the bed and feel humiliated." She blew a puff of smoke toward the door. "He's wrong about that, though. I might wet the bed. But I wouldn't feel humiliated."

She'd never felt ashamed of anything her body did, as best Alan could tell. Just as he was thinking about that, she said, "Of course as far as you're concerned, I've never exhibited any sense of propriety. So why would that change now. Right?"

"I didn't say that."

"But you thought it, didn't you?"

He sighed and sipped his coffee. He hated making these trips, hated sitting there alone with her in the café and trying to find a topic they could safely discuss. She hadn't regularly attended church in close to forty years and, if he mentioned anything about his work as a deacon, she'd grin annoyingly. She purchased books he wouldn't have been caught dead with. He'd seen her buy one called *Bastard Out of Carolina* and another entitled *Bleachy-Haired Honky Bitch*. He hoped that if she intended to buy anything today, Veasey would return in time to take her to the checkout stand.

"You thought it," she said again, thumping ashes onto her saucer. "And you know what, Alan? You're right. I have no sense of propriety. I don't know if I was born without it, which seems likely, or if I just lost it back when you were a boy. But I don't have it. And it does not have me."

He decided not to waste his breath arguing. His mother, whatever else you might say about her, had never shrunk from the truth. "What's Marlon going to do?" he said. "About his pain, I mean. Is he a candidate for hip replacement?"

"Lord knows. If you wanted to start replacing everything on Marlon that doesn't work anymore, you'd need to manufacture a completely new man."

Most people got red in the face when embarrassed, but Alan's ears always gave him away. He could tell she'd noticed they were glowing. She smiled at him, and when she did she looked a lot younger and was almost pretty again.

"It's a problem you'll face one day too," she said. "Don't pass up a chance to nail Nancy now. Morning, noon or night. The time'll come when you won't even remember what it felt like."

"Momma," he said.

"Yes?"

He just shook his head. "Nothing."

She laid her cigarette on the rim of her saucer, then lifted the cup and took a swallow. "Actually," she said, "Nancy called me the other day."

His wife hadn't mentioned talking to his mother. "What about?"

She set the cup back down. "Seems there are some new faces around town. Or should I say some old faces have returned?"

He wasn't finished with his coffee but got up and walked over to the counter, where the stainless steel thermoses stood in a row, and squirted some decaf into his cup. He stood there long enough to take three or four swallows, then he squirted in a little more and walked back to the table. She watched him as if she were a drama judge grading his performance.

He sat down across from her. "Yeah," he said, "I can think of one old face that's returned."

"And what do you intend to do about it?"

"What's to be done? It's a free country. He can live where he wants to." He sipped his coffee. "I haven't thought about the guy three times in fifteen or twenty years."

"Oh, honey," she said, reaching over and laying her hand on his, "you're lying."

Stunned, he sat there looking at the back of her hand, wrinkled now and covered with liver spots. She hadn't touched him like that or called him *honey* since he was twelve or thirteen. Everything that went wrong between them had started right then, at the moment he ceased to be a child. "Why do we need to talk about this, Momma?" he said. "Why bring it up now?"

She let go of his hand and sat back in her wheelchair. "Nancy called to ask me if there'd ever been a problem between you and Pete Barrington. You've got her scared, Alan. Her and Mason both."

The table was flimsy, standard-issue café furniture, with a single metal leg supporting it. He could've flipped it over and kicked it halfway across the room, and for just an instant, as scarlet fog filled his head, he thought maybe he would. He didn't care if hot coffee spilled in her lap. Worse stuff had been. He smacked the table with his palm. Both cups jumped, but Edie didn't move. "What did you tell her?" he demanded.

"You know, Alan, you better go read your Bible. I sure don't know everything that's in there, but I bet you'll find something somewhere about the need to let bygones go bye-bye. Am I right about that or not?"

The espresso machine hissed as somebody made steam for yet another latte. He hated seeing people drinking stuff like that. The craze had swept east from California. You even saw it now in Loring. People were drinking espresso and wine and eating God knows what at Sandra Jean Sturdivant's fake French café. Meanwhile, an entire way of life was being whisked aside. Folks bought the *New York Times* on Sunday at McCormack's over in Greenville. Drove over there and back just so they could say they'd spent six dollars on a newspaper, when they could've gotten the *Clarion-Ledger* at Mr. Quik for a buck twenty-five.

"I know what's in the Bible," he told his mother, "but I'll be damned if I'll tell you."

"That's a hell of a thing for an evangelical to say."

"This is a hell of a day."

She stared at him for a moment or two, then reached down and lifted her purse off the floor. She placed the bag in her lap, then unzipped it and pulled out a small book bound in imitation leather. "Do you want to know what this is?" she asked.

He didn't answer.

"Of course you do. So I'll tell you. It's a catalogue of sorts, Alan. Or to put it differently, it's a record of who I was when I didn't know who I wanted to be. And so we start out, right here, with a picture of me. Recognize it?"

She flipped the little book open and turned it upside down so he could see.

The picture had been taken on the day she married his father. He'd grown up with that photo, had looked at it countless times when it sat in a frame on the desk in his father's office. She'd trimmed it down and you couldn't see much of the background, but the photographer had snapped it on the front steps at the church where Alan now served as a deacon. His mother had just swept her veil aside and was smiling at somebody not in the picture, and he knew it was his dad.

"September seventh," she said, "1958." She turned the page. "And here's what I looked like six months pregnant."

He'd seen that photo too. She was sitting in a boat with his dad, who was paddling backwards away from the dock and grinning at the camera. Her stomach was big, and she held one hand to the side of her head, as if in amazement, while the other pointed straight at her belly.

"I've looked at all this stuff before," he said. "I don't want to see it again. Besides, I don't understand your point. I just don't get it at all. What's this got to do with Nancy or Mason? Or Pete?"

"You know something, Alan? You were always impatient. If I had to point to one quality above all others that in my mind defines you, it's that. A total lack of patience. You remind me of myself at your age. It's scary."

He couldn't let that comment pass, even though it meant engaging her on her own terms. "I remind you of *yourself*? Now, let me see if I get this." A couple other patrons turned their heads to look, but he didn't care. "I've been married to the same woman for almost a quarter of a century. She's the only person I've ever gone to bed with. I never even look at another woman. My wife knows where I am every moment of every day, and my son does too. I'm devoted to them. First comes God and then comes family, but in my case maybe the order's reversed. So tell me, if you can, where the resemblance lies between me and you?"

She turned the book around again and, smiling, began to page through it. Clearly, what she saw there gave her pleasure. "When you've got a problem, Alan, you want it solved right now, right this instant, today. That's what's behind your religion. It gives you an answer to every single question. And because you've got the answer, you don't have to trouble your head, much less your heart. Well, I was looking for answers too. I just found different ones than you."

He'd never hit a woman. He'd never hit another person, period. But right then the desire to slap her face almost overcame him. He shut his eyes and tried to pray for help but he couldn't find the words.

"You see?" she said. "Now you're out of answers, and there's not much you can do except sit there wishing you could stuff a rag in my mouth and shut me up. Isn't that what you're wishing, hon? Or is it something worse?"

He opened his eyes to find her staring at him. The book lay on the table.

"I'm wishing," he said, "that you were not my mother."

"I used to wish the same thing. See how much alike we are? Back when I was about thirty-eight or thirty-nine, when I was screwing boys your age, I used to wish it all the time." She looked down at the book, at whatever picture she'd found there. "Look at this, Alan," she said. "Take a long look, and then see if you can answer one question for me."

She picked the book up and turned it over in her hands, to show him what she'd been looking at. There were two pictures, one on each page. On the left, she was standing in the basement of the house he'd grown up in. You could see the air-conditioning unit behind her and, beyond that, his father's tool chest, which rested on a ledge underneath a joist. The picture showed his mother from the knees up. She was wearing a purple long-sleeved blouse with its top buttons unfastened, and you could see a good bit of her breasts. Though the blouse covered her crotch, it was apparent that she'd taken off her panties.

In the picture on the right, a young man stood directly in front of the stairs leading down from the kitchen. He wore a pair of cutoff jeans. His chest was completely hairless. His stomach was flat and hard, his waist narrow, his arms and shoulders huge. He had the body of a god but the smooth unmarked face of a boy, staring into the camera with a look of helpless longing.

"If that was your son," his mother asked him, "would you want him held responsible for whatever he did next?"

DRIVING BACK FROM MEMPHIS, Alan pulled off at the big Love's Truckstop near Senatobia, parked as far away from everybody else as he could get, closed his eyes and prayed silently. He told the Lord he knew he was walking in darkness and begged for deliverance from the hatred that consumed him. He hadn't made love to Nancy for close to two weeks, and the last time they'd tried he'd grown soft. Mason was looking at him strangely, as if he expected another eruption at any moment, and Alan knew his son was lying to him and seeing the Barrington girl when he claimed to be over at somebody else's place studying. He'd yelled at Reggie McDonald for slitting a bale of flour with a box cutter, and had turned away after catching sight of Wade on the frozen-food aisle the other day, prompting the reverend to call him at home later on and ask if he was still mad about the conversation they'd had after church.

His heart had grown large with the passage of time as he'd learned to love and forgive, to ask for and accept forgiveness, but now, he knew, it was a hard, dark thing, small and cold and empty of all besides anger. And so he asked that the anger be drained from it, and as he sat there listening to the sound of air brakes sighing, doors slamming, a voice over the loudspeaker alerting some truck driver that shower number six was now ready, he experienced the sensation of expansion, the capacity to give and receive love returning.

He opened his eyes and saw a small boy standing in a parking space nearby, beside the open door of a brown Dodge pickup. The boy wore blue jeans and a red Ole Miss jersey that hung down to his knees. When he saw Alan looking at him, he grinned and waved, then ran off after his father, who was walking into the truck stop.

———

At dinner that night, Alan made a point of asking Mason lots of questions about school, football, whether or not he was thinking of college yet. Mason was reserved at first, answering with little more than *yes sir* or *no sir*, but the question about college produced a more animated response.

"I think I'd like to go to Stanford," he said.

Alan slit a piece of corn bread and buttered both halves. "Why Stanford?"

"Well, it's got a really great history department. And I'm into that. I checked a book out of the library last week that one of their professors wrote. And it's great."

"What's the name of it?"

"*Freedom from Fear*. It's all about the Great Depression, Franklin Roosevelt and World War Two. And I think I'd like to take a class, you know, from the guy who wrote it."

"Well, you've got the grades. It's expensive, though. We'd need help, and from what I've heard, a place like that pays a lot of attention to where you went to school. Loring High's not exactly Exeter."

"Yeah, but they're also looking for a diverse student population. And they don't get a lot of applications from the Mississippi Delta."

Alan knew that the phrase *diverse student population* was one Mason had heard from somebody else. Somebody from a place where people said all kinds of high-minded things like that and then went out and elected as their chief executive a former bodybuilder with a reputation for grabbing women's breasts. Nevertheless, he said, "You're probably right about that. But do you think you'd fit in out there?"

"You never know," Mason said. "There are lots of things you just don't know until you experience them for yourself."

Alan thought about that comment later, as he lay in bed waiting for Nancy to emerge from the bathroom. There was plenty he hadn't experienced, and for the most part he felt thankful that he'd escaped it. He read a fair amount of military history, for instance, and guys kept saying again and again that nothing they'd ever done in their lives could quite match the exhilaration, much of it born of terror, that they'd known as young men on the battlefield. He never envied them the exhilaration one bit. He knew plenty of people in Loring who'd visited cities like New York, San Francisco, Paris and London, and he didn't envy them either. He liked to look at pictures of those places, especially aerial photographs, but as far as actually going to any of them, he really felt no interest in that because he hated crowds and traffic and high prices.

He knew, too, that most men had slept with a lot more women than he had. Just last week, in the barbershop, he'd heard a man he respected sigh and say how glad he was that he'd "poked around" in his youth, that it gave him a more realistic perspective on sex and commitment and that otherwise he might not have appreciated just how solid and secure his marriage really was. Alan didn't believe in waging those kinds of discussions in public places, or anywhere else, for that matter, but if he had, he would've said he didn't need to "poke around" to appreciate his wife, that the only thing he needed to do was enjoy the act with her, just as he so often had in the last twenty-two years.

When Nancy came out of the bathroom wearing her red night-gown, he climbed out of bed, walked over to the vanity, where she was reaching for a bottle of moisturizing lotion, and put his arms around her from behind. "Squirt some of that stuff on your hands," he whispered, "and rub it on me."

Color rose into her cheeks. Into her forehead, too. "Where?"

"You know where."

So his wife pumped a large puddle of the stuff into the palm of her left hand, set the bottle down, then reached into his boxer shorts. While he stood there, she knelt on the carpet and began to rub the cool creamy lotion over his genitals, using both hands, rhythmically pulling and kneading as he steadied himself against the wall and fought back the tears he felt coming. After a while he became aware that she'd removed one of her hands, and when he opened his eyes and looked down, he saw that her other hand had disappeared into the folds of her nightgown, and he groaned and lurched forward, grabbing the back of her neck and calling her name.

———————

The next morning, in the incinerator room at the grocery store, he did his best to make up with Reggie, asking him if he knew how many yards he'd gained this season (he did) and whether or not he was passing all his courses (he wasn't). He ribbed Wayne Collier about a new girl he'd seen him with the previous Saturday in front of Pizza Hut, and he told both of them that if they graduated on time, he'd stand each of them to a steak dinner and might even buy a case of cold beer as long as they promised not to drive after they drank it.

In his office he phoned the church, and when the secretary put Wade Phelps on the line, Alan said, "You know I've been out of fellowship lately."

"Yeah," Wade said, "but I couldn't tell if you did. Have you and the prime minister settled it—or is my input required?"

"It might be something I'd like to talk about sometime, but for right now I think it's under control."

"You know my number."

"And I won't hesitate to call it."

For the rest of the morning he busied himself completing paperwork, reviewing the stock boys' orders, coming down out of his cubicle from time to time to greet a customer or shoot the breeze with his assistant manager or one of the checkout clerks. A few minutes before eleven, he went out and got into his truck.

He hadn't been making his regular morning trip to the catfish plant for several weeks now. The first time he failed to go, it had just slipped his mind. That evening Nancy had acted strange but hadn't said anything, and the next morning, when he realized it was almost eleven and that he hadn't gone the day before, he picked up the phone and called to say he was going to quit driving over for the time being, because he could tell things were getting lax around the store in his absence. But last night, while she lay in bed with her head on his chest, she told him she missed those small exchanges, and they agreed to renew the practice.

She was out there waiting, right where she'd always been, and she smiled and waved and he knew she was thinking of what they'd done the night before, how they'd ended up on the floor, him on his back while she straddled him and closed her eyes and threw her head back and he ran his hands over her belly, her hips and her thighs, the parts of her body that he knew she felt ashamed of. You couldn't beat that kind of excitement, he thought, waving at her one last time before driving off. This could only come from loving what was familiar—loving it for its flaws, rather than in spite of them.

He didn't know why anybody ever went looking for anything else.

————

His truck was low on gas, and he always tried to fill up at the only independent station left in Loring, which belonged to Grady Stewart. It stood only a block from the fire station, and that was probably a good thing, because with so many grease rags and old tires lying around, it constituted the worst fire hazard in town. Mr. Stewart had been old when Alan was young. Now he was truly ancient. Some days he didn't even bother to open the station. He'd just nail up a sign saying NO GAS—GO SOMEWHERE ELSE. He was grouchy and foul-mouthed, and sometimes he'd pick his nose while he talked to you, but Alan had never forgotten that when his father disappeared, Mr. Stewart had once refused to accept payment after Alan filled up his tank. "You got enough troubles," he'd said, "without scrounging for gas money. Get on away from here. See if you can't chase you down some pussy, take your mind off what ain't right."

He was there today, in as nasty a mood as he ever fell prey to. "I'm sick to my soul," he said, jamming the nozzle into Alan's tank, "of goddamn nigger boom-boom."

"I'm afraid I don't follow you, Mr. Stewart."

"That shit they listen to. Boom-boom. Boom-boom. You know, where they don't actually sing the words but just kind of talk 'em?"

"You mean rap music?"

"Nigger boom-boom's what it is." The old man's face, covered with white stubble, broke into a brown-toothed grin. "You hear about what that big nigger with the cell phone done?"

Alan had no idea what he was talking about and said so.

"Nigger that drives the live-haul truck for the catfish plant. He picked up one of the women off the filet line, got her to spend the night with him and perform all manner of abominations. She didn't know he had one of them little cameras in his cell phone, though. He been showing pictures of her all over town."

"You've seen them, I take it?"

"No such luck, but I've heard from folks that has. And they say that nigger girl missed her calling, that she ought to been a drainpipe."

Wishing for once that he'd patronized Shell or Exxon, Alan paid and started the truck and pulled into the street.

He wasn't looking for trouble—afterwards, he could tell himself that with complete certainty. He was just doing what you do when you drive through a town you know so well that you could shut your eyes, should you choose to, and still skirt every pothole. He wasn't paying a lot of attention to the street itself. Nothing was coming toward him, so he let his eyes rove a little, noticing that the sidewalk in front of the Legion Hall had buckled, that somebody had tossed a Slurpee cup onto the pavement near the fire station and that in the run-down apartment complex in the next block, Tim Kessler, the alcoholic lawyer who doubled as a football coach, had just stepped out onto the landing and was scanning the parking lot as if somebody from the *National Enquirer* was lurking down there with a camera.

The woman who stepped out of the apartment behind him didn't act nearly so worried. As Alan lifted his foot off the gas, she put her hand in Kessler's hair, ruffling it a little bit, then leaned toward him and kissed his ear. Her own hair was plenty rumpled. Alan noticed, as he'd failed to before, how much she and her daughter resembled each other, though the daughter might have been a little taller. But then, after all, the girl's father stood six-four.

THE THIRD WEEK OF OCTOBER, a cold front blew through the Delta, accompanied by a band of tornadoes that destroyed several mobile homes near Greenville, tore the roof off a school in Indianola and toppled the Mississippi ETV tower just east of Inverness. Overnight, the temperature dropped into the thirties. When Pete walked into the kitchen the next morning, it was still cold, Angela having just turned on the heat.

His terry-cloth bathrobe smelled of their old house. He'd put it on now, for the first time since they'd moved, and its odor was affecting in ways that he couldn't explain. The man who used to wear it didn't exist anymore. When he and his family climbed into the Volvo and drove across country, he'd thought of the move as major surgery, but in truth the patients had all been consigned to death. And he was the one who'd certified their demise.

"Want scrambled eggs?" Angela asked. She seemed a lot more alert now in the mornings. The other day, rummaging through the cabinets for a jar of olives, he'd located her Toprol. He shook the pills out and counted them, and she still had seven. A prescription for thirty had been filled at Long's Drugs in Fresno right before they left, so he knew she'd quit taking them or at least dialed back. "Scrambled eggs'd be great," he said.

"Bacon, too?"

"Sure."

She put a few strips on, poured him some orange juice and put the glass down on the table. Then her hand grazed the back of his neck and lifted off quickly, only to settle there again a moment later. "You need a haircut," she said. "It's getting a little shaggy in the back."

At first he couldn't speak—it had been so long since she'd touched him like this. "All right," he finally said. "I'll go get one."

Backpack slung over her shoulder, Toni walked in and stood looking at them for a moment. "Do I smell bacon burning?"

Angela moved toward the stove. "It's not burning. It's just cooking. Would you like some?"

"No, bacon's unhealthy." She dropped the heavy backpack on the floor. "It ruins your complexion and clogs your arteries, and I want mine to stay clear so I can live forever."

Where his daughter was concerned, Pete could never quite determine when he ought to keep quiet. "To what," he asked, "should we attribute your newfound love of life?"

Toni's lips puckered into a sullen O. "I've always loved life. Sometimes life has not loved me."

After that he kept his mouth shut, except when forcing some food inside.

———

Following the loss to Yazoo City, the team had surprised everybody and put together a four-game winning streak. Reggie McDonald was leading the conference in rushing and scoring, and Cody Blackstone was fifth in total offense. Around town, Pete and Tim were receiving a major share of the credit. After all, most of the starters had played the year before, and Killingsworth hadn't been able to accomplish much with them on his own, so the win streak must be due to the two new volunteer coaches.

Pete hated hearing anything along those lines and did everything he could to convince people it wasn't true, pointing out that the head coach analyzed the opponents' game film, designed the offensive and defensive schemes, made all the decisions about who started and who rode the bench. But a lot of them were preconditioned to find fault with Rashard Killingsworth because he was black.

Rashard surely knew what was being said, and Pete figured his awareness could account for the testiness that he'd begun to display toward his crack volunteers. That afternoon, Pete got to the field at his usual time, just as the offense started running through the week's game plan, but Tim hadn't arrived yet and Killingsworth made no attempt to hide his unhappiness. "Kind of hard," he said, "to insist on the players being punctual when one of their coaches takes a notion to show up late."

"He might have been in court this afternoon, Rashard. And I imagine he had to go home to get some warmer clothes." Pete was wearing heavy sweats and a fleece jacket that didn't quite protect him from the biting cold. "Damn, I forgot it could get like this down here in October."

"You forgot how a lot of things work down here." Killingsworth stood with his hands in his pockets, the clipboard tucked under one arm. The day was overcast, but he wore dark glasses anyway, and Pete couldn't see his eyes.

"Are you trying to tell me something, Rashard?" he asked. "Because if you are, I'm all ears."

Killingsworth laughed. "All ears," he said. "Now that's flat-out funny." The head coach stepped over to the huddle. "Blackstone, if I'm the free safety, all I need to do to learn the contents of your last wet dream is watch your eyes. How many times I told you to look off the goddamn coverage?"

Tim appeared fifteen or twenty minutes later, dashing across the field, leaping mud puddles like a boy bent on play. His defensive backs were milling around hugging themselves to try and stay warm. By then, Pete was down at the far end working with the outside line-backers, who on Friday night might find themselves covering wide receivers because Greenville ran the spread offense. He saw Killingsworth glance at Tim and shake his head.

When the team came back together to work on the defensive game plan, Pete and Tim stood behind the free safety, as had become their habit. Pete said, "Killingsworth acted kind of unhappy about your being late."

"I didn't intend to do it."

Shontell Clemons threw a forearm in Depot's face and would have bulled into the backfield, but Depot stuck his leg out and tripped the big kid just like Pete had taught him. "Good stuff, Depot!" he hollered.

On hands and knees, Shontell turned around and faked insult. "Aw, Coach Barrington, you know that ain't legal."

"Sometimes," Pete said, "necessity's at odds with legality."

"Yeah, and that's usually when somebody goes to jail," Tim said. "Or, in this case, draws a penalty."

"Depot's already being penalized enough by having to block him." Pete watched the defense huddle while the scout teamers got ready to run another play. "When Rashard got testy, I told him you probably had a court date. Or something."

"Or something's what it was."

"Yeah?"

"Yeah. Toilet over at my place was running like O.J., and the whole post came off when I stuck my hand in there to jiggle the float. Had me a regular river flowing down the hallway."

"That's why they make shutoff valves."

"I can't think as fast as you do. Don't forget, son, you're in the business of life and death."

"Thought you were too."

"Nope. My business is life in Parchman."

Tim, Pete noticed, had lost a few pounds. His cheeks and jaws weren't so soft, and it had been a good while since his breath smelled of whiskey. He'd bought some new leather loafers and a blazer he'd hung in the coaching staff's locker room yesterday after practice, and he'd washed and waxed his pickup.

Suddenly it came to Pete that he had a woman in his life. The next revelation was accompanied by the odd sensation that his relationship to his surroundings was being altered, that the black jerseys worn by the first-team defense had somehow grown lighter while the gold ones worn by the scout team were darker, and the numbers had lost definition and become fuzzy, as had the goalposts and the blocking sled and the orange Gatorade barrel. There must be a damn good reason why his friend of more than thirty years hadn't told him about something this important.

The scrubs ran plays against the starting defense for another fifteen minutes, then the team ran through goal line drills, followed by wind sprints. Afterwards, Killingsworth called them together and told them the game against Greenville on Friday would practically determine who won the Delta Conference championship. If anybody had predicted during the summer that at this point they'd be tied for first place, he said, nobody would have believed it.

"A hell of a lot," he concluded, "has changed since August."

———

That evening Angela sat at her vanity looking at her face, as she often did these days. At first she'd been startled that her appearance had not changed. Visible evidence ought to accompany a transformation of the type she'd experienced, but no such evidence existed. At least not to her eye.

His eye saw what her eye missed. Normally, she did things when she sat there, examining her skin for blemishes, squeezing a pustule if she found one, rubbing cold cream on her neck, plucking her eyebrows. But lately she just looked. Her movements around the bedroom had grown languid too, and she no longer guarded her nakedness. Right now, for instance, she wore a white silk pajama top but was naked below the waist. Last night she'd stepped straight from the shower and walked over to the dresser with water dripping from her pubic hair. If she was still ashamed of her thin legs, small breasts or the fold of fat beneath the transverse scar from her C-section, she no longer showed it.

She could feel him watching her. She could even see his face in the mirror. He lay in bed, his head propped up on two pillows, his ragged paperback copy of *The Last Picture Show* open on his chest. He reread the book every year or two because, he told her, it was the last word on life in a small town. The last word on life in any town. She'd read it herself and hadn't much liked it. The pages felt dirty. Everybody fucked, but nobody loved. Everybody knew what everybody else did or didn't do.

Knowing she'd caught him watching her, he felt a twinge of excite-

ment. He could've explained what was happening to him in physiological terms, but the truth was he didn't understand it. Something
was in the air that possessed neither the status of romance nor the
allure of lust. He waited for her to step into the closet and pull on her
pajama bottoms.

His reflected image shifted. His right hand rose, the index finger
tracing a long, aimless line along his jaw. His chin tilted. He blinked.
Was an emotion struggling to gain entry, looking to breech the firewall? Did he *know*?

Jesus. He might.

See? she wanted to tell him. See how it feels? Even if you don't
care? Can you imagine how it hurts when you do?

He wished she'd just say it. It surprised him how much he longed
to hear it, how the thrill junky burned to be doused in those same
waters.

She did and did not want to satisfy his curiosity. Despite the chill
creeping into her naked legs and hips, she might sit there all night,
looking from his face to hers, then back at his again, playing chicken
with the image in the mirror.

As if he grasped the essence of the punishment she had in mind,
he sighed and took up the paperback.

"You know what?" she asked.

He closed the book, leaned over and laid it on the floor, then sat
up in bed, pulled his knees to his chest and wrapped his arms around
them, getting ready. "What?"

She'd never seen a more helpless sight. She stood up and walked
over to the closet, lifted her pajama bottoms off the hook and stepped
into them. Wasting no time, then, she turned out the light.

When she crawled into bed beside him, he didn't move, just sat
there as if braced for disaster.

Which was exactly what she served him. "I still love you, Pete,"
she said. "You know, I never stopped."

ON THURSDAY NIGHT, Toni waited in a booth at Pizza Hut, where she and Mason were supposed to eat dinner. This morning, in the hallway, he'd told her that when practice was over he was going home to tell his dad that they'd been meeting at various places around town and doing their homework together, that he'd taken her to a movie and they'd made a date for tonight. He'd ask his father, too, what had happened between him and Coach Barrington. Maybe she'd do the same thing?

She hadn't said whether or not she would. Mason didn't know exactly how she felt about her father, and sometimes she didn't know herself.

Up until two or three years ago, they'd gotten along just fine. He'd done the things she thought fathers should do, taking her to the zoo and movies and to Fresno State football games, where at halftime a bunch of skydivers would leap out of a plane and try to land on the big Bulldog painted in the middle of the field. They'd gone to the San Francisco Ballet together, just the two of them, and afterwards he took her to her favorite San Francisco restaurant, a little place near Davies Hall called the Blue Muse. That evening she'd felt like a woman, though she was only twelve or thirteen.

Then, on a warm Saturday afternoon, he'd left her in the car at Save Mart while he went in to buy ice cream, and he didn't come back for eons and eons, so finally she opened the door and the car alarm went off. Hot tears stung her eyes. She left the Volvo and stormed inside, where she found him in the vegetable aisle. He was talking to a small, trim woman with the blackest hair she'd ever seen. She had on a pair of white shorts and a black blouse, a nice pair of sandals and three or four bracelets. The instant she spotted Toni staring at her, her face seemed to freeze like one of those images on the computer when the mouse won't let you click. She whispered something to Toni's father, then rolled her cart off down the aisle and around the corner.

Her father's eyes were red, something she'd never seen. It scared her. "Who was that?" she said.

"One of my patients."

"What's her name?"

"I can't tell you that, hon." He tried to nudge her in the direction of the ice cream freezers. "I can't talk about my patients. It's kind of like attorney-client privilege. You must've heard of that."

"Don't talk to me like a child," she said.

She could tell when he was starting to get mad. It didn't happen often, mostly when another doctor had made some dumb mistake. But he was getting mad now.

"I'm talking to you like a child," he said, "because you are one."

"Then you shouldn't have left me locked up in the car. Don't you know it's hot out there?"

"You're right, I shouldn't have. And I'm sorry. Now let's get some ice cream and go."

"Who was that woman?" she asked again.

"I already explained." He laid one big hand on her shoulder. "I can't talk about my patients."

She shook it off. "I've heard you talk about your patients lots of times. Yours and Mom's friend? Mrs. Anderson? She has hepatitis C." Her voice was loud but she didn't give a damn. "The vice president at Fresno State has nodules on his vocal cords."

"Toni, hush."

"Father Alex? From St. Ann's? He's going to need a pacemaker."

At opposite ends of the aisle, people had stopped to stare.

"See?" she said. "I know a lot. Everything but one thing. I don't know that lady's name, and I want to. I don't want to know what's wrong with her, just who she is."

She stood toe to toe with him, looking up as she'd been doing her whole life. Only now he seemed much smaller.

"She had cancer," he said. "She doesn't have it anymore. Her name's Edie. Now, can we go get some Häagen-Dazs and get out of here?"

The woman's name was Nora, not Edie, but it would be another few months before Toni found that out. And by then so much else had gone wrong that she never thought to ask him where the fake name came from.

———

Mason was late. She'd just decided to call her mother to come get her when she spotted him through the window. He stood in the darkness on the far side of the highway, hands jammed in his pockets while he bounced up and down, waiting for a break in the traffic, then finally sprinted across.

To her dismay, after pulling off his coat, he sat down and buried his head in his hands. "Damn," he said.

"What?"

He ran his palms over his face, as if he were washing it. "I had a real argument with my dad."

"Over me?"

"Kind of."

"Either it was or it wasn't."

"Well, then, I guess it was. He told me he didn't want me to see you."

"And what did you do?"

"It's not so much what I did—it's what I said back."

"So what'd you say?"

He lifted the fork off his place setting, stuck the tines into his water glass and stirred the ice. "I told him to go to hell."

He sounded so tormented that it was hard not to laugh. But she knew hell was no laughing matter for him. He really believed in it. Whereas she bet if you traced the concept back to its origins, you'd find it was something somebody's father dreamed up, just to keep his kids in line. "What'd he say when you told him that?"

"He didn't say anything. He got all trembly, and then he got tears in his eyes, and Momma was crying too. I just walked out and came here to see you."

"I sure am a positive force in your life."

"Yeah," he said, "you are." He reached across the table and took her hand in his.

She was tempted to jerk it free, because two of the black girls Mason used to eat lunch with were sitting on the other side of the room, watching them through the space between the salad bar and the plastic hood that kept you from slobbering on the lettuce. But then she looked into his eyes. Her hand stayed where it was. "Did you ask him what he had against my dad?"

"Yeah."

"So?"

"So nothing. He wouldn't tell me."

He was still looking at her, but his eyes lost their focus, and she knew he was lying to spare her feelings. She said, "It probably involved a female."

He spoke softly: "What makes you say so?"

"I know my dad. I bet he took a girlfriend away from your father."

"Maybe so."

Then she knew it was something much worse. "On the other hand," she said, "most people wouldn't stay mad about that. Not if they were in their forties, with families of their own. They'd get past it. Don't you think?"

"Probably."

Mason's friends got up and went to the salad bar, and one of them looked over her shoulder and told him hello. Then she nodded at Toni with a pained expression and said, "How you doing, California?"

"Just fine."

"Bet you cold down here, huh?"

"A little bit."

The other girl said, "Better wear you something warm to Greenville tomorrow night."

"I will."

They both waited until the girls went back to their booth, then Toni said, "So it most likely wasn't girlfriend-related. You agree?"

"Look," he said, "I don't care what it was. It doesn't matter. I think your dad's a great guy. I don't care what he did twenty-something years ago, and I don't care what he did last year, either. I know how good he's been to me. I was always scared of bigger guys until I met him, but he's helped me get over that. And it's a great thing not to walk around feeling scared." He lifted his water glass and took a swallow, then set it back down. "Your mother I don't know. But I'm sure she's also a nice person. After all, she gave the world you."

His compliment whizzed right past her, like an errant spitball. "Mason," she said, "why did you mention my mother? Did your dad tell you something about her too?"

THE THING THAT KIND of amazes me," Tim told her, sitting on the couch in his bathrobe, his bare feet propped up on the coffee table, "is that you never tried to clean this dump up."

She was coming back from the kitchen with two more bottles of Budweiser. She handed him one, then took a swallow from the other and sat down beside him. The heat was on full blast but she was wrapped in a big beach towel that had the Lady Luck Casino logo on it. "Trying to clean this place up," she said, "would be a losing proposition."

He sipped his Budweiser, set it on the coffee table, then reached over and cupped his hand around the back of her neck. "You're equal to the task."

"I may be equal to the *task,* but it would still be a losing proposition. Because the truth, Tim, is that you're naturally messy. Getting you to be something else would just make you unhappy. No molding. Didn't I tell you that from the outset?"

"Yeah," he said. "I reckon having an extramarital affair's potentially analogous to grandparenting. You know how they say that when you have grandkids, you avoid all the mistakes you made with your own children?"

The dimple in her chin deepened, and she looked away, at the window, where the blinds were securely closed. He'd known her from the moment they met, and knew her even better now, and could tell she didn't relish this turn in their conversation. She still loved Pete and would as long as she lived, no matter what. He wanted to tell her she was wasting herself in her marriage, that sometimes you just needed to give up and start over, but he couldn't. She wouldn't have listened anyway. It was something she already knew, and it was something she'd never do.

"I thought people in our situation," she said, "always pretended what they were having wasn't an affair. Isn't that how they're supposed to behave?"

"It's not an affair for me. But that's what it is for you."

"Not now." She laid her head against his shoulder. "That's not what it is right now, Tim."

He accepted the lie in the spirit in which it was offered, and embraced this gift of illusion along with her. He tipped her chin up and kissed her mouth, then her dimple too. "You'll need to head home pretty soon, won't you? Fix dinner and get ready to take Toni to the game tonight?"

"No," she whispered, "I've got a little more time. Pete plans to eat with the team again, and Toni left a message saying she was going to the game with a couple of friends. I'll just stay home. I don't understand football anyway."

"The only thing you need to know about football is that boys start playing it in the throes of puberty."

"From which a few of you never recover."

D'Nesha and Essence had borrowed the car from D'Nesha's dad, Loring's first black chief of police. It was a six- or seven-year-old Mercedes sedan, a fact that Essence found hilarious. "Ever notice how many black people drive around in some old Mercedes?" she asked Toni, who was sitting behind her.

"I hadn't really thought about it."

D'Nesha glanced into the rearview mirror. "California's color-blind," she said.

Essence laughed. "Have to be plumb blind not to tell *you're* black."

D'Nesha was several shades darker than her friend, but it amazed Toni that they talked about such things. In Fresno, on the first day of school, you were handed a list of topics you should never bring up with classmates, and "racial or ethnic difference" was always number one. Unless you could broach it in "a sensitive, empowering manner."

"I guess I just haven't been looking," Toni said. "Or maybe I don't know a Mercedes when I see one."

"They all got that little three-cornered piece up yonder on the hood. You don't see it?"

"Yes, I can see it."

"Well, when you see one of them in Loring, odds are the car behind it's being driven by somebody looks like D'Nesha's daddy. Around here, folks like you drive American cars or pickup trucks."

"Our car's not American."

"I know that, but you from California. And your daddy's already got him a pickup to drive just 'cause he moved back home. See what I mean?"

Toni didn't. She felt major discomfort in the presence of these girls, but because they were Mason's friends and she'd seen them last night at Pizza Hut, she'd worked up enough courage to ask for a ride to Greenville.

Mason wouldn't answer the question about her mother, no matter how hard she pried. "Nothing," he kept saying. "My dad didn't say anything about her." She refused to order dinner until he produced whatever evidence his father had confronted him with, but he was too stubborn, or too kind, to give in. "Okay," he finally said, "we'll go hungry." He stood up, put on his coat and walked right out.

She followed, running across the highway after him as drivers slammed on their brakes. Her volume control had broken. She berated him at the top of her voice, calling him all the names she could think of—fundamentalist freak, the Baptist Osama bin Laden, a little Billy Graham in drag.

He spun on her near Loring Implement Company, grabbed her around the waist and pulled her off the pavement, into the lot where they displayed tractors for sale. Backing her into a big cotton picker, he pressed himself against her and shoved his tongue into her mouth, so she bit him. "Ouch!" he cried.

"I won't let Pat Robertson kiss me! I won't!"

He shoved his tongue back in, so she bit him again.

"Please stop doing that," he said, wiping blood off his lip. "Goddamn it, I don't have much confidence."

The next time he stuck his tongue in she sucked it.

"Ouch! That hurts too. But I like it. Do it again."

She turned and ran then, and he chased her through the darkness from tractor to tractor. She vaulted into a driver's seat and felt around for the key, a switch, anything that might start it. He grabbed hold of her ankle and tried to pull her off. She clung to the steering wheel and was still holding it when the beam of a searchlight hit her in the face and a voice barked over a bullhorn, "Y'all little shits leave them John Deeres be!"

He walked her home through backyards, crisp leaves crunching beneath their feet. Dogs barked, a few porch lights came on. They slipped into a garage behind the house where the principal lived. Inside, they sat on a stack of tires and kissed some more. His tongue was sore, but he said he didn't care, that it beat the hell out of getting his nose busted.

Her dad answered the door when they got home. "Hello, Depot," he said, as if boys with blood on their chins often brought his daughter back at a quarter till ten on a weeknight. This, she guessed, was the kind of thing her father understood, and for once she couldn't hate him for it.

How she felt about her mother was an altogether different matter, as she expected rather more from her. No matter how much else changed at home, she had remained the same, at least to Toni's watchful eye. Now, if she was changing too, Toni didn't want to know it, even though she'd felt obliged to try to milk information out of Mason. She didn't go in to wish her good night, didn't wish her good morning today, either. After securing a ride to the ball game, she left a message on her mom's cell phone, which should've been on but wasn't.

D'Nesha pulled into the parking lot at Greenville High. The Loring Leopards' bus had already disgorged its cargo, the players in the end zone warming up. Toni looked through the fence for number 84 and spotted Mason in the back row doing stretching exercises. Her father stood there clapping his hands and hollering encouragement, and the other coaches prowled around among the players issuing last-minute reminders.

Giggling, Essence grabbed her by one arm while D'Nesha seized the other and they lifted her off her feet and began carrying her toward the gate.

"What are you guys doing? Are you crazy? Put me down."

"California," Essence said, "guess what?"

She tried to struggle free, but they wouldn't relent. "I have no idea."

D'Nesha tickled her rib cage. "Tonight, white girl, you're an honorary sister."

———

Tim watched Greenville's offense run plays at the opposite end of the field. The backups formed a line behind the starters, limiting his vision, but he could see well enough to know that they were bigger, faster and more polished than any team they'd face. Greenville boasted a Division I prospect at quarterback, and the kid filled the air with footballs, throwing to four and sometimes five wideouts. He sensed a large presence nearby and said, "I hate that damn spread offense. I guess you saw a lot of it out there on the West Coast."

"It's not that uncommon even for high schools to run it. Clovis got a lot of mileage out of it."

"And Clovis is?"

"A suburb of Fresno where football's all the rage. Might as well be the South. They've even got the KKK."

"A little regional stereotyping?"

"Could be," Pete said. "You ever go in for that?"

"Regional stereotyping?"

"Yeah. Like telling yourself that folks from California have lax morals and so on?"

"May have."

"When?"

Tim dug his toe into the sod, testing its firmness, as if he were about to play on it. "One time or another. I mean, hell, Pete—you know how we felt about California when we were kids. Couldn't any of us wait to get out there, and you know why."

"You tell me. I don't remember any burning urge to get out there. Just so happened that's where they offered me a scholarship."

"Man, we wanted to get out there and lay on those broad sandy beaches and listen to Creedence and the Dead and watch women stroll by in bikinis. Figured if we got lucky, one of 'em might invite us to some cave to smoke dope or shoot up and then she'd crawl all over us."

"That's what we had in mind?"

"I believe so. But you were the only one to make it. Been there, done that and now you're back home. And me, I sure am glad." Despite the cold, Tim's armpits were soaked. He gestured toward the far end of the field. "What you reckon we can expect from these guys," he asked, "on third and short?"

Pete stepped up beside him. Half a head taller, fifty pounds heavier, a lot more successful at every task they'd ever undertaken. Except for one. And with any luck, he'd never know about that. Tim prayed to God he wouldn't.

"When you're in that kind of offense," Pete said, "it doesn't matter if it's first and ten, third and one or fourth and forever. We're talking high-risk. You just rear back and heave it and hope for the best."

———

The store looked like hell. On the glass aisle, instead of a solid wall of fronted labels, what Alan saw resembled photos of Berlin after the Red Army hit town. Huge gaps yawning open on the shelves, Vlasic dills standing on top of salad dressing, French's mustard mixed in with Heinz ketchup. Over in fruits and vegetables, somebody had dumped two bags of Kraft marshmallows in a grapefruit bin, and none of the stockboys had sense enough to pick them up. A bag of Mahatma had busted in dry foods, spilling rice all over the floor. He entered everything in his pocket notebook and decided to call a staff meeting on Monday. He had half a mind to let a few folks go.

"Alan? Alan?" Truman Wright, his assistant manager, stood in the glassed-in office, waving the telephone at him. "Your wife want to talk with you."

His cell phone had been off all day. He'd left home this morning before dawn and, after downing four cups of bad coffee at the truck stop, driven by the Barrington house. The lights were on inside, and he actually stopped his truck near the end of their driveway and briefly considered walking up and knocking on the door. What stopped him was the awareness that if Pete said the wrong thing or even looked at him sideways, he might well lose what was left of his cool. And there was no future in that. He still remembered the lick he'd taken on the football field back in tenth grade. You never forgot a hit like that.

"Tell her I'm busy," he said, "and hang up."

Truman was sixty years old and had lived his whole life in Loring, and it didn't matter how much he thought of his boss or how enlightened Alan might be, there was no way a black man his age could tell a white woman her husband was busy, then hang up the phone. He clutched the receiver to his chest. "Alan," he said, "please. Nancy sound upset."

"All right." He jammed the notebook into his pocket, climbed the steps to the office and took the phone from Truman, who wasted little time leaving. "Yeah? What's up?"

"What's up?" she said. "Well, let's see. It's Friday. Or have I confused the days of the week?"

"You may be confused about some things, but not that. Friday it is."

"Alan, what's the matter with you? There's a ball game tonight. Your son's playing. Are you coming to pick me up or not?"

"I can't go. The store's a mess. I'll have to stay here after we close and straighten things up."

"We've never missed one of his games. Never."

"And there's no reason for *us* to miss this one. You've got a car and a driver's license, and I believe you know where Greenville is. You'll know you're close to the stadium when you see a bright glow in the sky."

"Alan," she said, "sometimes you scare me. And lately I'm wondering if I even know who you are. Are you my husband or a total stranger?"

"Well, seems like this isn't the first time you've had trouble figuring out your relationship with family members."

There came a bad moment when he thought she was going to cry. Then an even worse moment when he realized she wouldn't. Quietly, she hung up.

He stood there holding the receiver. It was closing time, the store was silent and he could feel several pairs of eyes on him. Both of the checkout clerks knew he'd been hung up on and so did Truman, who was standing near the door, dangling his keys and acting like something out front had caught his attention, though the street was empty.

Alan placed the receiver back in its cradle. "Everybody can go," he announced. "Nobody's been doing much work anyway."

The crew cleared out of there just as fast as possible.

Rather than tidy up the store as he'd said he would, he turned off most of the lights and took a seat in his office. He kept a Bible there and for many years, whenever seeking guidance on a particular problem, had opened it and flipped to the concordance to see what Scripture said. Tonight he didn't bother to pull it out of his drawer. Whatever advice was in its pages, he knew he wouldn't take it. Last night, when his son told him to go to hell, he'd crossed over a line. The Lord claimed vengeance was His and His alone, but Alan wanted to exact a little for himself. And so he'd spewed filth all over Mason, telling him everything he knew about Pete Barrington, including his life in California, which anybody who owned a computer could find out, and then he'd told him what he learned about his girlfriend's mother just by driving down the street. "That's the kind of trash her parents are," he'd concluded. "And trash never produces anything but a real bad odor."

He glanced at the small stereo on his desk. He also had a few gospel CDs, but the last thing in the world he wanted to hear about right now was the old rugged cross. Around eight, he switched the radio on and turned the dial to the local station.

". . . and those slot receivers are having trouble finding seams in

Loring's secondary," the announcer was saying. "First down on the Greenville thirty-two-yard line. Furman's two of six so far. He's in the shotgun now, and there's a snap. He fakes to his running back, pulls it down and sprints out to his right . . . looking, looking—and he's got number eighty in the open! *Overthrows* him, ladies and gentleman. There wasn't a Loring Leopard within five yards. Coach Kessler's kneeling on the sideline, like he's saying a prayer."

Alan switched it back off. He sat there for three or four minutes, trying to figure out what to do next. Finally, he picked up the phone, dialed his house and after four rings the answering machine came on. "You have reached the DePoyster residence," Mason's voice intoned. "We're unable to come to the phone, but if you leave your name, number and a brief message . . ." He hung up. Obviously, Nancy decided to go on her own.

He walked to the back of the building, let himself out and climbed into his pickup. For a while he just sat there, tapping his fingers against the wheel, considering a range of possibilities: calling Wade Phelps and telling him he needed to talk, or going home to listen to the play-by-play, or driving out to KFC and reading this morning's Jackson paper—he hadn't even looked at it yet—while eating a quiet dinner. But Wade would probably be at the ball game, which Alan himself felt zero interest in. He wasn't hungry and couldn't care less about the paper. So he started the truck, drove through the parking lot and turned into the street.

It never crossed his mind that anybody would be at home, but the Volvo was standing in the driveway when he stopped in front of the Barringtons'. The outside lights were on, and the living room glowed from within. A figure passed behind the curtains. Without giving it much thought, he climbed out of his truck.

Every other house up and down the street was dark—everybody most likely in Greenville—but he heard a dog bark as he strode across the lawn. Standing in a circle of light, he composed himself, raising a hand to knock on the door.

He never had to. Maybe she'd looked out the window and seen the pickup parked at the curb, or perhaps noticed him walking across the yard. For whatever reason the door opened, and for an absurd moment he stood there with his fist in the air.

She was wearing a white bathrobe and furry white slippers and holding a glass of wine. He saw her in soft focus, as if she were surrounded by a nimbus. Despite whatever she'd been up to with Kessler, this woman was the absolute opposite of trash. You could see it in her eyes and feel it from being close to her, and he knew instantly she was someone he could reason with.

"You're Mason's father?" she said.

He nodded. "Could I possibly come in and talk to you for a few minutes? That's all it would take. I'd just like to discuss our children with you. Could we do that?"

"Sure," she said, then stood aside so he could enter. As he pulled off his coat, she asked if he'd like a glass of wine.

"No, thank you," he said. "I don't drink."

———

Up in the press box, wearing the headset, Pete found it hard to keep his mind on the game, even after Reggie McDonald took a pitchout from Cody on his own fourteen, slipped past the corner and outran everybody to put Loring up by a touchdown on the first play of the second quarter.

The team was where it wanted to be right now, though he was anywhere but there. He'd once convinced himself that if only Angela found somebody else, someone who could talk to her as she needed to be talked to and touch her as she wanted to be touched, he could sign over everything he'd ever earned and walk away with a clean conscience. There would be inevitable wreckage—a few lost friends they'd shared, the mangled relationship with his daughter—but none of that was anything to feel ashamed about. It happened all the time.

Well, as far as he could tell, that escape turned out to be more of a trap, and the best he could look forward to now was being stuck in the same town with her, knowing that she'd left him for his best friend. The perfect medicine for a man with his disease.

The Loring defense rendered the Greenville attack anemic for two quarters, using a variety of zone blitzes to confuse their hotshot quarterback and staying physical with his receivers, knocking them off their routes and disrupting the timing patterns. Loring went into the half leading 10–0 after kicking a field goal on their last possession.

Pete got to the locker room to find chaos reigning, players jumping up and down, showering one another with ice and Gatorade and banging their helmets against the flimsy metal lockers. Killingsworth, for once, had lost the ability to scare them. He was standing on a bench, hollering at them to tone it down because the game wasn't over yet.

A large metal trash barrel stood near the door, overflowing and stinking to high heaven. It was outrageous that it hadn't been emptied, that they had to smell that awful odor. But their own behavior was also outrageous. The whole goddamn evening was outrageous. Pete hefted the barrel above his head and, as the noise fell several decibels, hurled it across the room, where it knocked a paper towel dispenser off the wall and bit out a hunk of cement, garbage cascading onto the floor. "Will you guys shut your fucking mouths," he bellowed, "and listen to what your coach is trying to tell you?"

Killingsworth steadied himself against a locker. His mouth moved but nothing came out. Over in the corner, Tim froze, his face pale as milk.

Pete walked over to the trash barrel, stood it upright and began stuffing the garbage back inside. "Coach Killingsworth?" he said over his shoulder. "What do we need to do to keep winning this ball game?"

———

D'Nesha and Essence kept Toni wedged between them, up near the top of the bleachers in an otherwise all-black section. Most of the white kids were down in front, which stood to reason, D'Nesha said, since that's how it used to be in movie theaters. "Colored folks—that's what they called us, when they were acting nice—sat up in the balcony, and the white folks got to be down on the main floor, closer to the screen. Your daddy ever tell you about stuff like that?"

Her father had told her almost nothing about his hometown, up until the day he told her they were moving there. By then she didn't care where they went, as long as nobody knew her. "No," she said, "I'm afraid he didn't."

"He was probably sitting down below my daddy. And from time to time, my daddy might've thrown popcorn at him. He said they used to do that." She pulled a few kernels from the box of popcorn in her lap and, giggling, dropped them on Toni's head.

Toni brushed them off and watched them fall beneath the bleachers.

"Smile, California," Essence said, throwing an arm around her shoulders. "We're just telling you stories about the good old days."

———

"Your husband and I, we've got some history between us," Alan DePoyster said.

They were in the living room. She was sitting on the couch, and he'd taken the armchair at the end of the coffee table. She'd left the music on, Friedrich Gulda's 1955 recording of Debussy's Preludes. At Fresno State she'd taken classes from a professor who dated Gulda in Vienna when the pianist was a young man. She'd been thinking about that when she looked out the window and saw the truck parked by the curb, wondering what it felt like to brush up against such greatness.

"What kind of history?" she said.

"It doesn't really matter. If he never told you about it, it wouldn't be right for me to bring it up. The thing is, it's not something that I look back on with good feeling. I'm sure you can understand that. There must be things that happened between you and somebody else that you just have a hard time getting past. I imagine that's true of almost everybody. Don't you think?"

She noticed that his features were similar to Mason's—sandy hair, walnut-colored eyes, nicely shaped cheekbones and nose—but whereas his son's face suggested openness, his seemed somehow closed. Tastelessly, he wore a red-white-and-blue bow tie. "I guess we all have some things we'd rather forget, if that's what you mean," she said. "But I'm not sure what you're getting at, Mr. DePoyster."

"Please, call me Alan."

She lifted her wineglass and took a sip. "All right," she said. "Alan."

"What I mean," he said, sitting forward now, his fingertips tapping the coffee table's glass top in a manner she found mildly annoying, "is that our family, Mason and his mother and me—I think we kind of operate under a different value system. I'm not saying ours is better. I'm just saying it's different. I think a lot of that has to do with the environment down here. Y'all have been living in California. Life's faster, people think differently about a lot of things and they're more likely to take up new ideas. Down here things move more slowly. And Mason's mother and I, we kind of prefer it that way."

"Mr. DePoyster—"

"Please, couldn't you call me Alan?"

"Alan," she said, "have you ever been to California?"

"No, can't say that I have."

She could tell he was tempted to add that he'd never wanted to, either, but somehow he managed to restrain himself. "Well, if you'd ever been to the part of California that we lived in," she told him, "you'd know that it's an agricultural region, just like this is, with extremely conservative values. Believe me, Christian fundamentalism, if that's what we're talking about, is alive and well in Fresno."

"Mrs. Barrington—"

"My first name's Angela."

"Angela. *Fundamentalism* is a word I don't really cotton to. It's like *Hispanic.* It doesn't mean anything. Anyway, I wouldn't have to be a fundamentalist, as you put it, to believe in some values and disapprove of others. There are a lot of folks with no religion at all who'd see this just like I do."

"Since we've gotten into syntactic analysis, why don't you tell me what the antecedent of the word *this* is in your last sentence."

For a while he didn't answer. The Gulda recording was over, but she'd lost interest in the music anyway.

Finally he said, "I'm going to be really candid."

The last man who'd said that to her was her husband, after candidness had been forced on him. Whatever was coming now couldn't be as bad as that.

"I can tell you're a decent person, but you and your husband operate with a different set of sexual mores than the ones we try to live by," he said. "You know what I'm talking about, don't you?"

She sat there on the couch, regarding him with considerable detachment. When she finally moved, it was with grace, her motions smooth and silky, not jerky or frantic. She lifted her glass off the table and calmly tossed the wine in his face.

IN ORDER TO APPRECIATE VICTORY," Rashard Killingsworth preached, his voice hoarse from shouting, "you have to snatch it back from the maw of defeat."

Depot waved his clean jersey at him. "Coach," he hollered, "what you got against defeat's momma?"

Two or three other players laughed, but most just looked puzzled.

"We almost succumbed," Killingsworth continued, with a broad sweep of his arm. "But in the end we learned who we are. And who we *are,* men, ain't boys."

"No sir!"

"That's right, Coach!"

"Who we *are,* right now, is the only team in this conference that controls its own destiny!"

If you'd heard one victory speech, Pete guessed, you'd heard them all. But he couldn't recall one that didn't sound a hell of a lot better than the speeches that followed a loss.

Greenville had come out in the second half determined to do one thing: make Loring conscious of the ground game. They had one basic running play, a draw to the single setback, and they ran it five times on their first drive, letting the kid delay until he saw a lane open up in the pass rush. He gained eighteen yards the first time and, later in the drive, twenty-one yards for the touchdown. They would have scored on their second possession, too, had their quarterback not lost control of a deep snap on the Loring twelve. As it was, that touchdown got deferred until their next drive, putting them up 14–10 with six minutes remaining in the game.

Then disaster struck: after Reggie McDonald brought the kickoff back to the twenty-five, he had to be helped off the field. He'd twisted his knee in the pileup.

"I imagine that just about does it," Killingsworth said in Pete's ear.

"Maybe not. Now we'll see what Cody can do on his own."

What Cody did was complete two fourth-down passes to keep the final drive alive, then take it in himself from the five on a bootleg with less than a minute left.

Now, in the locker room, the team was planning a celebration, and for once Killingsworth didn't even caution them about drinking. He hopped down off the bench and went outside to talk to a handful of reporters and do the postgame radio show.

Mason came up to Pete. "Coach," he said, "would it be all right if Toni came with me to the party?"

Pete felt real affection for this kid. He hadn't been able to get him into the game, but it didn't look like Mason cared one bit. He was just happy to be part of the team. "Sure," Pete said, "but I don't know where she is. Her mom called this afternoon and said she was coming with some friends."

"I talked to her just now. She's with my buddies D'Nesha and Essence."

"You talked to her? I didn't see her."

"Neither did I." Grinning, Mason stuck his hand under the waistband of his game pants and pulled out a cell phone. "If I'd had to play, I would've left it on the bench."

Pete knew he ought to be angry, but could only shake his head. "They'll fine you for that in the NFL."

Mason's grin spread even wider. "I think we can safely say I'll never cause the NFL any problems."

———

He got home at a quarter till twelve. Tim had asked him on the bus if he'd like to go out for a beer, but he'd just shut his eyes and said he was tired. After that neither of them spoke.

He pulled into the driveway. She'd left the Volvo there, so he hit the garage door opener and drove the truck inside, then went back out and drove the car inside too.

He entered through the utility room, and the house was dark and chilly. Neither of them liked to sleep with the heat on, so they always set the thermostat to turn off at nine o'clock.

He walked into the kitchen, flipped on the light and poured himself a shot of Wild Turkey to warm up. He carried the drink into the living room, intending to put on some quiet music. He had a taste for Bill Evans this evening. Or Keith Jarrett, playing just like him.

When he switched on the track lights, his brain failed to process all the available information. That wasn't all that surprising, Chief Henderson said the next day. If the place had been turned upside down, he would've noticed immediately. As it was, almost everything looked normal: the CDs neatly arranged in their racks, the lid on the Petroff closed, as both Toni and Angela insisted it must be when not in use. No lamps had been turned over, nothing seemed to be missing, no blood stained the floor or the walls. The only thing wrong, as far as he could see, was that the beveled glass top of the coffee table, which had been custom-made someplace in Washington State, had broken loose from its fossil-stone mount and shattered on the floor.

He stood there staring at the thick shards for several moments. Then he noticed something else. Stooping, he reached into the broken glass and lifted out the stem of a wineglass.

BETWEEN NOW AND THEN

Living in fresno, you learned a lot about black widows, the places they hid, how they made their webs—dense, adhesive constructions that clung to you if you stumbled into them in the dark.

Toni woke to widow webs that morning. Her mouth was full of them, her eyes too, and the moment she swung her legs out of bed she felt the sticky substance in her hair, her nostrils, on the surface of her skin. It hung from all four corners of the ceiling, covered the floor, formed a thick film on the windows. Through that glutinous layer the people standing on the street watching her house were little more than shadows, vague, gray, ill defined.

She pressed a palm to the pane and the web disintegrated. When she pulled her hand away, a moist print remained on the glass as evidence of an iffy existence. Through it she could see Mason DePoyster in the driveway across the street, keeping his distance from the other onlookers, his hands in his pockets, his gaze unwavering. He was staring at her window, right into her eyes, yet he seemed not to see her. Probably no one would ever really see her again. Or if they chanced to, they'd look right through her, as though her presence in their midst were a source of embarrassment that might, if they ignored it long enough, finally fade away.

Burping, she tasted tomato paste and mozzarella. Jesus, when it happened she'd been feeding her face. Letting the curtain fall, she spun away from the window.

Back in August she'd placed a potted plant on her dresser. The plant was dead now—she'd forgotten to water it—so rather than unlock her bedroom door and run down the hall, she dumped it out in her trash basket, dirt and all. She set the pot down, lowered her face over it and disgorged the undigested remains of the pizza she'd eaten last night at the postgame party.

BAD CAKES: he associated them with deaths in the family. When his father and grandfather died, people had showed up on the doorstep loaded down with chocolate fudge, devil's food, butter golden or spice cakes as if they thought Betty Crocker possessed strange healing powers. Sickly sweet concoctions covered the kitchen table, the countertops, the top of the refrigerator and, finally, the lids of the washer and the dryer. His grandmother had even shoved one—a strawberry supreme—into a linen closet, where it was discovered only after a column of ants conspicuously reminded her.

He was sitting in the living room with Frank Henderson, the chief of police, when the first round of cakes arrived in the arms of Sandra Jean Sturdivant. The doorbell must have rung—he noticed the chief looking at him, as if expecting a reaction—but he hadn't heard it. Nevertheless, he glanced out the window and saw her standing there, hugging a plate hooded with Saran wrap.

"Want me to answer that?" Henderson asked. He laid aside his notebook and stuck his pen in his shirt pocket.

Waving him off, Pete got up and walked into the hallway. The door to Toni's room was still shut, and she hadn't answered when he knocked and begged her to come out. He'd jiggled the doorknob and probably would've broken in before now if he hadn't heard her moving around. At some point during the night, with the house full of police officers and crime-lab technicians, Donny Alexander had appeared, gently pushing Pete out of the room where Toni lay balled up near the foot of the bed, rolling from side to side and bellowing every time her dad tried to touch her. Donny told him later what he'd given her, but Pete couldn't remember. Valium, maybe?

He opened the front door. Rather than shove the cake toward him, Sandra Jean continued to clutch it, as if she knew perfectly well that nobody wanted a cake at a time like this, that she'd satisfied her own needs by bringing it and was embarrassed at having done so. "Pete?" she said. "Pete, honey, I'm really sorry."

He reached out, took the cake and set the plate down just outside the door. He imagined it was pretty good, as cakes went, but was not about to allow it into the house. Sometime tomorrow it and two or three others would disappear.

"You're in shock," she said. "You look like you just took a thousand-volt jolt."

Stepping closer, he put his arms around her. She wore a long, flowing horsehair overcoat, and beneath it her body felt soft, spongy. No sharp angles to her now, no blind corners to negotiate with care.

"Can you talk?" she said. "You can't even talk, can you? It'd help you if you could make a little noise."

Up close, he could see that her dirty blond hair was graying at the roots. She wore too much perfume, and her mascara was inexpertly applied. "You poor thing," she said, as her face, rather than his, became wet and he heard Chief Henderson step into the hallway behind him. "I bet you're wishing you'd never come home. That you'd just stayed in California."

———

"I've seen folks react all kinds of ways," the chief was saying. Sandra Jean had left after asking if she could call Pete tomorrow to check on him, and he and Henderson were again seated in the living room. "One of those people who was here last night from the crime lab? Billy Vardell, quiet little guy with the black-rimmed glasses? We had him down here about three years ago, when I was still in the sheriff's department. Called him in after the oxygen man at one of these catfish ponds shined a light down in the water one night and spotted a white hair ribbon floating on the surface and then realized it was attached to a headful of blond hair. Billy and them get here and somebody turns up a purse in the Johnson grass, and all it takes is one look at the wallet and poor Billy knows that girl's his niece, from down in Belzoni, and he's the one that'll get to tell her daddy. He walked right off that pond levee, just took off down the gravel road on foot, and it was two or three hours before me and another deputy found him sitting on a rusty propane tank at the edge of a cotton patch." The chief shook his head. "Lord God, I guess you can imagine what that poor child looked like after two or three days in the fishpond."

"I don't have to imagine," Pete said. "I took a class in forensic medicine."

"See, that's what I mean. Most folks never have to go through a thing like that. They may think they know how they'd behave if they had to, but they don't. Whereas you and me both know we don't know. Yeah, you might've predicted you'd pick up the phone the minute you walked into that bedroom, but you could just as easily have guessed you'd sit there on the floor for forty-five minutes or an hour or however long it was before you finally made that call. You had worse things to worry about than the ambient temperature."

The length of time he'd allowed to pass before dialing 911 had already become an issue, as had the fact that when the police arrived, the temperature inside the house was in the mid-fifties.

"Like Miz Sturdivant said," the chief continued, "you're in shock. I don't know who wouldn't be. So whatever you tell me, I figure it's subject to reevaluation on your part. Something that may look hazy today's liable to come clear this time next week. Right now, all you can see is splotches on the canvas."

In fact, he was seeing splotches on the face of the woman he'd once loved to the point of distraction. Pinpoint red dots on her cheeks and under her eyes, which bulged slightly and leaked fluid through their tear ducts. Her bathrobe securely knotted at her waist, the froglike appearance of her neck telling him that the cartilage and trachea must be broken. Her right hand lying placid on her stomach, her left arm hanging off the bed, fingertips grazing the floor. He'd grasped that hand with his own, knowing full well what was coming, promising himself he wouldn't recoil, and he didn't.

He'd held on to her hand for a long time, sitting on the floor in a pool of light cast there by the bedside lamp. He thought, for reasons that would remain forever obscure, of something else that had happened on this street, how he'd gone trick-or-treating here when he was seven or eight, because this was where the biggest homes in town were and he believed the people who lived in them would dispense more candy. Instead, almost all the porch lights were turned off and no one, as best he could remember, had deigned to open their door. Two thousand miles away, the woman whose hand he now held must have gone trick-or-treating too. She'd grown up in a rough part of Fresno. Had she also ventured out that night in hopes of finding something better?

"What I'm looking for right now," the chief said, "is nothing more than approximation. So when you tell me that to the best of your recollection you walked through that door back yonder"—gesturing toward the utility room—"at about a quarter till midnight, I *know* approximation's all I'm getting. And all I'm asking here this morning's whether or not that's still your best recollection?"

"Yeah. That's what I'd say."

The chief was a short, heavyset man with a shiny bald head and surprisingly long, supple fingers. He wrote something on his notepad, then tapped his knee with the pen, leaving an ink dot on his gray Dockers. "And when you see the coffee table's broken and that wineglass too, what's the next thing you do?"

So Pete told him how he'd gone into the kitchen and looked into the cabinet beneath the sink, where they put bottles and plastic containers they'd later take out to the garage for recycling.

"And you were looking for what?"

"To see if there was an empty wine bottle under there."

"How come?"

"I thought maybe she'd had too much to drink and had either fallen onto that table or dropped something and broken it."

"But you didn't find one?"

"No."

"Just the one that was in the refrigerator when I opened it last night."

"That's right."

"Pinot Grigio," the chief said, flipping a page and squinting at something he'd jotted down. "Didn't look to me like there was more than about a glass of it gone. Was that pretty much your impression?"

Pete nodded.

"But you're telling me your wife sometimes drank a little more than she ought to?"

"Not often. But sometimes."

"Well, that's like me. Maybe once or twice a year I might have a little too much. I'm not a wine drinker, understand, it's strictly Bud Light." Henderson made another note. "Now, after you checked on the situation under the sink, you realized something more serious might've occurred."

"You could say that, I guess."

"But you don't really recollect what your thinking process was."

"I don't even remember going into the bedroom. I don't remember switching on the light, either, but I know I must have because the house was completely dark when I pulled into the driveway. That's one thing I can say for certain."

"And so you went into the bedroom, and that's when you saw your wife there on the bed."

Again, he nodded.

"And as soon as you saw her, you knew she'd passed on."

"It's not quite as simple as that."

"What's not?"

"The question of what I knew, or didn't know, when I saw her." He explained himself as best he could, which was not as well as he wanted. "In medical school, it seemed like they were drumming it into our heads at every moment that medicine's science. Talent got short shrift. Nobody encouraged us to believe that you could eyeball a patient and tell much of anything at all, though everybody secretly thought you could—if you had talent. Given the situation I walked into, there were things I was trained to do. And I would've done them, if she hadn't been my wife."

"I'm not sure I'm following you now. Have been so far, but this last part's got me scuttled."

"I did my residency at a hospital in Visalia, California, and one day an eight-year-old boy who couldn't swim was brought into the ER after falling in his parents' pool. It was the middle of winter, and it gets colder out there in the Central Valley than you might think, but it rarely freezes, so folks don't drain or cover their pools. The kid had been left alone at home for a couple of hours, and nobody was really sure how long he'd been in the water. But I knew he was dead the instant I laid eyes on him. And I would've known it without touching him. Still, I worked on him for I don't know how long. Did everything that was called for, even though it was useless. Endotracheal suction, for Chrissakes. One of the nurses was in tears, begging me to stop. And through all of this, his parents were waiting right outside. Hoping to God they still had a little boy."

"So what you're saying is that last night you didn't want to give yourself any false hope."

"I guess I'm just saying this was my wife. That's about all I can tell you to explain my reaction. Or my lack of one. If that had been your wife lying there—well . . ." He raised his hands, then let them fall into his lap.

The chief kneaded his left eyebrow, then asked what he was doing when Toni came home. Pete admitted he'd still been sitting right there on the floor, that he only got up after hearing the front door creak open.

"And what time was that?"

"Maybe twelve-thirty, a quarter till one. I'm not sure."

"And the door creaked open. Hinges need oiling?"

That seemed like an odd question, and Pete didn't answer.

"Reason I'm asking is you say the door *creaked* open, but I didn't notice any noise when you went to let Miz Sturdivant in just now."

"So maybe it wasn't a creak. I don't know. It was some kind of sound. Maybe she slammed it closed. She often does."

The chief made another entry on his notepad. "Your daughter's got her own key."

"No."

"So you'd left the door open for her."

Pete just stared at him.

"I assume y'all don't normally leave the door unlocked at night," the chief said. "So maybe you went and opened it yourself, knowing your daughter'd be home before long. Is that what might have happened?"

"No."

"So since she didn't have a key, that door must've been unlocked before you ever got here. Follow my line of reasoning, Doctor?"

Up until today, Pete had been *Pete* and the chief had been *Frank*. But this morning, when he'd phoned to ask if he could come over, Frank had called himself *Chief Henderson,* and Pete was now *Doctor.* Henceforth, he supposed, formalism would be the governing aesthetic. "Yeah," he said, "I follow you."

"Was your wife one to leave the front door unlocked?"

"My wife spent most of her life in Fresno, where the crime rate's higher than it is in Oakland. She never left the front door unlocked. Or the back door, either."

"Well, the back door was most definitely unlocked when I got here, and we checked it for prints. But now we need to check that front door too."

"Why didn't they do it last night?"

The chief laid the pad aside and crossed his arms over his stomach. "This isn't California," he said. "The crime lab's understaffed. And underpaid, but that goes without saying. We don't always have the resources to do things the way we'd like to. You're probably used to seeing yellow barrier tape on the scene whenever somebody gets his golf clubs stolen. Well, that stuff costs eleven ninety-five a roll, and my budget's busted, so we're doing without. Same as with the crime lab and the coroner's office. We wake folks up in the middle of the night, they're still half asleep when they get here, and they do what they think's most crucial, which for the coroner means trying to get an accurate body temperature under difficult circumstances and for Billy and them it means going through all that glass on the floor and sealing up the bedclothes and that white bathrobe so they can comb them for fibers. If they'd gotten here sooner, yeah, they might've been more thorough. But before they can come, they need to know they're needed. And for them to know that, somebody's first got to dial those three numbers. Nine. One. One."

Henderson let that statement resonate for a moment or two, then folded his pad and put the pen into his shirt pocket. He stood but didn't leave. "The young lady," he said. "How's she holding up?"

Slowly, Pete got to his feet. His back and arms and legs ached, as if he'd played a ball game last night rather than merely watching one. "Donny gave her something to make her sleep. I heard her moving around earlier, but she hasn't come out yet."

Henderson said, "Take care of her, Doctor. Poor child's got some hard times ahead."

———

He waited until twelve o'clock, then went and tapped gently on the door to Toni's room. No response. So he knocked again, louder this time. Again, no response. "Honey," he said, "if you don't answer, I'm going to break the lock. I hate to do it. I don't want to scare you, but I need to know you're all right. Can you just answer me, please?"

Nothing.

Sighing, he grasped the knob with both hands, turned it with all his strength and heard something pop. The door swung open easily.

Her bed was unmade, but she wasn't in it. Thinking she'd climbed out one of the windows, he stepped over to one and then the other, but both were locked. Then his eye lit on the door to the closet.

When he looked inside, at first he didn't see her. It was dark in there, and her closets had always been messy, providing her, he suspected, with a necessary degree of disarray in an otherwise orderly environment. Panties and jeans, socks and bras, Kleenex and Kotex lay strewn across the floor, skirts and blouses hung askew, the basket for dirty laundry empty. But back in the far corner, beyond a pile of smelly sneakers, flip-flops and sandals, beside the toy crate that held such remnants of her childhood as the one-eyed panda she'd named José, two coals emitted an accusatory glow.

TIM HAD DISCOVERED that going to bed sober made waking more difficult, probably because his dreams had turned pleasant. Nightmares rarely came to haunt him anymore, so when someone began banging on his door that Saturday he just stuck his nose a little deeper into the pillow, which still smelled faintly of perfume. The pounding never let up, though, and he finally rolled over and glanced at the clock on his bedside table. Ten past twelve. God, he'd slept eleven hours. "Yeah?" he hollered. "Hang on, all right? Don't knock it down, it's the only door I got."

He heaved his legs out of bed, pushed a bag of Ruffles aside and then picked up his bathrobe and put it on.

Susan wore no coat, just a red sweatshirt that said *roxy* on the chest and a pair of dirty jeans. Her sneakers were untied, and she kept hugging herself while bouncing up and down on the balls of her feet as if she needed to pee. "Let me in," she said, "I'm *cold*."

He never really stepped aside. Somehow, she walked right through him.

She kicked the sneakers off, flounced over to the couch and settled in, propping her feet up on the coffee table. "This place is a pigsty," she observed. "It feels weird to know your daddy lives like this."

"Wup," he said.

"Wup?"

"Wup." He walked over and sat down beside her. "*Wup*'s what your grandma used to say when I got myself in trouble."

"What's it mean?"

"I think it's a truncation of *Well, you fucked up.* Does your momma know where you are?"

"There are different kinds of knowing—that's what my English teacher said. It's the only thing I ever heard her say that made any sense. But it did. Sort of. So depending on what you mean when you say *know,* well, maybe she does and maybe she doesn't."

"Then let me rephrase the question, seeing as how I'm dealing with another attorney. Does your momma know you're in Loring, Mississippi, at this particular instant?"

"Not a chance, Lance."

"Then we're going to have to call her. And by the way, how'd you get here?"

"Well, that's an interesting story."

"Which I can't wait to hear."

"Okay." She crossed her arms over the *roxy* emblem and cocked her head. He could see she was proud of herself. Running away might be the first thing she'd done really well since the day she left Loring. "They've got a Starbucks now just off I-Fifty-five," she said. "Did you know that?"

"No."

"On County Line Road, so it's close to Kent's house. And you know I got my license back in the summer."

"Oh, Jesus Christ. Honey, you didn't steal Kent's car. Tell me you didn't, sweetie. Please?"

"Okay," she said, flashing her perfect whites. "I didn't steal Kent's car."

"Oh, God. You stole it. Do you know what can happen to you? If he wanted to, he could charge you. Is it out there in the parking lot?" He started to get up.

"Relax." She laid her hand on his knee. "I said I didn't steal Kent's car, and I didn't. They're building a new house down the street from Kent's place, right next to where one of Momma's new friends lives? And this friend's gone to Oxford to see the Ole Miss game, and she and her husband have this awful little dog? One of those little ratty things with a pinched-in face?" She scrunched her nose and mouth together. "But she's crazy about that little bastard—well, that's what he is, Daddy, he barks all the time—and because he's, like, her *child* or something, she won't put him in a kennel. She offered me twenty-five dollars to go down there this morning and tomorrow morning and feed him and let him out to pee and poop. So I went down there and did it. And afterwards, when I was walking back past the construction site down the street from Kent's house—well, I saw the pickup and realized the engine was running."

He pitched sideways, his shoulder smacking the arm of the couch. "Oh, my God in heaven, you stole a fucking *truck*."

"That's something I really do love about you, Daddy. You can be so demonstrative. I hate it when Momma's like that, but I love it when you are."

He forced himself upright. "Where's the truck? We've got to get it back to its owner. Right now. This instant."

"He's probably already got it. See, this is where the Starbucks comes in. You didn't forget Starbucks, did you? Because that's where I parked the truck. I just drove it down there and went inside and got myself a big caramel frappuccino. I left the engine running, figuring somebody would notice it just like I had, then go outside and see who it belonged to and get in touch with him somehow. The guy who brought me up here was just leaving Starbucks. He had something hot, I couldn't see what, a latte or something like that. He was driving a pickup too, and he works for Fruit of the Loom over in Greenville. That's why I hollered at him. I saw the Washington County tag and figured if he was going over there, he had to drive through here."

He decided to remain calm, and failed. "You hitched a ride with some guy in a pickup truck? Jesus, Susan, are you out of your fucking mind?"

"*You* drive a pickup."

"Yeah. And any sixteen-year-old girl who'd hitch a ride with me's out of her fucking mind."

"He drove just fine."

Once she'd convinced him that she hadn't been raped or forced to take part in a string of robberies or a murder spree—Patty Hearst came to mind, as did Charlie Starkweather and Caril Ann Fugate—he went into the kitchen, closed the door and turned on his cell phone. Curiously, Angela hadn't sent him a text message. He'd been getting one first thing every morning.

He sat down at the table and called his ex-wife. He could hear Susan moving around in the living room, pushing junk aside and rearranging furniture, expressing amazement, from time to time, that a biped could survive in such surroundings.

Jena answered the phone with a tone he knew too well. He'd heard it thousands of times, whenever he disappointed her in the performance of some task she considered essential, like scrubbing scum off the grate of his perpetually filthy grill or remembering to unroll his dirty socks before tossing them in the hamper.

"I've just got two questions," she said, before he could tell her that Susan was there, safe, alive and well. "The first is, has she been molested?"

"No, she's fine."

"The second is, can you enroll her in school up there?"

Taking on his daughter's upkeep would lead to a lot of headaches, and he'd lose the only place where he could safely be alone with Angela: Susan might run off from school at any minute, and there'd never be a time when he could say, with one hundred percent certainty, that she wouldn't barge in on them. But he didn't hesitate. His daughter was his daughter. His lover was his best friend's wife. "Yeah, I can enroll her up here," he said. "She'll just probably have to get her latest transcript sent to them, her shot records—you know, that kind of thing."

"I'll take care of all that. I just can't handle her anymore. Maybe after Christmas. Though, Jesus—I don't know."

After they said good-bye, he looked up to find Susan standing in the doorway, grinning. Between her thumb and index finger, she held an amber earring. "Now who," she said, "could this belong to?"

———

He showered and dressed, then went back out to the living room, where Susan sat on the couch channel surfing. "Jackson had more on cable," she said, "but I don't care. Momma didn't let me watch much TV anyway."

"What makes you think I'm going to?"

"Around you, I'll just do what I want. When you ask me to cease and desist, some of the time I will."

"Susan, I'm your daddy. You know that, don't you?"

"I've seen my birth certificate, if that's what you mean."

"That's not what I mean. Honey, we have to make some rules."

"Okay." She turned off the TV and set the remote aside. "You make five, and I'll make five."

"This isn't going to be a democracy."

"Okay, you make ten, and I'll tell you which ones I'm willing to follow."

"Sweetie, let's go have some lunch, and we'll take it from there."

"*Thou shalt not go hungry.* Now there's a rule I can live with." She jumped up and jammed a foot into a sneaker. "See?" she said. "Right now you're batting a thousand."

———

Montrose's usually drew a pretty good lunch crowd on Saturday, the one day of the week when you might see other white folks there, but he and Susan didn't walk in until almost two o'clock, and the rush had already receded. A couple black families were sitting at large tables at the very rear, and a guy he'd defended on pandering charges was eating alone near the front.

"How you doing, Mr. Kessler?" his former client asked.

"Just fine, Wesley. And you?"

"Can't complain. My old woman come after me with a pistol the other night, but I manage to juke her off."

"That's real good, Wesley. Bullet wounds can be nasty."

"Yes sir, they sure can. I done suffered me a couple, so I know just what you mean."

He led Susan over to his favorite table. She'd been in Montrose's a few times when she was younger, but not during that last year he and her mother were together. They hadn't gone anywhere then. Hostilities rarely lapsed long enough for an entire meal to be consumed, and neither he nor Jena wanted anyone else to witness one of their battles.

Montrose emerged from the kitchen and saw Tim and Susan sitting there. Strangely, he propped his hands on his hips and studied them for a moment, as if debating whether they merited service.

Tim slapped the top of the grimy table. "Get on over here, Montrose, before we take our business to one of the chains."

Montrose pulled a pad from a pocket in his dirty apron. Still, he stayed rooted.

"This isn't about race, is it? If it is, I couldn't be more disappointed. I always thought you believed in equal rights for rednecks."

Montrose finally walked over, taking his own sweet time.

"That's more like it," Tim said. "You remember this young lady here, don't you?"

"Yes indeed. I remember everybody you ever been in here with."

"You'll be seeing a lot of us from now on. We both got a taste for deep tang, and my daughter's discovered Jackson to be a lot less salubrious than her own hometown."

"Salubrious." Montrose turned the word over, tasting it. "I imagine that term refers to the overall health of a location?"

"Sure does."

"Well, I'd be the last to deny that Loring's pretty healthy. Still, looks like it's a town you can get killed in."

"Yeah? Who the hell do you know that ever got killed in Loring?"

Montrose laid his pad on the table. Then he laid a hand—large, soft and redolent of garlic—on Tim's shoulder. "Counselor," he said, "if I had to guess, I'd say you slept late."

Mr. alan?" reggie said.

The kid was standing right outside the office, head and shoulders visible through the glass. His eyelids drooped. Even though his knee was sore, he'd probably stayed out half the night celebrating the big win. He hadn't sounded particularly alert—or happy, either—when Alan called and asked him to come in. Nobody was happy today. The cashiers acted subdued, the customers crept along the aisles in dazed slow motion and Truman Wright, who always ran the store on Saturday, had gone home professing illness for the first time in memory. Everybody had heard the news by now, and it seemed to be making them all sick. Alan himself wasn't feeling at all well. His head hurt, and he'd already weathered four or five bouts of diarrhea and had pulled a can of Glade off the shelf and taken it with him before the last one. "Yeah?" he said.

"I counted everything. I got forty-eight cases of them one-pound cans of Crisco shortening on a pallet. Got forty cases of the spray stuff and fifty-one of the oil."

"Well, that's too much to have standing in the stockroom."

"Mr. Alan, you told me to order that stuff while they had it on special."

"Yeah, I know I did, Reggie, but it hasn't been moving fast enough, and now we've got a bunch of cardboard skyscrapers back there. What I want you to do is get as much of that Crisco out onto the aisle as you can, take the rest of it out of the cartons and stack it onto the pallet, then break down all that cardboard and burn it. It's a fire hazard."

"Mr. Alan, I can't stack bottles on top of bottles, and as for them cans, if they're out of the cartons like that, every one of 'em's gone get dented."

The boy's reasoning was correct. It pained Alan to be on the wrong side of right, but that was where he'd placed himself. "Well, if they get dented we'll send them back. Soon as you finish the Crisco, I want you to tear into that big mountain of Hi-Dri's. Get as many rolls as possible on the shelf, then pull the rest out of those cartons and burn them too. I'm declaring war on cardboard."

Reggie shrugged and began to limp off down the pet-food aisle.

"Reggie?" Alan said.

The kid stopped and turned around, his slope-shouldered stance suggesting that no matter how his day concluded, he would consider it ruined. Alan made up his mind right then to pay him double overtime. Spoiling a boy's pleasure like this constituted a crime.

"Yes sir?"

"When that cardboard starts burning, why don't you grab a can of lighter fluid and squirt a little on the flames? We'll get that stuff incinerated fast."

Reggie's jaw looked as if it were about to come unhinged. "Lighter fluid? Mr. Alan, that fire back there get so hot it'd make the devil turn on the central air."

"Just do it, Reggie." He gestured at aisle eight. "It's over there by the charcoal."

———

Last night, around three o'clock, Nancy had gotten up and walked into the kitchen, where he was sitting at the table with his head in his hands. The Bible lay next to his elbow, but he couldn't bring himself to open it. When he'd removed it from the drawer in his bedside table, just laying a hand on it had felt like an act of desecration.

He that hath clean hands and a pure heart. . . . He shall receive the blessing from the Lord.

He didn't want to touch anything or anybody, nor did he want to be touched. Yet he knew Nancy intended to come over and place one or both hands somewhere on his body, and if she did that, he believed, he would scream. "Don't," he said when she circled around behind him.

Her palm began rubbing the back of his neck. "Alan?"

"No."

"No what?"

He could smell his own breath when he exhaled. He'd never smelled his breath before, only the breath of others. His reeked of worse rot than tooth decay. "I don't want you to touch me," he said.

"Why? You've always liked it before."

"I don't know why. It's just how I feel right now."

"Why did you say that to me tonight, Alan? About what I did with Jimmy? I didn't know that was still on your mind. Couldn't we have talked about it?"

What, he wondered, was there to talk about? What could you say about sleeping with your brother or deserting your wife and son? Some acts demanded to be swathed in silence. To sit around and discuss them, like you were a guest on one of those afternoon TV shows where dysfunctional families turned grief into comedy, would rob them of their stature. They were big acts, committed by little people.

"We were just two hot teenagers, Alan," she said. "Jimmy was and I was. Both of us were just burning up."

He remembered that comment on Saturday afternoon as he stood at the incinerator, his foot holding down the door pedal, his face hot, his hair singed and stinking. He'd let Reggie take off. Out front, he knew, there were only four or five customers and two checkout clerks, business light as always on Saturday afternoon, most folks at home watching football or raking leaves.

The fire in the incinerator howled as suction drew it upward into the chimney. The burn chamber itself was cylindrical, five or six feet in diameter and most likely in violation of every rule the EPA had ever made. He'd stuffed a bunch of grocery sacks inside it last night, on top of his shirt, pants, socks, bow tie and jacket. At the last moment he'd pulled his shoes off and flung them in too, and they were what he'd begun worrying about earlier today, whether or not the small fire he'd started had ever gotten hot enough to burn leather.

He hadn't wanted a large fire like this one, because anybody driving down Main Street would see the chimney belching smoke, not a normal sight on a Friday night. Of course, it wasn't normal, either, to see the manager of the local Piggly Wiggly driving through town wearing only a raincoat, but nobody had witnessed that, as far as he knew, since folks weren't back from the game yet and he hadn't encountered another vehicle between the store and his house.

Staring into the flames, he concluded that last night he'd destroyed the wrong things. Burning his clothes accomplished nothing. If, on the other hand, he could force himself through the opening and into the incinerator—big enough, after all, for a man to crawl inside—his earthly torment would come to an end. What prevented him was the certainty that while God might forgive his sin, he could never forgive himself. Hell, from now on, would be wherever he was.

Even if he died and went to heaven.

———

Driving home that night, he passed the police station. A couple patrol cars were parked nearby in the alley by First Baptist church. It would be a simple matter to park his truck next to them, go inside and ask to speak to Chief Henderson. He'd thought the same thing this morning, when he passed by headed in the opposite direction. He'd told himself then, and he told himself again now, that he didn't have the right to do that. If they came to him, he would lie, and if they didn't believe him, he'd lie some more. That was the only real option that remained, unless he wanted to sentence his son to a far worse disgrace than he'd had to face when his father left town.

He drove on past and soon—too soon—was turning into his driveway. The lights in the living room were on, the curtains shut. Mason's window was dark. They'd been having fires for the last few evenings, but tonight no smoke rose from the chimney.

He pulled into the garage beside Nancy's car and cut off the engine.

He was going to lie to her if she asked the question he feared was coming. He'd lie to Mason too. He'd lie for the rest of his life, to everyone but himself. Telling anything other than the truth did not come naturally to him, but he could do it. He had to.

He walked over to the door and unlocked it. The laundry room was dark and so was the hallway beyond it. No lights on in the master bedroom. Still, it didn't occur to him that anyone might be asleep. Nobody in his family had ever gone to bed this early. Without thinking, he flipped on the hallway light.

They'd left the door to Mason's room open, perhaps because they believed the other person who lived in the house would not be coming home. She lay on her side, her knees drawn up to her chest, a wad of pink tissue clenched in her right hand. Other wads lay on the floor or on the throw rug next to the bed. Her eyes were red, her cheeks flushed and puffy. A woolen blanket covered everything but her feet, encased in a pair of furry slippers.

Mason wasn't exactly lying behind her, but neither was he sitting. He'd propped himself up against the headboard and was stroking his mother's hair. He didn't stop just because the light had come on and his father was staring at him. He continued to do it, whispering, "Don't cry, Momma. Please don't cry. Everything'll be all right."

THE GATHERING, as Toni would come to think of it, began that Saturday evening, when she collected various fragments and began to assemble herself anew. From this corner, a memory of the room she'd slept in until she was three, in the Tower District bungalow, how the bulbs in her ceiling fan tinkled when a train rolled by and her father reached up and stabilized the fan and told her he could stop the earth from shaking. From that corner, a moment in San Francisco after a concert late one night in her fourth or fifth year, when their car got stuck in traffic and her dad complained of being lost and her mother laughed and asked how could they be lost, since they were all three together? And the time they visited Ireland, when they took the ferry to the Aran Islands and the sea rolled over the bow and her father held her tightly and told her not to worry, that the waves seemed big only because she was so little. And she believed him when he said that, just as she'd believed everything else he and her mother had ever told her.

She had been that girl too. And she knew, just as surely as she knew her own name, that it was important to pick up those small fragments, right now, and secrete them away, or she'd lose them just like she'd lost her mom.

Earlier, as if she were a stray that had been kicked once too often, her dad had coaxed her from the closet. "Here," he'd said, squatting, holding out his hand. "Come on, hon. Please. You can't stay in there. You need to eat. We've got to. Both of us." Light from the overhead glinted off his wedding band. He read her mind. "I'll wear it for the rest of my life. I promise."

She wouldn't allow him to touch her. Palms out, she pushed at the air, letting him know he had to back away.

Rather than stand up, he duck-walked backwards, across the room, as if he realized it was important to remain near ground level, that the last thing she needed to see right then was her father standing upright.

When some floor space opened up, she crept forward, on hands and knees, facing him, her forearms quivering.

Once more he extended his hand. "There's not a lot to eat in the kitchen. But I found a few cans of Campbell's soup. Some pastrami. And there's a carton of eggs and some rye bread. Does any of that sound appealing?"

"A woman brought a cake," she said. Her voice, when she heard it, surprised her. Not the sound of it, just the fact that she still had one.

"The cake's outside. If you want it, I'll bring it in."

"I don't want a cake. Who in her right mind would bring us a cake today?"

"She meant well."

"But she's not right in her mind."

"I don't really think there's anything wrong with her mind," he said, and she accorded him one point for not patronizing her. Just a single point, true enough, but at least he was no longer stuck on zero. "She meant to help," he said. "When people don't know what to do, they fall back on what they've seen others do before them. Her mother would've brought a cake. So she brought one too."

"I might try the soup."

"All right."

She stood. To her surprise, her knees supported her weight.

Her father remained in that ridiculous duck stance, so she awarded him another point.

——— —

Eight p.m. now. The longest day of her life.

They sit across the table from each other at the Western Sizzler in Greenville, waiting for a waitress to bring whatever it is they've ordered. When it arrives, Toni imagines, he'll be as surprised as she is. Neither of them looked at the menu, he just asked for two some-things, though she recalls that he first inquired about her preference and she said she didn't have one.

While she stirs her drink with the plastic straw, he watches her. Once or twice he starts to say something, then decides not to.

Finally, she breaks the silence. "That woman I saw at Save Mart?" she says. "The one you told me was named Edie?"

"Yeah. Except, of course, I was lying."

"Her name was Nora."

"Nora Houston."

"She had cancer."

"That's right."

"What kind?"

"Breast cancer. Her surgeon had to do a mastectomy."

"Were you in love with her?"

"I thought I was."

She'll brook no equivocation, but he must not understand that. Because he proceeds to lift the salt shaker and set it on the table in front of his iced tea. Then he reaches for the pepper shaker, and she says, "Don't tell me love's not black and white."

He puts the pepper shaker down. "I was in love with her then."

"So much in love that you wanted to leave Mom?"

So much in love that when Nora walked out of a room, he'd stay behind as long as he could, just to keep inhaling her scent. In love with the silence that enveloped them when they were alone together, with the look that took the place of a gesture, her reckless nature, how she invested even the simplest words—*coffee, paper, dinner, pool*—with an air of danger.

"No," he says, uncertain if it's a lie. "I never wanted to leave your mom. Or you either. I wanted everything. All for myself."

"And now," she says, "you've ended up with nothing."

"That's about the size of it. Unless by some miracle I can hold on to you."

A group of guys wearing Greenville High letter jackets saunters in, all of them loud and trying to act cool. Seeing them, she thinks once more of Mason, how he stood there staring at her house. He hasn't called. If what happened to her mother happened to his, she'd call. At least she hopes she would.

Pete understands the kinds of calculations being performed in her head, knows that she's trying to arrive at the absolute value of those remaining in her life—which, for all intents and purposes, means him and Mason DePoyster. The boy hasn't phoned her, probably considering it too soon. Pete would call and ask him to come over, but he got a strange feeling from talking to Alan at the father-son banquet and suspects that even after all these years, his call would not be welcomed.

The waitress, who isn't much older than Toni, brings their orders—apparently they're having steaks and baked potatoes—and asks if they need anything else. He says no thank you. Heading back to the kitchen, she passes the table where the high school guys are sitting, and one of them reaches out to grab her bottom. She giggles, pulls the baseball cap off his head and drops it on the floor. He says, "Hey, whore, come back here."

Pete looks over his shoulder. "Gentlemen, I wish you wouldn't talk trash," he says, "not when my daughter and I are present."

The guy's face turns red. He has four companions, all good-sized and all pretty good at sizing up the situation. Simultaneously, they focus on their menus.

Toni picks at her steak, takes a couple of bites, then lays down her knife and fork after cutting off a piece that's on the wrong side of the dividing line between pink and red.

"You need to eat," her dad says. She hears him say that they've got to make certain they don't get run-down, that both of them need to compose a list of things to do tomorrow, even simple things, like getting up, having breakfast, finishing homework or scooping leaves from the pool. Their days will need structure, he says, otherwise they'll spin off into chaos.

"My mom's *dead*."

Though she knows it's absurd, she hopes he'll deny it. When he doesn't, she bows her head so deeply that a few strands of her hair dip into the butter on her baked potato. He reaches out to lift them free, but she bats his hand aside. "Who would do this? And why? Almost nobody here even *knew* her."

He's already asked himself those questions a few hundred times. Nothing was missing from the house, no evidence of a burglary. The only man who hates him enough to harm him or anyone in his family is two thousand miles away, receiving psychiatric treatment at the behest of a California court. "I don't know who," he says. "I don't know why, either."

"What happens to . . . her body?"

He lays his knife and fork aside too, and she sees he has no appetite either, that he was willing to eat only because he wanted her to. "In instances like this," he says, "they have to perform an autopsy."

"Have you ever done one?"

"No."

"But you know how they do them?"

"Toni—"

Her eyes swim in warm, salty tears. "Will we be able to see her again?"

"No."

"Why *not*?"

"She wanted to be cremated, Toni. They'll do that in Jackson. After the state medical examiner releases her body."

"Then I want to go to Jackson."

"We can't."

"Why?"

"There's no point, honey. She's gone. And you probably wouldn't be able to see her even if we were there."

She's dissolving. The last time her mother could have heard her voice was from the message she'd left on her cell phone saying she had a ride to the game. She'd tried to sound nasty. And she knows just how well she succeeded. "I never told her good-bye."

The quickness with which he can move has always surprised her. Before she fully comprehends that he's gotten to his feet, he's already squatting next to her chair. He wraps those hard arms around her, and for once she doesn't try to pull away. It would be pointless anyhow. You can't get away from him, not if he doesn't want you to.

"Daddy?" she asks. "You didn't do it, did you?"

His breath warms her neck. She doesn't just hear his next words, she also feels them.

"No," he says. "Not the way you mean."

———

That night he hands her a pill, and she swallows it without bothering to ask what it is. He tells her he'll sleep on the floor beside her bed if she wants him to, but she shakes her head. For the longest time, after she turns out her light, she can tell he's still in the hallway, probably hunkering down with his back against the wall. Eventually, around eleven, as she's about to doze off, she hears him leave.

When she wakes, the digital clock reads three-twelve a.m. She pushes the covers off, and her feet feel around on the floor until they locate her slippers. The door to her room is open: he must have returned after she fell asleep.

His door's open too. She expects to find him awake, but he's snoring faintly, his head resting on his forearm. When she slips into bed beside him, he doesn't move at all, failing even to register another person's presence.

As was his habit on Sunday morning, no matter the weather, Frank Henderson got up a couple hours before everybody else in his family. After going out front to get the Memphis paper, he returned to the kitchen, made himself a pot of coffee and poured it in a stainless steel carafe. Carrying the coffee, the paper and a large blue mug with the acronym NACP on it, he walked out back to the glassed-in gazebo, switched on the electric space heater and lowered himself into a deck chair.

He had a whole set of blue coffee mugs with this legend printed on them. He kept three or four at the office, and from time to time somebody, usually a white person who'd come to discuss some civic matter, would look closely at the cup and observe that the inscription was missing an *A*. "No," Henderson would correct his guest, "there's nothing missing. That stands for National Association of Chiefs of Police. Not the National Association for the Advancement of Colored People. Though the existence of the latter organization made possible my entry into the former."

The existence of the latter organization had made a lot of things possible for Frank Henderson, including his three-bedroom house in a previously all-white neighborhood. It had enabled him to send both of his sons to college and, in a couple years, his daughter too. And it had allowed him to assume leadership of a department that, for three awful weeks back in 1964, had tormented his own father.

When he first took over as chief, he called the entire department together, right down to the janitor, and made a little speech. He told them that during Freedom Summer, his daddy had taken part in the voter registration drive, one of only three or four locals brave enough to team up with Bob Moses and the kids who poured into the Delta from places like New York, Ohio, Illinois and California. His family lived on the old Stancill place back then, he said, his daddy maintaining farm machinery, and the first thing that happened as a result of his father's political activity was that Stancill's overseer came by one day and told them they had to move. His father hadn't argued, he'd just called a friend of his who owned a truck, and between the two of them they got the house emptied out in five or six hours, and for the remainder of that summer the Hendersons moved from one friend's home to another, leaving just as soon as their presence began to cause their hosts a problem.

On three consecutive Saturdays that summer, he told the department, his father had been arrested on trumped-up charges by members of the all-white Loring police force. Once, while riding in a yellow van with a student from UCLA, he got jailed because "the means of conveyance," as the arresting officer put it, was "too yellow" and might be mistaken for a school bus. Another time, after blowing his nose, he was hauled in for littering the sidewalk. It might have been funny, Chief Henderson said, except for one unfortunate circumstance: every time his daddy disappeared into custody, he came home bruised from head to toe. The last time, he collapsed downtown but managed to crawl into an alley, where he hid behind a row of garbage cans until he felt strong enough to walk.

"So it goes without saying," Henderson informed the assembly, "that I harbor strong feelings about the proper conduct of this department. We're here to serve the public. The public consists of white folks, black folks and everybody in between. It consists of the old and the young, male and female, dog and cat. There are people in this world that sit up high and wear robes, and we call those folks judges. They determine wrong and right, innocence and guilt. That's not our job. See, the folks that grabbed my daddy got confused. They thought they were the judges. Whereas the plain truth is that the police department, if it's functioning correctly, has a lot more in common with the water department and waste management than it does with the judiciary."

While the chilly gazebo began to warm up, he poured himself a cup of coffee and opened the paper. Turning to the Mid-South section, he looked to see if there was any mention of that Friday's event, but there wasn't. The day the mayor appointed him chief, he'd said, "Frank, it's my job to see that the town gets its name in the news. It's your job to make sure it doesn't." Thus far Henderson had succeeded. He'd gone about his business quietly, exhibiting the same kind of careful determination his father had shown forty years ago.

He spent an hour or so with the paper, drinking coffee and shaking his head every now and then at the mess in which the world found itself on this particular Sunday morning in October. Then he went back inside, showered, dressed and got ready for work.

———

He parked his Mercedes in the spot reserved for him behind the police station and climbed out. Across the alley, the congregation at First Baptist was singing "Oh, How I Love Jesus."

Cloell, the dispatcher, six months pregnant, was dozing behind the plate glass under a signed photo of Steve McNair, the Tennessee Titans' quarterback. Gently, Henderson tapped the glass and, as she jerked upright, he grinned and wagged a finger at her. "Good morning, Miss Cloell."

She rubbed her eyes. "Morning, Chief. How you doing today?"

"Doing just fine. Any excitement?"

"A couple press peoples called this morning."

"Which ones?"

"Retha Mackey, from Channel Nine. And somebody that say they work for the *Clarion-Ledger*. Tried to write their name down but they was talking too fast."

"I'll call Retha back when the mood descends on me. Anybody else, get their number and warn 'em I'm awful busy."

"Yes sir." Her voice dropped as if she were about to convey a piece of gossip. "That preliminary report from the medical examiner's office come in on the fax a while ago. It's in there on your desk."

He walked into his office. Pictures of his wife and children hung on the walls, along with a photo of him and the county sheriff shaking hands after last year's interdepartmental softball game. He liked the sheriff, an older white man who'd come a long distance in his life and was now to the point where he never said *nigger,* though he'd once confessed that he still sometimes thought it.

Henderson closed the door and sat down at his desk. For a moment or two he let the fax lie there. He'd worked a number of homicides during his years with the sheriff's department, but this was his first as chief of police. He'd never seen one yet that failed to take him someplace he would rather not have gone. It reminded him of being a kid and hefting the garbage can in the backyard—it being his job to haul the trash down to the bayou for burning—and knowing a cottonmouth might uncoil the moment he lifted that container. Seemed like it happened more often than not.

He picked up the fax and started reading.

———

That evening, at supper, D'Nesha said, "Daddy, have you found out anything who killed California's momma?"

He was on his second can of Bud Light. He'd finished the first in the living room, sitting there with the TV on, the sound turned down, images of Daunte Culpepper and Randy Moss flitting across the screen like purple phantoms. It was rare for him to drink two beers in an evening. Usually, it was just the one. If he drank two, he meant to drink several more. But tonight that wouldn't be possible.

He reached for another corn bread muffin. He'd already eaten two, while leaving his chicken untouched. "Hon," he told his daughter, "you know I don't like to mix official business with family life."

His wife let the remark pass, but not D'Nesha. "So how come you woke me up yesterday morning to ask when California left the party Friday night and who took her home? Isn't that mixing the personal and the public?"

He cut his muffin in half, intending to butter it. "I guess you could argue I shouldn't have done that," he said. "Except to make that particular argument, you would have to overlook a fundamental fact."

D'Nesha plucked a raw broccoli spear off her plate, put it in her mouth and crunched it. "Well," she said, her chin canted at an annoying angle, "I'm not a fundamentalist."

He put both halves of the muffin back down, removed the napkin from his lap, folded it and laid it on the table. He hated baked chicken anyway, he wanted his fried. He was going to drive across town and take care of the business he'd been dreading most of the day, and on his way back, if his appetite hadn't deserted him altogether, he'd drop by KFC.

Standing, he gazed down at his daughter. "You're right. I posed those questions yesterday morning in my official capacity. I probably should've gone to the office, called your momma and had her bring you in for interrogation."

As he left the dining room, he heard D'Nesha ask her mother, "What in the world's wrong with Daddy?"

———

Little black sacks hung beneath the doctor's eyes. At first, Henderson wondered if somebody had punched him. He dismissed that idea, though, because he didn't know anybody who'd risk hitting a man that size. Even if you were that big yourself, you'd think twice about it.

They were standing in the hallway, the doctor in a terry-cloth bathrobe. It had become obvious to Henderson the moment he stepped inside that this time around he would not be invited to sit. He didn't blame Barrington one bit. If their roles had been reversed, he wouldn't want the other man sitting down in his house, either.

Two or three feet of empty space separated them, along with a number of other factors including skin color, education, income and the trouble in California, which Henderson had learned about earlier today when he Googled the doctor after reading the preliminary report from the medical examiner. But despite all that, he somehow felt close to Pete Barrington and sensed that for some inexplicable reason the two of them looked at the world in a not-altogether-dissimilar fashion.

"Dr. Barrington," he said, "I'm going to have to ask you two more questions, and then I'll say good night and leave you be."

"Fair enough, Chief."

"When was the last time you saw Mrs. Barrington alive?"

"About seven-thirty Friday morning. I took my daughter to school, worked until about a quarter after four, then changed clothes at the office and went over to the high school. The team eats dinner together before all our games. Afterwards, we got on the bus and went to Greenville. I could've gone by the house that afternoon, but I didn't. I wish I had."

Rashard Killingsworth had already confirmed that the doctor ate with the team at four-thirty on the dot. Between the end of the meal and the moment they all got on the bus, he said, Barrington had never once been out of his sight. Hearing that made the chief breathe a little bit easier. But when he asked Killingsworth if he'd noticed anything unusual in Barrington's behavior in recent days, the coach cleared his throat and acknowledged that at halftime on Friday night he'd blown his cool, picking up a trash can and throwing it against the wall. And for a minute or two after hearing that, Frank Henderson didn't breathe at all.

"Doctor," he said, standing there in the hallway, "I don't like having to ask you this next question."

"You didn't like having to ask me the last one, either. But you've got a job to do, so go ahead and do it."

"When was the last time you had sex with your wife?"

The doctor's gaze did not waver. "Eighteen months ago, at a cabin in Lake Tahoe."

Henderson intended for it to stop right there. He'd bid Pete Barrington good night, and sometime tomorrow, in a matter-of-fact manner, he'd phone to tell him the investigation into his wife's death had produced certain evidence that would necessitate DNA profiling. This is just something we need to do, he'd say. Being a medical man, I know you understand. You can come by the police station, so we don't have to bother you at home again. Or we can send somebody to your house, if you prefer, and then you won't have to make a trip. You choose. Just tell us which is best for you.

But Pete Barrington did not stop where Frank Henderson intended. "It was about eleven-thirty on a Monday night," the big man said. "We'd all watched *Father of the Bride,* and Toni had gone to bed. And we had a couple of glasses of wine—more than a couple, really—and it happened right on the couch, in this A-frame we used to own."

They'd spent a lot of time up there over the years, Barrington explained. And they'd returned eighteen months ago, trying to recapture something missing from their marriage. For a few moments that Monday evening, he said, they'd had it within their grasp. "Right then, I believed it would last, and I think she did too. But it didn't. And you know the rest. Or if you don't," Barrington said, reaching for the door, "I imagine you will before long."

Soft gold and wispy, Toni's hair spread out on the pillow just inches from his own. The angel that graced the tops of his family's Christmas trees when he was a boy had hair just like that. A cheap angel missing part of one wing, it had come mounted on a cardboard cylinder like the ones toilet paper was wrapped around. Except for the nice hair it looked pretty bad, but he loved that angel, loved pulling it out of the box and then watching while his father positioned it atop the tree. The angel promised mystery and surprise, something new and exciting near the end of a year that had, almost always, been dull and forgettable.

Christmas, as he'd conceived it, was not really about gifts, because in a family as poor as his, what you got was modest. It was about the odor of cedar and candle wax, ham baked in Coca-Cola, about tangerines and oranges, cold air, Bing Crosby crooning "Silent Night," his grandfather crawling around underneath the tree, picking packages up and shaking them and asking, "What you reckon's in here, Pete? Reckon it's a mean motor scooter? Or a Ole Miss football?"

Christmas, as he'd conceived it, had a thing or two in common with California, which, as Ms. Marsh used to remind him and Donny Alexander and Tim Kessler and all the other history students, had always represented the last best hope. If you struck rock bottom here, you could always hope you'd strike it rich there. That was why folks streamed over its borders in 1849, kicking off the gold rush, droves of desperate men pouring in so that in no time its population was ninety-five percent male, and that was why people lit out for it again during the Great Depression, after going bust in the Dust

Bowl. As long as California existed, Ms. Marsh said, there was still room for dreams.

Now all he had left of California lay beside him in bed, in Loring, Mississippi. She'd said she wanted to go to school, but he hated worse than anything to wake her up to contend with that.

———

You just have to face it, she told herself when her dad took his foot off the brake and the truck began to pull away, leaving her standing there in front of the high school—*it* meaning the rest of her life, which she saw as an ordeal that she had to survive. Toward that end she'd made herself a set of promises, and she now rehashed them as the kids hanging around outside parted for her to pass.

She would play the piano every day, starting this afternoon, and she would practice an hour longer than she ever had before and not only fill sixty minutes that would otherwise remain empty but also enter into musical conversation with her mother.

She would learn to cook. Her father possessed no culinary skills, and this lack opened another avenue of guilt for him to travel. He *was* guilty—of loving another woman—and nobody knew it better than he did. But she didn't want him focusing on that or, for that matter, on anything else. She wanted him focusing on her. If he didn't, she believed, no one would.

She would not go to Mason DePoyster. He could come to her, if he chose. But if he failed to she would learn to live without him, just as she would somehow learn to live without her mom.

She grasped the handle on one of the double doors, pulled it open and he materialized from the shadows in the hallway, as if he'd been lying in wait. "I'm sorry I didn't call you," he said. "I didn't know what to say. Will you forgive me?"

The school had a rule prohibiting embraces between students of opposite gender. If the hall monitor caught you, you got detention. She didn't care, as long as she got detained with him. She stepped into his arms and discovered, to her surprise, that she was not the only one crying.

"You can't do that," she whispered, nose nestled against his chest. "I need somebody with dry eyes."

"I'll try," he said. The first bell rang and students begin straggling in, giving them a few looks as they passed. He waited until the clanging stopped. "I'll try," he said again. "I mean, I'm scared too. But I'll do my level best to keep my eyes dry."

He took her hand in his, and together they walked down the hall past the trophy case with the picture of her father on display. She didn't look at the picture, but Mason did. He bet quite a few of the athletes in those old photos had copies at home, that they took them out and examined them from time to time. In their own minds, some of them were probably the same folks now that they'd been back then. He felt certain her father didn't do that. And *his* father, as far as he knew, didn't have any pictures like that.

All morning Mason remained beside her, ditching a couple of his classes when their schedules diverged. During lunch they sat together at a table in the corner of the cafeteria, and as if by agreement the other students left them alone. He told her he had an important test next period in econ and asked if it would be okay for him to go ahead and take it. She said sure, and they agreed to meet at her locker between fifth and sixth period. Before saying good-bye, he kissed her on the forehead.

Afterwards, as she sat in American government trying unsuccessfully to focus on a discussion of the most significant presidential vetoes, she remembered Mason's comment about being scared. Why should *he* be scared? She decided to ask him later, but when the end of the period rolled around and she saw him waiting beside her locker like he'd promised, her relief was so great that the question slipped away.

———

The year after Pete's dad died, his grandmother woke one morning unable to talk. She was silent all through breakfast, as both Pete and his mother noted, though they didn't discuss it until later. She sat at her end of the table, frowning while she glanced at the *Delta Democrat-Times*. She'd attended school only through fifth grade, couldn't read very well and seldom paid any attention to the paper, so they figured something unusual must have caught her eye.

She was silent on the drive into town, and Pete let them out of the pickup in front of the dollar store. He was in algebra when the principal's voice crackled over the speaker, summoning him to the office.

He'd been called to the office exactly twice in his life, and both times a member of his family had died. It never crossed his mind as he hustled down the hallway that the news might be good, and it wasn't: his grandmother had suffered a stroke. An ambulance had taken her to the emergency room, and the principal told him to get over there just as fast as he could.

His grandmother had lived through the Great Depression and was tough as nails. She eventually regained her speech, though for the rest of her life she suffered mild aphasia and would occasionally say nonsensical things, like "Open the dog" when she meant "Open the door." She even got healthy enough to walk the floor again at United Dollar Store.

She told Pete later on, when he announced his plans to become a doctor, that the day she had the stroke she'd known something was wrong the moment she woke up. But her limbs worked just fine, except for a little numbness in her hands and feet, so it didn't occur to her that maybe she ought to stay home. She'd never missed a day of work in her life, even driving hoe hands to the field the morning after her husband died.

He thought of her as he parked in the lot behind his office. He hadn't been able to come up with anything better to do today than go to work, either. His nurse-receptionist had phoned Sunday night, certain that he'd want her to cancel all his appointments, but he told her he'd be there and hung up.

She was at her desk when he walked in. "The phone's been ringing constantly," she said. Just then it rang again, and she ignored it. "Folks assumed you'd be rescheduling this week's appointments. I'm telling them all to come on."

"I've never known illness to take a rain check."

She looked at him like Lassie used to when Timmy behaved abnormally.

"Are you going to answer that?"

Shaking her head, she lifted the receiver. "Dr. Barrington's office."

He picked up a stack of lab reports and X-rays, tucked them under his arm and went to his office. A few minutes later, when he stepped out to get a drink of water, he heard sobbing. Fran was sitting at the desk, her back and shoulders shaking.

"That's not going to do a bit of good," he said.

"So it won't, then."

"If I thought it would, believe me, I'd do it too. I'd be right there beside you."

He walked over and touched her shoulder, and she jumped as if he'd poked her with a cattle prod.

"It's unseemly," she said, her face puffy and red. "It's just unseemly for us to be here."

————

He worked through lunch, one patient morphing into the next. A few of them told him how sorry they were about what had happened. One of them, a retired farmer who'd known both his grandfather and his father, asked if the police had any leads yet. After Pete shrugged and said he didn't know, the old man reached out and clamped a bony but surprisingly strong hand around his wrist. "If you got any inkling who it was," he said, "you tell me, boy, and I'll take care of 'em. You've seen them X-ray pictures of my old gut. Like the hymn song says, I ain't got long to stay here." Pete thanked him and sent him off to the oncologist.

When four o'clock rolled around, he pulled off the white coat, told Fran good-bye and walked outside wondering if he should attend practice or not. He'd gotten an e-mail from Killingsworth expressing his and his wife's condolences and telling him to come back when he felt able, and Sandra Jean had picked Toni up and taken her home and would stay until he got there. If he wanted, he could go do what he'd been doing when Angela took her last breath.

In the lot, another pickup was parked beside his, the hood practically covered with fallen leaves. It must have been parked there for some time.

Tim opened the door and climbed out. He had clothes on, though Pete saw right through them to the naked boy underneath. Only God knew how many miscreants Tim Kessler had protected from the correctional powers, but everybody knew that he could not protect himself. Never had been able to. Never would be.

"Pete?"

"In a manner of speaking."

Tim had promised himself he wouldn't say much, that he'd let Pete say or do whatever he needed to, and then he'd take whatever medicine got prescribed. But he started talking and couldn't stop. "You probably don't remember this, there's no reason you would, but one time old lady Candido made us write an essay on the topic 'The Person I Most Admire.' I wrote mine about you, and it turned out she made us get up and read them. I said that when we were in a tight game, I'd always look at number eighty-eight and feel secure, like nothing too bad could go wrong as long as you were on my side. And then I talked about that time we played Murrah in the state finals. On the film, we'd noticed their DBs weren't wrapping up real good when they tackled. So Coach bought a few tear-away jerseys for all the backs and receivers. Remember that? In the third quarter you ran that little hook pattern you loved, and the strong safety came up to tackle you, but you left him lying there holding the back of your jersey. Since I was riding the bench, I loaned you my shirt. And there you were, wearing number twenty-four, and for the rest of that game I got a chance to see what I'd look like if I were you."

He'd said a lot, but as Pete opened his arms and eliminated the space between them with a couple of giant strides, he realized how much he hadn't said, and wondered how in the world he could ever put the rest of it into words.

ALAN RARELY WENT TO THE MOVIES, but whenever he did, it annoyed him that the folks running theaters thought they needed to flash an announcement demanding that cell phones be shut off. Everybody seemed compelled to do that these days. He'd noticed it listed among the requirements on Mason's course outlines, and the church had begun placing it in the bulletin each Sunday. Why so many people were eager to remain accessible at every hour of the day or night had always been beyond his ken. The company paid for his phone, but during the five years he'd had one, it was probably turned off ninety-nine percent of the time. Now, however, he kept it on, even at night, when it was plugged into the charger. Bad news would reach you if it wanted to. Trying to avoid it didn't make much sense.

One person with no apparent interest in reaching him was his wife. She hadn't called even once, though she used to leave him two or three messages a day. Around the house, he'd noticed her staring at him several times but they'd hardly talked at all since the conversation in the kitchen when he'd asked her not to touch him. He'd tried to engage her, forcing himself to bring up all sorts of innocuous topics, like the problem Wade Phelps had been having with the leaking baptistry or how several fishponds had overflowed during the heavy rain a couple of weeks back, allowing half the stock to swim away in the road ditches. That his subjects often involved water imagery would be lost on him until later, when he thought about the flood and realized that, unlike Noah, he would have to survive without an ark.

———

The cell phone finally rang on Tuesday morning, when he was in the storeroom. A glance at the number on the display window dismayed him. His mother. Not much point in letting it go unanswered. She'd just keep calling.

He pressed the green button. "Hello?"

She didn't say anything, and for one blessed instant he entertained hope that she'd hung up. Then she spoke his name. "Alan." Nothing more.

He looked for a place to sit. The storeroom was a total mess, spray cans of Crisco rolling underfoot, paper towels falling from on high. He brushed dust off a bale of flour and sat down.

"What paper do you read?" she finally asked.

"The *Clarion-Ledger*. When I read anything at all."

"I see there's been a momentous event in town. There was a little note about it this morning in the *Commercial Appeal*. In that section where they have news briefs from Mississippi."

Sitting there on the flour bale, he shivered. Coldness centered itself in his shoulders, forcing him to hunch.

"Alan?"

"Yeah."

"Did you hear what I said?"

"Of course I heard you."

"Why didn't you tell me about Pete's wife?"

"Why should I tell you? What's there to say? Awful stuff like that happens all the time. Until now, it just never happened here."

"Was it a robbery?"

"I don't know."

"The *Commercial* didn't say."

"Then I guess they don't know either."

"Do you have Pete's home phone number?"

His stomach gurgled again. At various times in the last few days, he'd lost control of his sphincter and had to run for the john. He shifted position. "What?"

"Pete's phone number. Do you have it?"

"My God, Momma," he said. "You think he'd still be interested in you? At your age—and with you in that wheelchair?"

As far back as he could remember, she could shake her head at him and simultaneously suggest pity, disgust and amazement, and in the silence that followed his remark he pictured her sitting in Veasey's big house on the fringes of Overton Park shaking it again. Only the Lord knew what might have happened if he'd been near her.

"Alan," she said, "it's impossible to name a thing that doesn't exist, so I can't say what's missing in you. But there's something you just didn't get. Or if you got it, you didn't waste any time losing it."

Like paper towels, she was on a roll. She intended to say a lot more, but he had no intention of hearing it. He pressed the red button, End Call, then stood up and headed for the bathroom.

———

A few minutes later, as he stepped through the door onto the loading dock, sunshine glared off the roof of his truck and forced him to shut his eyes.

And when his eyes were opened, he saw no man. But they led him by the hand and brought him into Damascus.

For an instant, his throat felt so full he had to brace himself against a stanchion. A soft haze hung in the air, a faint trace of moisture laden with the odor of lint from the town's only remaining cotton gin. He associated that smell with childhood, with fall mornings on the playground when it seemed recess would last forever.

In third or fourth grade, when his father was a youthful presence on the Board of Aldermen and the Chamber of Commerce, Alan had snubbed Pete Barrington on the playground, on a day much like this one. Back then Pete was just a country boy, the kind who lived on a farm his daddy didn't own. Unlike some of those kids, he always wore clean clothes, though they were occasionally a little bit faded, and his hair was always clean, never displaying that telltale matted look. Yet in every other respect he was just like all the rest. He said *fanger* when he meant *finger,* and when it was his turn to bring a record to school for what their teacher called "musical moments," he'd inflict some old country whiner like Merle Haggard or George Jones on you.

That morning, Alan was walking across the playground, probably heading for the monkey bars, though in truth he couldn't remember. He knew he enjoyed playing on them back then, that he could go from end to end faster than most of his friends, swinging from one bar to the next, never losing his grip, not even when a buddy on the ground grabbed his feet and tried to pull him down. He must have been heading in that direction when Pete hollered at him.

"Hey, Alan? Want to play on my team?"

At the time Pete was chubby, maybe even a little fat. That weighed against him, as did his clothes, his accent and the fact that he usually came to school on the bus instead of being driven in a new pickup like the better kids who lived in the country. He was surrounded that day by boys of similar circumstance, some of whose names Alan didn't even know.

What captured Alan's attention wasn't those boys—it was the football Pete kept tossing into the air and catching. People like him owned chintzy balls made of synthetic material, rather than leather ones boasting a recognizable brand name like Wilson or Rawlings. Synthetic balls didn't smell good, like a leather ball would. They reeked of whatever chemicals had gone into their creation.

"Barrington," Alan hollered, ambling right on past, "you can take that stinking ball and stick it up your rump."

If you'd asked him a week ago whether or not Pete remembered that morning, he would have said no. Why would anybody who'd been a college football star, slept with any number of attractive women, held patients' lives in his hands, made a fortune and traveled all over the world—why would anybody like that cling to a memory so insignificant? Now, though, Alan wasn't so sure. If he could remember every wound he'd ever suffered, maybe Pete did too. Maybe a lot less ground separated them than he'd always thought. When you got right down to it, they were both just sinners, and if you kept a running total of the damage they'd done to each other, Alan knew his own sum would forever remain the greater of the two.

He stepped down off the loading dock, walked over to his pickup and got inside. The truck was almost out of gas—the orange warning light had come on while he drove to work this morning—and he knew if he didn't fill the tank right now, while it was on his mind, he'd forget and end up walking home. He thought maybe after he gassed up, he'd get some frozen yogurt at the Sonic. He needed to put something in his stomach but couldn't face the prospect of solid food.

———

In front of the station, on an overturned Nehi crate that must have dated back to the late '70s, when he'd quit selling drinks and snacks, Grady Stewart sat with his hands on his knees. When he saw Alan he didn't budge, which suited Alan fine because he preferred to pump his own gas and avoid conversation. He opened the door, climbed out and reached for the handle.

"Goddamn it, boy," the old man sputtered, "you know I don't allow that." He rose, kicked an oil can out of the way, walked over to the pump and, leaning into Alan none too gently, shouldered him aside. "What's your fucking hurry? Aiming to run home and get a little noonday booty?"

Alan didn't answer, nor did he render judgment. Filth and spite might fill Grady Stewart's heart, but the old man held no monopoly on that.

"I used to slip off from here and get me some in the daytime," Stewart said. He screwed the cap off Alan's gas tank and jammed the spout inside. "Didn't nobody know it, neither. You remember Mrs. Stewart?"

Alan did, though dimly. She was one of those women who'd seemed small, old and gray from the first time he took note of her to the day they put her in the ground, which must have been about ten years ago. "Yes sir."

"After she got a little older, her Fertile Crescent turned into Death Valley. Claimed fucking hurt her. I told her I still had to have it, and she said it wasn't nothing but fair that if it was to hurt her, it ought to hurt me too. I studied on her reasoning and had to admit she was right. So you know what we used to do?"

Before the old man could tell him, a plum-colored Mercedes pulled in and stopped on the far side of the pump. The door opened, and the chief of police climbed out.

Stewart made a face at Alan and mouthed a three-syllable word. *Jiggaboo.*

"Good morning, Mr. Stewart," the chief said.

"It was."

The chief laughed. "Mr. Stewart here," he told Alan, "likes to maintain the façade that he opposed my appointment."

"Ain't nothing I hate much more," the old man said, "than when a member of the colored race starts flinging five-dollar words around."

"Used to be a member of my race didn't even *have* five dollars. Those were halcyon times, weren't they, Mr. Stewart?"

"If that means then beat now from hell to Clarksdale, then you and me's in agreement about one thing."

"Some people," the chief told Alan, "might be of the opinion that I ought to patronize another filling station, given Mr. Stewart's views on African Americans. But the truth is I'm here in an investigative capacity."

"That so?" Alan said, in what he hoped was an offhand manner.

"Indeed. Because racist elements are still present here in Loring, and I figure Mr. Stewart's the only one who'll say openly what all the others think."

The old man finished filling Alan's tank, then pulled the spout out and screwed the cap back on. "Instead of worrying who mumbles *nigger* in their sleep," he said, "you better get busy and catch the bastard that killed Pete Barrington's wife."

"Now, Mr. Stewart, correct me if I'm wrong, but I don't believe you've had access to the medical examiner's report. So I'm not sure why you label Mrs. Barrington's death a murder, since my department hasn't issued any statement to that effect."

"I don't need no medical report, nor statement neither, to know what everybody else knows. Some sick son of a bitch went in there and strangled her. Raped her first. Didn't even steal nothing. Now, much as I hate to admit it, that right there tells me it was a white man did it. Because if that killer was colored, he would of walked out of there with *something*. Even if it wasn't nothing more than a few fancy forks and spoons."

The chief shook his head, then smiled grimly at Alan. "See what I mean? I drop by here once a week and get myself a big dose of disillusionment."

Alan pulled two twenties out of his wallet and handed them to the old man, who looked at the bills, then at the pump—showing a total of $34.53—and said, "Ah, shit," before turning to trudge inside and make change.

Chief Henderson watched him walk away. "Some of that," he said, "is just a put-on."

"I know."

"And some of it's not." The chief crossed his arms over his stomach. "If you hear anything I need to be aware of, you'll tell me, won't you, Alan?"

He prayed his stomach wouldn't pick this moment to betray him. Dear Jesus, his guts began gurgling. "About what?"

"Anything that might be useful to me in my investigation. You see a lot of people there in the store. Sometimes regular folks know more than we do. Most times they do."

Alan shrugged. "Sure." His hands were starting to shake, so he stuck them in his pockets. Then he decided this looked unnatural, so he pulled them right back out. "Was she really raped?"

The chief made a sour face. "I'm asking *you* to tell *me* things. I know it's rude not to repay the favor, but unfortunately I can't."

"I know that. I shouldn't have asked."

"No need to apologize," the chief said as Stewart sulked back toward them. "Everybody's curious. Beginning with me."

When you had lived in the same town almost all your life, every single inch of it was layered, strata topping substrata, reaching as far back as the moment when you first became aware you were anywhere at all. That realization came to Alan as he sat in his pickup at the Sonic Drive-In forcing frozen yogurt down his throat.

He'd sat there before, at different hours of the day and night, at ages ranging from twelve or thirteen to forty-two, in all kinds of weather, winter, spring, summer and fall. He'd sat there even before twelve or thirteen, in fact, because the International Harvester dealership, located south of town these days, had once occupied this lot and the ones behind it and on either side of it, and he remembered going into the dealership with his father, to see a client who sold farm equipment and had once given Alan a little red die-cast Farmall for Christmas.

If, on the other hand, you were traveling through Loring going someplace else and just happened to stop at the Sonic, it couldn't be anything more than itself. Your task in viewing it would be absurdly simple, with nothing to absorb but the surface details. The plastic menus with pictures and speakerphone attached to red metal poles. The black kid who sat behind a plate-glass window inside the tiny brick building, hunched over a microphone. The two waitresses—one black, one white, both badly overweight—who shuttled in and out, carrying trays of food. The Sonic would be that and nothing more.

Not a single thing would prompt you to consider how you'd changed since prior visits to this particular space, or create a mental image of an adolescent male sitting in a pickup beside a man who looked just like him, or a later updated image in which an adolescent male resembling the first one sat in a more recent pickup beside an adult male who also resembled the older man.

If you were a onetime visitor, you'd put your vehicle in gear, back out and, a moment later, pull onto the highway. You'd head east or you'd head west, and before you reached the city limit sign and left Loring, Mississippi, behind, you already would have forgotten where you'd eaten your number-three combo meal, with the medium chocolate shake substituted for the soft drink. As far as you were concerned, once you'd extracted what you wanted from it, this particular place would no longer exist.

————

From a distance, the minister still looked like the athlete he'd once been. He was running along Bayou Drive, on the soft turf beside the sidewalk. He held his head straight and level, rather than letting his chin drop so he could scan the ground where his next step would land. He couldn't help but see Alan driving toward him.

Alan hoped he'd grin and keep on going, making it possible for him to do the same. Instead, the minister broke stride, stepped onto the sidewalk and waved for him to stop.

Sighing, he pulled to the opposite curb.

Wade, wearing black warmups with the Southern Mississippi Golden Eagle logo on the chest, trotted across the street. Using his sleeve, he wiped sweat from his forehead. "Hey," he said.

"Hi, Wade. Getting some exercise?"

"Doing a little running. I'm making a light day of it, though. I think I'm on the verge of pulling a hamstring. It's cool enough that I don't want to take too many chances." He hugged himself, pretending to shiver. "For a boy from the Gulf Coast, this weather's pretty darn frigid."

Alan could think of nothing to say. He felt sure he knew what was coming next.

"I noticed you weren't in your pew last Sunday."

"I was feeling like I might be coming down with a cold."

"A bunch of people were absent."

"Well, it's the time of year when folks get sick."

"I don't think that was it," Wade said.

"So what do you think it was?"

"Mind if I climb in there with you?" the minister asked. "I could use a ride back to the parsonage."

Saying no was impossible, so Alan didn't bother trying to come up with an excuse.

As they rode across town, Wade gazed out the window. "I think folks figured I might preach another sermon on crime and forgiveness," he said. "And I gather that after what happened to that poor woman the other evening, they're not in the most forgiving mood."

Liquid-Plumr could not have dissolved the lump lodged in Alan's throat. Maybe, if he was lucky, it would turn out to be a tumor that would grow until it finally shut off his air supply and he could go ahead and die. Then Nancy and Mason could collect his life insurance without enduring shame. "No," he said, "I doubt anybody's in the mood to forgive whoever it was."

"There's a small part of me," Wade said, "that hopes they don't catch him." Out of the corner of his eye, Alan could see that his friend had turned toward him. "You probably think that's an outrageous thing to say."

"I guess it does seem like an odd emotion."

"They'll all get drunk on vengeance. It'll poison their souls—the ones that aren't already poisoned."

"You really think whoever'd do a thing like that deserves to be forgiven?"

"Absolutely not. But then I don't deserve to be forgiven for my sins, or you for yours. When we repent, we're forgiven by the grace of God. A lot of people seem to forget that."

Despite Alan's determination to keep his mouth shut, the words rushed out. "What about 'Ye know that no murderer hath eternal life abiding in him'? That doesn't sound to me like an admonishment to forgive."

"First John, chapter three, verse fifteen. But you should read on down the page, Alan. What about verse seventeen? 'Whoso hath this world's good, and seeth his brother have need, and shutteth up his bowels of compassion from him, how dwelleth the love of God in him?' Sometimes I envy priests. I never met a Catholic yet who could recite a lick of Scripture unless he wore the collar." He gave the arm-rest a whack. "The Bible's not a self-help book, and it's not a manual for conducting a court-martial. It's a complicated literary text. You have to read it like a Dostoyevsky novel."

A multitude of possible responses presented themselves to Alan. He could have said that contrary to what Wade probably assumed, he did know who Dostoyevsky was and had even read a book by him back in high school. He could have told the minister he didn't like novels, that he wanted to read the truth and, as far as he was concerned, they didn't contain any. Or he could have delivered a little lecture of his own, informing Wade that his problems with the congregation had come about because the congregation spoke one language, while their minister, of late, had begun to speak another—one that was spoken on university campuses from Boston all the way to San Francisco. Any of those statements would have been accurate, but none of them seemed worthy of the breath he'd expend on them.

A feeling of heaviness swept over him. The springs in the seat seemed to sag beneath his weight. In another moment, he might sink right through the floorboard.

He stepped on the brake and pulled to the curb. At first he didn't know where he was, then he looked across a well-kept lawn and saw the house where he'd grown up. "Wade?" he said. "Jesus, Wade, I'm in trouble. I've done something terrible."

Recognition came slowly, but you couldn't say that anything dawned on the minister. What happened had more in common with the onset of darkness. You could see it in his face, as part of the weight Alan had been bearing was shifted miraculously onto someone else's shoulders.

FROM PREVIOUS EXPERIENCE, Pete knew you could tell when people began to view you in a different light. During idle conversation, those who'd once tried to stand as close to you as they could, as if they wanted to soak up your aura, started granting you a lot more room, until finally you realized that like it or not you were surrounded by your own personal firewall. Fewer and fewer messages appeared in your in-box. You also got fewer and fewer phone calls, and then one day somebody you trusted would put it all into words, and once those words were spoken you'd breathe them again and again, practically suffocating from all the poison.

On Friday morning, less than a week since he'd walked into the house and found Angela's body, he arrived at his office to discover that Fran wasn't there yet. Inside, a stack of mail lay on the counter, which was odd because her routine was to pick it up from the post office before coming to work. He thought maybe she'd forgotten something and returned home to get it, so he carried the mail back to his desk, laying it beside all the other unopened items that had piled up there over the last few days. Then he washed his hands, put on his white coat and stepped into the hallway, ready for work.

Fran had returned from wherever she'd been. She was laying a couple of keys down on the counter. Behind her, near the door, stood her husband, Jack, his jaw working hard on a piece of chewing gum.

Pete raised his hand to let her know she didn't need to explain, that he understood the situation and it was okay. He'd mail her a check that afternoon.

But either she missed the gesture or misinterpreted its import.

"I'm sorry," she said. "My mind's already made up. I'll keep praying every night for you and your daughter, but it just wasn't right for you to come to work two days after it happened. And then to go on coaching football . . . I've asked the Lord for direction, and He simply doesn't want me to be here."

"People get sick. Letting them suffer wouldn't have changed anything for my daughter and me." He meant to say more, telling her that he needed to work right now, that trying to help others also helped him. And as for football, at least it occupied his mind for an hour or two each day.

But Jack, who stood about five-seven and had played wingback on the junior high team when Pete was a senior, stepped forward. "There's different kinds of sickness," he said. "Like the kind they're looking for when they do DNA testing."

Jack had earned himself a black belt in karate school over in Greenville. He'd probably love nothing more than to take a big man down. And for just an instant—before Pete reminded himself that no matter who was left standing at the end, he'd emerge more damaged than Fran's husband—the little bastard came close to getting his chance.

"You're right, Jack," he said. "Illness comes in all varieties. Some folks are afflicted by what I call the amoeba complex."

Jack's face flushed. He looked for somewhere to spit his gum.

"Now before you start your Bruce Lee impersonation," Pete said, "there's one thing I ought to tell you. By virtue of having gone down to the police station the other morning to give them that DNA sample that was supposed to remain confidential, I got to know the dispatcher. And if you touch me, you better kill me. Because about two seconds after you leave here, I'll call Miss Cloell and charge you with assault and battery, and by the time I get finished, that black belt'll be all you have left, because I won't quit till I've got everything else."

Jack had never been a quick thinker. Coming up with an adequate reply took a while, but even Pete would have to admit he succeeded. "That's just like you, Barrington. Walk into a building full of men, and the only person you come out remembering's a woman."

They left him there alone to face his patients.

———

A couple of days ago, after he'd gone into the police station and let a technician from the state crime lab use a buccal swab on him, he'd walked back outside and flicked his cell phone on to find he'd missed a call from Tim. Standing there, he hit the Dial button.

"Hey," Tim said.

Pete could hear noise in the background, a bunch of voices chattering at once. "Where are you?"

"At the courthouse," Tim said. "But hold on, I'm going outside." Soon the noise subsided. "Listen, I was driving by the police station this morning when I saw the Volvo parked in the lot."

"Yeah. That's where I am now."

Tim's voice rose in pitch. "At the police station?"

"Outside it."

"What are you doing there, Pete? Did they tell you to come in?"

"They're running a DNA on me."

"Why?"

"You'd have to ask the police chief that. He didn't tell me. He asked me nicely, and I complied so he wouldn't have to serve me with a search warrant."

"What makes you think he would've done that?"

"The look I saw in his eye."

"Pete . . . Henderson's not treating you like a suspect, is he?"

Across the alley, at First Baptist, an elderly black man who'd been raking leaves paused to study Pete. When the man realized Pete was looking back, he started raking again.

"I wouldn't say he's treating me like a suspect. Nor would I say he isn't."

Tim's voice dropped to a whisper. "There's a rumor going around town that Angela was raped. That . . . that's not what happened, is it?"

Pete was standing right next to the Volvo. A well-made car, it could take a little bouncing. He pressed down on the roof as hard as he could. Once. Twice. Three times. The wagon rocked on its shocks, conducting some of his anger, though not all of it, right into the pavement. "Now that," he said, "is something you'd have to ask the medical examiner. Want to drive down to Jackson and do that? Go down there and ask what they found when they examined her body?" Cellular silence was deeper, it had always seemed to him, than the kind you heard on landlines. "Tim?"

"Yeah?"

"I'm sorry I said that."

"I'm sorry you had to."

"There's something else I need to say too. It's kind of in the same category. Are you in a listening mood?"

"I'll be in a listening mood the rest of my life."

"It's about Angela's cell phone."

"Yeah?" The reply sounded synthesized, as if it had been run through one of those electronic toys loved by rock guitarists in the '60s.

"Henderson asked me just now if I'd found it. They combed the house for hours the other night and I guess it was one of the things they were looking for, though they didn't mention it at the time. Anyhow, the thing is, I *did* find it. And it's no wonder they didn't, because it was in a pot under the stove, at the back of the cabinet. I came across it when I made soup the other day. I guess she kept it in there so I wouldn't ever pick it up and see her calls list or her text message in-box.

"I don't know what kind of retrieval technology Cellular South has. If Ken Starr could dredge up e-mails the president of the United States had already deleted, I guess anything's possible. But I wanted you to know I took the phone into the garage and threw it on the floor, which was enough to bust it open—"

"Jesus," Tim said.

"—and then I got a hammer and pretty much reduced the pieces to something that looked a lot like brake dust."

On the phone he heard a loud noise.

"What was that?"

"That was me getting into my truck," Tim said. "Now I want you to get into that Volvo."

"Why?"

"Christ, Pete . . . you're standing outside the fucking *police* station."

"Well, I don't have anything to hide. Everything I ever did that I tried to keep hidden's already entered the public domain."

"You've suppressed *evidence,* for Jesus' sake. Will you get into the fucking car? No, wait. . . . God, I can't think straight. Pete, I've got a *kid* to look after."

"Me too."

"Yeah, I know you do. Believe me, I'm thinking about yours and mine both."

Pete could almost see him sitting in his truck, holding a hand to his forehead as he faced yet another personal disaster, this one potentially larger than all the others combined.

"Let's get off these damn cell phones," Tim pleaded. "Can you meet me over at my place?"

Ten minutes later, they were sitting in his living room, Pete in a lumpy armchair, Tim on the couch next to a stack of bedclothes. He said his daughter was sleeping there now. They'd move just as soon as he could find a new place.

The room didn't look as bad as Pete had expected, given what Tim had said about his living conditions, but then his daughter had probably straightened things up. Still, there was dust in the corners, the rug needed cleaning and the walls were completely bare. For a moment, he tried to imagine Angela here, on that very couch with his oldest friend, unbothered by the squalid surroundings.

His imagination failed him. He couldn't see it. Which proved she'd known him a lot better than he'd known her. Because she'd had no difficulty imagining him and Nora together and had even recounted, with uncanny accuracy, what had occurred the first time they made love, how her scarred breastbone would have possessed magnetic properties, drawing his hands there as though he hoped to heal her with his touch.

Tim was saying something about Frank Henderson, how he could lull you into thinking he didn't know what he was doing, when in fact he knew exactly what he was doing and, more often than not, what you were doing too.

"Well, I'm not doing anything I'm ashamed of," Pete said. "Not now, anyway. And as for that cell phone, it's hard for me to see how destroying it would qualify as suppression of evidence when nobody had even asked me about it yet."

"That'd depend," Tim said, "on what you discovered when you looked at it. On what any reasonable person in that situation would've concluded about its importance or lack thereof."

"You know, I never have liked the way lawyers talk."

"Most doctors don't."

"A lawyer once tried to kill me."

"This'd be the guy who barged into your office out in Fresno armed for bear?"

"How long have you known about that?" Pete asked.

"Since the day you called me last spring and said you were thinking of moving back home. I figured something must have gone wrong. Because I never knew you to be crazy, and only a crazy person'd leave California for this place, unless he had to. So I did a little bit of checking around."

"You didn't tell Rashard Killingsworth what you found?"

"I didn't tell a soul. But that doesn't mean nobody knows. I can just about guarantee you that by now Frank Henderson does."

"I don't have much of a question about that."

"Got a question about anything else?"

"I got all kinds of questions." He rose and walked over to the window, pulled the grimy curtain aside and looked out. By now, probably half the town knew he'd driven over to his wife's lover's place and that the two of them were in here talking. He'd never understood why so many people were absorbed in the sex lives of others, but they were. Evidently every community needed a few folks who, through their inability to control their worst urges, could keep the rest of the population entertained. Rather than express their gratitude, though, the audience threw eggs at the performers, showing them no mercy. Whereas he pitied anybody who felt the need, at any given moment, to make love. His heart went out to lovers much as it did to those suffering from chronic pain. Sex was a sickness for which he knew no cure.

He let the curtain fall, then turned to face his friend. "Have you got anything you want to ask me, Tim?"

"Like what?"

"Like whether or not I did it."

"What?"

"Are you wondering if I killed her?"

Tim's face went through various stages of collapse: an initial quiver, then the grooves near the corners of his mouth deepened into ravines, then the whole structure sagged. "God, Pete. Are you out of your mind?" For a moment, it looked as if he'd cry. "Maybe you got a question for me along those lines. Is that where we're headed, Pete? You wondering if I was at your place the other day, before the team left for Greenville?"

Pete walked over to the chair and sat back down. "I know exactly where you were the other day," he said. "I know where she was too. And I know what time she left you here and went home."

"The thing is—"

Pete held his hand up. "The thing is," he said, "*I* know those facts, Tim. But Frank Henderson doesn't. And when he runs that DNA on me and doesn't get the match he's looking for, I have a feeling he'll look elsewhere."

HER FATHER'S FRIEND, Sandra Jean Sturdivant, drove her home on Friday afternoon, as she had every day that week. Ms. Sturdivant was a little hyper, prone to extravagant speech and sweeping gestures, but Toni had come to appreciate her. Like most adults, she made you feel that she had one face for kids, another for grown-ups and yet a third that nobody saw except herself. Toni personally would've liked the last better than the first, and felt pretty sure that she wouldn't like the second much at all. Unfortunately, that was the one the lady had to depend on, and you could tell it had not served her well.

"Hon, would you like me to fix you something to eat?" Ms. Sturdivant asked as they pulled into the driveway. "Maybe a quiche? I make a mean one."

She'd made a quiche on Wednesday. While she prepared it, Toni sat at the table watching her move around the kitchen, talking constantly and somehow managing to create the impression that she was onstage in a musical, one of those really corny ones like *Oklahoma!* or *Annie Get Your Gun.*

"You know, I'm not really hungry this afternoon," she said. She pretended to yawn. "I think maybe I'll just go in and take a nap."

"You'll be okay? On your own?"

"I think so. And my dad said he'd come home before the team's pregame meal."

"I admire your dad. I really do. Most folks'd just lie down and quit. But he never was the quitting kind." Ms. Sturdivant leaned over the transmission hump and hugged her. "Sweetheart," she said, "things won't always be as bad for y'all as they are this week. Ground that's brown today'll turn green tomorrow. That's what I always tell myself, and so far I haven't seen any ironclad evidence to convince me it's a lie."

On that cheerful note, she patted Toni's hand, then watched while she got out and walked across the yard to the house.

———

Rather than get in bed, she sat down at the piano but didn't take out any music. Her father used to tease her when she was younger, asking her to play "Danny Boy" or "Tennessee Waltz" just to hear her admit that she couldn't do either one, not without any music. He'd rifle through his CDs, pulling out Keith Jarrett's recording of Shostakovich's *Preludes and Fugues*. "See?" he'd say, waving it at her. "Keith can play this stuff." Then he'd lay it back on the shelf and pull another one out and pop it in the CD player. "But he can also play *this*." And Jarrett would cut loose on some old bebop warhorse like "Scrapple from the Apple" or "Bouncing with Bud."

"In life," he always concluded, "you need to learn to improvise. Sooner or later, everybody has to play without a score."

She had no score now. She'd be without one from now on out.

She played a couple of intervals that sounded good together—the E above middle C, back down to C, then the A—and instead of focusing on time signature was trying to add some dynamics. The results didn't sound all that good, but they didn't sound awful either.

She'd thought a lot these past few days about the music her parents preferred. Her mother's love of the great late romantics like Scriabin and Rachmaninoff had always seemed odd. By rights, given her formality, she should have been drawn to the rigorous logic of the Viennese classics. Her father, when not listening to country music, always chose Bill Evans and Keith Jarrett, yet professed an inability to identify with the music her mother liked, and she in turn could stand neither Jarrett nor Evans. Whereas to Toni's ear, works like Rachmaninoff's *Morceaux de salon* had a lot in common with modern jazz.

In her mind she'd listed traits each of her parents exhibited—their taste in food and books, the places they liked and disliked—in an effort to come up with the answer to one simple question: what made them different? She'd finally decided that while the question might be simple, answering it wouldn't yield much useful information. People could be different and get along just fine—she and Mason seemed to fall into that category—or they could be just alike and drive each other crazy. No formula for good music existed, and neither did a formula for happiness.

When her father came home, she was still sitting on the piano bench, but her head and elbows were resting against the music stand, her cheeks moist and hot. She hadn't even heard him walk in. She'd gone to sleep after all.

"Can I sit down there?" he asked.

"I don't know if it'll hold you."

"There's a lot less of me lately," he said, and she realized for the first time that he'd lost weight. His face was pale, and his cheeks had a sunken-in look she found alarming. She scooted over.

He sat down beside her and put his arm around her. "You've met Tim's daughter by now, haven't you?"

Just yesterday, she'd been standing by her locker with Mason, who was trying to convince her to let him skip this week's game and take her to a movie or just come over to her house and hang out. The team didn't need him, he said, and Coach Killingsworth had already okayed his absence. She was about to tell him she wanted him to do what he always did on Friday night when she became aware that somebody was standing right behind her.

"Don't let me intrude on your conversation," a voice said.

She turned to find someone she'd never seen before. The girl wore neither rouge nor eyeshadow, no makeup of any kind, and her clothes looked no different from Toni's. Yet something about her suggested that she'd been put together from pieces that didn't quite match. An arm from this mannequin, a neck from that one.

"Susan?" Mason said.

"Afraid so."

"What are you doing here?"

"The city of Jackson declared me a municipal hazard and sent me back. This was after I put the dead mouse in a jar of mayo at Winn-Dixie."

He shook his head. "Same old same old. Always trying to stick your foot into a glove, hoping everybody'll think it's cool." He put his arm around Toni then and nudged her in the opposite direction, and though it struck her as rude she allowed him to propel her down the hall. When she asked who the girl was, he said she was Coach Kessler's daughter, that she used to go to school here and was always on the brink of getting expelled. Teachers couldn't stand her. Neither could he.

"I met her yesterday," she told her dad, "but we didn't really have a chance to talk."

"Well, she's got her driver's license, and Tim's hoping you'll let her come over here tonight, that maybe the two of you could watch a movie or something and get acquainted. She was living with her . . ." His voice trailed off, as if he couldn't say the word. "She was living with Tim's ex-wife, but that didn't work out, and she'll be staying with her dad now. So what do you say, hon? I'd feel a lot better if I knew you had some company tonight."

"You're assuming I don't want to go to the ball game."

"Do you?"

"No," she said. "But I don't want you to make those kinds of assumptions. I want you to ask me."

"All right. I'll always ask from now on. Just as I'm asking you if you'll let Susan Kessler come over this evening."

Rolling her eyes when he made a request of her had become second nature, and she almost did it again. But at the last instant, she managed to blink instead. "Okay," she said.

She hadn't liked the girl and didn't want her to come over, but the presence of another person would clearly make her father rest easier. And after all, what could it possibly cost her?

———

"I've never been to California. But I *have* seen New York City, though I don't remember much about it, except one of our taxi drivers—we took taxis all the time, because Momma said the subway smelled bad—he told us he'd never *once* left New York, even though he was about two hundred years old. I mean, I know it's not like saying you've never been out of Loring, but still. Can you believe that? Kent—that's my momma's new guy—he says that's why New York and California vote the opposite of the rest of the country. They're kind of insular, you know what I mean? Like if you grow up in Mississippi, you kind of know you're nowhere and want to go somewhere else, so you pay attention to other places and how people think there, even if you disagree with them. But I guess maybe if you grow up in New York or California, you know you're somewhere, so you kind of naturally assume the rest of the country's nowhere and don't care about the people who live there or what they think. Does that make any sense?"

"Not really," Toni said.

Susan laughed, locked her hands behind her head and rocked back against the arm of the couch. "That's what my daddy said when I told him Kent's theory. He also told me not to try it out on you, since you're from California. But I can see you're not the type to get offended." Leaning forward again, she drew her knees up to her chest and rested her chin on them. "You aren't, are you?"

Her mouth had been running for at least thirty minutes. Toni hoped the frozen burritos she'd stuck in the oven would be ready soon. Surely the girl couldn't talk and eat at the same time. "I wouldn't say I'm *easily* offended."

"Which is not the same thing," Susan said, "as saying you're not offended at all."

"I'm glad to see you grasp the nuance."

"Oh, you bet I do." She lifted one hand and wiggled her fingers. "Growing up in a house like mine'll turn you into a regular seismograph."

That was the first thing Susan Kessler had said that sounded halfway intelligent. "I know a thing or two," Toni told her, "about those kinds of tremors."

"Do you think everybody does? Or just people like us?"

"What do you mean, *people like us*?"

"Oh, you know. Girls with indigent dads."

For the first time in recent memory Toni sprang to her father's defense, leaping off the couch and towering over the girl. "My dad isn't indigent. As far as that goes, yours isn't either. You don't know what the word means."

"On the contrary," said Susan, "I most certainly do. The primary meaning of the word is *impoverished*. But the secondary meaning is *lacking* or *deficient*. And it's the secondary meaning I was using."

"My dad isn't lacking anything except my mom," Toni said, as her eyes began to sting.

To her horror, the other girl stood up, reached out and—before Toni could push her away—put her arms around her. She smelled like cigarette smoke. "Of course your dad lacks something else," she said. "Because people say he's an interesting guy. Just like my dad. And it's what they don't have that makes them interesting. Now here's another word I know. *Raptorial.* Adapted to the seeking of prey. Most grown men are raptorial. But your daddy and mine? Hell, sweetheart, they only prey on themselves."

———

The team Pete watched from the press box bore little resemblance to the one that had worn Loring's uniforms the previous week. On their first possession, two illegal-procedure penalties and a quarterback sack pushed them back to their own six. Then the center snapped the ball over the head of the punter, resulting in a safety, and on the following free kick South Panola's return man brought the ball back inside the ten. Two sweeps and they were in the end zone, the home team down by nine.

On the next series Pete got confused about down and distance and tried to run the gimpy Reggie McDonald off tackle on third and long. Killingsworth never said a word, just signaled in his own play. He did the same thing in the second quarter too, substituting an option on second and one when Pete had called for the wideout to run a wheel route.

In the locker room at halftime, trailing 16–3, the head coach pulled Pete into one of the shower stalls. "Listen," he said, "why don't you go on home and see your daughter?"

"What?"

"Your head's not in the game, Coach. Frankly, I don't know how it could be."

Pete couldn't really argue with that assessment. At the office this afternoon he'd received a small silver box with a pull-out drawer containing ashes. Toni hadn't broached the subject yet, but it was only a matter of time until she'd demand to know what had happened to her mother's remains.

He was trying to find the words to tell Killingsworth that he needed the game now more than ever when Tim stepped into the stall. "What's going on here, Rashard?" he asked.

Killingsworth's jaw began to quiver. Like a lot of coaches, he'd spent many years in a world that consisted largely of two groups—those who wore the right color jerseys and those who wore the wrong color—and it might have been this factor that led him to see things so simply. Whatever the reason, he made it clear that a line divided him from Tim Kessler, though color had nothing to do with it. "Coach Kessler," he said, "I'm going to tell you something. In fact, I'm going to tell you several somethings. First, I didn't invite you into this shower stall. Second, I don't want you in this shower stall. Third, since you're in this shower stall with me and Coach Barrington against my wishes, you may as well know that a lot of these boys on our team have seen some bad examples set by men who could've made a difference in their lives. Assholes that run out on their wives and children, for instance, because they can't say no to booze and crack—or keep themselves from chasing skirt."

"I've been drunk a good bit," Tim admitted, "but I never did crack in my life, Rashard, and I didn't run out on my wife and kid either. My wife ran out on me. And my daughter's living with me again."

Killingsworth shook his head. "This is turning into *Judge Judy,*" he said. "I got to go figure out how to win this goddamn game." He walked out and left them standing there in the stall.

After a moment or two, Tim said, "Well, what do you think we ought to do, Pete? Take a shower?"

———

"Them boys kicking our asses," Shontell Clemons observed, pulling off his headgear and flinging himself onto the bench. "You lucky to be over here, Depot. That number seventy-five about done hurt my pride."

Mason DePoyster felt anything but lucky. On the sideline, where he'd spent most of his time as a football player, you could do a lot of thinking. For that reason more than any other, he wished somebody would get injured so Coach Killingsworth would have to send him onto the field. Like most backups, he rarely wished to enter the game, because when you sat on the bench play after play, watching your betters butt heads and listening to their grunts and cries, you'd be crazy not to get scared. But everything that scared him tonight was inside his head. He wouldn't have minded if somebody hit him hard enough to knock him senseless.

In the shotgun formation Cody Blackstone took the snap, held the ball for three or four seconds, then hurled a wobbly pass over the middle, hitting a South Panola linebacker right in the hands. Surprised, the kid stood there for a moment, then took off toward Loring's goal line. Cody ran him out of bounds near the five.

Shontell grabbed his headgear. "Coach K calling stupid plays," he said. "Even somebody dumb as me know that." He jumped up with the rest of the defense and jogged back onto the field.

Mason turned and looked over his shoulder—first at the press box, where the space normally occupied by Toni's dad was now vacant, then at the bleachers, row five, section C, where his parents sat together, just as always.

In the last couple of days, a feeling of suspension had set in around his house, as though real time had temporarily stopped. On Wednesday morning he'd opened his bedroom door and stepped into the hallway, and it was as if he'd wandered onto a soundstage. Sunlight was streaming through the window, and on the radio the weatherman was talking about dew-point levels and barometric pressure. From the kitchen came the odor of frying bacon and the sound of his mother's voice. She was speaking to his father. "Want orange juice?"

"Sure."

The Jackson paper lay open on the table. When Mason walked by, his dad said, "Well, son, looks like we're headed for a few days of good weather."

His mother was still in her bathrobe. She laid her spatula down, put her arm around Mason and offered him her cheek, which, out of habit, he kissed. "What about you?" she said, and he made some kind of animal sound. "What about you?" she said again. "Want some orange juice?" He must have nodded, because she set a second glass down on the counter and reached for the Minute Maid carton.

Each of the last few mornings had followed the same pattern, and so had each of the evenings. At dinner they said prayers, and both his mother and father included Toni and her dad in them. His father prayed for the soul of Toni's mother, asking God to grant her entrance into His kingdom, and while he prayed Mason watched him. His dad's eyes were shut, his face relaxed. "We pray that she's there with You tonight, God," he said. "We pray that she'll be there with You always, that one day she'll be reunited with those she loved, that between now and then their suffering will somehow be lessened, that they'll remember only the good in the lives they shared with one another, that somehow those memories will come to fill their hearts with joy until they rejoin their loved ones in Your eternal presence." His father's hands came together atop the table. "And dear God in heaven, we pray for the soul of the guilty. For the souls of all the guilty everywhere. Forgive all of us, God, for our sins, and please, dear Heavenly Father, remove the stains from our hearts."

On the field, a South Panola running back bulled past Shontell Clemons into the Loring end zone. A groan arose from the home-town fans.

Mason got up off the bench, walked over to the fence that sepa-rated the field from the bleachers and stood there watching his father until his dad's gaze met his own. For a moment they stared at each other. Then his father clapped his hands and shouted something. While Mason couldn't hear the words over the noise of the crowd, he understood them perfectly.

Come on, team. Let's go.

———

For good measure, Alan clapped again. "Come on, boys. You can beat these fellows, I know you can."

Nancy was eating like crazy these days, putting on more weight, and tonight she'd bought a bucket of popcorn. He reached down and grabbed a handful and stuck it into his mouth, and though the taste of rancid butter almost made him gag, he kept chewing and swallowing while his son observed him from the sideline.

"The day'll come when you face God, Alan," Wade Phelps had said the other day, as they sat together in Alan's pickup near a row of overflowing trash cans at the rear of the parsonage. "But you've repented, so you don't have to fear it. As for what you should do between now and then—that, my friend, I can't tell you. I can only tell you what you shouldn't do. You mustn't willfully cause more suffering. Notice I didn't say inadvertently. I said willfully. As you've discovered, being a Christian doesn't mean you're perfect. On the contrary, it means living every day knowing just how imperfect you are." The minister gestured at one of the trash cans. "The garbage in there's mine," he said. "I acknowledge it. And my trash stinks as bad as anybody else's. Yours does too. There's not a lot of love in garbage."

That neither of them would look for love in a garbage can, Alan understood now, was beside the point. Folks took their love where they could find it, and some found it on the refuse pile.

Let's go, guys. Play hard.

———

"I got these old things from my dad's place," Susan said. She lifted several large books out of the Clorox box she'd brought along. Each one was bound in imitation leather, with black and gold stripes across the cover. The one on top said *1980 Leopards' Ledger*. "That's the year our dads graduated. You won't believe what some of these people look like."

She started with the senior pictures. All of the guys wore black coats, white shirts and bow ties, and their hair was uniformly long. The girls wore black gowns that showed off their shoulders. Many sported fake lashes.

"Here's my dad," Susan said. "Doesn't he remind you of something like, I don't know, maybe a golden retriever?"

He certainly looked shaggy. Beneath his picture, in telegraphic style, appeared a passage intended to sum up his years at Loring High.

No. 24 . . . Pete's best pal . . . he's Ole Miss–bound . . . likes to ride the levee . . . "Hello, I'm me, may I kiss you please?" . . . wants to be a lawyer (so he'll know which laws to break) . . . a number-two chili cheeseburger, please ma'am, with double dills on the side . . . he ain't heavy, he's lighthearted T. K. . . . silliest senior . . . most likely to . . . ?

"If that last phrase had continued," Susan said cheerfully, "I imagine it would've ended with *fuck up*." She offered Toni the book. "Want to see your dad?"

Toni turned to the Bs. If he owned one of these yearbooks, he'd kept it hidden, and she'd never seen his graduation picture before. All the other boys were smiling, but not him. He looked at the camera in an appraising manner, as if measuring the distance between himself and the lens.

No. 88 . . . the good hands man . . . headed for Fresno State (don't worry if you never heard of it, he'll put it on the map) . . . senior class president . . . all-State . . . brains AND brawn . . . wants to be a doctor (and we know what kind!) . . . Sandra Jean . . . Ellen . . . Mitzi . . . Lee Ann . . . M is for MYSTERY . . . a real LADY's man . . .

She flipped backwards through the yearbook, looking for a picture of Mason's dad. He wasn't among the seniors, but she found him with the juniors. Alan DePoyster. He didn't look that much like his son. His features were smaller and kind of compressed, but you could see a faint resemblance. There was no information on the juniors, only the student's name.

She turned the pages again, flipping through Class Favorites, Athletics, Faculty and Parents' Organizations. Nothing much of interest, but to be polite she said, "I'm glad I got to see that," and handed it back.

When Susan leaned over to pull another yearbook from the stack, her hair fell forward, revealing her left ear. An amber earring dangled from it. The amber was embedded in an oblong silver locket, and you could see little greenish bubbles inside.

"That's an interesting earring," Toni said.

"You like it?"

"It's unusual."

"I've only got one." She giggled. "I found it between the cushions of my dad's couch," she said. "He won't tell me who left it there."

"Let's see how our girls are taking to each other," Tim said when they pulled into the driveway.

Pete switched off the ignition but didn't open the door. He sat there with his hands gripping the wheel, thinking how he'd pulled into the same driveway just a week ago tonight, of the scene he'd found inside.

Tim must have known what was going through his mind. He reached over and laid a hand on his knee. "This is now," he said. "Last Friday night was then. Sometimes it seems like trouble's got legs, Pete, but it doesn't. It can't run after you."

It seemed to Pete that trouble didn't need legs because it had wings. You could speed across the country trying to outdistance it, but it would be on the ground at your new destination, a dark angel waiting for you with a cold embrace. "One of my patients in Fresno," he said, "was an immigrant from Poland. He told me something one time I never will forget. He said that every year, a few days before September first, his grandmother would start stockpiling supplies, buying all kinds of stuff—meat, vegetables, eggs, butter, even a few bottles of vodka—and hiding it in her apartment. And when the first passed without another German invasion, she'd throw a big party."

"I guess I don't get it."

"I'm thinking that if I walk into that house and nothing's wrong that wasn't wrong when I left it, I might throw a party myself." He climbed out and shut the car door and started across the lawn, and in a few seconds he heard Tim get out and shut his door too.

He pulled his key out and stuck it in the lock and turned it. And as soon as he stepped inside and saw Toni sitting on the floor near a stack of old yearbooks, the other girl on her knees beside her, he knew he should never have left them alone together.

———

She held off posing the question until their guests left. She even waited until he'd gone into the bathroom and taken a shower and come back out in his bathrobe. That was when she asked him, as he stood near the foot of the bed he used to share with her mother, toweling his still-damp hair.

"Daddy?"

"Yeah, hon?"

She squeezed the amber earring she'd removed from the box on top of the dresser. "Had Mom become close friends with Mr. Kessler?"

EARTHLY EYES

A LOT OF WHAT HE KNEW about investigative work Frank Henderson had learned from watching the Loring Police Department in action forty years ago, when they kept arresting his father and other voting rights activists. On the one hand, they put to improper use almost every bit of knowledge they possessed. On the other, there wasn't much they didn't know. They came by their information the old-fashioned way: by talking to folks on street corners, in the barber shop, the grocery store and the pool hall, or just by walking around town and keeping their eyes open. They never stopped working.

"Off duty today, Officer?" his father had once asked a tall, skinny cop named Ernest Andrews as he and his son walked out of the drugstore downtown and saw the policeman leaning against a parking meter.

The cop was dressed in street clothes—a pair of khaki pants and a white short-sleeved shirt. "Till you showed up," he said, "I was just standing here waiting on my old woman, who's in the furniture store over yonder spending most of what I made in the last two or three months on a goddamn dinette set."

"And now?"

"Now I'm fixing to head into that drugstore and see who all's in there. Since you was, I figure there's the least little chance something's going on inside I might need to know about."

"Course an argument could be made," his father said, while sweat trickled down Frank's back and into the band of his underwear, "that there's more to be learned by following me home."

Several of the policeman's teeth were missing, and those that remained were stained and pointing in various directions. A few years later, in a bar out on Highway 47, he'd use a crowbar on a white man who told him he ought to buy some dentures and try to keep them clean.

"We got somebody else," he told Frank's father, "to follow you home."

Small-town policing in its most efficient form.

In the alley beside the police station, a little over three weeks after Angela Barrington was murdered by manual strangulation, Frank Henderson opened the door of his plum-colored Mercedes bound and determined to leave the office behind. Early that afternoon he'd learned that Pete Barrington's DNA didn't match the semen they'd found on his wife's body. This was no surprise to him, but it might be to the handful of patients who'd deserted the doctor in the last couple weeks and gone back to the Alexanders. Now Henderson would probably have to request a second DNA sample, though he already knew that due to what pathologists called "the window of probability," this sample, if in fact it provided a match, would not help him close his case either. Because the plain truth of the matter was that Tim Kessler was in Greenville coaching football when the woman died. You couldn't prove he'd killed her. Only that he'd fucked her, which by now everybody knew anyway.

These worrisome thoughts were going through his mind when he lowered himself into the Mercedes and somebody hollered, "Chief? Hey, Chief?"

Wade Phelps, the minister at First Baptist, had stepped out of the church's service entrance and was walking across the alley. Running into him was a fairly regular occurrence, due to their proximity. The congregation Wade preached to remained all white, a source of great embarrassment to him, and Henderson rarely missed a chance to needle the minister about it. Frank held churches in low esteem to begin with, remembering how few of the black faithful had supported his father back in the day. As for the whites, well, to hear them tell it back then, a handful of "good niggers" might somehow make it to heaven, but only a little heaven out behind the big one.

Oddly enough, Wade Phelps seemed eager to subject himself to Henderson's gentle ridicule, and ended most of their sparring sessions by inviting the chief to break the color barrier at First Baptist.

"What you up to this evening, Reverend?" Frank asked. "Crafting a sermon on the biblical justification for shoplifting?"

"No, I think I'll save that one for later. Right now I'm working up something to justify invading either Iran or Syria. I figure that'll make my congregation happy and lull them a little bit, then I'll come back again with something a little more progressive."

"Your congregation," Frank said, "represents a great argument for capital punishment, but I'd like to sentence all of them to life in our nation's capital." He laughed. "Man, can you imagine what some of those folks'd do if they found themselves out after midnight in Anacostia?"

"Speaking of sentencing," Wade said, "have you made any progress on your murder case?"

Henderson's laughter died in his throat. Put a black man in charge of anything more than a rake or a tractor, and the first time something went wrong, everybody, black and white alike, would start saying he wasn't up to the job. Rashard Killingsworth had been hearing it since he coached his first game, and now Frank was hearing it too.

The other night, someone had broken the lock on the back door at the mayor's house and left without taking anything, probably because the family's dog scared him off. The chief doubted it was anything more than a routine burglary attempt, despite the widespread panic that whoever had strangled Angela Barrington was planning to do the same thing to Loring's first lady. As the mayor put it, "Folks want some results in that murder case, Frank. Hell, *I* want some results."

Well, the ones he had back in his office weren't going to satisfy anybody. "We've learned a few things," he told Wade. "We're just not ready to make an arrest."

"But you're close?"

"*Close* is a relative term, Reverend. I could say yes or I could say no. And since either one works, I think I'll just keep quiet."

The minister squatted on his haunches by the door to the Mercedes. The whites of his eyes were streaked with red, and Frank caught a whiff of something sweet and minty. Jesus Christ, he thought, this Baptist's been drinking.

"If what I've heard's true," the minister said, "the poor lady was strangled, and there were traces of semen. Of course, you never know if what you've heard's true or not. So I'm going to speak speculatively."

Something about the look on his face and his tone of voice made Henderson recall how that chance encounter, all those years ago, had made Ernest Andrews quit leaning on the parking meter and go into the drugstore, to see what might be going on inside. "Speculatively?"

"Such as, is there any chance that the man who did the killing and the one who left the semen on the lady's body might not be the same?"

"In a purely speculative sense," the chief said, "I suppose I could entertain that line of thought."

"So when you catch the guy, if it turns out he hadn't raped Mrs. Barrington, that fact might play in his favor? When it came to sentencing, I mean."

"I'm not a judge, Reverend Phelps."

"But you know how the law works."

"Sometimes it doesn't work at all."

"Granted." Phelps gazed out at the street, where people were driving home from work, weekday traffic flowing away from downtown. Putting his hand on the pavement to steady himself, he leaned forward, until he was behind the car door. "What really worries me," he said, "is the possibility that whoever did it has so much anger stored inside himself that one day another woman'll do or say something to enrage him and he'll react the same way again."

The chief had already decided that tonight, he'd call one of his patrolmen who attended First Baptist, warn him that he'd lose his job if he breathed a word to anybody and ask for the names of every male member of the congregation. Once he had that list, Henderson would start checking off the names of those who'd attended that football game in Greenville. And after that he'd look long and hard at every name without a check mark beside it.

"What makes you so sure," he said, "that Mrs. Barrington did something to enrage him?"

Wade stood and shoved his hands in his pockets. Before turning and trudging off across the alley, he said, "I try to imagine myself committing an act like that. I'd *have* to be enraged. Wouldn't you?"

"Yeah," Frank Henderson said, "I imagine I would. Speaking speculatively."

THE CLOCK WENT OFF at six-fifteen. Pete groped, hit the wrong button and heard, instead of the buzzer, the radio, where some kind of Rush Limbaugh clone was saying the European elites, well, sure they opposed the war, but when you burned a little shoe leather and got out and talked to the people, you'd find out they supported it. "The man on the street," he assured his listeners, "has a moral consciousness you can bank on. Even in Europe."

The man on the street, if he happened to spot Pete Barrington coming toward him now, would probably drop his head, not knowing what to say. The woman on the street was, as always, a different story.

Yesterday, after football practice, he'd stopped at Wal-Mart to pick up some motor oil for his truck. He was rolling his cart to the checkout stand when somebody said, "Dr. Barrington?"

He'd noticed the woman around town once or twice right after he moved back but didn't know her name. She was tall, had thick auburn hair and long nails with a thick layer of purple polish. Though a little on the heavy side, she'd made enough of an impression that he remembered her now.

She had three or four bags of Hershey's Kisses in her cart, several sacks of popcorn and something labeled "Therapy Ball." A picture on the box showed an anorexically thin young woman balanced on top of a red sphere doing yoga exercises.

She noticed him eyeing the last item. "It says it's the biggest ball they've got. Though I don't know if it's big enough for me."

"Well, it's probably even big enough for me," he said. "But you can hurt yourself with one of those if you don't know what you're doing."

"Then I may get hurt, because I definitely don't know. By the way, I'm Mason DePoyster's mother."

If you'd lined up every woman he'd seen since coming back to Loring and asked which one he thought was Alan DePoyster's wife, she would probably have been the last one he'd pick. It wasn't just her size—taller than Alan, and she likely outweighed him—but something else, some quality he couldn't quite put his finger on. Something you didn't associate with Alan or imagine him valuing.

"Mason's a fine young man," he said. "I'm sure you're proud of him, and you should be."

She was moving alongside him down the wide aisle that paralleled the checkout stands.

"He really likes your daughter," she said. "I haven't met her yet, but I know Mason wouldn't be so crazy about her if she wasn't someone special."

He stopped beside a display of off-brand grape juice. For a moment, as he stared at the shelves filled with shoddy merchandise, he was transported back to the dollar store, where all those years ago another woman linked to Alan, whose first name he didn't know, had asked him, "Running today?"

Mason's mom stopped rolling her cart. "Is something wrong, Dr. Barrington? I mean, I know something's wrong, and I'm so horribly sorry, and I hope I haven't done or said anything to add to it. I just wanted to say hello, that's all. Because of Mason and your daughter, I mean."

He knew then why he would never have connected this woman with Alan. It had to do with how easily she'd fallen into step alongside him, how she'd stopped when he did, her willingness, even now that he was behaving in an embarrassing manner, to look him in the eye rather than focusing, as most people would have, on the floor or the junk in her shopping cart.

"Does it ever seem to you," he asked, "as if certain scenes in your life just keep repeating themselves?"

Rather than answer him, she said, "I was in a dramatic production at my church last year and kept flubbing all my lines. Had trouble with every scene I was in. I guess I'm doing it again."

"No, not at all. What role did you play?"

"Mary Magdalene."

He let her steer into the checkout stand first, and she paid with cash.

"I'm surprised you're buying things here," he said, because he felt like he had to say something and it was all he could think of. "After all, your husband runs a grocery store."

"If you were me, would you want your husband knowing you couldn't control your appetite?"

He could have told her there were different kinds of appetites, and his wife, when she was alive, knew all too well he couldn't control one of his. Instead, he kept quiet, just pulled out his platinum Visa and handed it to the checker, who turned it over and examined it front and back, as if she'd never seen anything quite like it. While she rang up his motor oil, Alan's wife waited, then they walked out into the parking lot together.

She stopped behind an eight- or ten-year-old Bonneville.

"Want me to put that stuff in the trunk for you?" he asked.

"Sure. All except one bag of candy."

She raised the lid, and he put the therapy ball and the popcorn and the rest of the candy inside, then pushed the trunk closed and offered her his hand.

She held it a little longer than she absolutely had to. "You haven't asked," she said, "but I thought I should mention that my name's Nancy."

———

The hardest part of every day was waking Toni. She continued to sleep in the bed with him, lying where her mother used to, and in the morning she clung tenaciously to her pillow. He'd been giving her .25 milligrams of Xanax every evening while taking .5 himself, but had already told her that next week they were going to stop medicating themselves: Xanax was addictive, and sooner or later, unless they upped the dosage, it would stop working anyway.

This morning he let her stay in bed while he made coffee, turned the radio on and poured two bowls of cereal. The NPR news was just signing off, and underneath the voice announcing the program's sponsors, he caught a few notes of a Chopin étude that Angela used to play, then realized he was finished for the day.

———

"I've seen the river," Toni said. "I saw it when we were moving here."

"Yeah, I know you did. But it's one thing to see it from the Greenville bridge and another thing from where I've got in mind."

He'd called the office and told his new receptionist to reschedule the day's appointments, and now they were driving north on 61, the old blues highway, heading up toward Cleveland. Toni hadn't been happy at breakfast to hear that he wanted her to skip school this morning. When he stepped out of the shower, he learned why: she was leaving a message for Mason, telling him not to worry, that she'd be back around noon.

On either side of the road, cotton fields stretched out to the horizon. Picking had almost been finished, and the fields had that bedraggled, leftover look, a few stringy white fibers hanging from each stalk. Growing up, he'd always considered fall his favorite season, and one big thing in its favor was that it preceded winter. When these fields had been picked down to a few broken gray stalks and all the leaves had fallen from the trees, the Delta was hell to behold. The wind came howling down off the Great Plains. Everything froze, and you could freeze along with it.

For several days now he'd been wanting just to climb in the Volvo with Toni and go, without caring much about the destination. He'd become, apparently, the kind of person who turned tail and ran away. That was what he'd done back in the summer. And when you've run once, his grandmother used to tell him, it's always easy to do it again.

"Hon," he said, "how are you feeling about where we are right now?"

"I wish I'd just gone to school."

He started to clarify his question, thinking she hadn't understood him, but then realized that in all likelihood her answer would remain the same. She'd been a stranger just a few months ago, but now, even after being hit by the worst tragedy one could imagine, she must feel like she belonged. He didn't need to guess who'd made her feel that way. "I'll get you back by lunch," he said. "I guarantee it."

In Cleveland, they turned west and headed for Rosedale. When they got there, he crossed Highway 1, drove over the levee and stopped in a small park on the riverbank beside an observation tower. The park was deserted today, as it almost always was when he used to come here twenty-five years ago.

"Let's get out," he said, "and climb the tower. You can get a pretty good view from up there."

She slogged along beside him to the foot of the wooden structure. Several times, in recent years, it had been partly submerged, and the condition of the lowest steps was parlous.

"You first," he said.

"Why?"

"If you fall on me, I'll catch you. If I fall on you—well, we're both in trouble."

"And with our luck," she said, "that's exactly what'd happen."

The faint tremors just below her maxillae suggested tears, but instead she laughed. When he tried to recall the last time that had happened, he couldn't. It seemed like years ago.

She turned and put a tentative foot on the first step, which groaned but didn't break. Holding on to the rusty handrail, she began to climb. He let her reach the first landing before following.

The tower stood thirty-five or forty feet tall. From the observation deck, they could see across the treetops on the Arkansas side to the cotton fields beyond. A sulfurous odor hung in the air.

Toni wrinkled her nose. "What's that awful smell?"

"Remember the town in Arkansas we passed through last summer, the one that kind of curved around a lake?"

"Not really."

"Well, that was Pine Bluff. It's about fifty miles west of here. There's a big paper mill near the city, and when the wind blows from the west, you can smell that thing for a hundred miles."

The Mississippi was fairly high, owing to all the recent rain. He'd hoped maybe a tugboat would be out there plowing the water, but the great river lay clear of traffic as far as they could see. "I used to come here every few days," he said, "the summer before I left for California. I'd just turned eighteen."

"That's a pretty long drive, to climb a rickety tower."

"The tower wasn't rickety back then. It'd just been built."

"You wanted to see the river that bad?"

"It's one of the tallest structures in the Delta, at least that you can get up on. Things like water towers and TV and radio towers, you know, usually have fences around them. And I wanted to be up high."

She was looking at him now like she used to as a child. He had all her attention. "Why?"

He'd been driven at the time by the determination to rise above the flat landscape, where the only thing that mattered was how many acres you owned and whether or not they were buckshot or sandy loam. He wanted to rise so high above it that nobody on the ground could touch him. At the same time, there was another consideration: he'd been banished from the basement where he'd stolen his first pleasure. She said he was getting too attached, something neither of them could afford. And he liked knowing he was higher than she was.

"This'll sound funny to you," he said, "because you've already been to a lot of foreign countries and seen Prague and London and Florence and so on. But when I was eighteen and getting ready to leave for Fresno, I'd never even been on the other side of the river."

"You'd never gone to Arkansas?"

"Not then."

"Had you ever been out of Mississippi at all?"

"Yeah, I'd been to Memphis a few times and even flew to Atlanta when Georgia Tech recruited me to play football, though they finally backed off. My coach sent game film all over the country, but I'd played against such poor competition in high school that in the end I got only four offers—Southern Mississippi, Ole Miss, Memphis State and Fresno State. I took the last one, sight unseen, because it was the farthest away."

The wind had picked up. Whitecaps were starting to speckle the brown band of water, and he watched a piece of driftwood, caught in an eddy, sink below the surface.

"I think when I was up here back then," he said, "I was trying to see out to California. Trying to imagine what awaited me there."

"For you, it wasn't real yet." She didn't pull away when he put his arm around her.

"In some ways," he said, "it still isn't." That didn't sound right, so he added, "There's just something about the place you grow up. It doesn't matter how long you've been away, when you come back it can start to feel like you never left. Like everything that happened to you someplace else is less real than what happened to you here. Except it wasn't. You're the proof of that." That didn't sound right either, so he decided to give up and stare at the river.

Toni stared along with him. "We read *Huckleberry Finn* last year," she said. "At University High. And my teacher said it was about the lines that divide us—black from white, north from south, east from west, slave state from free state. He said the river cuts the country in half but that in the novel it's kind of like a state itself. That when Huck and Jim were on their raft, what was happening on the shore didn't matter."

"I'd say that's pretty accurate," he said. "Though it's been a long time since I read it."

"I'd like to be someplace," she said, "where what's happened to us didn't matter."

"You think such a place exists?"

"No. But that doesn't mean I can't wish it."

"What about you and Mason? If you went to the Land of Oz, you wouldn't get to hang out with him."

"On a raft I would."

"Think you'd like being on a raft with him?"

"Possibly." For her, a bold admission.

"You think you could make a little space on it for me?"

"With you on it," she said, "we might sink. You'd probably weigh it down."

"I could just swim along beside y'all. I used to have a pretty good stroke."

"Daddy?"

He could tell from her tone of voice that the time for playful banter had suddenly passed. "Yeah, hon?"

"You never did answer my question about Mom and Mr. Kessler."

"I thought I did."

"No, you really didn't. You just said it was natural that they'd become friends. Then you changed the subject."

Please, he thought. Don't make me take anything else away from you. "Well, I didn't think the subject really needed any more explanation," he told her. "Mom became friends with Mr. Kessler because he and I are old friends. In fact, I guess he and I are best friends. Want to tell me why this has stayed on your mind?"

She put her hand in the pocket of her jeans and made a fist, like she was squeezing something. "Daddy?" she said.

"Yeah, hon?"

"Let's just say I miss my mother horribly and just leave it at that."

"All right," he said. "We can leave it at that forever."

———

He parked in front of the high school at a quarter till twelve. "Got you here for lunch," he said, "just like I promised. Need me to write you a tardy note?"

"No. Besides, what would you say? 'I took my daughter to climb a rotten tower so we could get a good whiff of a paper mill'? I'll be fine, Dad. Relax." She leaned over and kissed his cheek. "See you this afternoon."

After she disappeared inside the building, he sat there. For the first time in a good while, he had time on his hands and nowhere to go. No patients to see, no lover to meet for champagne and sex, no wife to go home to and deceive. Nothing to do except sit in the parking lot outside the school that still displayed his picture in the hall. If he wanted to, he could walk right in and stand there before it honing his math skills, subtracting the boy he'd been then from the man he was today.

Everybody knows about this place," Mason told her, "but hardly anybody's ever been inside it."

He was sitting on a wheeled mop bucket, pushing himself back and forth in rhythmic motion, a few inches here, a few inches there, dirty water sloshing against the galvanized metal.

A bare lightbulb dangled from the ceiling. Brooms and dust mops stood propped against the wall, and the tiny room beneath the staircase stank of disinfectant. The janitor had given him the key.

She pulled wax paper away from the soggy ham and cheese she'd made this morning, then remembered the elaborate sandwiches her mother used to prepare: roast beef with Roquefort and caramelized shallots, shredded pork with lemon coleslaw, softshell crab with almond mayonnaise. Toni usually stripped off most of the fancy stuff before she ate them, but that didn't matter. What mattered was that her mother had made them for *her*.

She laid the sandwich down on the wax paper and buried her face in her hands.

The mop bucket creaked, and immediately Mason was in front of her, pulling her hands away and pressing her face to his chest.

His woolen sweater made her nose itch. "I'm allergic," she said.

"To me?"

"To wool."

"You think I'm a sheep?"

She couldn't help laughing for the second time that day. "I'm all right," she said. "I just realized what a lousy sandwich I made."

"Want mine?"

It lay on top of his lunch box, grape jelly oozing from between two slices of styrofoam.

"No thanks. Yours looks even worse."

She was sitting sideways in an old student desk, one whose wooden writing surface was actually wooden, not the laminated kind. Generations of bored kids had scratched all kinds of inscriptions into it—*John + Connie, R. L. B. loves K. M. A., Coach Collier Sucks, I hope Larry Jeffcoat gets sent to Viet Nam.* Her dad's name, though, was nowhere in evidence. Sandwich in her left hand, she used her free index finger to trace imaginary letters.

"What would that say if I could read it?" Mason asked, sitting back down on the bucket.

"A...M...B...I...U...S...C."

He took a bite out of his sandwich, then wiped his mouth. "What's that mean?"

"Antonia Madelyn Barrington Is Up Shit Creek."

"You cuss too much. Probably comes from hanging out with Susan Kessler all the time."

"We haven't been *hanging out.* She just gives me a ride home. Plus I hardly ever cuss—and that hardly qualifies as cussing. Shit's a perfectly polite word in Middle English. You could even say it in church." She'd made that up—completely—but Mason seemed impressed.

"You've got a scholarly mind-set," he said. "I can see you when you're thirty, a professor of musicology someplace."

"I'll never be a professor. Or a musicologist."

"You've never told me what you want to be."

She wanted to be what he was: a normal kid with two parents, everybody alive at home, nothing to be ashamed of, no secrets to hide. She wouldn't even have minded if they made her go to Sunday school. Or she might have liked being a character in one of those old TV shows where nothing real ever went wrong. The camera closes slowly on a nice suburban home with a manicured lawn, then the scene dissolves and the next thing you know you're inside, where Samantha's worrying about who's going to sit next to Larry Tate at the next big dinner party. Darrin's job is on the line and Endora's mon-keying around with fate, but you know Samantha will come to the rescue. She always does.

"I think," she said, "I might like to be a witch."

He didn't say anything, just took another bite of his sandwich, the jelly dribbling onto his chin.

She reached over and blotted it with her napkin. "Aren't you go-ing to lecture me about the wickedness of witchcraft? I bet your preacher's had a thing or two to say about Harry Potter."

"Our preacher probably loves Harry Potter."

"I thought you were a Baptist."

"I am. Our preacher is too. But there are Baptists—and there are *Baptists.*"

"What kind of Baptist is your preacher?"

"Unfortunately, from my point of view, he's the kind who'll be gone before long."

"How come?"

"Because he's not preaching against Harry Potter."

"In other words, I'm right."

"About what?"

"How intolerant people at your church are."

"I didn't know we were holding a seminar in here."

"What *are* we in here to do?" she asked.

"To hide."

"From what?"

"Earthly eyes."

The rules forbade being where they were. You could get detention for eating anywhere outside the lunchroom, and the janitor could lose his job for giving them the key. He must've done it because he realized that occasionally a boy and a girl needed to go off somewhere by themselves. Ninety-nine percent of the time, Mason DePoyster lived by the rules. So did the janitor, probably. But in some instances you had to break them—that was the main notion she'd take away from that day, and one she'd fall back on numerous times in her life. You didn't really need to explain why you'd broken them, other than to tell yourself that some moments, some actions, should be concealed from earthly eyes. Mostly for your own protection. But sometimes for the sake of others too.

A two by four had been fastened to the wall behind Mason, just above eye level. A row of nails protruded from the wood, probably hammered in to serve as coat hooks. She got up from the desk and impaled her sandwich on one of them.

Mason stopped chewing and looked over his shoulder at the dangling ham and cheese. Finally, he swallowed what was in his mouth. "Why'd you do *that*?"

"Do you have any idea," she said, standing over him, "how many times you've asked me that same question?"

"Because you're always doing stuff I can't explain. I used to just tell myself, Well, she's from California. But I bet even folks out there don't go around hanging their sandwiches from nails."

Something was happening to her. Something that depended on their being in a tight little room full of strong odors, where a man who made his living cleaning up after people went to take the weight off his feet and rest his aching back. Maybe to do a little daydreaming, too. "For me," she said, "you're the perfect audience"—a remark she figured would make him angry, and it did.

"I'm not an audience," he snapped. "An audience is composed of many. I'm only composed of me."

"You're not composed at all." Then she pulled what was left of his sandwich from his hand and stuck it on the wall next to hers.

He was looking at her with wariness and fascination, as her father had looked at Nora Houston in the vegetable aisle at Save Mart. She hoped he'd looked at her mother like that at some point in their lives. He must have.

"You lost something," Mason said. "But the part that could be recovered—well, now you've got it back. I can tell."

"You don't know *what* I might do next," she said.

"No, I don't."

"And you don't want to."

"Not until you do it."

"What if I did this?" she said. Straddling his thighs, she sat down in his lap. "Like it? Or not?"

"Like it," he said. "Like it quite a lot."

"So what are you going to do about it?"

"Well . . . what if I did this?" Wrapping his arms around her, he pressed his mouth against hers.

Spots swam before her eyes, spots of various colors, all of them warm—red, purple, royal blue, emerald, burnt orange. Her relationship to gravity was in flux. She was floating, entering a realm reserved for angels. "Mason," she said, "don't ever turn me loose."

"I won't," he promised. "I swear it."

He was not the kind of person who took his vows lightly. He kept clinging to her even after the mop bucket tipped over, depositing them on the floor and soaking them in a flood of sudsy water.

MOST DAYS SUSAN'S DAD let her take the truck, which she said he called his "mobile garbage can." The interior was a mess—seat covers torn, the glove box door missing, wrappers and paper cups strewn all over—but it looked okay from the outside, and Toni thought it beat riding with Ms. Sturdivant. As for walking, she'd learned her lesson there the day she met the guy who lived in the junkyard.

"My daddy," Susan was saying, just then turning onto the highway, "he's talking about buying a house north of town, about five miles beyond the city limits? He might even make an offer on it this week. The guy who owns it's some kind of line foreman or something out at Southern Prime."

Toni shifted uncomfortably, her jeans still damp and smelly. "The catfish plant?"

"Yeah. So last night, this guy must've been drinking or something and started feeling guilty—you ever notice how when men drink, they get in this guilty mood, but when women drink, they just get mad? Anyway, about eleven o'clock he calls up and says, 'Listen, Mr. Kessler, there's something you don't know about my house. It's right by this big drainage ditch, and in the springtime the damn thing backs up and nobody can get in here without a boat.' Daddy, he just laughs and tells the guy, 'Well, that's why I want it.' Isn't that hilarious?"

"Why would your dad want to live in a house nobody can get to?"

"Because I'll be living there too! And when the road's underwater, he won't have to worry about guys coming to see me."

As best Toni could tell, that was something that shouldn't trouble anybody. Whenever Susan approached a guy, more often than not he took off in the opposite direction. After her parents got divorced, she'd been uprooted and her dad drank too much, and even though she'd lived in Loring most of her life, she was still viewed as an outsider. She didn't have any real friends but still managed, somehow, to maintain an optimistic attitude.

That was a quality Toni now valued, though she hadn't always. Optimism, it seemed to her, was the main thing separating those who were contented from those who weren't. Her dad didn't have that quality, and neither did her mother, at least not these last few years. Toni was trying hard to cultivate it in herself, fearing that without it life wouldn't be much more than a forced march through muck and mire, that you'd finally get bogged down and quit moving at all, just stand there and wait for your heart to stop beating.

"Well, it won't only be guys who can't come see you when the road's underwater," she told Susan. "I won't, either."

"You never come to see me anyway."

She'd never set foot in Mr. Kessler's apartment, and didn't intend to, but again she found herself wondering how much Susan knew. And for that matter, how much did she really know herself? Precious little, for which she was thankful. "I'll come see you at your new house," she said. "I just won't come if I need to take a boat."

Susan turned left onto Loring Avenue. Wrinkling her nose, she said, "Does it seem to you like this truck stinks of Lysol?"

———————

Susan would've stayed, but Toni didn't encourage it. She wanted to get out of her dirty clothes and take a shower, and she needed a nap. Lately, when she came home from school she felt like she was falling in on herself. Her limbs and eyelids grew heavy the moment she stepped inside.

She both wanted and did not want to leave this house forever. It was the setting in which the nightmare had occurred, a landscape she longed to put behind her, but it was also where her mom had last been alive. Leaving it would feel like breaking yet another connection.

She kicked off her jeans and threw them in the clothes hamper in her dad's bedroom, then pulled off her panties, blouse and bra, all of them reeking of disinfectant.

She took a long, hot shower, letting the spray pummel her, hoping it would maybe wake her up enough that she could stay on her feet till her dad got home. He was worried about the amount of time she spent sleeping and after this week was cutting off the Xanax. She doubted she could fall asleep at night without it, but if she seemed alert in the afternoon, he might change his mind.

She climbed out, toweled off, put on her bathrobe and was about to dry her hair when the phone rang. Barefoot, she stepped over to the bedside table and lifted the receiver. "Hello?" she said.

The voice on the other end sounded androgynous. "Honey, could I speak to Pete Barrington?"

"I'm sorry, he's not here. May I take a message?"

"I bet you're his daughter, aren't you?"

Her fingers and toes began to tingle. "May I ask who's calling, please?"

"This is just an old friend of your father's."

It was a woman—middle-aged, she figured. "Yes, but could I have your name?"

"Sure you can, honey. I'm sorry. I'd actually like to give you my phone number too. Have you got something to write with?"

A pen lay on the bedside table, next to a prescription pad with her dad's name and office address at the top. "Yes," she said. "I'm ready."

The woman gave her a phone number, then one for her cell too. "Tell him to try the cell phone first. It's almost always on."

"Okay," she said, "but would you mind telling me who this is?"

"Oh, I'm sorry, honey. Just tell your dad Edie called."

She was wide awake now. "Edie?"

"That's right, dear. Edie DePoyster. I believe I know my grandson?"

Frank henderson's relationship with Loring's black teen-agers had gone through certain unpleasant changes since he assumed his current position. When he was still in the sheriff's department, he'd only rarely been aware that these kids viewed him as a potential adversary. He worked out in beat five, where fish farming had largely replaced row crops, cutting into the demand for field labor, and close to eighty percent of the population was white. There weren't a lot of meth labs out there to shut down, so mostly you dealt with Bubba drinking a little too much Bud and slapping Earlene around and then locking her out of the double-wide. They'd both call you *nigger* when you tried to straighten them up, but about half the time one of them—almost always Bubba, which surprised him at first—would end up apologizing for that. All in all, it was a pretty tranquil existence.

Being chief was a different story. Two gangs operated on the South Side, and at one point or another he'd had run-ins with most of them. The older scum that called the shots—guys in their late twenties or early thirties who often didn't even live in Loring but holed up over in Greenville at the Ramada or the Holiday Inn—used teenagers and even preteens to make deliveries and pick up change, so the kids who would've been cutting white folks' grass when Henderson was young were now bringing them grass, and a lot worse, in plastic bags. Some of those kids would turn tail and run if they saw Frank driving by or walking down the street. Those he could tolerate. Others would plant their Air Jordans on the sidewalk and stick their chins up and their chests out, their eyes screaming *White Man's Nigger!*

Neither Reggie McDonald nor Wayne Collier had ever caused an ounce of trouble, but Wayne's older brother Johnny, who called himself M. John, like he was some kind of corporate exec, had done more than enough to make up for his brother's good behavior. M. John was currently serving five to ten in Parchman, where Frank sincerely hoped he got force-fed all-meat weenies every night of the week.

Wayne played basketball, and when Henderson spotted him that afternoon he was dribbling down the sidewalk beside Reggie. Both boys wore backpacks over their raincoats, and Reggie was limping a little. He'd not yet recovered from his sprained knee, which was a major reason the football team had lost three of their last four games.

He was the first to notice that a car was inching along behind them. After glancing over his shoulder, he laid his hand on his friend's forearm, and Wayne lost his rhythm, the basketball bouncing into the street.

Henderson hit a button and the window on the passenger side slid down. "You aim to drive the lane," he told Wayne, "you got to keep control of your dribble. It can get kind of crowded in there."

"Yes sir," Wayne said, "it sure can."

"I hope y'all run the floor a little bit this year. All those games that end up in the forties just about put me to sleep."

Both boys had stopped walking. They were good kids, and right now they must have been wondering how long their bad luck would last.

"Y'all ever ridden in one of these cars?" Henderson asked.

"Been in a BMW once," Collier said.

"Yeah? Whose was that?"

The kid's mouth moved but no words came out. Reggie stood there, shaking his head.

"Never mind," the chief said. "Climb in and we'll go for a spin."

———

This was what he knew on that cold, drizzly day in November, with Thanksgiving just around the corner:

He knew that a certain downtown merchant had never missed one of his son's football games until the night Angela Barrington was killed. He'd attended every other game the boy ever suited up for, starting back in PeeWee League, but he was one of the very few regular attendees who'd missed the one in Greenville.

He knew that this man and his minister, Wade Phelps, were extremely close—according to one of his patrolmen, he'd gotten Wade hired, and the minister had never forgotten it. You'd see them together a good bit, his patrolman said, and in the last few days, since Henderson started paying attention, the merchant entered the church on five or six different occasions, all on weekday afternoons.

He knew that the man's father had deserted him and his mother, and that at the time most folks thought he left because his wife was fucking Pete Barrington. Frank knew this not because he remembered it—from the other side of the color line, nothing white folks did mattered as long as they weren't doing it to you—but because the patrolman who attended First Baptist was able to dredge it up when asked if there'd ever been any bad blood between the merchant and Pete.

He knew that the man's son had fallen for Pete's daughter, and he suspected he wasn't too happy about it. Frank probably wouldn't have been too happy, either, had he been in the same shoes. Some hurt just couldn't be healed.

He knew that none of this was evidence of anything, that if evidence existed, he'd have to find it. And even if he did, most folks weren't going to believe it. He probably wouldn't believe it himself. There wasn't a white person in town he held in higher esteem. And not too many black people, for that matter.

Turning onto B. B. King Road, which would take them beyond the city limits in two minutes tops, he glanced into the rearview mirror and saw Wayne hugging the basketball and mopping his lips with his tongue. Henderson had insisted Reggie sit up front, because he didn't want them making eye contact with each other. He intended to give both of them, especially Wayne, an opportunity to go one-on-one.

"Now, I know you guys probably asking yourselves, 'Why the hell is this crazy so-and-so bothering me? I ain't done nothing wrong.' Well, guess what? I know you ain't done nothing wrong."

"I figured you wanted to ask me about M. John," Wayne blurted. "Like was it true about him operating from inside and so on. I don't know nothing about that."

Reggie put his chin in his hand and stared out the window.

"No, I'm not too worried about Johnny," Henderson said. "Where he's staying, the property management's pretty efficient. I'm actually concerned with local businesses. See, I've been hearing rumors about black workers not getting equal treatment from some of the white merchants, and the only way of finding out about that stuff's to talk to the people who know."

He turned onto Highway 47 toward the Sunflower River. There was an abandoned country store just south of the bridge, with enough gravel in the lot for him to wheel in there and park without getting the car all muddy. A Mercedes caked with mud just didn't look right. "Now, I'm gone ask y'all right up front to keep this confidential. You think y'all can do that?"

"Yes sir," Wayne said.

"What about you, Reggie?"

Reggie turned and looked at him. The chief couldn't have said he actually saw himself reflected in the young man's eyes, but he could tell from Reggie's demeanor how he'd been perceived. The kid knew he was being lied to. What he didn't know was why.

"Yes sir," Reggie finally told him. "I can keep stuff to myself."

Henderson didn't have any doubt about that. Truth was, he'd never paid much attention to the boy, except when a football was tucked under his arm, but he might merit a little more scrutiny.

He turned off the highway and pulled up in front of the store. A couple of rusty signs still clung to the weathered boards, advertising Barq's Root Beer and RC Cola, but the front steps had rotted clean away. "I used to go in there when I was a kid," he said, "and get me a dime's worth of baloney and oatmeal cookies. Hard for you young men to imagine a day when a dime could buy anything, I guess."

Neither of them responded.

"Used to be a man named Will McPherson that worked behind the counter," he said. "A black man. He was about eighty years old, and his momma and daddy had been born in slavery. Short and skinny as he was, you did *not* want to arm wrestle that old man. He'd drive your wrist right through the counter and never break a sweat.

"I never will forget the day when the fellow the store belonged to, this white farmer named Gordon Bumpus that owned the land around here back then, happened to walk in while me and a friend were in there fooling around with Mr. Will, as we called him. Bumpus took one look around, like that sorry little storeroom was heaven and he was God Almighty, and he said, 'Will, what you running here? A colored kindergarten?' He was laughing when he said it, he wasn't trying to be mean, understand—wasn't even trying to make us leave. He'd got hot out in the field and was probably wanting to drink something cold before heading back to work.

"I don't know what got into Mr. Will. He'd been hearing white men say things like that his whole life, and I guarantee you he'd never done anything before like what he did that day, else he never would've lived to be eighty. Because what he did was, he got up off his stool, drew himself up to his full five-foot-four or five-five or whatever he was, and he looked old Gordon Bumpus right straight in the eye and told him, 'No sir, I'm running a kindergarten for white children, and I got me one pupil, and that's you.' "

Henderson started laughing—and, once he'd started, had a hard time stopping. The steering wheel dug into his stomach.

Reggie McDonald was observing him as if he'd slithered up from the sludge of prehistory. "What happened?"

"What you think happened?"

From the backseat, Wayne said, "Mr. Will lost his job."

"No sir, he did not."

Reggie said, "I thought white folks'd fire you for stuff like that back then."

"You bet they would. But the thing is, Gordon Bumpus never got around to it. Y'all want to know why?"

Both boys just sat there, but he knew he had them hooked.

"He never got around to it," Henderson said, "because about

three or four seconds after Mr. Will said that, old Bumpus suffered a heart attack, keeled over and died."

"I ain't believing that," Reggie said.

The chief pointed at the sagging building. "Right in yonder. And if y'all think I'm lying, carry yourselves down to the public library and go through the newspapers from 1959 or '60, and read the obituary for Gordon Bumpus saying he dropped dead of heart failure while stopping by his store. What it won't say, which only me and one other living person know, is what caused his heart to fail."

He sat there for a moment or two without adding anything, letting the story sink in. It wasn't totally fictitious. Gordon Bumpus and Will McPherson *had* made the remarks attributed to them. Bumpus said what he had to say and went on back to work, and after he left, Mr. Will said exactly what the chief had reported. Two days later, Bumpus did indeed drop dead inside the store. Being police chief, Henderson had always felt, gave him poetic license.

"That's how things used to be around here," he told the boys. "You worked for a white person, they more or less owned you—or thought they did, anyway—and could say whatever they wanted to. They expected you to keep your mouth shut.

"That was then. This is now. Things are *supposed* to have changed. And that's what I wanted to talk to y'all about. To find out if y'all been encountering any kind of treatment like that where you work."

Wayne said, "Mr. Alan ain't never talked to us like that. Has he, Reggie?"

McDonald shook his head.

"He's been treating y'all just like everybody else?"

"Yes sir."

"That's pretty much what I figured," Henderson said. "If there were a few more white folks like Alan DePoyster, this'd be a much nicer place." He reached up and scratched his head. "Wonder what it is," he said, "that accounts for a fellow like Mr. DePoyster being so open-minded? You know, they say we're all products of our environment, but it's hard to see how this environment could've produced a guy like him."

"Coach Barrington growed up here too," Wayne said. "He's pretty open-minded."

"Yeah, but Coach Barrington spent half his life in California," Henderson replied. "And if your mind's not open out there, they drill a hole in it to create a little space."

"Sure was sad what happened to his wife," Wayne said.

"Yes, it sure was." In the rearview mirror he could tell that the Collier kid was starting to feel comfortable, that he'd decided it might not be so bad to ride around in a Mercedes and sink into that nice leather seat. "That killing's got everybody off-kilter," Henderson said. "I mean regular folks that didn't have a thing in the world to do with it. It's just got 'em acting different, doing stuff they wouldn't ordinarily do. Take my next-door neighbor, for instance. He's a big executive out at the catfish plant. In charge of media relations. Fellow stands about five-eight, weighs maybe two hundred and twenty pounds, and likes to relate to the media, best I can tell, sitting down. I mean, this gentleman's suffering a long-term energy crisis. But ever since that poor woman's murder he's been a regular whirlwind, cleaning out his garage one weekend, painting his picket fence the next. I even saw him crawling around under his car the other day. Looked like he might have got pinned beneath the oil pan. Beat anything."

"Mr. Alan was kind of hyper afterwards," Wayne said. "First thing was, he got the squirts."

"The squirts?"

Wayne clamped his fingers around his nose. "Got to stinking up the bathroom. Sprayed some air freshner in there, but it didn't help much." He leaned over and tapped Reggie on the shoulder. "You remember what you told me about him making you burn all them boxes? That Saturday after the Greenville game?"

McDonald didn't reply, turning his face away again to stare out the window at the highway.

"Reggie?" the chief said. "Could you turn around to where I can see you? Is that the kind of thing I might persuade you to do?"

It took a while, but Reggie finally looked him in the eye. The chief made up his mind right then that no matter what happened here in the car, he was going to keep an eye on how this kid developed. He didn't give a flying shit about grades or SATs. What he cared about was mettle, and this young man had it.

"Y'all normally burn your boxes, don't you?"

"Yes sir."

"In the incinerator back there at the rear of the building?"

"Yes sir."

"So what was so unusual about Mr. Alan asking you to burn a few more?"

"Wasn't just a few," Wayne said. "And we didn't need the stock yet."

Henderson said, "Is that right, Reggie?"

McDonald barely nodded.

"Back room's *still* cluttered," Wayne chimed. "Everything rolling around all the time. I tripped on a can of Crisco spray the other day and like to bust my butt."

"Y'all burn boxes every day?" the chief pressed Reggie.

"No sir."

"When *do* you burn 'em?"

"After we stock the store."

"And that'd be?"

"Monday night and Thursday night. We might do a little minor restocking on Wednesdays too."

"Everything changes when there's a holiday," Wayne said. "Like during Thanksgiving week? We gone be working our tails off then. See, there's—"

"So y'all normally burn on Monday and Thursday evening?"

"No sir," Reggie said. "It takes us all night to stock the store. We burn on Tuesday and Friday morning."

"And what about Wednesday?"

"We might burn a little bit that night, after we refill the shelves. But we always try to get out before midnight, and sometimes we just stack the stuff up by the incinerator and wait till Friday morning."

Suddenly, Henderson grasped a fact that had been hovering just beyond his reach: Reggie McDonald didn't think it was strange that the chief of police was asking him these questions. "So it was the day after Coach Barrington's wife got killed," he said, "when Mr. Alan asked you to do all this extra burning?"

"Yes sir."

"A Saturday."

McDonald nodded.

"You normally work Saturdays?"

"No sir."

"So Mr. Alan called and asked you to make a special trip in?"

"Yes sir."

"You notice anything unusual in the store?"

The young man hesitated. Henderson remembered the day the boy's dad died, killed when that tractor rolled over on him, and somehow he knew the kid was thinking about that himself, how wrong it was for a child to be deprived of his parent.

"No sir," Reggie managed. "Everything was pretty much normal."

Henderson waited.

From the backseat, Collier said, "What about Mr. Alan's bow tie?"

THE PEACE WHICH PASSETH all understanding had not been granted to Alan DePoyster.

No matter how long or hard he prayed, kneeling beside Wade in the minister's office or sitting alone on the overturned washtub in his own backyard, he couldn't banish the images that haunted him. His inability to do so called to mind what he'd heard another preacher say years ago: "I've been reading in the paper that out in San Francisco, there's all these psychologists now that specialize in helping professed homosexuals overcome their feelings of guilt. Well, brothers and sisters, I've got news for those folks. Feelings of guilt are not *supposed* to be overcome. Guilt is to our minds as fever is to our bodies. It's the Lord's way of telling us something's wrong."

Alan's guilt had become feverish. At first, the worst assaults occurred at night, when she came to him as he slept. She always wore white—long flowing robes or diaphanous gowns. Her skin, too, was white and looked as if it had been powdered. One night she finally spoke. *You never got to know me. We weren't all that different.* After making that observation, she sat down on the edge of the bed, lifted her arms and drew the gown over her head, then let it fall to the floor. Shivering, she hugged herself. He wanted to hug her himself, to pull her beneath the covers and wrap both arms around her, warming her with the heat of his body, but he knew that his wife was sleeping beside him. The naked woman waited, eyes searching his face, her body quivering from the cold. He woke soaked, the sheets so damp that at first he thought he'd wet the bed. He got up, walked into the bathroom in the hallway and took a shower before stretching out on the couch to weather the next nightmare.

Before long, though, he was also seeing her during his waking hours. The other day at church, he'd been sitting in his pew, staring across the aisle at a stained-glass panel in a nearby window, when gradually her body took shape, her form becoming visible in the multicolored shards—one leg green, the other one blue, her limbs splayed at odd angles, her torso a pulsing red splotch. He began to rise, intending to run, but Nancy reached up and clamped her hand around his wrist, and her touch, for the time being, resettled him.

His head hurt night and day. He'd lost more weight—his pants now sliding down his hips, even with the belt tightly buckled. He made himself eat, because he didn't want to saddle Nancy with sickness on top of everything else, but his body burned calories faster than he could ingest them.

The truth, he knew, was that he was being consumed.

———

Under ordinary circumstances, he enjoyed Thanksgiving week. Sales rose, and he was, after all, in the business of selling groceries. He'd always liked the holiday bustle as well, though it bothered him that nowadays people started putting up Christmas decorations while they still had turkey in the fridge, instead of waiting until December 11, as they had when he was a boy.

But there was nothing ordinary about Thanksgiving this year, and on Monday before the holiday, his aching head resting in his palm, he sat in his office more or less oblivious to the hubbub. He heard the cash drawers opening and closing, but it was just noise and nothing more. For all he cared, folks could walk in, fill their carts and roll the stuff right out the back door.

His name was nothing more than noise, either. Whoever'd just said it—a woman, he knew that much—said it again. He turned and looked through the glass, and there stood Norma Salter, in black jeans and a black leather jacket, with a pretty pink muffler thrown around her shoulders. She was smiling at him.

She must have been in the store many times since the morning they'd talked about her grandkids, but as far as he recalled they hadn't spoken. That was the day he'd first seen Pete Barrington, and even though he'd written Norma's name in his notebook, he hadn't remembered to pray for her. He'd been too focused on himself.

He stood and leaned over the glass. "Norma," he said, "how are you?"

"Oh, I'm just fine, Alan."

"Are you really?"

"Yes, I am."

"Bought your turkey yet?"

"You won't sell me one this year. I'm going to have Thanksgiving dinner with the Alexanders."

"Donny, Mark or Fred?"

She laughed. "All of them. At Donny's house. He plans to barbecue the turkey. What I'm supposed to do is bring a sweet-potato casserole. I need marshmallows for that, though, and I don't see any on the shelf. Do you think you've got some more in the back?"

"I don't know," he said, "but we can sure find out."

She followed him down the pet-food aisle. "There's something I've been meaning to ask you," she said. "Do you remember the first time you ever set foot in here?"

"In the store?"

"Yes."

He knew he'd read his first comic book in here and that he'd once stolen a package of M&M's without anyone ever finding out. "I don't know exactly when. But I'm sure I was coming in here by the time I started first grade."

"Did you know it wasn't called Piggly Wiggly back then?"

"No, I can't say that I did."

"It was just known as the 'Blue and Gold.' A man named Farish Crowder used to own it. He died when I was in college. Have you ever heard of him?"

They'd reached the aluminum doors that opened into the back room. "No," he said, "I don't think so."

"Well, he appropriated everything about Piggly Wiggly except the logo, and he stopped just short of stealing that too. In place of the pig with the grocer's hat, he designed a cat with a similar hat, but the cat looked more porcine than feline. And that same logo was on everybody's apron. Eventually, Piggly Wiggly threatened to sue him, and somehow or other he settled with them and they bought him out. I can't believe you never heard about all that. But then I'm a lot older than you are, and it would've happened when you were little. It's ancient history, in other words."

He paused before stepping through the doors. "I wouldn't really call it ancient. We're talking, what—mid-sixties?"

She laid her hand on his forearm. "Alan, these days, the mid-sixties aren't much different than the Golden Age of Athens. Nobody remembers what happened last week, let alone forty years ago."

"Then why did you just tell me you couldn't believe I never heard about this Crowder guy?"

"Well, for one thing, it's your store." She moved an inch or two closer. He could smell her perfume and could see she'd spent a lot of time on her face, applying eyeliner with an artist's touch. She must still harbor some hope for the future. "And to be completely truthful, Alan, I probably associate a lack of historical awareness with shallowness, and you've always struck me as one of the least shallow people I know. Maybe that's why I tried talking to you that time I was feeling so down."

"And I let you down a little bit further by not coming up with anything to say."

"Oh, well," she said, "don't worry about that, Alan. I could tell you were having a bad day too."

He could've pushed through the aluminum doors and stayed in the back room until he got a grip on himself. She would've waited patiently near the Puss 'n Boots display or whiled her time away on the next aisle over, perusing *Good Housekeeping* or *Southern Living* or something else from the magazine rack. He might've walked back out a few minutes later with a bag of Kraft marshmallows and sent her happily on her way, or else told her he didn't have any right now but would get more tomorrow.

Instead, he dropped his head and said, "Norma, that's no excuse for my behavior. Because right then I didn't even know my day would be bad."

"Alan?" she said, and he could hear the concern in her voice, even if, by virtue of staring at the floor tiles, he couldn't see it on her face. "What's wrong?"

"That was the day I ran into Pete," he told her.

"Pete who?"

"Pete Barrington."

"So?"

He had no choice but to look at her then, and what he saw on her face wasn't concern but sheer confusion. She remembered who used to own this store, what the aprons worn by clerks looked like in 1965, but she'd either forgotten, never knew or didn't care what Pete used to do with his mother. It probably held no more significance for any person on the face of the earth, except him.

He'd always prided himself on being civic-minded, the kind of guy who'd step in and give a hundred dollars to a good cause, because he could remember a time when good causes, especially those designed to benefit black people, went unsupported. He prided himself on knowing history too. Having read a good bit of it, he knew the precise moment when the Union had been saved, with Joshua Chamberlain standing firm on Little Round Top. He knew he lived in a better world because the Twentieth Maine had repulsed his forebears. He understood he hadn't been born in a vacuum, that his own personal history was distinct from that of the human race. Yet for the past few months he'd behaved as if it weren't.

He hated to tell another lie now, to add to all the others he'd told lately, but he had to. So he put forward the best he could come up with, only later realizing that like all the most convincing lies it was laced with truth. "I hadn't seen Pete in years," he said. "And when I saw him—well, I started thinking about how much of my life had slipped away. And that's when it turned into a bad day."

"That'll do it," she said, leaning against him, and hugging her seemed both natural and, once he'd done it, wonderful. "Hon, that'll do it every time."

———

He hugged her again twenty minutes later, this time in the parking lot, where he'd rolled her shopping cart and unloaded both sacks of groceries into the trunk of her Cadillac. He said something to her, too, but from where Frank Henderson sat in the far corner of the lot, down close to Indian Bayou, it was impossible to know what. Whatever it was, it brought a smile to Norma Salter's face. She took Alan's hand in hers before getting in her car and backing out.

After she drove off, DePoyster continued to stand there. The day was cloudy and cold, close to freezing, but he wore no coat, just dark slacks and a white long-sleeved shirt. He'd never replaced the red-white-and-blue bow tie that Reggie McDonald noticed among the incinerator ashes.

The cold must not have concerned him. Neither, apparently, did the many pickups and cars in the lot. Because while the chief watched, Alan DePoyster dropped to one knee, closed his eyes and bowed his head.

WHEN HE LEFT THE STORE that night, Alan noticed the big Mercedes parked down the street in front of Delta Jewelers, but he couldn't tell if anyone was inside. He saw the car again the next morning: it pulled into traffic as he passed the post office, and followed him for three or four blocks before turning onto Loring Avenue and heading, presumably, to the police station. The car had always been noticeable—of the few Mercedes in town, this was the only plum-colored one—and Alan couldn't say, with any certainty, whether or not his awareness of it now was significant. It was just out there. It didn't scare him that much.

What scared him a lot more was the realization, which he expressed Tuesday afternoon to Wade, that no matter what he did from now on, the life of his family had already been ruined. "I can't look my son in the eye," he said, sitting across the desk from Wade. "I try. I tell myself to play my old role, that I have to act the part for his benefit, but I can't help it. I always look away, and I know it's scaring him."

Wade pulled a bottle of Jack Daniel's from his desk drawer and poured a shot into a McDonald's cup.

The first time Alan had seen him do that, he hadn't been able to stop himself from saying, "My gosh, Wade." Whereupon the minister smiled, stuck his hand inside the drawer again and withdrew a rock that must have weighed at least two pounds. He laid it on the desktop and pushed it toward Alan. "I've had it in my drawer now for a couple of months. It's kind of a stage prop. I figured the first time one of my brothers or sisters saw me pour a drink and they expressed

surprise, horror or outrage, I'd offer them the rock, so if they wanted
to . . ."

"They could cast the first stone?"

"Forgive me," Wade said, "for being quite so obvious." He took a
sip of his whiskey. "I'm lucky it's you sitting there, Alan. I can think
of a couple folks who'd pick that thing up and turn into Roger
Clemens."

Today, after pouring the drink, he put the bottle back in the
drawer, where it clinked against the rock. "Do you think Mason has
any idea," he asked, "that you're responsible for what happened?"

"A part of me says why would he? I never hit him or his mother,
never did anything violent my whole life. I only yelled at him a couple of times in all these years. On the other hand . . ."

"On the other hand, what?"

"I think he knows. I don't know how or why. I just think he does."

"What about Nancy?"

"Nancy's not one to dig too deep. She knows I'm not myself, but
she thinks it's because of something she did a long time ago."

"You mean having sex with her brother?"

It was as good a measure as any of the changes inside him over the
last six weeks that he felt no flame light his face. "Yeah," he said.
"That's what I mean."

"She knows it's not that," Wade told him. "She's been to see me a
couple of times."

"Obviously."

"In my position, you learn a lot of things you'd rather not know."

"What else did she tell you?"

"She said that before you ever got married, you forgave her for the
thing with her brother and that she knows you well enough to know
you really meant it. She's in a great quandary, wondering what's happened." He took another sip of whiskey. "She told me you quit making love to her, Alan."

"I don't make love to her because I can't. I don't think I'll ever
make love again."

"Convinced yourself it's a sin?"

"For me, maybe."

"Well, what about for her?"

The words, when they emerged from Alan's throat, sounded less like the language of humans than some kind of primal groan: "I'm gone, Wade. I'm not myself anymore."

The minister eyed him coolly, as if even such anguish should be viewed with detachment. Later, Alan would wonder if Wade already suspected what awaited him personally in the next few months and was preparing himself for his firing by the board of deacons, the loss of his wife and children, the rapid slide into alcoholism.

"Well," he finally said, "I'd say we need to figure out how you can get yourself back. Because truth be known, Alan, you were the only man left in town that I could stand."

ONE OF MANY THINGS PETE didn't know how to do was cook a turkey. Fortunately, Tim did, so after closing his practice at lunchtime on Wednesday, Pete climbed into the Volvo and drove downtown to Piggly Wiggly. Afterwards, when he tried to figure out why he'd gone there instead of the big Kroger out on the highway, where he'd been shopping ever since he returned, the best answer he could come up with was nostalgia. He still remembered making trips to the old Blue and Gold with his grandfather. The owner, Farish Crowder, who sometimes gave him a free lollipop, had never been good with names. He called all the boys in town "Butch," all the girls "Honey."

If Pete had been avoiding the store, he wasn't aware of it. His office was on the other side of the highway, closer to the Kroger. Once or twice, after Toni started hanging out with Mason, he'd thought of stopping by and trying to talk to Alan, but in the end it seemed unwise. They might one day be in-laws. If so, they could talk then.

He'd been surprised the other day when Toni handed him the sheet from his prescription pad with two Memphis phone numbers on it and said, "This lady named Edie called and wants you to call her back." He waited for her to say more, but she didn't, so he couldn't tell if she knew this Edie was her boyfriend's grandmother.

He had no intention of calling her back. He'd thought about Edie often enough down through the years, more often than he ever would've admitted to anybody, but always as she remained in his imagination: a woman in her late thirties, naked and sweating. As for having anything to say to her, he hadn't said much to her back then and had even less to say now. Together they'd engaged in an athletic endeavor—the only one he could think in which the goal of both contestants was to end in a tie.

———

Pulling into the parking lot, he noticed the Mercedes. It was idling, smoke curling up from the tailpipe and drifting out over the bayou. Rather than take a vacant space close to the street, he drove down to the end of the lot, parked and climbed out.

Henderson watched him walk across the asphalt and motioned him around to the passenger side. They hadn't spoken since he'd called Pete to say his DNA wasn't a match.

He opened the door and got in. The car smelled of leather and aftershave. A CD was playing. Soft jazz piano. " 'Waltz for Debbie,' " he said. "With Scott LaFaro on bass and Paul Motian on drums?"

Henderson nodded his approval. "You a Bill Evans fan?"

"You could say so."

"I noticed you had quite a few of his CDs at your place. Even those last two boxed sets. You know, from the club dates he played in San Francisco right before he died. What are they called?"

"*The Last Waltz* and *Consecration*."

"That's the ones. I looked those things up on the Internet one night and both of 'em are over a hundred dollars." The chief whistled. "If you've got a CD burner, I might ask you to copy 'em for me sometime. Why you looking at me funny?"

"Because," Pete said, "you're the first black person I ever met who admitted to loving Bill Evans. You know what the knock is—an interloper, too classical, couldn't play the blues and so on."

"Yeah, well, if I want the blues, I know right where to find 'em." Henderson reached over and turned off the music. "I imagine you're wondering how the investigation's going. Fact is, I was planning to come see you on Friday."

"Why Friday?"

Sitting back, the chief crossed his arms over his belly, resting his elbows against the steering wheel. "Because tomorrow's Thanksgiving," he said. "And pretty soon there's going to be some news that won't make anybody at your house thankful."

I WAS IN MY TWENTIES," Tim said, "before I ever tasted a turkey with juice in it." He stood near the counter, rubbing spices on the big Butterball. Following his conversation with Henderson, Pete had bought it at Kroger after all. "My momma used to get up at five o'clock on Thanksgiving morning, stick ours in the oven and bake it all day long. By the time she finished, that poor bird was shrunk to the size of a Cornish hen and hard as a rock. My daddy had this weird thing about poultry. If he bit into a drumstick and felt any softness, he'd put it back down and say, 'Well, I can tell this chicken's still capable of laying an egg.' He liked his poultry well done."

Pete sat on a stool doing his best to concentrate on his friend's monologue. This morning, he'd woken up thinking about last Thanksgiving. Dinner at home, a little tense but not too bad, then over to a friend's house with Angela for a party. Nora and her husband were there too, and once or twice he noticed his wife chatting with his lover, Nora reaching up every now and then to brush that dark hair off her forehead, Angela confessing God only knew what. Afterwards, Nora refused to say if she'd complained about him or not. When asked why, she said, "Because I think she trusts me. She shouldn't, but I think she does."

She shouldn't have trusted Nora, nor him, and maybe not even Toni or Tim. It was as if she'd been born to be betrayed.

"This bird's ready to fly," Tim said, wiping his hands on the candy-striped apron that had belonged to Angela. He'd tied himself into it earlier this morning, and if he'd thought much, one way or the other, about the woman who used to wear it, you couldn't tell. He seemed pretty happy these days. Frank Henderson hadn't knocked on his door demanding DNA, and he'd gotten his daughter back.

"Tim," Pete said, "you mind if I ask you a serious question?"

"Not as long as you know I might lie."

"I figure either one of us might lie at any given moment. We're men."

"That's some pretty dark spin."

"These are pretty dark times. In this house, anyway."

Tim walked over to the refrigerator, pulled a Bud out, popped the top and took a big swallow. "All right," he said. "Shoot."

"Were you in love with Angela?"

The question produced an effect similar to the ones Pete had witnessed back in junior high, when their math teacher, Mrs. Cignetti, sent his friend to the board. Tim seldom did his homework and never had the slightest idea how to solve a problem. He'd just get a blank look on his face and shuffle his feet. *Good-time Tim,* Cignetti liked to call him. *A fraction of a frat boy already.*

"You don't know?" Pete asked. "Or you don't want to say?"

"I just wish we didn't have to talk about it. Susan's liable to show up over here any minute, and Toni may wake up and walk in on us too."

"If Susan shows up, we'll shut up. As for Toni, she's drugged. She'll sleep till noon if I let her."

Tim carried his beer over to the counter, stood it there, turned on the tap in the sink and squirted some liquid soap onto his hands. While Pete looked on, he washed them, then tore a sheet off the paper towel rack and dried himself off. "There wasn't much point in falling in love with her," he said. "Hate to sound like Hank, but she was still in love with you. You've had a surfeit of riches, as they say."

"I think *surfeit* and *riches* in the same sentence are redundant."

"They're redundant in life too. But the fact remains, that's what you had."

In Tim's mind, he was still number 88, a man too big to tackle. The only way you could stop him was if he happened to drop the ball. Otherwise he'd waltz into the end zone on air. He walked over to the refrigerator, opened it and looked inside. He didn't feel like a beer yet—too early in the day—so he pulled out a bottle of Crystal Geyser, twisted the top off and turned it up. The bubbles caused him to hiccup. Then he made a statement he figured he'd regret for the rest of his life: "I once took your jersey. So I guess you just had to take something of mine."

Tim flushed. "You didn't take my jersey. I gave it to you."

"You suggesting I should've been willing to give you my wife?"

"For all practical purposes," Tim said, "you did. Loaned her, anyway. And she knew it. And as for taking something—as you put it—that wasn't mine, well, look who's talking. You've taken plenty that wasn't yours. That's why you had to come crawling home. Hell, it's why you left in the first place. Because you fucked DePoyster's momma."

Pete threw the Crystal Geyser on the floor, the bottle shattering into every corner of the kitchen. He knew he was wrong to take pleasure from the twitch that appeared at the corner of Tim's mouth, but he couldn't help it.

They were standing there breathing hard, like two little red-faced boys, when Toni stumbled in. She looked at her father, then at Tim, then at the broken glass. "Stop it!" she erupted. "For God's sake, stop it!"

"Sweetheart—" Tim began just as Pete said, "Honey—"

"I don't want to be *your* sweetheart," she said, "and I don't want to be *your* honey. I just want to be an ordinary, everyday, unremarkable *girl.*"

———

"She's different," Mason said that morning when his father asked what had drawn him to Toni Barrington in the first place.

They were riding in the pickup to the grocery store. In a sign of the distraction gripping them all, Nancy had forgotten to pick up celery and onions for her stuffing.

"Different how?"

"I don't know," Mason said. He wouldn't look at his dad, just watched the bayou sliding by outside, the Christmas floats already in position, ready to be lit tomorrow or the next day. "It'd be easier," he said, "to tell you how she's not different."

The Mercedes pulled out of an alley and fell in behind them. Apparently Frank Henderson worked on holidays. Alan ignored the car, just as he had for much of the past week. "Okay," he said. "Tell me how she's not different."

"When her momma was killed, she felt like shit. Just like most folks would."

Alan chose not to remark on the foul language, which was one more thing he couldn't blame on anyone but himself. He'd used it in the presence of his son, and now his son had picked it up. What else had he taught him? What else might he teach him? "Anybody'd feel like that," he agreed. "I remember how I felt when your grandfather left town."

"Yeah, but he *left*. Nobody killed him. You always knew there was a chance he'd come back."

"I didn't want him to."

For Mason, the bayou lost its interest and went back to being a ditch full of muddy water. Now he was looking at his father.

"I remember when I tried out for the long jump my sophomore year. I didn't have much athletic ability, but I wanted to earn a letter and the long jump looked easy. Just run thirty yards or so, throw yourself through the air and land in the sand. What could be hard about that? I practiced every day for three straight weeks, and then we had the tryouts and I came in dead last. Jumped something like fourteen feet and sprained my ankle on my last attempt. The track coach put his arm around me and said, 'Alan, you just don't have a lot of natural spring in your legs.' Well, I don't have a lot of natural forgiveness in my heart, either. It took me a long time to forgive my father, and when I did it wasn't because of anything inside me. It was due to grace and grace alone."

He knew what Mason was going to say before he said it, and he knew that when he did say it, his tone would reveal everything. So he took his foot off the accelerator and let the truck coast down the street toward the store he'd run for more than fifteen years and listened.

"Dad?" his son asked softly. "How does a person come by that kind of grace?"

——— ———

Susan Kessler had somehow made herself a T-shirt that had a picture of her and Brad Pitt on it. In the photo, which looked a little faded, they were standing together at some fancy-dress party—Brad in a tux, Susan in a sheer pink gown sprinkled with glitter. The actor held a glass of champagne and Susan was leaning toward him, about to whisper something. She told Pete the actual body in the dress belonged to Jennifer Aniston. She seemed to think he'd know who that was.

While she stood at the sink peeling potatoes, her dad stuck the turkey in the oven. They had their moves down pat. You could tell they'd done a lot of cooking together, though Tim said most of it had occurred outside. In recent years he'd eaten primarily from bags. "In other words," he said, "I'm rusty."

"That's because you've spent too much time in the rain," his daughter quipped.

"I need oiling." He pulled another beer out and popped the top. That was his fourth or fifth of the day, and it wasn't even one o'clock.

Toni stood on the far side of the kitchen with her hands in her pockets, her hair still damp from the shower. She hadn't spoken to either of the men since her outburst that morning. She hadn't said much to Susan, either. Now she announced, "I think I'll go to my room for a while."

Susan looked over her shoulder, then went right back to peeling potatoes. Pete waited a moment or two before excusing himself.

All he intended to do was check on her. He'd never eavesdropped on his daughter, not once, and wouldn't have wanted her eavesdropping on him. Nevertheless, when he heard her voice through the door, he paused in the hallway.

"Don't imagine things," he heard her say. And, a moment later, "Yes, I swear I will. No matter what . . . Yes, I know what I'm saying." She must have lowered her voice, because he couldn't quite make out her next response. Then, just as he was about to turn and walk back down the hall, she said, "Don't be silly. I won't. For me now, this is home."

———

Whenever Mason thought back on that Thanksgiving, he'd remember that his father had sat down to dinner without his shoes on. He wore socks—thick white ones, with fuzzy gray bottoms. If Mason or his mother had done the same thing it wouldn't have seemed extraordinary, but his father never appeared at the table without being fully dressed, and for him that meant wearing outdoor shoes.

The turkey was overdone, the stuffing soggy, the sweet potatoes cooked to mush. His mother made apologetic sounds that washed over him. Her face was flushed, the fabric beneath her armpits damp. She'd worn her apron to the table, another odd sight.

He'd sat down to the meal afraid that, for the first time in memory, no one would say a prayer. He didn't know why he thought that, but he did. And if that's how things developed, he'd made up his mind to insist on a prayer, even though he'd often regarded it as a nuisance. The truth was that his own religious faith had steadily ebbed away, and that for at least the last couple of years he'd participated in the ritual devotions of his family mostly out of respect for his parents. He wasn't exactly a nonbeliever, but neither could he have honestly claimed to know there was a heaven or that he would one day wind up there. Still, his parents' faith had structured their lives, and he feared that if they lost it, chaos would reign. He had to try to help them hang on to it.

As it turned out, he needn't have worried. Because his father bowed his head, just as he always had, and though at first he said nothing, you could tell he was formulating his thoughts.

Finally, he began. "Our Heavenly Father, we thank You for the years that led to this one. For the minutes and the hours that made up our days and nights. If we were to sit and list all our blessings, none of us at this table would have good enough math skills to arrive at the final sum. We thank You for the joy You've bestowed on us and for the joy You've enabled us to offer one another. We ask forgiveness for all those moments we didn't live like we should have. We ask forgiveness for whatever pain we've caused, or may cause, and we pray that one day those times when we were less than we should've been will be subtracted from whatever we add up to."

He fell silent then. As always, Mason waited for his mother. When a minute or two passed without her saying anything, he opened his eyes and looked across the table. She was sitting there with her head bowed, tears rolling down her cheeks. His father had reached over and taken her hand in his.

Mason didn't want them to see him watching. So he closed his eyes again and said, "Dear God, I thank You for my mother and my father."

———

"Where I went to school in Jackson," Susan was saying, spearing a slice of white meat, "we had this girl named Melissa? And she couldn't stand being called that? So she changed it to Meleya. Well, she wrote this poetry cycle about hating holidays. Her anti-Thanksgiving poem was titled 'Bitches Basting Buzzards.' "

Her father said, "Hon."

"Well, it was, Daddy." She passed the plate to Toni. "For Easter she wrote one called 'Your Cross Is Just Lumber.' That kind of thing. Real transgressive stuff."

Toni took the smallest piece of white meat she could find, then handed the plate to Mr. Kessler. She could tell from the glow in his eyes that he was drunk—he'd switched to whiskey after pulling the bird from the oven. Her own father was sipping whiskey now himself, but she'd never once seen him in the type of etherized fog Mr. Kessler was in. She wondered what it felt like to be in that state. Her mom had drunk quite a bit, but she'd only seen her *act* drunk one time in the last year or so, and that was on the day she overslept and left Toni waiting by the flagpole. That seemed like years ago now, like it had been lived by another girl.

That was the same day she'd run into the homeless guy near the junkyard. What had happened to him between then and now? Was he still sleeping in the El Dorado? If so, she hoped he'd found some blankets, that the roof didn't leak and the police, if they knew about him, would just lay off and leave him alone.

Her dad said, "These garlic potatoes taste great, Susan."

Susan's face turned a variety of shades, ranging from grapefruit pink to fire-engine red. "Thanks, Doc. Nothing much to it."

"Susan," Mr. Kessler said, "you're being a little too informal."

"It's all right," her dad said. "She can call me *Doc* if she wants to."

He was just being nice, Toni knew, but she could see what effect even that much of his attention was having on Susan, who fluttered her fake lashes, lifted her sagging shoulders, slung her bangs out of her eyes. She was putting on what she must have considered her worldly look, trying to come up with something memorable to say, hoping to hang on, a little longer, to whatever it was she believed she'd won, not understanding that Pete Barrington, impressive as he probably seemed to her, was just another wreck.

———

The car'd had that luxury-sedan smell, the odor of leather combining with the scent of the polish that Henderson must have buffed into the burled wood trim. Pete was used to cars like that, had once driven a Mercedes himself before deciding it was too showy.

They'd sat there the previous day, Henderson watching the loading dock at the rear of the grocery store. He'd said what he had to say, then waited for Pete's response. But Pete didn't have one. So finally the chief said, "I could have a search warrant in about forty-five minutes, go in there and get some fingerprints and so on, but I don't want to do that. You understand what I'm saying?"

"Yeah. But I don't believe it. Alan doesn't have it in him to do something like that."

"Oh, you'd be surprised. We've all got it in us. Some of us are just unlucky enough to stumble into situations that bring it out."

I've been just fine for almost twenty-five years.

"What *I'm* trying to do," the chief said, "is help this man preserve at least a little bit of dignity for him and his family. Trying to help him reach the right decision on his own, see, because there's nobody in this community that's done more good for other folks. He knows I'm out here, and he's bound to know why. I'm willing to give him another day or two, let him spend the holiday with his wife and son. If I have to, I can always walk down the criminologically correct path."

"You think he killed my wife."

"I'm in the realm of certitude."

"Then tell me, if you will, why you made me come in and give you a sample of my DNA the moment you entertained the slightest suspicion about me, and now you plan to let him enjoy Thanksgiving with his family."

Henderson's face contracted into a tight mass of muscle. "When I look at Alan DePoyster," he said, "I see a man who's tried his best to lead a mistake-free life. He's the kind of guy who thinks long and hard before he puts his foot down because he's worried he might step on an ant. And to me, men like that have great value. Assemble enough of them in one place and you get a smoothly functioning community in which the ants don't get stepped on. I'm just guessing, mind you, but I bet you never felt like an ant."

That was true, Pete thought, as he stood at the sink washing pots and pans while Susan Kessler dried them with a dishrag. He had never felt insignificant. If anything, he felt as if his significance grew greater day by day, as if some force, like gravity, drew others toward him. Once they entered his orbit, their navigational systems went haywire.

According to Henderson, he might soon have to try explaining to Toni how it was that her boyfriend's father, a man who'd lived an otherwise exemplary life, had lost his bearings and gone berserk right here in their house. He'd have to tell her that her mother's life had gone to pay off his own bad debt.

He lifted the big pan in which the turkey had been roasted. Grease and congealed fat caked the corners, and the bottom of the pan was burned.

Susan whistled. "Man," she said, "that is one nasty mess."

From the living room came the sounds of a movie preview, Toni and Tim getting ready to watch a DVD just as soon as he and Susan finished up.

"You know," he said, "I've got a good mind to throw this pan away."

"Oh, you don't want to do that. It's too nice. Besides, didn't it belong to your wife?"

She was right, and Angela had taken great care of all her cooking utensils, making sure they never got scratched or mislaid. Every single item had its own place and had to be put back there once it was no longer in use. "I wasn't serious," he said. He squirted dishwashing liquid into the pan, ran some hot water in it, then picked up the sponge and began scrubbing. He worked on it for at least ten minutes, putting body English behind his efforts, getting red in the face and sweating. Still, a layer of black grime covered the bottom. "Damn," he said, "this is amazing."

Susan stood there looking at it. Finally, she shook her head. "Some stuff can stick forever," she said.

The heart-shaped box of chocolates was small, but it had cost close to forty dollars and was the most expensive thing Alan could find, even at the Pecan Shack, where prices always verged on the absurd. He'd bought it the previous day and hidden it in his underwear drawer. As soon as he knew Nancy was in the shower, he pulled the box out and laid it on the bed. Then he walked through the hallway. Passing his son's room, he heard him typing, probably writing the Barrington girl an e-mail.

He opened the door to the garage and, slipping inside, flipped on the light. The ice chest was over in the corner, right where they always kept it, and nobody, least of all Nancy, would have suspected that anything was inside it. He raised the lid and there stood the bottle, tipped a little to one side but still covered by ice. He pulled it out and stuck it inside his bathrobe. It was so cold it burned his nipple.

He made it back down the hallway without being discovered. Once inside his bedroom, he locked the door. Nancy was still in the shower, so he grabbed a towel from the closet and laid it on the bed-side table. Then he pulled the foil off the bottleneck, loosened the wire cage, lifted off the hood, picked up the towel and wrapped it around the cork.

He'd seen champagne opened in movies and on TV—corks flying, bubbles spewing—but that wasn't what he had in mind. The Web site he'd looked at last night said that if you were careful and followed directions, you should be able to avoid it. So he did as instructed, gently twisting the bottle, feeling the cork start to move. Two or three more turns and it popped out. He felt moisture under the fabric, but not too much. When he removed the towel, the bottle smoked a little.

He stood it on the bedside table, next to two water glasses he'd brought from the kitchen. His hands, which had stayed steady as he rotated the bottle, were beginning to shake. Thinking it might calm him, he lifted the bottle and took a small swig. He almost gagged. He'd never tasted anything worse.

When the shower shut off, he poured the glasses full, then slipped out of his robe and his underwear. Carrying the two glasses, he walked over to the bathroom door and knocked.

"Just a minute," she said. "I'm drying off."

Without waiting, he opened the door.

Her face colored slightly when she saw him. She held her towel in both hands, and at first he thought she'd try to cover herself with it, but in the end she let it fall to the floor. "Not much point," she said, "in trying to wrap it around me. We don't have anything big enough for that."

The last time they'd made love, weeks ago, most of the excess weight had been in her hips, legs and breasts. Now, he saw, her stom-ach was bulging.

He was bulging too. The sickness that had festered inside him all those years had worked its way to the surface, deforming him beyond recognition. This was as good a time as any to get drunk.

He handed her one of the glasses.

She eyed the bubbling liquid. "What's this?"

"Champagne."

"What?"

"Champagne. Only it's not really champagne unless it comes from France, and this came from Napa Valley." He raised his glass, intending to take a swallow.

"Don't people usually make a toast?"

"I guess so. But I can't think of one."

"I can," she said. "To our son." Closing her eyes, she turned the glass up and drank most of it in one swallow.

In bed, he poured her another glassful and loosed the gold ribbon binding the box of candy. "Any of this look good?" he asked, removing the top.

"All of it."

He selected a nougat.

Keeping her eyes on him, she opened her mouth, and he laid the chocolate on her tongue. Slowly, continuing to watch him, she chewed.

For the first time in weeks, he felt that old blessed stirring in his groin. He laid his hand on her belly and began to massage her.

"I'm ashamed," she said, "of that part of myself."

"I'm ashamed," he said, "of myself in its entirety."

She said, "I like for you to know I'm ashamed."

"Well," he said, "I'm afraid I don't like for you to know I am. I don't like for anybody to know. I'd rather have nothing to be ashamed of." He didn't want to talk about his troubles—not here, not now. Those troubles could be discussed at length later on. To forestall further discussion, he popped a piece of candy in his mouth—some kind of awful cream-filled dark chocolate—and forced himself to chew it. When he finished, he tossed down the remainder of his champagne.

They emptied the bottle in thirty minutes. By then he was stretched out on his back, his arms at right angles to his body, her head resting against his shoulder, her knees spread apart. She had one hand between her legs, the other between his. Her eyes were wide open, staring blankly at the ceiling. Every few seconds her lips expelled air.

For the first time in his life, his wife's touch failed to produce an effect on him. While she began to moan, he shut his eyes and said the last prayer he would ever say in this place he'd called home for so long:

Please lift me above myself.

AT A QUARTER PAST NINE, he woke tangled in the covers, alone in bed, his head feeling strangely light, as if it contained less matter than it had the night before. He was naked, his shorts on the floor where he'd dropped them, his robe nearby. Dimly, he recalled hearing Nancy dress for work. She'd stood before her vanity humming and before leaving had walked over to the bed and kissed his nose.

The stock crew would have reported for work this morning, since he'd given them Thursday night off, and he almost reached for the phone to call and ask Truman Wright if he'd gotten there in time to let Reggie and Wayne and the other guys in. But Truman didn't need to be called. He'd handle things at the store just fine.

He swung his legs out of bed and sat there on the side of it, looking around the room. The walls were white now, but they'd been pink until two years ago, and before that, back when he first bought the place, they'd been covered by horrible light green wallpaper, with darker green stripes that suggested the previous owner had a watermelon fixation. Those first few years he and Nancy used to lie there making jokes about it, calling it "slime lime" and looking forward to when they could afford to tear it off and get the room repainted. They had a lot to look forward to then. They knew the day would come when they could choose their color and get things exactly like they wanted them.

Over the years, they'd put massage nozzles in both of their showers. They'd installed a carbon filter on the kitchen faucet, bought a new compressor for the central air, summoned Chuck Klingler from Loring Electric and had him install a burglar alarm that they forgot the code to and never used. They had a handyman build permanent bookcases for the den, though they didn't own enough books to fill them. They bought a fireplace insert. They bought a Renoir print— *Luncheon of the Boating Party*—at a little shop in the Greenville Mall, had it framed and hung it over the mantel. They put a ceiling fan in Mason's room.

This place where they lived was different because they'd lived here. Evidence of their presence would not be wiped away for many years, no matter who inhabited this space. Like the watermelon wall paper, some things would hang around.

He got up and took a shower, which did nothing to banish his headache. He was getting dressed when he heard Mason knock on the door. "Just a minute," he said, having forgotten that today was a school holiday. He finished buttoning the clean white shirt he was wearing, then stepped over to the door and opened it.

Mason's backpack was slung over his shoulder, and he had on his Loring High windbreaker. "I saw the truck in the garage," he said, "and wondered if you were sick."

"No, I just overslept."

Mason's mouth curved into a frown. His father never overslept.

"Where you headed?" Alan asked.

"Mrs. Anklan said she'd open the school library today because a bunch of us have research papers due on Monday. We're going to meet over there to work together."

Alan knew the identity of at least one of the other scholars. "How'd you plan on getting over there?"

Mason shrugged. "Thought I'd walk."

Alan picked his keys up off the dresser. "Let me grab a cup of coffee," he said, "and I'll take you."

He'd made the offer reflexively, as any decent parent with a vehicle at his disposal would have. But the words had hardly left his mouth before he realized that the last thing he wanted to do today was drop his son off in front of the school.

Driving across town, he kept the metal coffee mug clamped between his knees, unable to face the thought of that hot sour liquid in his stomach. He should have made himself a cup of tea, or eaten a Clif Bar. Or jumped off a cliff.

"I just read a great book for my paper," Mason was saying. "It's called *Lee Considered.* Have you heard of it?"

"I don't think so."

"It's about Robert E. Lee. It was written by a lawyer who applies his courtroom techniques to a study of Lee's actual record and concludes that a lot of what we think we know about him's just mythology."

"A lot of what we think we know about anybody's just mythology," Alan said. "So is a lot of what we think we know about ourselves. As far as what you learn about somebody in the courtroom—well, a lot of that'll be mythology too. Because we're more than just our records."

He wouldn't have been able to explain what he meant if his son had asked, but Mason didn't. Instead, he busied himself pawing through his backpack, trying to make sure, he said, that he hadn't left his notes or his cell phone at home. Either Alan's comments had failed to capture his attention or, more likely, they'd embarrassed him.

A couple of cars and one pickup stood in the teachers' parking lot. Rather than pull up to the front doors, Alan stopped at one end of the building.

Mason said, "Could you let me out up there?" He pointed at the main entrance. "The end doors'll be locked."

So Alan took his foot off the brake and the pickup moved forward.

And then he was exactly where his father had been all those years ago, about to say good-bye to his son and disappear from his life, and he thought he understood now why he'd left. His dad, as he remembered him, had been a man of strong conviction. He knew right from wrong—he often said so—and was willing to make a judgment about the difference between what was good and what was bad. Sobriety was a good thing, drunkenness wasn't. Fidelity was a virtue, betrayal a sin. When you gave someone your word—a client you'd insured, say—you stuck to it. When you saw someone in trouble, you extended a helping hand. You obeyed the law of the land.

His father had borne the weight of moral clarity. Deviation by others from the standards of behavior to which he held himself could drive him to the point of red-hot rage. He never did violence to another person, but there was violence in his means of working his anger off—going out back and chopping the wood they never seemed to burn in the fireplace, or lopping branches off trees that overhung their backyard, or ripping weeds from the ground in his tiny vegetable garden. When he'd performed those actions long enough, he'd come back inside and collapse on the couch into a sleep that resembled death.

His father had left town because he knew that if he didn't, he was going to kill someone.

"Dad?" Mason said, his hand on the door. "You think you could drive back by here this afternoon and pick me up?"

Alan's own father had not known how to tell him what was coming. He wanted to do better by Mason, so he sat there searching for the proper language, trying to find words to convey something so unspeakable. He'd never know how much time passed before Mason said, "Look, Dad, don't worry about it, okay? I'll see you when I see you."

THE DAY AFTER THANKSGIVING, Frank Henderson tipped the scales at 186, four pounds heavier than the previous morning. Still, he mused while carrying his cup of coffee into the police station, he'd fared better than last year, when he'd picked up six pounds. It wasn't the turkey that made him gain weight. It was everything else. He loved cranberry sauce and sweet potatoes, thick gravy and corn bread dressing.

Cloell, the dispatcher, had gotten so big near the end of her pregnancy that she couldn't squeeze into her swivel chair. Her husband had brought in a wide armchair, and she was sitting in that, with her headset on, and reading the *Delta Democrat-Times*.

"Good morning, Chief. Look like you done ate you some turkey."

"It's that obvious?"

"I ain't talking about your belly. Person got a belly like mine, they not likely to joke about somebody else's. No sir, I mean you just have that happy just-fed look on your face."

He wasn't aware of being particularly happy, but as he sat down in his office and pulled the plastic lid off the McDonald's cup, he had to admit that life was not bad. He still loved his wife, and his kids were doing well in their studies. He drove a nice car and owned a nice home, nobody in his family was sick or in trouble, most folks he met on the street smiled and called him *Chief,* plus basketball season would start in a few more days.

He'd just taken the first sip of the by-now tepid coffee when he happened to look out the window. Wade Phelps was stepping out of the church, followed an instant later by Alan DePoyster. They were dressed alike, each of them wearing white long-sleeved shirts and khaki pants, neither of them in a coat or jacket. As if they were about to walk down the aisle together, they locked arms and started across the alley.

By the time Cloell ushered them into his office, Henderson already had two chairs pulled up beside his desk. "Good morning," he said, putting out his hand. "What service can I perform for you gentlemen today?"

THE END OF CALIFORNIA

ON THE SCREEN, her father stoops, a spoon in his hand, his hair longer than he wears it these days. "Come on, little lady," he says. "Time for dinner." He glances sideways, mugging for the camera, which she knows is being held by her mother. Laughter explodes from the baby in the high chair. Playfully, she swipes at the spoon but, because he's quicker than she is, she misses.

That makes her angry. What baby wouldn't be? Both fists crash down onto the tray table, and her dad jumps backwards, dropping the spoon on the floor. "Shit," he says.

The baby cries, "Thit!"

She hears her mother's voice. "You'll eventually have to stop cursing around her. She'll start to pick it up."

"Believe me," her dad says, "if that's the worst thing she learns from me, we'll be doing okay."

Jump cut to a Christmas tree in the living room of the house they lived in until she was three, a Douglas fir decked out with multi-colored lights and lots of tinsel. The tree's taller than her father, who's standing right beside it. He grins, bends down and picks up a large box wrapped in peppermint-candy-striped paper. To someone you can't see, he says, "What do you think this is? A miniature dollhouse, maybe? Or could it be a giant panda?"

She hears her mother laugh. "Who's the kid? You or her?"

She hits the Stop button, then turns off the VCR and the TV. It's the twenty-third of December, exactly fifteen years since the video was made. Her dad will be home in a while, and she's going to make a special request of him to which she has no idea how he'll respond. She gets up off the floor, goes into the kitchen and brews herself a cup of tea—thinking maybe it will fortify her, if it turns out fortification is required.

———

On the Friday following Thanksgiving, while lingering with Mason in a Pizza Hut booth after their study session, she looked up to see her father. He was standing by the door, still in his white coat. He never wore a white coat except at work.

Mason, with his back to the entrance, couldn't see what she did. Which meant that he missed the tell-tale tightening of the muscles in her father's jaws. Anybody who saw him in that moment would have known he'd embarked on an unpleasant task.

Motion swirled around her. Near the salad bar a couple of elderly women frowned at the food particles that had invaded all the dressings, at a table for four a harried mother tried to reconcile the urges of three little boys, each demanding his own selection of toppings, and up front her father began his slow march toward her booth.

"I'm not that hooked on grades," Mason was saying. "I mean, I've always made A's, but if I made a B and still learned a lot I'd feel just fine. A grade's not the only way to measure knowledge."

"You're right," she said, and was halfway out of the booth before he realized something was wrong. He turned and looked over his shoulder, at the big man moving toward them.

Afterwards, it would seem to her that their motions had been choreographed, as if there were marks on the floor where each of them understood his or her feet belonged. Her role was to move as quickly as possible to a position between her father and Mason, who'd now slid out of the booth. Her dad spread his legs apart like the captain on the Aran Islands ferry, as if bracing himself against the sea, whereas Mason assumed the posture of a chastened schoolboy, his head already beginning to droop, his left foot virtually on top of his right.

"You don't have to tell me," she told her father. "I already know."

Of the many surprises flung at him in the last year, that had to be the toughest to fathom. She watched it hit him harder than an ocean swell.

"I didn't want to," she said, "but I did. I knew when that woman called. Edie. Maybe even before."

He stood there like a rock, an elemental mass, as all their private misery once more became public. The woman with the boys at the nearby table was trying hard to appear disinterested. The two old ladies were watching with the kind of rapt amazement they generally reserved for afternoon TV.

Behind her, Mason said, "Has anyone noticed me?"

There were worse things than invisibility, and he'd soon find out about some of them. While being washed in the blood might have sanitized his spirit, it wouldn't do a damn thing to clean his family's name. As soon as she was able, she promised herself, she'd urge him to leave all that baggage behind.

"Yeah," her father said, "I've noticed you, Depot. I noticed you right from the beginning."

"What's that supposed to mean?"

She could imagine what her father was thinking. He must have been wondering if somebody, somewhere, was keeping a ledger on him, noting each of his misdeeds, then placing an equal sign between the crime and the designated punishment. An eye for an eye. A large death for all the small ones.

Rather than answer Mason, her father said, "Come on, Toni, let's go home."

He laid his hand on her shoulder, but she held her ground. "You mean back to Fresno?" she said. "Or just back to our house?"

His gaze traveled from her face to Mason's, then back again. Later on, she'd ask herself if he already knew that from Mason's point of view, a baggage tag had been attached to her as well.

"To our house," he said. "That's the only home we've got."

Driving home two days before Christmas, Pete wonders how many patients he's seen in the last ten years who, upon learning they were terminally ill, wanted him to assure them that their smoking hadn't led to the cancer in their lungs, that all the whiskey they'd drunk hadn't rotted the holes in their livers or that they hadn't contracted the virus that was killing them by having unprotected sex with a few hundred strangers. They wanted to assign illness to malevolent nature, rather than chalking it up to their own misbehavior.

Nature, in reality, is neutral. Time is what's malevolent, and if you live long enough it will always take you down. What you've done, he sometimes wants to tell them, is hasten your own destruction. But you can't say that kind of thing to a patient. You can only say it to yourself.

In the back of the Volvo, he's got a stack of packages he ordered from Amazon. For Toni, a couple of CDs by Piotr Anderszewski, a Polish pianist who's supposed to be hot. Also a new book by Alice Hoffman, her favorite writer, and a history of Paris by Alistair Horne, since he plans to take her there when spring break rolls around, anything to get out of town. He's got the collected novels of Alan Furst for Tim, who enjoys suspense fiction but until now has never read anything good, and for Susan he's bought a bunch of oldies her dad thinks she'll like: Creedence Clearwater, Steely Dan, Little Feat.

They'll be spending Christmas together, the four of them, at Tim's new place. Unless it rains, and it's supposed to. Then they might have to do it here, though Pete hopes it won't come to that. He knows he should've bought a tree but just didn't feel like it, so all they've got is a small plastic one that stands on the kitchen counter, as it had in Fresno. Their real estate agent gave it to them after they bought the house, and because he never failed to come by and wish them happy holidays, they always felt like they had to put it out. As soon as he left, Angela would stick it in a garbage bag and return it to the garage. Toni found it in the closet, and he has no idea how it ended up in Mississippi.

All the houses on the block except his are strung with lights. A fat Santa rotates in his next-door neighbor's yard, and one of those pathetic-looking skeletal deers stands directly across the street. One guy—probably the richest man in town—has hired somebody to cover his lawn with fake snow. It'll be interesting to see what happens to that if the rain hits.

He parks in the driveway and gets out. He's thinking that once he's unloaded the car, showered and changed, he'll take Toni to dinner in Greenville, where there might be a halfway decent restaurant. For a while now they've been eating junk—Coleman's BBQ, KFC or, at the lower end, Wendy's. He knows he shouldn't be feeding her that kind of garbage. He knows what her mother would say.

Inside, she's sitting at the kitchen table over a cup of tea. Her eyes are dry. She hasn't cried for weeks, or if she has he hasn't seen it.

"Tell you what," he says. "I need to go back out and bring some Christmas presents in, and I'd like you to stay here while I do it, because they're all unwrapped. I'll get them stowed away, clean up and then we'll go over to Greenville and eat a better dinner than we've had in a while. How's that sound?"

She takes another sip of her tea, then sets the cup back down. "Normally," she says, "that'd sound just fine. But tonight I've got something else in mind."

"And what's that?" Whatever it is, he will not tell her no. For the rest of their time together he has ceded control, but he hopes it'll take her a while to figure that out.

"I want us to go on an errand of mercy," she says. "To the DePoysters."

He walks over to the refrigerator, pulls a bottle of Sierra Nevada out, grabs the opener and pops off the cap. He takes a sip of cold beer and leans back against the counter. "No," he says, "absolutely not. You can ask anything. But you can't ask that."

———

Driving over, she wonders what Mason's house will look like inside. She's seen it from the outside—if you're walking along the south bank of Indian Bayou, as she has several times in recent weeks, it's visible through the willows—but for obvious reasons she's never stepped in the door. She imagines a set of praying hands in the middle of the dining table, pictures of a long-haired Jesus on the walls. The one thing she assumes she won't see is a cross. She's heard that Baptists consider the image idolatrous.

Her father hasn't spoken since they got into the car. After refusing to come with her, he followed her into the hallway, watched her pull her heavy coat out of the closet, slip it on and reach for the door. "Would you let me get those packages out first?" he asked. A few minutes later they were headed across town.

He pulls into the driveway behind the truck that belongs to Mason's father. The house is dark, all the blinds shut, but a few shards of light appear between the cracks. She knows they're in there. You never see them around town now. In his last e-mail Mason told her they've been buying their groceries at night, at a store over in Indianola.

"Okay," her dad says, "we're here. Now what is it you want us to do?"

From the pocket of her jacket she pulls a small wrapped package. Inside it is the CD. The sound quality's not great—she recorded it on her laptop—but it's not atrocious, either. She made a couple of mistakes in tricky passages but consoles herself with the knowledge that he'll never know. It won't matter how well she's playing Shostakovich. What will matter is that she's playing just for him. "I want to give Mason a present," she says.

"If that's all you want to do, then I don't think you need me. I'll just sit out here and wait."

"That's not all I want to do," she says. "I also want to give him you."

Her dad props his elbow on the steering wheel, then rests his head in the palm of his hand. "So now the truth emerges. I'm on exhibit. A bull with a bow around its neck at the Loring County Fair." He shuts his eyes. "Or should I say a steer?"

"What's the difference?"

"Let's just say the difference matters less and less with age."

He opens the car door. She gets out too, and together they walk across the yard.

She rings the doorbell. No one answers. She waits a minute or two, then rings it again.

"Hon," her dad says quietly, "we probably aren't doing them a favor. I imagine we're the last people in the world they want to see."

A little desperate now, she raps on the wood. "Mason," she calls, "it's me. Can you *please* open the door?"

For a while, nothing happens. At various times in her life she's going to face disappointment, and whenever she needs to soothe herself this is the moment she'll return to—the interval between her plea and the sound of the deadbolt snapping open. When the minor modulates into the major.

You can tell from his eyes he hasn't slept a lot lately, which comes as no surprise to her since his e-mails have been arriving around the clock. He hasn't whined or said anything about how this is affecting him, not even when she asked, except to tell her that as bad as it might sound, he still loves his dad.

"Can we come in?" she asks. "For just a minute?"

He glances over his shoulder. In the hallway, a door that was open a crack is silently closing. "Sure," he says. "I mean, I guess."

He steps aside, and she crosses the threshold. At first she thinks her dad isn't coming, that he means to hang back, but then he's beside her.

She can see into the nearest room, a wood-paneled den with a fireplace in which there's no fire. Numerous cardboard boxes are stacked in piles three deep. In one corner stands a small Christmas tree, lit by a single string of white lights. There's no furniture of any kind. In the last e-mail, he said, *My uncle came and got a bunch of our stuff today. The rest will go tomorrow morning. I'll stay online just as long as I can.* The house hasn't sold yet but they're leaving anyway, moving to Atlanta to live with his mother's brother. He'll start school there in January.

"Hello, Depot," her dad says.

"Coach," Mason says.

She assumes they'll shake hands, since that's what males do. Mason must be expecting that too: his hand is moving toward her father when suddenly it pauses midair.

Her dad is just standing there looking at something, and for an awful moment she thinks there must be a picture of Mason's dad somewhere, that it's hanging on the wall in the den and she failed to see it. So she follows her dad's gaze, but the only thing there is the Christmas tree.

"I put it up," Mason says. "My mom didn't want me to. If you think it's in bad taste, I'm sorry. I was just trying to keep one thing normal."

Her father doesn't answer. Instead, he moves toward the tree so purposefully that she's afraid maybe he'll pull it from its base and hurl it against the wall or through the window. But all he does is stand before it.

"Depot?" he says.

"Yes sir?"

"Where'd you get this angel?"

Why anyone would notice the angel on top of the tree must be a mystery to Mason, because it surely is to her. It looks like it's about fifty years old, a ragged little thing that's missing part of one wing. It has hair that must once have been about the color of her own, but now it's dirty blond and frayed.

"I don't know," Mason says. "It's just always been in the family. We've had it as long as I can remember. Why?"

Pete doesn't answer. He's assuring himself there's a logical explanation. After his dad and his father died and he left town, his mother and grandmother quit buying green trees and started putting up a synthetic one that stood only about five feet high. All they had for decoration, as best he can recall, was a few colored balls. They didn't hang tinsel, didn't even use lights. At some point around the time he got married, he noticed the angel was gone.

They must have had a yard sale. The town, after all, is small, and there aren't that many people who could conceivably have bought it. Somehow or other, it ended up in Alan DePoyster's hands. Who knows how many others it passed through before it got there? Who knows why he kept it all this time, when better-looking angels were available?

"Coach? Are you okay?"

Mason sounds puzzled, even troubled, but Toni knows what must be going through her father's mind. He's remembering that night all those years ago in California, when an old friend led him across a marbled floor toward a woman he'd never seen before, telling him to come meet an angel.

ACKNOWLEDGMENTS

For their friendship and support during the writing of this novel, I would like to thank Linnea Alexander, Bob Bennett, Craig Bernthal, George Booker, David Borofka, Luis Costa, David Anthony Durham, Lillian Faderman, Diana Fisketjon, Gail Freeman, Corrinne and John Hales, Coke and James Hallowell, Sam Howell, Phyllis Irwin, Beverly Lowry, Bill Nichols, Ina Roy-Faderman, Vida Samiian, Tim Skeen, James Walton, Liza Wieland and, especially, Ania Wilczynski.

Thanks to my daughters, Lena and Tosha Yarbrough, for their valuable insights into the behavior of teenagers and the information they so graciously provided about music their father wouldn't be caught dead listening to.

My deep gratitude goes to Sloan Harris, once again, for being the best agent any writer ever had, and to Katharine Cluverious for her sound advice. Thanks to Liz Van Hoose for reading the book so insightfully and for always being there when it mattered.

Lastly, special thanks to my friend and editor, Gary Fisketjon, who has amazed me through three books and more than a thousand manuscript pages. He's the best, bar none.

PRISONERS OF WAR

It is 1943, and the war has come home to Loring, Mississippi. As German POWs labor in the cotton fields, the local draft board sends boys into uniform, and families receive flags and condolences. But for Dan Timms, just shy of 18, the war is his ticket out of town and away from the ghosts that haunt him. As he peddles goods from a rolling store for his profiteer uncle, Dan tries to understand his friend L.C., a young man who, on account of his skin, feels like a prisoner himself. But one day, Dan spots Marty Stark, just returned from Italy, mysteriously reassigned to guard the POWs he was once trained to kill. As Dan soon learns, Marty's war is far from over and threatens to erupt again.

Fiction/978-1-4000-3062-0

VISIBLE SPIRITS

In 1902, deep in the Mississippi Delta, nearly a generation after the end of slavery, events obscured by time but impossible to forgive or forget echo in the lives of blacks and whites alike. Bound together by history yet separated by mutual distrust, the citizens of Loring face present tensions as they look toward an uncertain future. Into this charged atmosphere rides Tandy Payne—prodigal son of a prominent planter, brother of the current mayor, and a dissolute gambler looking to reclaim the family estate. When he takes advantage of a perceived slight from the town's black postmistress, the ensuing clash with his principled brother results in a harrowing confrontation.

Fiction/978-0-375-72577-6

VINTAGE CONTEMPORARIES
Available at your local bookstore, or visit www.randomhouse.com.